# NO SECRET TOO SMALL

## A Novel of Old New Mexico

Loretta Miles Tollefson

PALO FLECHADO PRESS

ISBN: 978-1-952026-03-4

Library of Congress Control Number: 2020919180


Palo Flechado Press
Santa Fe, NM

# Other Books by Loretta Miles Tollefson

## Old New Mexico Fiction
Not Just Any Man
Not My Father's House
The Pain and The Sorrow
Old One Eye Pete (short stories)
Valley of the Eagles (micro fiction)

## Other Fiction
The Ticket
The Streets of Seattle

## Poetry
But Still My Child
Mary at the Cross, Voices from the New Testament
And Then Moses Was There, Voices from the Old Testament

# A Note About Spanish Terms

This novel is set in northern New Mexico in the late 1830s and reflects as much as possible the local dialect at that time. Even today, Northern New Mexico Spanish is a unique combination of late 1500s Spanish, indigenous words from the First Peoples of the region and Mexico, and terms that filtered in with the French and American trappers and traders. I've tried to represent the resulting mixture as faithfully as possible. My primary sources of information were Rubén Cobos' excellent books, *Refranes, Southwestern Spanish Proverbs*, (Museum of New Mexico Press, 1985) and *A Dictionary of New Mexico and Southern Colorado Spanish* (Museum of New Mexico Press, 2003). Any errors in spelling, usage, or definition are solely my responsibility. A glossary of Spanish terms used in this story is provided at the end of the book.

# DEDICATION

For all the world's children who are caught in the cross fire of
adult squabbles

# NO SECRET TOO SMALL

Loretta Miles Tollefson

# PART I

## APRIL—MAY 1837

## MORENO VALLEY

# CHAPTER 1

"And what have we here?" a man's voice says from the cluster of greening narrow leaf cottonwoods beside the small creek.

Alma's head jerks from her fishing line. She's supposed to stay alert when she's away from the cabin. Her mother will be furious. But then her heart settles. She feels no sense of danger from the dark-skinned, curly-haired man smiling at her from the edge of the trees. In fact, he seems oddly familiar.

Then a squinting face under a battered brown hat appears beside the man's shoulder and she laughs aloud. "Old Pete!" She drops her willow fishing pole, jumps up, and flings her arms around the mountain man's thick waist.

"All right, little missy." Old One Eye Pete sounds a little embarrassed and she giggles as she squeezes him again. He pushes his hat back from his tangled faded-brown hair, grasps her shoulders, and holds her at arm's length, his good eye twinkling. "You look like you've been growin' agin. Still fishin'?"

"I'll be fishing until the day I die!"

"Your ma all right with that?"

She laughs. "I have six trout. That's enough for the midday meal."

"You suspicion there's enough t' share with me and my pal here?"

Alma beams at him. "There's always enough to share with you, Old Pete. And anyone you bring with you." She moves toward the stream. "Let me collect my catch and my sunbonnet, and I'll come with you."

When she joins the men on the dusty road, Old Pete's friend has remounted his mule, but Pete stays on foot. He and Alma chat happily as they move up the narrow dirt track that runs north-south through the center of the valley.

Alma turns occasionally to peer out from her flapping sunbonnet and give the stranger a friendly look so he won't feel left out, but he doesn't catch her eye. He seems to be examining every inch of the landscape, its greening late-April grasses, and the cattle and fields below the hillside cabin on the valley's northeast edge.

"Your ma still tryin' to grow her corn?" Old Pete asks as he scratches his beard.

Alma grins. "She was in the field yesterday, trying to decide if it's warm enough yet to plant."

"Those pesky raccoons leave her enough for seed?"

Alma's laughter peals into the open air. "They tried not to. They kept Chaser Two working hard all last summer. Those pests sure kept that mastiff busy!"

"I bet she's glad to get out in the sunshine, though."

"It's been kind of a rough winter," Alma says somberly. Then she perks up. "But Papa says we're getting close to having enough money for glass windowpanes, and that will make it easier for her."

When they get to the cabin, the men lead their mules into the steep-roofed adobe and timber barn and Alma runs to the house.

As she rushes in the door, her mother looks up from her dusting. "What have I told you about running?" she asks. She pushes a stray black tendril into the bun at the back of her neck. "Your hair is down again. You look like a veritable hoyden. And that fish is dripping all over the floor."

Alma hoists the string of fish a little higher, as if this will keep the floor from getting wet, and uses her free hand to shove her unruly black curls back under her sunbonnet. "Old Pete's here!"

Her mother brightens and begins folding her dust cloth. "How nice! I wonder if he'll have any news." She tucks the cloth into her apron pocket. "Did he come east from Don Fernando de Taos or north from Mora?"

"I don't know. We were talking about fishing."

Her mother's lips twitch. "I should have known. Go warn Ramón that we'll have another person at the midday meal."

"Two, actually."

"Two?"

"He has a friend with him. Well, he calls him his pal."

"Two travelers will mean two sets of news. That will be doubly nice." She reaches to untie her apron from her slim waist. "Now please get that fish out of here and bring back a wet cloth to wipe up the mess it's made."

Alma looks at the floor. There's a pool of slime on the planks. She wrinkles her nose, lifts the string higher, and moves down the room to the kitchen.

Ramón, her godfather, her father's business partner, and the family cook, looks up from the rough-hewn plank counter. His face brightens. "What have you brought me, nita?" It's his special word for her, the one that means 'little sister.'

She hoists her catch. "Six fish and two guests!"

Ramón chuckles. "Excelentisimo. And who are our guests?"

"Old Pete and his pal."

"It will be good to see Old One Eye Pete again and hear of his travels. Have those fish been cleaned?"

"Of course." She crosses the room and settles the trout into the dry sink. "They're good-sized ones, too!"

3

"You did well."

She beams at him, then grabs a cloth from the counter and heads for the water pail in the corner. "I dripped fish slime on the floor. Mama was not pleased."

Ramón's eyes twinkle. "When you've finished cleaning, go find your brother and tell him we'll be eating soon. Your mother sent him to the garden to weed the potatoes."

Alma straightens from the bucket. She and her godfather exchange a conspiratorial look. Andrew is probably crouching in the grass beside the potato patch listening to prairie dogs whistle or sitting next to the shallow irrigation ditch to observe the dragonflies.

"I'll find him," Alma promises. She slips into the other room, wet rag in hand.

Old Pete and his friend are settled on the brightly-painted wooden chests by the fire. Her mother is in her mahogany rocking chair, knitting.

"And now, Suzanna, where is your good man?" Old Pete asks.

"He took a load of hay to Mora. We ended up with plenty left over from the winter. He and Ramón thought a trade venture south might be worthwhile."

"He's that sure it's not goin' to snow again and keep the cattle from the pasture?"

Her mouth twists. "Nothing's ever certain about the weather in these mountains. But Ramón believes we're going to have an early spring."

The other man raises an eyebrow. "Early? Hasn't spring already arrived? It was warm when we left Don Fernando de Taos." His voice is rich and warm. Soothing, somehow. Alma glances up at him. That slightly amused look in his eyes seems so familiar though she doesn't understand why. She watches him out of the corner of her eyes as she cleans.

"We're only two days east of Don Fernando, but up here in the mountains, spring comes much later than it does there," her mother says.

Old Pete chuckles. "Much to your aggravation."

She gives him a thin smile. "You could say that." She turns to the other man. "I fear I didn't catch your name."

"They call me Smith." He hesitates. "Gerald Smith."

"My husband's first name is Gerald." She smiles. "It's a nice name."

An odd look flicks across the man's face. He turns his head away. Alma's mother glances at Old Pete, but he's studying the fire. "Gerald should be home tomorrow," she says. She looks at Alma. "Did you wipe up all those drips?"

"I think so."

"Go find your brother and tell him it's almost time to eat. I set him to weeding the potato patch, although I doubt he got much of it done before he was distracted by a prairie dog, coyote, or dragonfly. Or found a reason to go visit that steer of his."

Old Pete swings his gaze back to her mother. "He's still the little naturalist, is he? Still'd rather watch a beaver than trap it?"

She grins. "He is. And now he has a brown-and-black beef yearling named Brindle. Slaughter time may be a challenge. But we won't starve. Alma is still our trapper and hunter child."

Alma swipes at the floor one last time, then gets to her feet and heads for the door as the adults continue their conversation. She really doesn't want to hear her mother reflect on the differences between her and her younger brother.

She hangs the wet rag over the porch rail to dry and heads down the hill to the potato patch. Personally, Alma doesn't think she and Andrew are all that different. They both like being out-doors. It's just that Andrew is more able to sit quietly and ob-serve, and Alma can only keep still if she's stalking something or fishing.

During the midday meal, they sit side by side on the bench across the table from Old One Eye Pete, Alma's sturdy body contrasting with her brother's slighter one, both of them watching the mountain man eat. He shovels pieces of pan-fried fish into a tortía, adds red chile sauce, takes a bite, and humphs contentedly. "That's good trout." He winks at Alma with his good eye. "You're quite the fisher girl, ain't you, little missy?"

"Don't encourage her," her mother says. "She spends far more time outdoors than is good for her complexion."

Old Pete purses his lips and studies the siblings. Alma tenses, waiting for comments about the dark blotches that mottle her brown skin, but all he says is, "Andrew's hair seems to like the sun. It's bleached those curls the color of straw."

Alma grins. "Brown-skinned towhead. That's what Papa calls him. The only six-year-old boy with brown skin and curly blond hair in all of Nuevo México."

Andrew laughs and sticks his tongue out at her. "And you're the only curly-haired eight-year-old with a heart on her cheek."

"Eight and a half," Alma says firmly. But she touches her left cheek self-consciously.

Old Pete reaches across the table, gently lifts her chin, and turns her face to the side. "Yep, it's still there." He looks at Mr. Smith. "She's had it since she was born."

Alma feels her face flush, but Ramón comes to her rescue. "And what news do you bring of events?" he asks the two men. "Have Governor Pérez and the militia returned from the cam-paign against the Navajo?"

"They came back all right," Old Pete says. "But they didn't bring anything back with 'em. There's folks callin' it the worst campaign that ever was."

"It doesn't sound like it went well," Mr. Smith agrees. His voice is smooth and comforting even when he's giving bad news. Alma sees her mother give him a puzzled look, as if she also senses something familiar about him.

"Apparently they didn't run into any Navajo, but they did run into bad weather," he continues. "Gregorio Garcia told me some of the men came close to losing their fingers from frostbite."

"Gregorio Garcia!" Alma exclaims. Her mother gives her a sharp look for interrupting, but she plunges on. "Jesús Gregorio Garcia from Don Fernando de Taos?" She looks at Old Pete. "Our Gregorio?"

Old Pete and Mr. Smith both chuckle. "He did mention that he knows you," the black man says.

Alma smiles happily. His skin isn't really black, she realizes suddenly. More a rich reddish brown. Like the mahogany of her mother's rocking chair. Like a darker version of her father. She squints at him. Are they related? That would be nice.

But the adults have returned to their political gossip. "Governor Pérez was gonna put his mark on the wild tribes," Old Pete says. "He had the presidio soldiers and the village militias and the Pueblo warriors all in tow, but they didn't find a single Navajo anywhere they looked. Armijo and them told him winter wasn't a good time to campaign, but he knew better, bein' a colonel from Mexico City an' all." He shakes his head. "He's been here two years. You'd think he'd cogitated a few things by now."

"He's in a difficult situation as a result of the campaign," Mr. Smith observes. "There's no money left in the treasury to pay the presidio troops. So he had to furlough them after they returned.

7

They're going to have to find other ways to feed their families for the time being."

Old Pete nods. "I was in Tomás Valencia's mercantile before I left Santa Fe and Sergeant Vigil was working there as a clerk. That's a bit of a comedown fer a soldier."

Alma's mother frowns. "Aren't the troops paid out of the customs receipts from the Santa Fe Trail merchants?"

"Yep, but I reckon there just weren't as much left over from last year as usual." He reaches for another tortía. "Or some of the money's gone to more important things. They say Pérez has some mighty nice carpets and mirrors in the palacio now. And he's bought a fancy carriage from St. Louis along with the horses to pull it." He shakes his head. "Good looking set of horseflesh, too."

"That appaloosa of his is a real beauty, as well." Smith turns to her mother. "They say it has a real affinity for the governor. A man with a way with horses can't be all bad."

Old Pete chuckles. "You just ain't gonna say anything negatory 'bout the man, are you?"

Smith's eyes twinkle. "It won't do any good, as far as I can tell."

"And what of last year's charges against Treasurer Francisco Sarracino?" Ramón asks. "Have those been resolved?"

Smith strokes his chin. "Well now, that's an interesting thing."

Old Pete grins at him. "Even you have to wonder about that."

"Por qué?"

Alma's mother reaches for another bit of trout. "Wasn't he charged with defrauding the treasury or peculation or something?"

Smith grins. "Back in Missouri I suspect they'd call it creative bookkeeping."

"I had hoped it might all come to nothing," Ramón says.

"It still may," Smith tells him. "Especially now. They say the Mexican law has changed again and Governor Pérez will soon have the authority to check the accounts himself and not rely on investigators who may have their own axes to grind."

"Their own axes!" Old Pete hoots. "That almost sounds like a criticism!"

Smith's eyes twinkle. "It's just an expression."

She leans forward. "The governor has the authority? Where did that come from?"

"Oh, it's part of a whole collection of laws the Congress in Mexico City's been spewing out," Old Pete says. "Gives the governor more authority than he already had. And I'm sure he'll use it. He's already thrown the oldest of the Santa Cruz Montoya brothers into the calabozo for agitatin' against the ricos havin' to donate money for this last Navajo campaign."

Ramón raises a gray-and-black eyebrow. "Antonio Abad? That Montoya?"

"That's the one." Old Pete rubs his forefinger against his thumb meaningfully. "Montoya got himself out, though. From what I hear, the alcalde down there just happens t' be a cousin of his." He tilts his head at Ramón. "Ain't that alcalde also related to you? Name's Esquibel. Juan, I think."

Ramón frowns slightly. "I don't know that Antonio Abad and Desiderio Montoya are related to him, but yes, Juan José Esquibel and I are distant cousins on my father's mother's side."

Alma's mother chuckles and turns to Smith. "But then, Ramón is related to at least ninety percent of New Mexico's population."

Ramón laughs. "But not to Governor Pérez, I think."

# CHAPTER 2

After supper the men settle onto the carved wooden chests by the front room fire. While Ramón twists thin strands of elk rawhide into rope, Old One Eye Pete carves a cottonwood whistle for Andrew. Mr. Smith stares into the fire a long while before he pulls out his pipe and tobacco pouch. "May I?" he asks Alma's mother, who has settled into her rocking chair beside the small table and its oil lamp.

She looks up from her mending. "Of course. My husband smokes a pipe also, and I miss the smell of it when he's gone."

"Are you expecting him soon?"

"Oh yes. He'll probably be back tomorrow, if he hasn't swung through Don Fernando de Taos to see about beaver prices."

"He got twenty peltries this winter," Andrew says from the floor by the fire, where he's petting the mastiff's brown-and-black head. "And that's just from around here. He's a really good trapper, when he has time."

"Do you go with him?"

Andrew shakes his head. "Mama says I'm too young."

"And what does Papa say?"

Andrew brightens. "Maybe next year."

Old Pete looks up. "You can come along with me, if your pa don't go out."

Andrew gives him a doubtful look. Chaser Two lifts his head and looks at the boy, then licks his hand.

"You don't hafta kill 'em," the mountain man says. "There's plenty t' learn besides clubbin' and skinnin'."

"Perhaps," Andrew's mother says. "We shall see. Winter is a time for schooling, not wandering around in the snow getting frostbite."

"You school them?" Mr. Smith asks.

"I do my best. As my father did for me." She glances at the small bookcase below the mica-paned window. "We have primers, Shakespeare, and Latin and botany texts. I find them sufficient for the purpose."

"And the Bible?"

"That also."

"And newspapers when Grandfather Peabody visits from Don Fernando de Taos," Alma says. She moves closer to the lamp on the small table at her mother's elbow and frowns at her knitting. "I've dropped a stitch again."

Her mother shakes her head and takes the needles. "Perhaps you'd rather read us something."

"A Psalm?" Mr. Smith asks.

Alma crosses to the bookcase. Mr. Smith watches her and puffs his pipe. She runs her fingers over the Washington Irving, the Shakespeare, and the botany book, then obediently pulls down the big leather-bound Bible.

She loves to read, even if it isn't Irving, and soon Alma is lost in the magical black marks on the page. As she speaks the words, her mother knits, her brother helps Ramón with his rope, Old Pete whittles, and Mr. Smith smokes his pipe and stares into the fire. Once or twice, she looks up to see his eyes on her face.

When he smiles at her, she again feels that sense of familiarity. He doesn't seem like a stranger at all. The room is as comfortable as it is when her father is home.

Alma reads three Psalms, then her mother announces that it's time for bed. Old Pete and Mr. Smith retire to the barn, where male visitors sleep when her father is away. Ramón goes with them, to make sure they're settled, then lets himself into the kitchen from the back door and goes into his own room.

"Mr. Smith seems very nice," Alma remarks to her mother as they prepare for bed in the loft.

"Yes," she says absently. "Come and let me comb your hair."

"He thought I was old enough to go trapping," Andrew says.

"Go to bed, Andrew," she answers.

He settles onto his pallet at the other end of the loft and watches sleepily as his mother combs Alma's hair and braids her curls into submission. He's asleep by the time Alma crawls into her own blankets. As she drifts into sleep she wonders again why Mr. Smith seems so familiar to her, so comfortable.

Late the next day, her question is answered. Old Pete has gone off to investigate the beaver ponds in the small river that flows out of the marshy area down slope and northeast of the cabin. Mr. Smith has stayed behind. He and Andrew are replacing the strips of worn rawhide that secure the corral poles to their posts.

Andrew is inside the corral, bracing the poles for Mr. Smith, who's outside the fence. He cuts away the old rawhide, then pulls new strips from the basket Andrew has lugged from the barn and wraps them carefully around the post, then the pole, then the post again. Finally, he ties the ends off and uses a stick to twist the lacing even tighter. When they've done one post, he and the boy move on to the next.

Alma is tending the narrow bed of worked soil below the cabin's drip line, weeding the spring grass away from the strip of tiny new pea plants and the little mounds of dirt where the wrinkled pink rhubarb plants are starting to poke through. The mastiff lies on the porch, sleepily watching them all.

Suddenly, Andrew's head jerks toward the valley below. His hands move at the same time and the pole he's holding wobbles out of position. Mr. Smith looks up.

"That's Papa!" Andrew's on tiptoe now, peering down at a man driving an empty wagon up the dirt road in the center of the valley. As Andrew twists to see more clearly, the pole pulls completely away from the post.

Mr. Smith reaches for it through the fence. "Go on. I've got it."

Andrew barrels toward the cabin. "Mama, Papa's coming!"

His mother appears in the doorway. She shades her eyes and peers down the hill. "He seems to have found a market for the hay. He'll be glad of a chance to talk with Old One Eye Pete." She smiles at Mr. Smith and raises her voice slightly, so he can hear her. "And you, of course."

Mr. Smith smiles and nods. Then he looks at Andrew and tilts his head toward the pole. "I think we have time to finish this set before your father arrives. I can't do it without you."

Andrew beams at him and trots back to the corral. His mother chuckles and looks at Alma. She lowers her voice. "The man seems to have a gift for getting that boy to actually work. I'm going to have to pay attention to just how he does it."

Alma giggles and her mother goes back in the house. But she never can stay away when her husband is approaching. Five minutes later she's back on the porch with her mending basket. "This sunlight sure is a blessing," she says as she settles onto a bench near the dog.

They all work quietly for a while, with one eye on the man and wagon below. When he turns east and begins moving up the road to the cabin, Mr. Smith says, "That'll do it." He pats Andrew's shoulder. "I'll take the basket to the barn."

Andrew nods and heads to the well in the middle of the yard. He draws a bucket of water, takes a drink, and leaves the bucket beside the well. Then he crosses to the porch and drops onto the top step. "I expect Mr. Smith'll want some water, too," he tells his mother. "That fence repairing is hot work."

She gives him an amused glance. "I expect he will."

But when Mr. Smith comes out of the barn, he doesn't turn toward the house or the well. Instead, he walks to the end of the barn and gazes at the approaching wagon. He moves toward the road, stops where it meets the track to the cabin, and stands waiting.

"He seems to want to speak to your father in private," Alma's mother observes.

Alma reaches for more weeds. "I wonder why?"

"Men do that sometimes." She looks down at her work. Alma and Andrew share a grin. They know she's just as curious as they are.

But all of them have their curiosity more than satisfied when the wagon slows to take the turn to the house.

Alma's father pulls hard on the reins and the mules toss their heads impatiently, but he doesn't speak to them as he usually would. Instead, he stares at the man beside the road. "Papa?" he asks. Then he yanks the hand brake into position and is off the wagon, his arms around Mr. Smith's shoulders, hugging him tightly.

On the porch, Alma's mother drops her mending onto the bench and stands in one swift motion, almost tripping on the mastiff, who's stood with her. She takes a step toward the edge of the porch. "What in tarnation?" she mutters.

The two men climb onto the wagon seat and Alma's father releases the brake. As the buckboard moves toward the cabin, her

14

mother's chin lifts. She turns, crosses stiffly to the cabin door, and disappears inside.

Alma stands, moves to the steps, and peers into the house through the still-open door. Her mother is climbing the ladder to the loft.

As Alma watches, Ramón emerges from the kitchen and says something to her mother but she doesn't reply. He crosses to the door and looks out, then gives Alma a puzzled look. "What is it, nita?"

She shrugs. Ramón glances toward the end of the barn, where Alma's father and Mr. Smith are getting down from the wagon. Alma's father sees him, smiles, and waves. "Ah," Ramón says.

Andrew drifts down the porch steps to stand beside Alma. "I guess he's only just called Smith. It's not his real name."

She frowns. "Or Papa's last name really isn't Locke."

Ramón steps onto the porch. "Just wait and see."

"What is it Mama says? Patience is not a virtue I possess in any great measure."

Ramón chuckles. Then his smile fades as the children's father and Mr. Smith cross the yard. They stop in front of the children and look down at them.

Alma blinks. Yes, the almost-square face, the slightly amused something in the corners of the eyes. And they're almost the same height. That's why the older man seemed so familiar. Except her father's eyes are gray. And his skin is a lighter color. More honey-brown like Ramón's. But the two men watching her are incredibly alike.

"Hola, Papa," Andrew says. His eyes flick to Mr. Smith's face, then to his father's. "Did you have a good trip?"

His father smiles, first at the children, then Ramón, then at Alma and Andrew again. "The best part came at the end." He puts a hand on Mr. Smith's elbow. "Chamacos, this is my father, your grandpa."

Andrew puts his hands on his hips. "You told us your name was Smith."

"I said that people call me Smith," the man says gently. He spreads his hands, palms up. "I'm sorry. I wanted to speak to your father before I made myself known to you and your mother."

Alma turns toward the doorway behind Ramón. It's still empty. There's no sound from inside the cabin. She bites her lower lip, then turns back to the men and smiles up at the older man. "I thought you reminded me of someone I loved." She moves toward him, her arms out. "Just like my father." As he wraps his arms around her, she buries her face in his chest. Then she tilts her head to see his face. "Buenos días, abuelo."

Her father's hand touches her head as he speaks to Ramón. "I thought I saw Suzanna on the porch."

"Sí," Ramón says. "She was here. She saw you."

"She's in the loft." Andrew scowls. "You made her cranky."

Alma breaks away from her grandpa as the three men exchange somber looks.

"I wasn't sure—" her abuelo says.

"She never asked," her father says.

"She is part Navajo herself," Ramón points out.

"She said my background didn't matter to her."

Alma's grandpa looks questioningly at Ramón, who shakes his head. "I do not provide information that isn't requested of me."

Andrew moves directly in front of his grandpa and puts his hands on his hips. "I have a question."

"Yes?"

"What's your real name? Is my last name still Locke or is it really Smith?"

The man's lips twitch. "I see you are a man who likes facts."

The boy scowls. "What is it?"

"It's Locke. I am Gerald Locke, Sr. and your father is Gerald Locke, Jr., so you are still Andrew Locke."

"Andrew Ramón Locke," the boy says, emphasizing his middle name.

"Andrew, because that was my mother's father's name," her father says.

Andrew gives him a long look. "I hope so." He turns on his heel and brushes past Ramón into the house. He runs to the ladder and scrambles into the loft. They hear his voice, then his mother's, then silence.

The dog goes to the door and looks in. His head tilts to one side as if he's trying to find the boy. Alma bites her lip. Her grandpa's voice is somber. "Will you go to her?"

"Not just yet," her father answers. "I'll wait a bit. She'll need some time to adjust."

# CHAPTER 3

A week later, the children's mother has shown no sign of adjusting. She spends her time reading her Caesar or hoeing the still-unplanted potato patch. She does not speak to her husband, Old Pete, or anyone else, unless she's lashing out at one of the children for misbehaving in some small way. Even Andrew, who's almost as silent as she is, feels the sting of her anger.

The boy's way of dealing with upsetting news or circumstances is to retreat to the pasture to pet Brindle or to one of the tiny valley streams to study the flying insects that hover there. Chaser Two is usually with him.

When he and the big dog wander up the hill late for dinner one night, his mother drops her book and darts out of her chair. "Where in tarnation have you been, you careless boy? Don't you know we're all waiting on you?" she says accusingly. "You could have been lying out there half-eaten by a mountain cat and no one would've known!"

Alma, who's been reading beside the fire, looks up in surprise. It's still daylight. There's little danger of mountain lions wandering the valley at this time of day. And Ramón hasn't actually told them dinner is ready.

Andrew's eyes are wet with tears. His mother puts her hands on her hips. "And don't you start crying like a baby!"

"I'm sorry," he says. "I didn't mean to worry you."

Her hands drop. For a brief moment, she looks like she'll burst into tears herself. Then her chin lifts. She stomps to the door, grabs a coat from the row of pegs on the wall, and yanks it around her shoulders. The heavy wooden door shudders as it closes behind her.

Andrew and Alma look at each other. "For a minute there I was sure she was gonna switch me," he says.

Alma tries to laugh. "She hasn't switched you in forever. Not since that time you stole the black hen's eggs."

"I didn't steal 'em, I just borrowed them. I wanted to see if I could hatch 'em. I was only four and a half. I didn't know about hens."

Alma wrinkles her nose, glad to have found a way to distract him. "When the eggs started smelling bad, you must have known they weren't going to hatch."

He grins. "Mama found them just about the time I figured that out." Then his face drops. "She was awfully mad, but she wasn't as mad as she is now."

"She's not mad at us."

"It sure feels like it." He looks around the empty room. "Where is everybody?"

"Papa and Grandpa are in the barn and Ramón's in the kitchen." She lifts her book. "I wanted to help him, but Mama said I should read my botany lesson."

He moves to stand at her elbow and lowers his voice. "Are they going to sleep out there?"

"Out where?"

"In the barn."

"It's too cold to sleep in the barn. Grandpa was down here last night."

"So was Papa."

She lifts an eyebrow.

"I was awake when he came up the ladder this morning to get clean clothes. He was still in his pants and shirt from yesterday."

"Was Mama with him?" This happens occasionally during the summer months when their parents want some 'privacy of their own,' as her mother calls it.

Andrew shakes his head. "She was in bed asleep, like usual."

She's been sleeping a lot lately, going to bed before the children instead of overseeing their nighttime routine. They haven't minded. She can't snap at them if she's sleeping, although Alma does miss having her hair combed.

Alma bites her lip. "How long's she gonna stay mad at him?" She knows she's too old to sound so plaintive, but this is beginning to frighten her. Mama's temper is legendary, but so is her ability to get over her aggravation. She should have calmed down by now.

"Well, he lied to her. I'd be mad, too."

"He didn't lie. He just didn't tell her everything." She looks at him. "We don't tell her everything, do we? When you go down into the canyon to watch the beaver, you don't tell her where you're going, because you know she'll say it's too far. And I don't always tell her where I'm planning to fish."

He gives her an impatient look. "That's different." He frowns. "Why'd Grandpa Locke have to show up now, anyway?"

Andrew's question is answered a few days later. They're all sitting in the living room after the evening meal. Old Pete and Ramón are side by side on a big wooden chest near the fire, each braiding leather to make hackamores. Gerald Sr. and Jr. sit opposite them, the children's father on the other chest and their grandpa in a chair beside him, both pulling on their pipes.

The children are doing their schoolwork at the small table beside the bookcase, with the oil lamp between them and Chaser on the floor at their feet. Their mother is in her rocking chair. Her knitting needles click against each other like tiny swords fighting.

Old Pete's hackamore is a complicated six-strand braid that alternates dark and light strips of cured leather. Alma's grandpa leans forward to study it. "That's quite a design you have there."

Old Pete grins at him. "Nice, ain't it? But it weren't me that come up with it. Ramón here's got a gift."

Ramón looks up. "It's mostly scraps from one thing and another. Together, they'll produce a good length. As my grandmother used to say, "Un grano no hace granero pero ayuda a su compañero.""

"One grain doesn't make a granary?" Alma's grandpa asks.

"But it helps its companions," Alma says from the table, completing the translation.

Her mother looks up. "Have you finished those sums?"

Alma bends back to her work. Her mother's needles click in the silence.

"That's a good proverb to explain why I showed up now instead of sooner," Alma's grandpa says. "Or later."

The children exchange a glance. A log drops in the fireplace. Their father moves to add a new piece of wood. When he returns to his seat, he glances at his father. "Are you going to elaborate on that?" There's a touch of something between amusement and apprehension in his voice.

Alma's grandpa gives her mother, then her father, a cautious look. "Well, I wasn't certain how I'd be received. Seeing how I left you in Missouri on your own, and all."

"I don't know that you had much choice," Alma's father says. "Given the way you were being pushed out of blacksmithing by the white landowners, and the way the country was being flooded with slaves. Living as a free man was becoming more and more difficult. Besides, I was fifteen and apprenticed to that farmer.

21

Old enough to be on my own and set up as safe as you could make me, given the conditions."

Old Pete looks up from his work. "Conditions?"

"Missouri was a good country when I first arrived," Alma's grandpa tells him. "Back before it was even a territory. But then some Washington politicians decided it should enter the Union as a slave-holding state. After that, things went from good to bad, then bad to worse." He glances at Alma's mother, then returns to Old Pete. "So when I heard about how things were here in Nuevo México, I made sure my boy was set and I—"

"Headed for the high country."

"Something like that."

There's a long silence. The two Geralds puff on their pipes. Alma returns to her sums while Andrew makes endless penmanship loops on his slate and surreptitiously watches his mother's face.

"I was sure glad when I knew you were in Nuevo México." Alma's grandpa looks at her father. "It sure was good to see you again and know you were safe, even if I only stayed around long enough to get a glimpse of you."

Alma's father nods. She can't see his face but there's something about the set of his shoulders that says he's holding back on his words.

"I figured you'd want to make your own way, though," her grandpa continues. "So I headed for the low country. Ended up in California for a spell."

"So I heard," her father says.

Old Pete drops the braid he's been working on and rubs his hands together. "This here's hard on the fingers." He looks at Alma's grandpa. "So how was Californee? I've heard tell it's a right land of milk and honey."

The other man snorts disparagingly. "Long on milk, short on honey."

"A real pleasure to live there, huh?"

"It was all right. But they've been having some tussles between the ricos and the peónes, and we Americans started getting pulled into the fight. It wasn't any place I wanted to be." He turns to Alma's father. "And of course, we'd heard about the rebellion in Texas and there were rumors that the same thing was happening here. I didn't know exactly where you were and I got to worrying that you'd get caught up in a fight."

Alma's father's eyes glimmer in amusement. "This isn't Texas."

Old Pete chortles. "Not by a long shot."

"I'd heard folks were getting riled about taxes, then when I got here I realized it was just folks in Santa Fe not wanting to pay school fees."

"Well, it's a little more'n that," Old Pete says. "There's always gonna be folks here who don't figure they oughta' help pay for a govmint that's clear down in Mexico City. But the governor slapped a tax on fandangos and other public entertainments and that pretty much had everybody ruffled up for a time there."

The other man shrugs. "There was just a sense of trouble abroad and I became a trifle concerned." He grins at Alma's father. "I didn't know you were in a mountain valley about as far as you can get from any trouble that's likely to build up."

Alma's mother sniffs. He looks at her, then turns back to Alma's father. His voice drops. "And when I heard you had a wife and young ones, I decided it was most definitely time. I've missed you, son. I'm sorry I didn't make it back sooner."

23

Loretta Miles Tollefson

Suddenly, the rocking chair stops moving. Alma's mother stands, drops her knitting into the basket beside the chair, and stalks from the room and into the kitchen.

Andrew's slate drops to the table. His chair scrapes back and he runs after his mother, the mastiff close behind. As the boy opens the door to the kitchen, the one that leads to the hillside behind the house shuts with a thud.

"What are you gonna do?" Old Pete asks in a subdued voice.

"I don't know," Alma's father answers. "I truly don't know."

# CHAPTER 4

Although the children don't agree on the righteousness of their mother's anger, they do agree that it's best not to turn her sharp gaze on themselves. So when they're in the barn feeding the chickens and collecting eggs two days later, they don't go running to the house to announce that the black hen has once again escaped the pole-latticed chicken pen and is in the hayloft.

Instead, Alma dumps the rest of the feedgrain into the chickens' narrow cottonwood trough and follows Andrew out of the pen. She latches the door behind them, then pushes the sides of her sunbonnet away from her face to see into the loft above the chicken enclosure. The hen is trotting along the edge of the loft. "Tarnation!" Alma says. "We're going to have to go get her."

Andrew is carrying the woven willow basket of eggs. The yellow barn cat rubs against his feet. He looks down at her. "You'd just love to have an egg to eat, wouldn't you?"

"Cats don't eat eggs," Alma says absently. She's still watching the black hen.

Andrew eyes the cat, who looks much thinner than she did a few days ago. "I wouldn't put it past her." He turns and studies the barn interior. "There ain't no place really safe from a cat, is there?" He lugs the basket to the tack room at the other end of the big dusty space, unlatches the door, sets the basket down next to Old Pete's gear, and pushes the peg firmly back into the latch. Then he nods at the cat. "Try to get into that, why don't ya?"

Alma looks over her shoulder at the closed barn door and jiggles impatiently. "We're wasting time. If Mama comes in, we'll have to tell her about the hen."

"Come on, then." Andrew scrambles up the ladder and she follows close behind. As he swings into the loft, the hen begins to squawk angrily.

"What'd you do, step on her?" Alma laughs. She's on the top rung now.

But Andrew is still next to the ladder and the hen is in the far corner, hopping along a small ridge of hay and peering at something behind it. She flaps her wings irritably.

Andrew begins unbuttoning his shirt. "We need something to cover her head."

"She'll scratch your bare chest with her feet," Alma says. "Just a minute." She swings into the loft and reaches for her sunbonnet. "This stupid thing turns out to be useful after all."

She hands the floppy cotton to Andrew. He grasps a side flap in each hand and moves cautiously toward the chicken. She's too busy scolding the hay to notice him. He swoops the sunbonnet over her head and bundles it tight against her wings before she can react. Her feet scrabble at empty air as he lifts her, then she goes still. Alma grabs the dangling strings, wraps them around the hen's enclosed body, and ties them in a neat bow. "That should do it."

Andrew grins and hefts the chicken in his arms. "Maybe this will teach her to stop trying to get out." He turns and leans to look into the space she'd been fussing at. "Oh look! It's kittens!"

The children have their heads together, examining the blind babies in their nest, when a door hinge squeals below. They look at the trussed hen in Andrew's arms, then each other, and sink onto the hay-strewn loft boards so whoever is below can't see them.

"We need to talk." Their father's voice has a grim weariness to it. The children look at each other apprehensively. There's only one person he speaks to in that way.

"How could you not tell me?" Their mother's voice is low and furious. There are no tears in it. Alma looks at Andrew, who has closed his eyes. He looks like he'd put his hands over his ears if he wasn't still clutching the hen.

"How dare you not tell me such a thing?" their mother continues. "How could you keep such a thing from me? Why, what you've done is downright criminal!" A hand slaps the side of the empty cow stall, rattling the boards. "You lied to me! Not with words, but with every action you took!" Her voice rises. "You lied to me! How dare you!"

"Suzanna—" He sounds almost like he wants to plead with her. Alma leans forward, wishing she could see, but Andrew jabs her ribs with his elbow. His eyes are wide open now. He shakes his head at her urgently.

"Don't you touch me!" their mother snaps.

There's a shuffling sound, as if their father is moving as far away from her as he can without actually leaving the barn. "I'm sorry." His voice is stiff now, not pleading.

"That's all you can say?"

"If you'll recall, I tried to tell you." Then his voice changes, becomes sadder. "I was a coward. I see that now. But I didn't want to lose you. And you said you didn't care about my past, my background. That it was me you wanted. That my character was all that mattered." There's a long silence, then he says quietly, "And I wanted to believe you."

A piece of harness jingles as he paces past it. The children look at each other and smile slightly in spite of the tension. Papa paces when he's thinking. "Enoch Jones would have told you all about me," he says. "Given half a chance."

"Is that why you tried to kill him in the Gila wilderness?"

He stops moving. "Of course not! Jones was attacking Gregorio Garcia. I had to do something to stop him. Then when he came at me, I had no choice. You know that. I told you what happened." He begins moving again. Another piece of harness jingles as he brushes past. "I'm surprised he didn't tell you about me when he attacked you in the cornfield six years ago. But I suppose he had other things on his mind."

"He did say there was something about you I didn't know. But I thought he was just trying to distract me. I never expected anything like this." She snorts. "And I was in no position to give him a chance to explain."

There's a short pause. Then her voice hardens. "All right. I suppose I invited you to not tell me the truth. But the fact remains that you've been living a lie all these years, letting me believe your Irish mother was married to a man of the same race. That you simply had skin that tanned well and stayed that way. Not bothering to explain just where Alma's skin color and those so-called freckles on her face came from."

She pauses as if she's waiting for him to answer. When he doesn't, she says, "But now it turns out that you're negro, of all things. Son of a man who's a runaway slave." Her voice rises. "What in tarnation did you expect? That I'd simply say 'oh my goodness, what a pleasant surprise'?"

"My father isn't a runaway slave. His mother was. His father was Cherokee."

"It's still in the blood."

"What, the runaway part or the African part?" There's a harshness in his voice that Alma's never heard before. She bites her lip.

But then he seems to catch himself. His tone changes. "I wanted to tell you," he says quietly. "So many times. But when that first opportunity passed and you didn't seem to care, well, I thought I'd wait a while, until we'd been married a bit." He begins pacing again. "I thought you'd guessed and that it truly didn't matter. That it wasn't something even worth discussing. That with your own Navajo grandmother, you'd understand."

There's a long silence. When he speaks again, there's bitterness in his voice. "But it's not the Cherokee part of me that's the problem, of course. It's the negro, the blackness. Not telling you was sheer foolishness. I should have known you were just like all the others."

"What others?" she snaps. "What in tarnation is that supposed to mean? And skin color has nothing to do with this! You lied to me!"

"And if I hadn't? Would you have married me anyway?"

There's a long silence. "I—" Her voice catches as she speaks. "I don't know."

"Probably not."

"But you'll never know, will you?" Her voice rises. "Because you didn't have the courage to find out!"

Alma's breath catches. Her mother has just called her father a coward.

In the barn below, his hand thuds against a board. "What the blazes, Suzanna? You said then that you didn't care where I came from and now you say that if you'd known, you wouldn't have married me! I gave you what you said you wanted and now you throw it in my face! What's a man supposed to do?"

29

There's another long silence. When she speaks again, her voice is icy. "We have clearly come to a parting of the ways in terms of our perspective on this matter. I think—"

But just then, the outer door rattles. Alma cranes her neck. A sliver of light dances upward from the opening.

"Children?" Ramón's voice calls. The door swings farther open. "Ah, perdóneme," he says. "I sent los chamacos to gather the eggs and they have not yet returned."

"Those two are so irresponsible," their mother says irritably, though her voice sounds oddly relieved.

"They're probably down in the canyon watching beaver," their father says.

Their mother's skirts swish as she crosses to the door. It swings farther open. "Alma!" she shouts. "Andrew!"

Andrew's mouth opens instinctively. He leans forward, but Alma grabs his arm and pulls him back. She shakes her head and he nods reluctantly and sinks back onto the floorboards.

"Ah well, they will return when they are ready," Ramón says. "Perhaps the black hen has escaped again and they have gone in search of her."

"I wouldn't put it past that hen to keep trying to get out," their mother agrees. "She ought to go in a soup pot, then we wouldn't have—" Her voice fades as the three adults leave the barn.

The hen clucks nervously and twitches her feet. Andrew chuckles as he strokes the cloth. "Don't worry, I won't let them eat you," he whispers.

Alma moves cautiously to the edge of the loft and sticks her head out far enough to see the dim interior below. The door is firmly shut.

"Did Ramón know we were up here?" Andrew asks.

Alma shrugs. She suddenly doesn't want to talk anymore. She touches the heart-shaped freckle on her face. Light flickers from the roof and she glances up. There are holes between the wood shingles. Like her heart. "Let's get out of here," she says.

# CHAPTER 5

In the following days, Alma does her best to avoid her mother, but then one morning Alma's sitting on a bench on the porch, her botany book in her hands when her mother marches across the yard and stops at the bottom of the steps. She has a hoe in each hand. "The cornfield needs to be turned over," she says abruptly. "Today's as good a day as ever. Put the book away."

There's a grimness in her face and a stiffness in her shoulders which make it clear Alma had better do as she's told. She nods and stands. As she moves to the cabin door, her mother adds. "And put your sunbonnet on! Your skin's splotchy enough as it is!"

Alma's stomach tightens, but she obeys. She follows her mother down the hill. "You can start down there." Her mother waves a hand toward the western end of the patch. "Break up all the clods. I'm going to start seeding next week, whether the weather's warm enough or not."

Alma nods and moves to the lower end of the field. Her mother marches to the upper end and positions herself in the northeast corner. Alma steps sideways until she's at the very end of the furthest row opposite. She wants to stay as far away from her mother as possible.

Her sunbonnet flaps against the sides of her face. She pushes at it impatiently, folding the flaps back against her head. Then she glances up the field. If her mother sees sunshine on Alma's face, she'll be even more cranky than she already is. Alma drops her hands and lets the cloth fall forward and flatten against her cheeks.

She bites her lip. She's too old to cry. But she hates the way the bonnet slaps against her face and blocks her view. All she can see are the clods of winter-hardened dirt immediately in front of her. The only sound is the slap of her mother's hoe lashing at the mounds of soil at the top of the field. Alma blinks back her tears and goes to work, her stomach a dead weight of misery.

Two hours later, her mother stops working and leans on her hoe. She's turned over the dirt in perhaps a fifth of the plot. Alma has completed only half what her mother's accomplished, but her mother's shoulders are looser now and more relaxed. Alma begins working slowly toward her.

"That's enough for today," her mother says when Alma's close enough to hear.

She nods and pushes her sunbonnet flaps out of the way. Her mother's face seems calmer, too, although she still looks unhappy. But resolved, somehow. Like she's reached a decision. The knot in Alma's stomach eases a little. Maybe she's decided to forgive Papa for not telling her about Grandpa Locke. After all, nobody can help the color of their skin or who their grandparents were.

She follows her mother up the hill toward the cabin. As they reach the top, she sees her father in the corral, working with his favorite two-year-old gelding. It's a pretty thing. Chestnut red with a blaze like a white starburst that half covers its face. Her mother turns and reaches for Alma's hoe. "I'll take that. You go on into the house."

"I want to watch Papa with the horse."

Her mother's jaw tightens. "I told you to go in the house."

33

Alma pushes the sunbonnet flaps away from her face again. Her mother glares at her. Alma turns and heads toward the cabin. When she reaches the steps, she looks back. Her mother has moved to the corral and is leaning the two hoes against a post. Her father turns and gives her a tentative smile, but then his face drops into a sad wariness. He pats the gelding's shoulder, releases the rope from its halter, and moves toward his wife.

She says something that Alma can't catch and his head jerks as if he's been slapped. He looks toward the cabin, sees Alma, and flaps a hand at her, waving her inside. She bites her lip and obeys. Whatever decision her mother has made, it isn't what her father hoped for.

The noon meal is a silent one. Her mother's face is stony and her father's is grim. Alma can barely swallow. The little bit of Ramón's fresh tortías and queso she's able to force down sit in her belly like a pile of rocks.

After the meal, she escapes the cabin as quickly as she can and climbs the hill behind it to her favorite rock, a flat piece of light brown sandstone that juts at an angle from the hillside. It's the perfect location for viewing the long valley below, the green-black mountains that hug its sides, and the mountains that fold around its southern end, a mere suggestion behind a blue haze.

No matter how cantankerous her mother is, Alma always has this. She drops onto the rock, pulls off her sunbonnet, and lets the breeze push through her black curls. Then she folds her legs to her chest, wraps her arms around them, puts her chin on her knees, and soaks in the May sunshine. A golden eagle circles overhead and a hawk flies over the marsh below, searching for prey. A red-winged blackbird trills over and over again, defining its territory. Alma's muscles relax.

When her father appears, climbing toward her, she uncurls herself and stretches luxuriously. Then she sits back down on the rock, to one side this time so he'll have room to join her. His face is stiff with anxiety, but she refuses to acknowledge it. Instead, when he gets closer, she smiles up at him and says, "This is my favorite view."

"It's mine, also." He drops down beside her and looks sadly at the landscape below. "This is the view that I showed your mother the first time she came to the valley."

Alma laughs. She knows the story of her parents' arrival here. And, if he's talking about that, maybe things aren't as bad as they seem. "But you came from Don Fernando de Taos through Palo Flechado Pass! That's eight miles south of this hill! How could she not have seen the valley before she got here?"

A smile flickers across his face. "She hadn't seen it from this vantage point. I made her close her eyes as we climbed the hill."

She raises an eyebrow. It's hard to imagine her father making her mother do anything. "That was a long time ago."

He nods, his face sad again. "It was." He reaches for Alma's hand. "I have something to tell you, niña." It's her favorite nickname, because it means she's the apple of his eye, but the way he says it makes her belly feel rocky again. He gently squeezes her hand, then releases it and leans back to brace his palms on the flat rock. "Your mother has decided to move to Don Fernando."

Something inside her freezes. "Move?"

"Well, not move permanently. At least I hope not. Go to stay for a while."

She feels her breath begin again, cautiously now. "With Grandfather Peabody?"

"That's the idea."

35

"It would be nice to see him again." He hasn't visited since she was six, two years ago. But the thought of leaving the valley squeezes an anxious feeling into her chest. "I wish he'd come here instead." She brightens a little. "Maybe he'll help Mama to not be so angry." She looks up at him. "You can convince her together."

His eyes glint in sad amusement, then he looks at the grassland below. He suddenly seems very tired. "I'm not going with you."

She frowns. "Is Ramón staying here?"

"Yes."

"And Grandpa Locke?"

He nods.

"Then you don't need to stay. Grandpa Locke can help Ramón with the cattle and the chores."

He keeps his eyes on the valley fields. "She—" His voice sounds choked, then he swallows hard. "She wants to go alone."

"It's days and days to Don Fernando and nobody lives between here and there. She can't go alone. It isn't safe."

He nods. "Old One Eye Pete has offered to go with you."

"Us?"

"Your mother and your brother and you."

Something twists inside her. She can't bear to look at him. She bites her lip and turns her face away. North of the cabin, the pyramid-shaped cone of Baldy Peak has a shadow of snow at its top. She blinks twice, trying to bring it into focus. "But not you."

"No. Not me."

She takes a deep breath and pushes the tears away. She looks up at his bleak brown face, his hooded gray eyes. "But it's just a visit? Just until Mama stops being so angry?" She can't keep the pleading from her voice.

He nods. "And Old Pete will go with you." He turns his head and gives her a small smile. "That will be fun. He'll tell you stories about trapping and fending off grizzlies and Apaches—"

She chuckles in spite of the pain in her chest. "Most of which won't be true."

"He's quite a character," her father agrees. "But he's been a good friend to us."

"'Specially to me. He made me my first fishing pole and he never treats me like I'm just a girl." They're on safer ground now. She twists sideways to look up at him. "How old *is* Old Pete, anyhow?"

His face softens slightly and she rushes on. "I know why he's One Eye Pete. One look at the empty space on the right side of his face explains that. But he doesn't look much older than you. How come we call him Old Pete?"

He gives her a bemused glance, as if he knows what she's up to and is grateful for it. "He's been Old Pete as long as I've known him. The story is that Old Bill Williams started calling him that in '26 when they were trapping with St. Vrain and his bunch north of the Gila. Pete was giving Williams a hard time, wanting to know just how old he was. Finally, Old Bill got aggravated and started calling Pete 'Old Pete.'" He grins, leans down to pluck a piece of grass from a tuft beside the big rock, and looks it over carefully. "And he's been Old Pete ever since." He puts the grass stem in his mouth, bites down, and gazes again at the green valley.

His face seems a little more relaxed now. Alma feels a glow of satisfaction. She's distracted him from his pain. "Those mountain men are somethin' else again," she says.

He gives her a sideways grin and takes the grass stem from his mouth. "They are, aren't they?" Then he shakes his head. "Though they're not all the same. Old Bill now, he's a loquacious opinionated old coot who isn't afraid of anything, even your mother, for all his soft heart." He looks glumly down at the cabin. "On the other hand, Old Pete knows a thing or two about tracking and fishing, but he's all gruffness and no bite. He'll do anything a woman asks of him, even if he doesn't think it's a good idea."

Alma bites her lip and tries to find something else to take her father's mind off his troubles. "How did he get to be Old One Eye Pete?"

He tosses the chewed stem to the ground. "He's never told you that story?"

"Well, I've heard a tale about a grizzly and one about a cougar. And also a yarn about an Apache with three eyes who wanted a fourth one. So I'm not inclined to believe anything he tells me about his eye, and I've stopped asking."

He chuckles. "I can understand that."

"So do you know what happened?"

"The story I heard is that he was down around Coyote Creek somewhere—"

"Our Coyote Creek? The one south of here where the Martínez family keeps their summer sheep?"

"Yes, that one." He looks at her sideways. "Are you going to let me tell this story or not?"

She grins at him. "I was just making sure I knew the location of the tale."

He chuckles. He looks even more relaxed now. Her lips twitch with satisfaction as he continues. "So, he was up in the hills around Coyote Creek with a couple of mules. One of them got testy. She didn't want to cross a patch of wet shale."

"Smart mule." She wrinkles her nose. "Shale can be mighty slick when it's wet."

"There was really no other option. They were on the side of a steep hill and that's where the trail led. There wasn't room to turn around and head back down the mountain."

"And Old Pete got stubborn."

He gives her a fake-exasperated look. "Who's telling this story?"

She giggles. "I suspicion I know where it's headed."

"All right, you tell me. What happened next?"

She tilts her head, considering. "Old Pete got mad and yanked on that mule's head and they both ended up halfway down the side of a cliff."

He chuckles. "The way I heard it, that's more or less what occurred."

"And Old Pete lost his eye? Did he fall on a piece of rock or something?"

He shakes his head. "I've never been clear on that point. There was a mountain lion involved and also a bear, though I doubt it was a grizzly. I heard him say once that the mule saved his life and that's why he didn't shoot her, even though she started the whole thing."

"But he ended up with no eye and all those scars on the right side of his face."

"Yep." He reaches for another blade of grass. "And that's all I know about that."

She leans against him. "You tell good stories."

He slips an arm around her shoulders. "You told a good part of that one."

"We tell good stories together." He squeezes her, but the sadness has descended on him again. She can feel it through his arm. Like he doesn't want to let go of her. Her throat wobbles. "I don't want to go, Papa," she whispers.

39

"I know, niña," he says softly. "And I don't want you to go. But hopefully, it will only be for a short while."

She leans her head against him and follows his gaze toward the mountains on the western side of the valley. The sun is setting and the sky behind the black peaks is a blaze of orange and yellow and red.

Finally, he squeezes her shoulders again and lifts himself from the rock. "We'd best get down the hill. Ramón's cooking those rabbits Old Pete trapped yesterday."

Alma's belly is hurting again. She's not sure she'll be able to eat. But she follows her father down the hill toward the cabin anyway.

# CHAPTER 6

They leave early in the last week of May. Her mother has planted no corn in the patch below the cabin, but the peas in the strip under the eaves are starting to flower. She ignores them as she follows Old Pete from the house to the buckboard wagon in the yard. He's carrying the wooden chest that's stored the children's clothes in the loft for as long as Alma can remember.

"And I'll want my box of herbs and salves, and the rocking chair," her mother says.

Alma, standing on the porch next to her brother and the dog, blinks in surprise. "Doesn't Grandfather Peabody have a rocking chair you can use?"

Her mother scowls at her. "That's my chair. It's solid mahogany and my father imported it from St. Louis on my fourteenth birthday. I am taking it with me."

"What about Chaser Two?" Andrew asks. "We're taking him too, aren't we?" The mastiff sniffs at the boy, who puts a protective hand on the big black-and-brown head. "See, he wants to come with us."

"There won't be room for him to ride in the wagon. He'll have to walk."

"We'll walk together."

"Well, you're coming, so I guess he's coming too." She sniffs. "It's not as if there'll be any crops here that he needs to protect." She moves up the steps. "Or that I care if he protects or not." At the door, she turns toward the children. "Andrew, go tend to the mules. Alma, come and make yourself useful."

41

The girl bites her lip and follows her mother into the main room. A wicker basket sits on the floor in front of the little wooden bookcase. "Choose what you want to take," her mother says. "I want the Caesar and of course we'll need the Latin and the botany. See what else you can fit in, along with your and Andrew's slates." She turns and heads toward the kitchen.

Alma bites the insides of her cheeks, brushes the dampness from her eyes, and kneels in front of the books. She places her mother's copy of Caesar, the battered Latin grammar, and her own copy of Mrs. Phelps' *Botany for Beginners* in the bottom of the basket, then slips the slates in next to them. She frowns. That won't work. The fragile writing boards will crack if the books jostle against them.

She looks up at the row of outdoor clothes on the pegs next to the door. Sunbonnets will protect the slates nicely. She grins. It's a good use for the stupid things. She hurries across the room and grabs all three. Then she stops. Will people in Don Fernando de Taos think her skin is too dark? Does the sun really make her as splotchy as her mother says? Her shoulders slump. She puts the headgear back and goes in search of a cloth to use instead.

Once the slates are in place, the basket is almost half full. Alma studies the bookcase, trying to decide what else to take. She doesn't need Padre Martínez' handwriting primer or his mathematics book anymore, but Andrew does. And then there are some novels by Jane Austen and Fanny Burney, and a collection of poems by William Cullen Bryant. These are all gifts from Old Bill and Ceran St. Vrain to her mother. And something by a lady named Mary Wollstonecraft that her mother likes to read. Grandfather Peabody gave it to her.

But Alma's in no mood to care what her mother likes. Personally, she prefers Mr. Irving's history of Christopher Columbus and especially the one about the Alhambra in Spain. She grabs the books and puts them beside the basket. Then she turns and pulls the Bible from the shelf.

She bites her lip. Just holding it makes her feel better, makes her see her grandpa's kind face, feel her father's arm around her shoulders. But her mother won't think it's as important as the Latin and the botany. And Grandpa Locke seems to take great comfort from it. She gently puts the book back on the shelf. She runs a finger down its spine. She'll be back. There will be other nights to read it aloud for him. Won't there?

Tears blind her eyes. She swipes at them with the back of her hand, then wedges the Irvings into the basket and goes outside to ask Old Pete to carry it to the wagon.

The buckboard is packed by midafternoon, although the mules are still in the barn. Andrew has said goodby to Brindle and is perched on the long board seat, swinging his legs and watching Chaser Two, who's sniffing at the wagon's wheels.

Alma is crouched beside the pea plants in front of the cabin, tending them one last time. Her father stands on the porch and gazes at the valley below, his face a dark mask of something between anger and grief. Ramón and Grandpa Locke are nowhere in sight.

Her mother comes out of the house and hands another bundle to Old Pete. He settles it next to the rocking chair, then steps back, pushes his battered hat from his forehead, and looks up at the sky. "Probably oughta wait 'til tomorrow to actually head out. If we leave now, we won't make it up and over Palo Flechado Pass before nightfall."

Her jaw tightens. "If we stop wasting time and leave now, we can camp at the base of the Pass tonight and be ready to tackle it first thing in the morning."

43

"I'll get the mules," Andrew says. His mother nods and he scrambles down from the wagon.

As Andrew trots toward the barn, Grandpa Locke comes out of the cabin. His daughter-in-law's lips thin when she sees him.

He heads down the steps, straight toward her. "I'm sorry I've caused all this trouble." His eyes flick over the valley, then back to her. "As I've said before, I'll leave, if that will help." She's tall for a woman. Their eyes are level, his full of pain, hers narrowed and sparking with anger. "I'll leave and never come back," he says. "No one else needs to know about our connection."

"As I told you before, it's too late. I'll know."

He winces. "I'm truly sorry I've caused this trouble."

She shakes her head. "You aren't the cause." She looks pointedly at the cabin porch, where Alma's father is watching them, his hands in his pockets. Her voice rises slightly. "It isn't your fault. You just wanted to see your son."

Alma's father's jaw tightens. His gray eyes are dark with anger. When he speaks, his voice is bitter. "Nothing I say is going to make you see my side of things. Maybe you should just go."

Her head jerks as if he's slapped her. Then her chin lifts. She turns toward the barn. "Where is that child?" She moves toward it as if she can't get away from the cabin quickly enough.

Alma's throat chokes. She pushes herself to her feet, stumbles to the porch, and wraps her arms around her father's waist. He pulls back a little, as if the feel of her arms is too much for him, but she just clings more tightly and leans her head into his chest. "I don't want to go, Papa," she moans.

"I know, niña." His hand strokes her curls, then drops to her shoulders. "And I don't want you to." Then his voice changes, as if he's trying to convince himself as much as he is her. "But you need to be with your mother. I can't keep you safe here, what with the hunting and firewood gathering and tending the animals and all. Ramón and I have a lot to do to keep this place going, even if your grandpa stays to help. You'd end up alone too often and for too long a stretch." She feels his chest expand as he takes a deep breath. "Besides, you won't be gone forever."

But he doesn't sound like he believes this. Her chin trembles. He strokes her head again, his fingers lingering on her hair, then gently pushes her away.

Her mother appears, leading the two brown mules. They twitch their ears as they near the wagon. They're not used to a woman handling them. They balk a little as she tries to maneuver them into the traces, then Old Pete steps forward. Alma's grandfather retreats to the porch.

Alma's mother watches Old Pete's movements intently, clearly trying to remind herself how the harnessing is done. She turns her head slightly to speak to Alma. "Go in and tell Ramón we're leaving. He's packing some food for us. And put on a sunbonnet."

Alma pulls away from her father and gives him a pleading look. He shakes his head bleakly. She moves slowly into the house and across the main room. It looks empty without her mother's rocking chair. Half the books are missing from the shelves. She crosses to the big painted chests in front of the fire and trails her fingers over the one on her right, the one with the bright-red flowers. She blinks hard, bites her lower lip, and heads to the kitchen.

Ramón is at the counter, wrapping tortías in a cotton cloth. She's going to miss this kitchen, the stone fireplace, the rough wooden counter, the cheerful painted doors of the food cabinet, the shelves with their simple pottery dishes. Even the battered table and benches.

She swallows and tries to make her voice steady. "We're leaving now. Old Pete is hitching up the mules."

He nods without looking at her. She moves alongside him, gazing at his brown and kindly face. He almost always has a smile for her. But not today. Today his lips droop at the corners and he keeps his eyes on his work.

"I don't want to go," she says to his profile. Maybe he can convince her father to let her stay. "I want to stay here."

"I know, nita." He looks up. "I wish you could. But it is not right for a girl to be without her mother. You must go with her."

"If that's true, then it's also not right for a boy to be without his father," she says stubbornly. "Andrew should stay here."

His lips twitch. "He is young still. He should be with his mother. And he wishes to go with her."

She braces herself against the counter, feeling the solidity of the thick wood, the goodness of it. She opens her mouth, but the tears threaten again. She clamps her lips tight and focuses instead on Ramón's hands as they carefully tie the cloth around the food. He lifts the bundle and places it before her on the counter. "This is what I am sending with you for today."

"I wish you didn't have to send anything."

He smiles at her sadly, reaches to pat her shoulder, then turns away and picks up the basket of longer-term provisions he's also prepared—dried corn and pumpkin and meat. When he turns back to her, his own eyes are damp. "You will return," he says gently. "All of you. I feel it."

Her chin quivers. He smiles again, then gives her a sharp nod. "And when you return, you will appreciate your home more than you already do."

"I don't think that's possible," she says. But she's a little calmer as she follows him out the door, the bundle of tortías in her hands.

# CHAPTER 7

Even though it's late May, snow begins to fall the next morning as they climb Palo Flechado Pass. For a brief and giddy moment, Alma thinks they'll turn back. But Old Pete only eyes the steep grade ahead and speaks encouragingly to the mules.

Alma's on the seat beside Old Pete, but Andrew and the dog are walking, following the wagon up the slope. The mountain man looks back at them, then turns to Alma's mother, who's on her other side. "You might oughta tell that young 'un to level up with the wagon," he says. "Him and the dog. These here mules are plenty strong enough to keep us from rollin' backward down the hill, but I wouldn't want t' risk it."

She nods and twists on the seat. "Andrew!" she calls. "This snow is going to get your shoes wet. Come get in the wagon!"

"I can't stop on this grade," Old Pete warns.

She nods. When Andrew and the mastiff trot up beside her, she leans down, grabs the boy's hands, and swings him up. He laughs gleefully. "You're strong!" Then he looks around. "Where'm I gonna sit?"

"I'm strong enough when I need to be," his mother says grimly. She pats her lap. "Sit here. I'll hang on to you."

"What about Chaser?"

But the dog has already bounded up the slope beside the rocky track and is sniffing at a game trail.

"He'll be back," Old Pete says. "I ever tell you about that black mangy-haired Ute dog I had me one time?"

He keeps them occupied with one story after another as the wagon works its way over the Pass, then down the long stretch that drops into the canyon of the Don Fernando river. He's still talking that night around the campfire and the next day, as they follow the river west toward Don Fernando de Taos.

Andrew listens intently, but Alma, usually eager for Old Pete's stories, drifts into her own thoughts. This landscape is different from home. A little rockier, more prone to juniper than pine. And drier. It reminds her of the lower canyon of the Cimarron, the little river that forms in the marsh below the cabin. She bites the insides of her cheeks and turns resolutely to looking more closely at the grasses and flowers.

But even the passing plants and trees can't keep her attention. Her mind keeps drifting to the valley. It's not that she really wants to think about home. That hurts too much. But she's tired. Tired and sad. She doesn't want to think about anything, really.

Her mother isn't listening to Old Pete's stories, either. But her quietness isn't sadness, exactly. It's more like her mind is somewhere far away.

The next day, when the wagon trundles out of the mouth of the river canyon and they all catch their first glimpse of Don Fernando's adobe houses, her mother's quietness changes. Her back stiffens and her chin lifts as if she's bracing herself for something bad, preparing to defend herself. Alma gives her a puzzled look. They'll be at Grandfather Peabody's in another hour, the house she grew up in. Shouldn't she be excited and happy?

It's too confusing. Alma bites her lip and looks away. Then her gaze drifts west and lands on a black gash in the earth, a kind of canyon that drops away from the middle of the flat valley and cuts it into two pieces, east and west.

Andrew, who's standing on top of a large rock beside the road, has seen it too. He jumps down and runs to the wagon. "What is that?" he demands, pointing.

"That there is what they call the gorge," Old Pete says.

"The what?"

"I s'pose you could call it a ravine, but it's deeper'n that. A good mile or more, top to bottom."

"It looks like a big black mark from here. What's down there?"

"Rocks, mostly." Old Pete barks a laugh. "Rocks and mountain sheep."

Alma's mother turns her head. "There's a river at the bottom of it. The río Grande del Norte."

"The big river of the north?" Alma asks.

Old Pete points a finger north. The tops of the nearest mountains are still white with snow. Others are so far in the distance they're a mere haze of blue. "It comes out o' there, so it's the river of the north." A note of nostalgia creeps into his voice. "Where the beaver was. And the otter. May still be, for all I know."

Andrew stretches to see more. "That's where you hunted beaver?"

"There and yonder."

"I wish I could of hunted with you."

"Could have hunted," his mother says absently. "Not could of."

The boy and the mountain man grin at each other.

"Maybe you can someday," Old Pete says. "Maybe you can."

Alma's still studying the black gash called the gorge and the flatness beyond it. This so-called valley is too broad. It feels empty. She scowls at her brother. "You don't like to hunt. You don't like to kill things."

49

"I like to see new places and find out about the animals that live there. And I can bring in meat if I need to."

"Explorin' is half the fun of huntin'." Old Pete's good eye twinkles at Alma. "You jest enjoy the huntin' half a little more, that's all. And the fishin'."

He's right. It's the chase she likes, the excitement. But she doesn't want to think about that right now. She moves her gaze to the low brown adobe buildings in the town off to her right. She's never seen them before because Grandfather Peabody has always gone to the valley instead of them coming here. He says it's easier for one person to make the trip than a whole household. Besides, they have cattle and fields to tend.

And pea plants. She takes a deep breath, steadying herself. She won't think about them or the wide-openness of this place. She'll think about the town instead.

She turns to Old One Eye Pete, who's flicking the reins at the mules. "So, tell me about Don Fernando." She pushes the sun-bonnet flaps away from her face. "Don't tell me a story that may or may not be true. Tell me something that really happened here. Or how it was settled."

"Well now." He scratches at his beard. "There's been Indians here as long as anyone can remember." He points the whip north. "They live up there at the pueblo of Taos, about three miles out of the town, which is called Don Fernando or Don Fernando de Taos, though I hear tell some people say it really oughta be San Fernando." He looks at her sideways. "And that's all I can say about it, unless you want a story that may not be true."

He sounds a little put out, like she's spoiled his fun. She chuckles and pats his arm. "Maybe later. How long has Don Fernando been here?"

He frowns. "Well now, I'm not sure I know the answer to that." He looks at her mother. "Who was Don Fernando, anyhow?"

She gives him a blank look, then frowns at Alma. "What was that?"

"How long has the town of Don Fernando de Taos been here?" Alma tilts her head. "And why is it called that? Most place names in Nuevo México don't begin with 'Don,' do they?"

"I can't recall any others. They're usually named after a whole family, like Los Chavez or Los Lunas. Or a really important person, like Spain's Duke of Alburquerque."

"Or a saint," Old Pete says. "Like Santa Fe."

She gives him an unwilling smile. "You mean la villa real de la Santa Fe de San Francisco de Asís?"

"That's a long name," Alma squints at Old Pete. "So Santa Fe is really named after Saint Francis?"

"I reckon so."

"But nobody knows who Don Fernando was?"

"There was a Don Fernando Duran y Chavez who settled here back in the 1600s, but he didn't come back after the revolt," her mother says.

Alma knows about the Indian revolt that kicked the Spanish out in 1680 and how they came back. She doesn't want that story right now. She wrinkles her forehead. "Why would they name their town after someone who didn't live here anymore?"

Her mother looks away. "I have no idea." She's clearly through talking.

Alma bites her lip. She refuses to let her mother's moodiness unsettle her stomach. She turns to Old Pete. "So tell me something about the town of Don Fernando that you know for a fact."

"Well, let's see." He's concentrating on the road ahead. He maneuvers the mules across a muddy patch, then pushes his hat back and scratches his forehead. "Once upon a time—"

Alma giggles and pokes him in the ribs. He pretends to jump in surprise and grins at her. "Oh, that's right! You wanted a true story, now didn't you?" He chews on his lip. "Well, I guess I could tell you about the bailes—"

Her mother comes out of her trance. "She's too young to care about dances."

He grins. "How about Old Bill and one of his sprees?"

"And she doesn't need to hear about Bill Williams' debauchery."

"What about María Rosa Villalpando?"

She's studying the town below. She nods absently.

"I think I know that story," Alma says. "Wasn't she the girl who was carried off by Comanches and then married a Frenchman and went with him to live in St. Louis?"

"I guess you do know that story," he says.

"Gregorio Garcia told it to me when he visited us last summer. But he said she lived a couple miles south of Don Fernando , near Ranchos de Taos."

"She was from somewhere around here. That's all I know."

"Hmm." They've reached some outlying buildings now. The adobe walls glint in the afternoon sunlight. Alma squints at them. "Why do they sparkle like that?"

"They've got bits of mica in them," he says. "Makes 'em shiny when the sun hits just right."

"They sure don't look like the sheets of mica in the window at home."

Her mother sniffs. "They certainly don't. These reflect the sunlight instead of blocking it out." She turns her head and gazes at the broad sweep of the land that slopes from the mountains they've just come from. There are mountains west of them too, but they're so far away their blue peaks are barely visible on the horizon. "But then, there's more sunlight here."

"Fewer mountain peaks hoverin' right overhead," Old Pete agrees. He twists around on the seat. "Where's that boy and his dog? We're almost there."

As he speaks, Andrew and Chaser bounce out of a nearby field. He runs up to his mother's side of the wagon and thrusts a stalk of what looks like thick, prickly grass into her hand. "There's fields and fields of this stuff!" he says. "What is it?"

His mother glances at it. "It's wheat. See the grains?" Her face softens as she turns it over. "It's a beautiful green color this time of year, isn't it? Like green sunshine." Then she frowns at him. "But this is someone's crop, Andrew. You can't be running through it or picking it, either. It doesn't belong to us."

"It's not like at home," Alma says.

Her mother gives her a withering look, then turns back to Andrew. Her voice softens. "You need to stay out of people's fields. The farmers won't like it if you and Chaser Two trample their crop."

Andrew's lips twist guiltily. "Chaser did knock some down."

"It'll probably spring back," Old Pete says. He gives their mother a sly look. "'Sides, they're just gonna use it t' make whisky."

"Hopefully, some of it will go for bread," she says drily. Then she glances up the street ahead and her back stiffens. "We're almost there."

Old Pete reins the mules to a stop in front of a big double-doored wooden gate set into a long brown adobe wall. One side of the gate is cracked open. Alma's mother takes a deep breath, scrambles off the wagon, and helps Alma down after her.

As Alma straightens her skirts, the gate creaks. She looks up into the surprised and smiling face of Gregorio Garcia. His narrow face and brown eyes are as beautiful as ever. Her heart lurches, but he's looking at her mother.

"Señora!" he says. "How good to see you!"

She nods and gives him an anxious smile. "Buenos días," she says formally. "Is my father at home?"

"Yes, señora." He looks at Old Pete. "Will you bring the wagon inside?"

"I reckon that'd be the best thing for now," Old Pete says. He nods at Andrew. "Help him with that gate, son."

Andrew runs to assist Gregorio with the gate as Alma and her mother walk into the rectangular courtyard beyond. There's an open space for the wagon to park and, to the left, a well with a bucket beside it. Firewood is stacked neatly behind the well. Farther down the adobe wall is a blue door and a window with blue shutters.

The courtyard is lined with flowers and other plants. A small garden plot at the far end contains neat rows of peas, lettuce, and chile seedlings. A wooden bench sits by a short brown door on the wall facing the gate. It's all just as inviting and peaceful as her mother has described it. Chaser Two is already settling himself beside the bench.

The blue door swings open. Her mother takes Alma's hand and reaches for Andrew, who moves toward her. A tall, thin man with a graying chin beard and wearing a somewhat-worn black suit stoops out of the door and straightens.

"Grandfather Peabody!" Alma drops her mother's hand and flings herself across the courtyard.

He bends to envelop her in a hug, then holds her at arms' length. "You have certainly grown since I saw you last!" He looks over her head at her mother and brother. "What a wonderful surprise!" He releases Alma and holds out his arms to Andrew. "Come and greet me properly, joven!"

Andrew gives his mother a questioning look and she nods. He trots across the courtyard to his grandfather and Jeremiah Peabody wraps his arms around the boy. "It is so very good to see you!" He holds out an arm to their mother. "Come, come, let me greet you as well. And where is Gerald?" He looks toward the wagon and nods to Old Pete, who's climbed off the seat and is unhitching the mules. "Peter, how are you?"

"I'm well, thankee," Old Pete says somberly. He glances at Alma's mother. "Me and Gregorio here'll take these ol' mules around back and give them some feed."

As Jeremiah nods in agreement, his eyes stray to the back of the wagon and the rocking chair. He turns to Alma's mother. His voice changes, cautious now. "And Gerald?"

"He's in the valley."

He looks into her face, then at each child. Andrew's chin lifts defiantly but Alma's eyes fill as she meets her grandfather's gaze. She blinks and looks away. He frowns a little and turns toward the door. "But you are tired from your journey and surely hungry, as well. Come inside and we'll get you some food and black tea."

Alma smiles as she follows the adults and her brother into the dim hallway. This is how her mother has told her he greets every visitor to his home.

The first door they come to is open. "This is Consuela, my cook and housekeeper," Alma's grandfather says. A plump woman with streaks of white in her hair looks up from the table in the center of the room. "My daughter and grandchildren," he tells her. "They've come down from the mountains to visit me. Could you bring in tea and some biscuits?"

Then he escorts them further down the hall and into the parlor her mother has spoken of with such affection. Chairs line the wall left of the door. To the right is a round table covered with a white cloth. Opposite the door, two tall well-filled bookcases flank the fireplace. Cushions brighten the adobe window seat below the mica-paned windows. Except they aren't mica.

"You've replaced the mica with glass!" Alma's mother says. "How wonderful!" She turns slowly, looking at the room. "It all looks so different. So much brighter!"

He smiles a little guiltily. "When St. Vrain offered them to me, I couldn't refuse, even though they cost more than I could really afford. But the extra light has been a blessing and I'll probably make up for the cost because I won't have to buy so many candles."

She laughs in delight. "It makes such a difference!"

Consuela comes in with a tray that holds a pitcher of water, teacups, and saucers. "I thought you'd be thirsty for water." She sets the tray on the table. "I'll bring the tea shortly."

"An excellent plan." Alma's grandfather rubs his hands together. "Suzanna, will you do the honors?" He settles himself into an armchair by the fireplace. "Now, tell me all your news."

Alma and Andrew look at each other, then their mother, who has moved to the table. They all watch as she pours water into the teacups and hands them around. Alma retreats to the window seat and Andrew drops into a chair beside the door. Their mother fills a cup for herself and settles next to Alma.

Her father takes a sip of water, then places the cup on a tiny table beside his chair, next to a book and a pair of spectacles. His eyes narrow slightly as he looks toward the window. She drinks her water in one gulp, then stands up. "I was more thirsty than I realized." She looks from one child to the other. "Does anyone want more?"

Alma shakes her head and runs a finger along the edge of the cup's handle. Andrew jumps out of his chair. "I do! I'll get it!"

As he heads toward the table, Alma looks at her grandfather, who's studying her mother. "Perhaps the children should go to the kitchen for their tea," he says.

"They can stay if they like." A note of bitterness creeps into her voice. "There's no privacy on that farm. They know what's happened and why we're here."

His mouth thins. He looks so much like her mother just now that Alma would giggle if she wasn't so sad. "Andrew," he says. "Alma. Go ask Consuela to give you your tea in the kitchen. Or you can take it out to the courtyard if you like."

# CHAPTER 8

When the children appear in the doorway to the kitchen, Consuela looks up in surprise.

"Grandfather said we should have tea here," Andrew tells her.

The cook waves a hand at the table. It's covered with flour, baking utensils, and a tray that holds a blue-flowered teapot and a plate piled with biscuits. "There is no room." In the corner fireplace, a big copper kettle begins to burble. She turns toward it. "And I am baking. It is not a good time."

"We can go into the courtyard," Alma offers. "We can have our tea there."

"Two places," the cook sniffs. She lifts the teakettle from the fire, moves to the table, and begins filling the flowered pot. She glances at the corner cupboard, where there's another pot, a simple brown one. "Two teas and not one."

"I can help." Alma moves to the cupboard, lifts the pot from its shelf, and carries it to the table.

Consuela picks up the flowered pot, pours the water from it into the brown one, then drops tea leaves into the first pot and adds more hot water. She looks up and jerks her chin toward the cupboard. "The tea is in the wood box."

Alma returns to the corner, lifts down a flat ornately carved container, and carries it to the table. When the cook lifts the lid, the rich scent of black tea fills the air. Alma leans forward to examine the oblong of compressed leaves inside. Three of the squares have been cut out and used already, so the block is no longer rectangular. The piece that juts out has been reduced to perhaps half its original size.

Consuela drains the water from the brown pot, then reaches for a small knife. She carefully slices a sliver of tea off the block, places it in the pot, and pours more hot water in. As she pours, she nods toward the pot on the tray. "You should take that in now. Before it gets bitter."

Alma looks at her in surprise, then realizes the cook doesn't know why she and Andrew were sent out of the room. She takes a deep breath and gingerly lifts the tray. When she nears the doorway, Andrew snatches a biscuit from the plate, then retreats into the hall and out the courtyard door. It thuds behind him as she moves carefully toward the parlor.

The tray is heavy and requires both hands. Alma pauses outside the door, uncertain how to hold it and open the door at the same time. She braces the edge of the tray between the adobe wall and her hip and reaches for the door.

Then she stops. Inside the room, her mother's voice rises in frustration. "Tarnation! You haven't heard a word of what I've just said!"

"I have heard you very well," Alma's grandfather answers. "However, I believe you are not being entirely truthful with yourself or with me."

"Truthful! How dare—" There's a short silence, then she speaks again. "Would you care to explain yourself?"

"Before Gerald asked me for your hand you made it very clear that you saw no need to pry into his background." His voice drops. Alma has to strain to hear him. "You were in love."

"I didn't want you to discover something that would make you refuse him." Her tone sharpens. "You were convinced I was too young. You would have latched onto anything to make us wait."

"Hmm." It's the voice he uses when he doesn't want to say what's really on his mind.

"My age at the time is not relevant to this discussion." Her mother sounds downright sulky. "He lied to me."

"He wasn't completely forthcoming. It's not quite the same thing."

A chair squeaks. When she speaks again, it's clear she's moved across the room. Her voice has changed. She sounds more puzzled than angry. "Doesn't this news surprise you, at least? Concern you in any way?"

His tone is carefully neutral. "Why would it?"

"You knew." There's a pause, then she says again, "You knew! And you didn't think I should be told?"

"You said you didn't want to know anything about him but what you had seen with your own eyes and heard with your own ears. Perhaps not in those words. But that was clearly your intent."

"Tarnation!" she says again.

There's another moment of silence. Then suddenly the door to the room flies open. Alma straightens and lifts the tea tray. Her mother glares down at her. "You undoubtedly knew, also!" She stalks into the hall and toward the courtyard door. "Everybody seems to have known but me!"

The next morning, she stays in bed. Old One Eye Pete has gone off to visit friends at the pueblo. The children and their grandfather eat breakfast in silence at the kitchen table, although Alma stirs her porridge more than she eats it. There's a hard lump in her belly that's been there since her mother stormed out of the parlor.

Alma watches Andrew gulp down his food. When he eyes her dish, she scoots it across to him. When the bowl scrapes the table top, her grandfather looks up but doesn't comment. Alma sits with her hands in her lap, waiting dully for whatever is going to happen next. She's very tired. The night was a long one.

Finally, Grandfather Peabody puts his spoon in his bowl, drains the last of his strawberry leaf tea, and nods to the cook. "Thank you, Consuela. That was a fine repast."

"I am sorry there were no eggs for you this morning, señor," she says. "Gregorio is still trying to understand where the snake is entering the coop."

"I'll manage without eggs every morning," he says. "Though I do enjoy them when they're available." He turns to Andrew. "I wonder if that dog of yours might help to locate the reptilian entrance point."

Andrew nods eagerly. "Chaser can find anything!"

Consuela sniffs. "He is so big, he will destroy the nest boxes."

Alma's grandfather strokes his chin beard. "He might at that. Perhaps that wasn't such a good idea." He turns back to Andrew, whose mouth is twisted in disappointment. "But I know he is an excellent companion. Perhaps we should take him to the plaza with us and introduce him to mis vecinos."

On the way to the center of town, their grandfather explains that the Don Fernando de Taos plaza consists of joined abode buildings constructed around a large hollow square. It has four entrances, each with a big wooden gate that can be barred and locked.

"To keep the Comanches out?" Andrew asks.

He nods. "Comanches or Utes or Navajo. It was constructed many years ago. Nowadays, the only Indians who raid in New Mexico are the Navajo and they're more interested in the pastures than the towns. They primarily want sheep."

Alma reaches for his hand. She's heard the stories. "And boys to herd them and girls to spin and weave the wool."

He squeezes her fingers in his. "But you have a mastiff to protect you. At any rate, I'm certain you aren't foolish enough to wander the fields by yourself."

Alma thinks wistfully of her mountain valley streams and their fat trout, and nods. Chaser Two loops around behind Andrew and her grandfather and nudges at her hand. She smiles at him and pats his big head.

They're at the northeast corner of the plaza now. It looks like a much larger version of her grandfather's courtyard, except instead of plants and woodpiles on its edges there are long, covered porches and people sitting or squatting in their shade.

Some of the people have laid out blankets and arranged produce, pots, or other goods on them for sale. Others stand talking or move from vendor to vendor, shopping. The sun beats down from a bright blue sky with a single white cloud in it.

Andrew steps to one side to investigate the contents of a blanket. He picks up a wooden whistle and turns to show it to Alma. "It looks like the one Old Pete made me!"

His grandfather gently takes the whistle from the boy's hand and returns it to the blanket with an apologetic word to the vendor, a man wrapped in a big red-striped white blanket. "You must not touch something unless you are interested in purchasing it," he tells the children. "It's not polite."

"Oh." Andrew puts his hands behind his back and turns to the man. "Perdóneme."

The corner of the man's eyes crinkle as he smiles at the boy, then his sister. "De nada."

"Are your grandchildren stealing again?" a deep voice says from behind them.

The children jerk around, but their grandfather only laughs. "Ah, Padre," he says. "You've caught us at last."

A thick-chested man with a high forehead and wearing a long black robe smiles at Andrew, then Alma, benevolently. There's a sharpness in his eyes that doesn't match his expression. Alma offers him a small smile anyway. Andrew studies him wide-eyed.

"Padre, these are my grandchildren, Alma and Andrew Locke," their grandfather says. "Children, this is Padre Antonio José Martínez."

Alma gives him a small curtsy, as her mother has taught her, and the priest laughs in delight. Andrew says, "I've heard about you!"

The Padre chuckles and gives their grandfather a sideways glance. "Only good things, I hope."

"You share books with Grandfather Peabody and talk with him about important things," Alma says before her brother can repeat the gossip Old One Eye Pete and Bill Williams have brought to the cabin. Things about women and money and power that she doesn't really understand. Padre Martínez smiles at her, then turns back to her grandfather. "She looks remarkably like her father. That square-shaped face and that hair."

Alma takes her grandfather's hand and turns her head so the priest can't see her left cheek. She should have worn her sunbonnet.

But the men aren't paying attention to her anymore. Another man has joined them, a man taller than Grandfather Peabody. She tilts her head to get a better look. His skin is almost as pale as her New England grandfather's, and he has dancing brown eyes and wavy black hair. He's standing still, but it almost feels like he's moving. Energy seems to radiate from him. He gives her a bright glance, then nods respectfully at something her grandfather is saying. Next to Gregorio, he's the handsomest man she's ever seen.

Then Grandfather Peabody turns to her and says her name. "This is Señor Donaciano Vigil." He gives the man a questioning look. "I believe he's a relative of Ramón."

"Juan Ramón Chavez of Don Fernando de Taos?" The man laughs and spreads his hands, palms up. "Isn't everyone in Nuevo México related to Ramón?"

"I thought you were in prison for insubordination," Padre Martínez asks. "Or can they jail presidio soldiers for insubordination when you aren't being paid?"

Señor Vigil laughs again. "I am in town for only a short time, on an errand for the governor, but I have to report to el calabozo as soon as I return to Santa Fe."

Padre Martínez looks at Alma's grandfather. "Surely you've heard the story." He nods toward the newcomer. "This one here didn't give his superior officer due deference and the credit the officer thought he deserved at Valencia's mercantile. As a result, the señor here was arrested for insubordination."

Vigil spreads his hands, palms up. "Because Governor Pérez ran out of money for the troops, I was assisting my cousin in his store, translating and clerking, fetching and carrying." He grimaces. "Now I'm either sitting in jail or running errands for the governor." Then he grins. "Actually, working in the store and being in jail are much alike. Both involve a great deal of sitting around, interspersed with activity. Except for the pay and not carrying a weapon, I still have the duties of a soldier."

"You're a soldier?" Andrew breaks in. He stares at the tall man in admiration.

Alma's grandfather frowns. Donaciano Vigil gives him a swift glance, then nods at the boy. "I am. But right now there is no money to pay me, so I do other work. Soldiering is not a good livelihood if one has a family. And it's often quite boring."

"Like the Navajo campaign you returned from in March," Padre Martínez observes.

Señor Vigil grins. "That was both boring and cold." He turns to Alma's grandfather. "Although your man Gregorio Garcia comported himself well. I was glad to make his acquaintance."

"He is not my man," he answers. "Although he does work for me occasionally. But I will pass your kind words on to his mother, who was not pleased when he joined the militia."

Padre Martínez frowns. "I will speak to her also. It is a man's duty to participate in the militia when it is called upon. The Navajo are a constant danger to us and must be repelled at all costs. I and my brothers have lost many sheep and even cattle to them over the years."

Señor Vigil is looking past Alma's grandfather to the northeast entrance of the plaza. "Ah, but here is the man himself."

Alma turns. Gregorio moves toward them, a bundle of linens in each hand. She smiles brightly at him, but he's focused on her grandfather and the other men. He moves his hands toward his back, making the bundles seem smaller.

"Gregorio Garcia!" the priest says playfully. "It's been a long time since I've seen you at mass!"

Gregorio nods respectfully to each of the men in turn. "Sargento," he says to Señor Vigil.

"We were just speaking of you and military service," Alma's grandfather says.

Gregorio smiles slightly. "Although the campaign last winter was a cold one and we didn't see any Navajo, I found I enjoyed it."

Señor Vigil claps him on the back. "Good man!" He peers at Gregorio's bundles. "And now, like me, you have returned to town and all the duties pertaining thereto." He grins conspiratorially. "We do what we must to keep our households fed and warm."

Gregorio gives him a rueful look. "My mother launders, I deliver." Then he turns to Alma's grandfather. "And assist others where I can. I will come this afternoon to search again for that snake."

"Ah, Consuela will be glad to hear it." He nods toward Chaser, who's still standing patiently beside Alma. "Andrew and the mastiff may be of some assistance to you, also."

"I can help too." Alma looks into Gregorio's face. "I'm not the least bit afraid of snakes."

"Like mother, like daughter," the priest chuckles.

Alma's head jerks toward him. She certainly hopes not. She opens her mouth to say so, but his eyes are sharp as a serpent's, even though his lips are smiling. She looks at Gregorio instead.

He grins back at her. "Of course you can help, nita." He glances at her grandfather. "If your abuelo agrees."

He nods and gives the children a stern look. "Catching a snake is serious business. You must exercise caution and obey Señor Garcia in whatever he tells you to do."

# CHAPTER 9

The chickens are housed in the section of the compound that includes the stable and is accessed through the brown door in the courtyard. There's a small wood-latticed window above the bench beside the door, with shutters to cover it at night. The door has two sections, above and below. Right now the upper portion is open and the lower part is shut.

Gregorio unlatches the lower piece and the children follow him into the stable's cool interior. It's a big space with loose hay at one end. A big wooden door is open on the far side, opposite the courtyard. Through it, Alma sees a pole corral and the wagon mules nosing at the water trough. Chickens peck in the dirt nearby.

Gregorio turns to the right. The children follow him through another half door into a small adobe-walled room. The latticed window that sits above the bench outside is on their right. Light slips from it in a golden dust-flecked stream. Andrew chuckles and swipes at it with his hands.

"At first I thought the snake was getting in through the window," Gregorio says. "But I've lined the edges of the shutter and both the doors with strips of buffalo pelt and now this room is tight as a barrel when everything's closed up at night." He shakes his head. "And still the snake enters."

Alma moves toward the wall on her left. It contains rows of shelves made of round sticks crisscrossed over each other. Thin blocks of wood are positioned at intervals to form nests for the chickens. The straw in them is empty.

She frowns. "Aren't there any eggs at all?"

"Consuela has already collected what few there were this morning." Gregorio points to the floor below the lowest shelf. "See the shells? That's the sign a snake has been here."

The children bend over the fragments of brown shell. They're very clean.

Andrew squats down and peers under the shelf. "I see a crack in the wall." He pulls back and squints at Gregorio. "But a snake couldn't get through something that small."

Gregorio squats beside him and bends toward the floor, twisting his neck to see, but he's too big. Alma giggles and he pulls himself up and grins at her. "Can you spot it?"

She bends, folding herself in two, and peers under the shelf. "It looks like someone scratched a line in the clay, almost straight up and down."

As she straightens, Andrew flattens himself onto the dirt floor and squirms his head and chest under the wooden ledge. "There's a kind of a hole at the top. Right up under the shelf." He pulls out and scrambles to his feet. He scrunches his three middle fingers together and shows them to Gregorio. "It's about this big."

"That would be large enough. Thank you Andrew! I would not have found it without your help." He turns toward the door.

"Aren't we going to get to see the snake and catch it?" Andrew asks.

"If that's the only hole, then the problem is solved. I'll mix up some mud and patch it and the snake won't be able to get inside anymore."

"Maybe that's not the only hole," Andrew says. Before Gregorio can stop him, he drops back onto the floor, scoots all the way under the egg platform, and begins working his way from one end to the other. "Nope, that's the only one," he says as he reaches the far wall. He begins to push himself backward into the room, then suddenly stops short and makes a choking sound.

Gregorio waves Alma back as he moves toward her brother. "What is it?"

"A—" His voice wobbles. "A snake."

"Move away slowly. Slowly now."

Andrew takes a deep breath but doesn't budge.

Gregorio tries a different tack. "Can you see what color it is?"

Andrew's foot twitches. "It's got stripes."

"What is it doing?"

"Just laying there. In the corner. Blinking."

"It isn't poisonous. Poisonous snakes don't eat eggs. It's probably still digesting its meal, which means it can't move very fast."

"Are you sure?"

"Just move slowly backward into the room."

Andrew shudders. His legs twitch. Then he edges cautiously backward and stands up, wobbling a little. His face is pale in the light from the window. Gregorio reaches to steady him and Alma lets out a breath she didn't know she'd been holding.

"It has white stripes and two kinds of dark stripes." Andrew frowns, concentrating. "I think one of them is black and the other is maybe red." He shakes his head. "It's too dark back there. I couldn't tell for sure."

"It must be a milk snake," Gregorio says. "I'll go ask Señor Peabody for his pistol."

Andrew's eyes widen. "Why?"

"It's eating the chicken eggs." He chuckles. "It's digesting one right now."

"I thought you were going to catch it. Can't you catch it and take it someplace where it can eat mice and things like that?"

Gregorio studies the boy, then smiles a little and nods.

"How will you do it?" Alma asks.

"Go get me a stick that has a fork or a crook at one end and I'll show you."

The children dart into the stable and return a few minutes later with a three-pronged wooden pitchfork. "That will do," Gregorio says. "Now go to the kitchen and ask Consuela for a sack from her storeroom. We'll use it to keep the snake safe until we release it."

As they enter the courtyard, Alma looks at her brother and laughs. His shirt and trousers are covered with a layer of dirt, straw, chicken poop, and bits of feather. "You'd better brush yourself off!"

He looks down, laughs, and beats at his clothes with his hands. A cloud of dust and feathers flies up. He laughs again, shrugs, and trots toward the house door.

They run into the hall and turn toward the closed kitchen door. Then they pause and look at each other in alarm. Their mother's voice is loud and furious. "I can go where I like and take my children with me! This isn't the United States! I have rights!"

The women must be at the end of the table nearest the door. The cook's voice is lower, but the children can hear her answer. "But they are his children, too. Surely you cannot stay here with them without his agreement. Not permanently."

"We'll see about that!"

Alma's stomach twists. She looks at her brother, who blinks at her, then backs toward the door to the courtyard.

Alma follows him. As they emerge into the sunlight, Gregorio comes out of the stable. "Did she have a bag for you?"

The children shake their heads. He tilts his head at them questioningly. When they both look away, he turns back toward the stable. "We'll find something here, then. Perhaps a saddle blanket we can turn into a pouch."

Andrew's hand slips into Alma's as they cross the yard toward him.

# CHAPTER 10

"This is just like the old days," Alma's mother says as she pours out the tea. She looks up and smiles at Carlos Beaubien, who's sitting in her rocking chair.

Alma and Andrew are perched on the banco, the adobe bench built into the wall below the window. They roll their eyes at each other. They've heard about the old days in their grandfather's parlor often enough. This is where their mother met Old Bill Williams, Ceran St. Vrain, Peg Leg Smith, and all the other trappers. And their father. Alma's eyes drop and she touches the heart-shaped freckle on her cheek.

"Not quite like the old days," William Workman says in his thick North England voice. He grins at their mother, but there's a hint of malice in the very placidity of his broad forehead. "I was persona non grata in those days."

She smiles at the teacup she's filling. "And are you still producing Taos lightning and smuggling in goods under the noses of the customs officials?"

Old Pete, who's in a chair by the door, chuckles, but Mr. Workman says, "Well, I wasn't, but I may need to go back to doing so."

Charles Bent shakes his head. His thin black hair is flat above his knotted eyebrows. "I'd think twice about that. If you're caught, Governor Pérez will take everything you own and then some."

"Ah, but William has coin, and le gouverneur does not," the Frenchman Carlos Beaubien says. "He has not been going into debt to you and St. Vrain and the other merchants, as Pérez has."

Mr. Bent's eyes twinkle in spite of his perpetually skeptical look. "Pérez hasn't borrowed from you?"

Carlos Beaubien's smile splits his narrow face. "I have managed to keep my distance up to this point. But if he does approach me, I doubt I will have much choice in the matter."

Mr. Bent shakes his head. "These enforced loans are not good for business."

Alma's grandfather raises an eyebrow. "But from what I understand, business is booming"

"Well, yes," William Workman concedes. "That's quite true, as far as it goes. The trade to Missouri and Chihuahua, and now to California, are all doing well enough." His face darkens. "But the Mexican ricos are trying to cut in on our trade. In fact, our sheep-rearing former Governor has done quite well for himself in that regard."

Alma's mother gestures to her and then toward the plate of bizcochitos beside the teapot. Alma slides off the banco and crosses the room. Her mother hands her the plate. "I assume you mean former Governor Manuel Armijo?"

Alma stops in front of him and proffers the anise-flavored cookies. He takes one and nods at her mother. "From what I hear, Señor Armijo is doing quite well."

"Now that's a typical British understatement," Alma's grandfather says. "My understanding is that the flocks Armijo has sent to Chihuahua in the last few years have resulted in quite a handsome return."

"As have the woven goods he and others have transported south," Charles Bent says. "Everything from fine blankets to

73

jerga floor coverings." He shakes his head at Alma's proffered plate. "We should start a weaving manufactory here in Don Fernando like they have in Chimayó."

"I hear tell they're totin' 'em to Californee, too," Old Pete says. He grins at Alma and takes a cookie. "I'm tempted to try it my own self. Buy goods cheap from the Chimayosos and haul 'em west and then bring me back some of those wild horses I hear are ripe for the takin' out there." He glances at Alma's grandfather. "Ramón Chavez told me about a widow lady cousin of his in Chimayó who weaves. Even told me where I can find her."

Alma offers a cookie to her brother and completes her circle of the room. She places the half-empty plate on the table and returns to the banco. As she passes Carlos Beaubien, he says, "Woven goods are always in demand, but the wild horses in California may be scarce. I suspect Peg Leg Smith and his compagnons d'armes have already collected all the mustangs to be obtained there." He glances at Charles Bent. "The word is that the herd they sold at your fort on the Arkansas last year was considerable." He glances at Alma's mother, then refocuses on the trader. "Was not Old Bill Williams part of that gang of thieves?"

"The last I heard, Old Bill was trapping in Yellowstone country," Mr. Bent says. "I haven't laid eyes on that old coot in a couple years now." He stands and stretches. "It's time for me to get back to the store." He turns to Old Pete. "If you're serious about doing some trading, I'd recommend going south rather than west. The route to Chihuahua's more established and you're more likely to find a group to caravan with. Neither route is advisable without a good-sized party around you."

Old Pete raises the eyebrow above his good eye. "Why's that?"

"The Navajo are acting up again," William Workman puts in. "Escaping Pérez' troops last winter seems to have bolstered their confidence."

Mr. Bent nods. "They're been ranging far and wide. I hear tell they've even been nosing around the Martínez flocks here in the valley."

At the word 'valley,' Alma's head swings toward him. Then she realizes he's not talking about her valley, but the broad plains around Don Fernando . "Are there really Navajos this far east?" she asks.

Her mother gives her a sharp glance, then looks at the Frenchman. "Just how difficult would it be to set up a weaving enterprise here?"

"You'd need wool," William Workman answers for him, his eyes twinkling. This time the rest of his face reflects his amusement. "I probably have some I could sell you."

Her lips quirk. "But only if I don't ask where it came from."

"You'd need someone to weave that wool," Charles Bent says. "Unless you plan on acquiring Navajo slaves, that would be difficult."

"Isn't there weaving done at the pueblo of Taos?"

"Yes, but they don't sell much of it. At least, they don't offer it to St. Vrain and me at the store. Most of what we carry is from around Chimayó."

She looks at her father. "Don't you have friends at Chimayó?"

"I'm sure I know someone there, but Ramón is the one with connections in that area."

"It's not an easy skill to acquire," Charles Bent says. "And those Spanish looms the Chimayosos use are big and heavy." He turns toward the door. "It's a man's work, really."

75

As he leaves, the other men follow his example. Alma's mother shoos the children into the passageway after them. The men say their goodbyes in the courtyard and she turns back to the blue house door. Alma moves to follow her, but she waves her off. "I need to talk to your grandfather."

Alma scowls and crosses to the bench by the brown door, where Andrew is tootling on his whistle, trying to produce more than two notes on it.

Alma leans back on the bench and restlessly moves her feet back and forth, scraping the dirt beneath. "Now she wants to set up a weaving workshop," she grumbles. "It sounds like she wants to stay here forever."

Chaser trots into the courtyard, gives them a welcoming woof, then comes to snuffle at Alma's skirt. She pushes his head away.

Andrew stops tootling and reaches for the dog. He scratches behind the mastiff's floppy ears. "It's not Chaser Two's fault you can't hear what Mama and Grandfather are talkin' about," he says. "Besides, I like it here. It's sunny and that makes Mama feel good. And there's lots to do, with the market and all."

Alma sniffs and touches her cheek. Lots to do and lots of people looking at her. "Adults don't talk about anything important if they think children will hear," she complains.

Andrew gives the dog's head a double pat. "We know what to do about that, don't we Chaser?"

"What are you talking about?"

He grins at her. "The fireplace in the storage room behind the kitchen shares a chimney with the parlor."

"But Consuela's always in the kitchen."

"There's another door." He gestures toward the stable. "On the back wall beside the hay."

Her eyes widen, but she shakes her head. "We'd be eavesdropping."

"Like we did at the kitchen door."

"That was different. It was accidental."

He shrugs. "You're the one who wants to know what they're saying in the parlor."

"But it's not polite."

"Like Papa not telling Mama about his daddy?"

"She told him she didn't want to know."

"But she really did, didn't she? Secrets are never good. And listening is the only way we're gonna find out. She isn't going to tell us what she's thinking." He bends over Chaser's head, scratching the dog's chin.

Alma studies her brother's profile. It's the first time since they learned their father's secret that Andrew has said anything even slightly negative about their mother. "Does your stomach hurt, too?" she asks quietly.

He glances sideways at her, then focuses on the dog. He nods his head and scratches Chaser's chin even harder.

She scoots off the bench. "Let's go then."

# PART II

# JUNE–JULY 1837

# CHIMAYÓ

# CHAPTER 11

The storage room is quiet and dim. It's crowded with slightly dusty barrels of food and coils of rope. Two saddles are draped over poles attached with ropes to the vigas overhead. There's an open space by the adobe fireplace in the left-hand corner, beside the narrow path from the kitchen to Consuela's room. The thick wood doors to both rooms are firmly shut, but Alma still eyes them nervously.

Andrew tugs at her elbow and points to the empty hearth. The children arrange themselves in front of it. They tuck their legs up, wrap their arms around their knees, and lean forward, holding their breath.

The voices are small, as if they're very far away, but they're remarkably clear. Chaser snuffles at Andrew's shirt. He gently pushes the dog away and puts his fingers to his lips. The mastiff snuffles again, then moves off to lay beside a wicker basket filled with unhusked corn. The children lean further into the empty fireplace.

"We can't stay here indefinitely," their mother's voice says. "You've made that abundantly clear."

"As I recall, I said you couldn't stay away from the valley indefinitely," their grandfather says.

"That I most certainly can do."

"I don't have the resources—"

"To support me and two children. Yes, I know." There's a pause, then her voice becomes apologetic. "I didn't come here to be a burden to you, Papa. I just didn't know what else to do."

"You could go home."

"He lied to me!"

Even though Alma can't see him, she knows how her grandfather is responding to this: the lips grim and tight above the graying chin beard, the pain in his eyes before they close, then open again. "It will serve no purpose for us to discuss the issue of contention between you and Gerald," he says. "However, if you are determined to remain here in Don Fernando de Taos, we need to evaluate options for potential ways for you to sustain yourself and the children."

Andrew's eyebrows quirk at Alma. She grins. Grandfather's language always becomes formal when he's trying to keep his temper.

"I've thought about teaching," their mother says. "You've certainly prepared me for that."

"As you know, Padre Martínez provides that service here. In addition to his seminary for young men who want to become priests, he also teaches children of both sexes to read, write, and do simple arithmetic."

"In Spanish."

"Yes. Those whose parents can afford to have them learn English come to me."

"And Latin?"

"No one studies that unless they're preparing for the priesthood." There's a short pause, then he says drily, "After all, it is a Catholic country."

Alma and Andrew exchange a grin. Grandfather may be friends with Padre Martínez, but he's still Protestant to the bone. Then their heads jerk back toward the chimney as their mother says, "So there's no room for me in Don Fernando's crowded educational market."

"Not particularly."

"There are other things I could do."

"Such as?"

"I could take Consuela's place."

The children roll their eyes at each other as their grandfather says, "That would require cooking."

"It's your fault I can't cook! You wouldn't let me near the kitchen! Latin and botany were more important. That certainly hasn't done me much good."

Alma's belly churns. She bites her lip.

"Perhaps you could get a clerking position in one of the mercantiles," her grandfather says.

"I've already talked to Charles Bent and Carlos Beaubien about that. They have all the help they need." There's a short pause, then she adds. "I even talked to Antonia Garcia about taking in laundry."

"Laundry?"

"I've had plenty of experience."

"Doing your family's wash and taking in other people's laundry are two very different enterprises."

"I know it. And it's unlikely to pay enough to keep us. Unless we lived here with you."

"I don't have room for that kind of operation." There's a long pause, then he says mildly, "You could also go back to the valley."

"I'm not going back!" It's practically a shout. Alma bites the insides of her cheeks and Andrew drops his forehead to his knees.

"You can't remain away indefinitely. Children need their father." Grandfather Peabody sounds tired. As if he's said it before and knows there's no use saying it again, but is doing so anyway.

"You kept me from my mother."

"I kept you from spending much time with your mother, but I didn't banish her from the household or take you elsewhere to live. Given her morals, I had every right to take either of those options. She pursued every man who came within—"

Now she's the one who sounds tired. "Yes, Papa, I know. But I'm not going back. At least not for a long time."

Alma takes a deep steadying breath. At least she's not saying 'ever.'

"So what is it you plan to do?" her mother's father asks.

"I thought—" There's a little pause, then she starts again. "It seems to me that weaving might be an option. If I can go to Chimayó and learn to do that, I could come back and perhaps set up a loom here. I could buy wool from the Martínez family and probably make enough to at least keep the children in clothes and shoes."

"Do you know someone there who would be willing to teach you?"

"I can ask Ramón's cousin, the one he told Old Pete about."

"Weavers are usually men."

"She apparently took over her husband's loom after he died."

"Ah." A chair scrapes. Alma pictures him standing, moving to one of the tall bookshelves beside the fireplace, lifting a volume, then putting it back. Then he speaks again. "But a loom will cost money, as will the wool. And if the woman is willing to teach you, she ought to be compensated for her time."

"I have funds."

The children exchange surprised looks.

Grandfather must also look surprised, because their mother's voice is a little apologetic now, although also defensive. "I wasn't sure what lay ahead of us, so I took the money we'd saved for glass windows."

Alma's jaw drops. Her parents have been scraping money together for glass windowpanes since before she was born. Her mother has always hated the thick pieces of mica in the cabin windows. It's something she complains about regularly, especially during the winter months. If she took the money for them, she really doesn't plan to return. Alma's chin trembles and Andrew lifts his head and pats her hand. "She hasn't spent it," he whispers.

"She's planning to!" she hisses.

Then their mother is speaking again. They tilt their heads toward the sound. "Gerald knows I have it. I didn't take it without his knowledge. I wasn't sure what lay ahead and it seemed wise to have something to fall back on."

"You'll need someone to accompany you to Chimayó. It's dangerous for a woman and children to travel alone."

"I'll ask Old Pete to go with us. He doesn't seem to be in any hurry to get back into the mountains."

"I've observed that also," he says. "None of the mountain men seem very anxious these days to return to the wilderness. Trapping is being replaced by trading as the best way to make the proverbial killing. The next thing we know, Old One Eye Pete will be on a caravan heading south to Chihuahua with a cargo of Chimayó woolen goods." Then his voice changes. "Though Chimayó isn't the safest place to be at the moment. I hear that there's a great deal of unrest there."

Alma's chest eases. Mama won't go if it's dangerous. Will she?

"You mean because of the government tax policies? There's always unrest about taxes in New Mexico. Taxes or tariffs on the merchants' goods. That's why people like William Workman can get away with smuggling goods in through the mountains. The complaining and the smuggling have been going on for as long as I can remember."

"This is worse. Surely you've heard the rumors, even in the valley."

"We've heard them. Every time someone comes through on their way to Missouri, we hear complaints about the governor's interference in local affairs and the imposition of new import duties and new fees. People in Santa Fe are even complaining about the levy to pay for schools. They ought to be delighted that schools have finally been organized there."

"They've had schools."

"For the children of the ricos. Not for the poor." Then her voice changes. "I wonder if they have enough teachers."

Andrew straightens and looks at Alma, his eyes bright with hope. Alma scowls at him. Santa Fe is far to the south, farther than Chimayó. Even farther away from the valley and her father.

The anxiety in her stomach is echoed in her grandfather's voice. "Surely you wouldn't go so far as Santa Fe?"

"It was simply an observation. It would be more useful for me to learn a trade. Something that would be physically active and not require that I sit still for long periods of time."

"Weaving certainly seems to meet those criteria. And Chimayó is at least closer to Don Fernando de Taos." A pleading note enters his voice, something Alma has rarely heard from Grandfather Peabody. "And when you have learned what you can, you can return here."

Alma holds her breath, waiting for her mother's response, but there is only silence in the other room. Alma bites her lip, slips off the hearth, and moves toward the door to the stable.

Andrew scrambles after her. "Chimayó!" he hisses, his eyes bright. "That's a long way from here!" Alma scowls at him and turns away.

# CHAPTER 12

She cheers up slightly when Gregorio Garcia volunteers to accompany them to Chimayó. Old Pete will come also, but he plans to push on to Santa Fe almost immediately, to make arrangements to head south with a trade caravan. Gregorio might stay longer. He has relatives there on his father's side.

They pull out early on a crisp June morning, Gregorio driving the buckboard and Old Pete on his mule beside it, moving south toward Ranchos de Taos between fields of spring wheat and barley, past plots of new corn and potatoes.

Alma twists around to study the plains of Taos Valley one last time. It still doesn't seem like much of a valley to her. It's too flat, too broad. But the morning light streams golden on the grain in the fields and touches the cows in the pastures beyond them. And it's closer to home than Chimayó will be.

She bites the insides of her cheeks and turns back to face the road. She puts her hands on either side of her head, flattens the sides of her bonnet closer to her face, and closes her eyes. She doesn't want to see anymore.

They're taking the wagon road into the mountains southeast of Don Fernando instead of following the narrower and rockier track straight south on the hills above the río del Norte. Pine trees close in as they move into the foothills, but Alma doesn't stir. Not even the sound of the stream beside the road, or Gregorio and Andrew's discussion about how it's used to operate the local grist mill, can open her eyes.

They may be in the mountains again, but these aren't her hills. And this road is taking her further from home, not toward it. Even the spicy resin smell of pine needles in the sun can't comfort her.

A wagon journey from Don Fernando to Chimayó usually takes two days. Alma's mother wants to arrive in full daylight, not dusk, so Old Pete advises three days on the road. Andrew is excited about sleeping under the summer stars. Alma isn't. They'll just remind her of her valley's vast stream of overhead nighttime brilliance.

Her only comfort is that the extra day will give her more time on the buckboard seat beside Gregorio. It's true he treats her like a younger sister, but she can still take sideways peeks at his kind brown face, his dark eyes, and long lashes, the shy quirk of his mouth when he smiles.

Most of the time, Old One Eye Pete is on his mule, riding behind the wagon and keeping a querulous eye on Chaser, who threads his way through the boulders and trees beside the road, following scent trails.

Andrew's perched in the back of the wagon on the wooden chest that holds the children's clothes. When they stop at noon to graze the mules and eat a quick meal of jerky and bread, he announces that he's going to join the dog.

"Stay within calling distance," his mother says.

"You need to keep up now," Old Pete adds. "We don't need t' be trailin' after you when you get lost in the trees and rocks, or step on a rattler."

"I won't get lost," Andrew says. "And Chaser can smell a rattlesnake a mile away."

"It's the human rattlers I'm talkin' about."

"Chaser'll take care of those, too." Andrew stuffs the last of his jerky in his mouth. "C'mon, boy. Let's get a head start." He and the mastiff trot onto the road and head south.

Old Pete shakes his head and lifts his canteen to his lips. He takes a long drink, wipes his mouth with the back of his hand, and looks at Alma's mother. "I didn't realize that boy had such an adventurous streak."

"He's never been out of the valley. This is quite an experience for him."

He turns to Alma. "You ain't never been west of the valley yourself, have you, little missy?"

She shakes her head and looks away.

"And don't have a hankerin' for it neither," he says, but she doesn't answer.

Gregorio stands and heads toward the mules. They lift their heads expectantly. Alma follows him. "Can I help with the harness?"

The rest of the day is quiet. The road winds through the mountains, clinging to the valley bottoms as much as possible. The slopes above are dark with pine. Old Pete mutters about dogs, boys, rocks, and snakes, but Andrew and Chaser appear from time to time, crisscrossing the road ahead, and after a while the mountain man stops fussing.

The rim of the western canyon is black against the lingering light when the mastiff appears at the top of the next hill. He drops onto his haunches in the middle of the road and sits looking down at them, his mouth slightly open.

"Now where's that boy?" grumbles Old Pete, who's now riding beside the buckboard.

Then Andrew appears beside the dog. Small rocks skitter away from his feet as he runs toward the wagon. When he reaches the mules, he slides to a stop and looks up at his mother. "I found us a camping place for the night!"

"The paraje with the creek?" Gregorio asks. "The one on the side track?"

Andrew's face drops.

"Is the creek running?" Gregorio glances at Old Pete. "If there is no water, we should move on to another location."

"There's a stream bed but it's got nothin' in it," Andrew says.

"Has nothing," his mother says.

"We'd best keep on goin' then," Old Pete says.

Gregorio nods to Andrew. "Gracias, amigo. You have saved us some time."

The boy gives him a brilliant smile and turns to run back to the dog, who rises and lopes down the road beside him.

The shadows are long and quite black by the time the wagon rumbles into the next paraje. The camping space is right next to the road, in a dip on the north side of a hill. It's been cleared of everything but grass and a few junipers.

Andrew is there already, standing next to a small pile of firewood and brush.

"Good man!" Old Pete says. "You been busy!"

"It was already here," Andrew says. He looks disappointed.

"It is the way of travelers to leave behind what they don't need so the next party will be provided for," Gregorio tells him. "If you will gather more in the morning, we can leave some for those who come after us."

"But for now, whyn't you get a fire goin'?" Old Pete fumbles at his waist and tosses Andrew a flint. "There's your starter. Let's see what you can do with it."

Andrew grins at him and heads off to find tinder as Gregorio helps Alma and her mother from the wagon. "We don't truly need a fire," her mother says. "We still have jerky and bread and the moonlight's enough to see by."

"Ah, it won't hurt him t' make himself useful," Old Pete says. "And I could do with some tea, if you brought any. 'Sides, in these mountains a fire is handy even in June. It'll warm us and keep the varmints away."

But the fire doesn't keep them from having company. It's almost full dark when a voice from the hill farther down the road calls, "Hola! Hello the camp!"

There's a thick British sound in the voice. Alma wrinkles her forehead. It seems familiar.

Old Pete calls, "Come on in, but come in easy!" and a few minutes later William Workman rides a tall gray mare to the edge of the firelight.

He grins at them sardonically. "Well, well." He looks at Alma's mother. "Did Don Fernando get too small for you so soon?"

She frowns slightly, then says formally, "Mr. Workman. How are you?"

"Come on down and pull up a seat!" Old Pete says. "We got tea, if you want some."

The other man swings off his horse and leads it off to the side. He returns a few minutes later with a saddle in one hand and saddle bags in the other. He drops them onto the ground, then grabs a piece of firewood, balances it on one end, and sits on the other. He nods at Old Pete. "A spot of tea would be quite tasty." He slides Alma's mother a grin. "Unless you have something stronger. I'm afraid I don't have any of my own production with me."

"You comin' in from points south?" Old Pete asks as he empties his mug onto the ground. He refills it from the pot and passes it to Mr. Workman.

"Just from Santa Cruz. I tell you, after all that commotion, I'll be glad to get back to Don Fernando and the comparative quiet."

"Commotion?" Gregorio asks.

"There's some kind of new voting restriction. Only men with money can participate in the elections or be on the town council." He shakes his head. "And there are new taxes comin' in, too. The Santa Cruz folks aren't the only one who'll feel those. That's going to affect business."

"Even smuggled goods?" Alma's mother asks with a small smile.

He grins at her. "I have to admit, this all might benefit me."

"New Mexico is exempt from such taxes," Gregorio says. "It has been for as long as I can remember."

William Workman nods. "Twenty years or more, or so they say. But not now." He shrugs. "There's a rumor the ricos are askin' for another exemption, but the governor's not enthusiastic about sending the request on to Mexico City. He plans to start collections up any time now." He reaches to adjust his makeshift seat. "On top of that, Congress has handed him a whole new set of powers. He's appointing the local judges now, instead of the villages electing them."

Gregorio frowns. "Appointing alcaldes is the way of Spain, not Mexico."

"It sounds like somebody in Mexico City is feeling an urge to govern more directly. The word is Pérez's going to appoint Ramón Abreú the prefect for the whole north, including Don Fernando."

Gregorio's frown deepens. "His brother Santiago is already one of the chief justices. That will put the courts here all in one family."

"Sounds like trouble waitin' to happen," Old Pete says.

"It certainly looks like it to me." William Workman shakes his head. "That Antonio Abad Montoya's still feeling riley about being thrown in prison last year. And rather smug, too, since he got himself out again."

"With a little help from the alcalde," Alma's mother says.

He nods and grins. "That Montoya's something of a firebrand, even if he is a rico. He's been out and about, making speeches about the right to self govern and the plight of the poor. If he's not careful, he's going to get himself clapped in jail again and this time he won't get out so easy, now that there's a prefect settling in." He cocks his head at her. "Where'd you say you were headed?"

"I didn't," she says drily. "But it's not the first time in history the situation in Santa Cruz has been a little tense. The people there seem to rile easily."

"Ramón has relatives in Chimayó," Andrew pipes up.

Mr. Workman grins at him. "Where doesn't that man have relatives?" He looks at Old Pete. "Be that as it may, my advice is to get through that area quick as you can and head to Santa Fe. You should be safe enough there, if things get hot. The governor will find funds for the presidio troops if he has too."

Old Pete looks at Alma's mother. The Englishman follows his gaze and shakes his head. "But I wouldn't go anywhere near Chimayó or Santa Cruz, if I were you. They may be eight miles apart, but everyone in that valley's related to each other in one way or another. If one place flares up, the other will follow. And those Chimayosos are all a little crazy, anyway."

Old Pete and Gregorio glance sideways at her, but she looks William Workman square in the face and says, "I'll take your advice into consideration," in a voice that says she's unlikely to take his advice about anything.

94

Alma and Andrew exchange glances. They've heard that tone before.

"The people of Chimayó are not any different from anyone else," Gregorio says.

"True enough." William Workman grins. "It's just that they're all related and none of them are kin to the new Governor."

"Howsomever, this here ain't Mexico City and he don't have a whole lot of soldiers backin' him this time," Old Pete says. He looks at Gregorio. "Wasn't he somethin' big in the Mexico military before he got here? A colonel or such like?"

Gregorio nods. "His Excellency's mind is that of a military man. He believes if he waves his sword, the peasants will obey him." The firelight flickers on his grim jaw. "He and his officials know nothing of us."

"Well now, some of his officials have been here a while," Mr. Workman says. "Sarracino and Manuel Armijo have both been governor here."

"And Armijo was born in Alburquerque to an old New Mexico family," Alma's mother says mildly. "I believe Sarracino was, also."

"They're both ricos." Gregorio's jaws are still tight. "They don't know what it is to be poor, to have to work for one's living. To be torn away to fight in the militia campaigns and get nothing from it but memories."

William Workman chuckles. "I don't know about Sarracino, but that's certainly true of Armijo, though I do hear he's an officer in the Alburquerque troop. A lieutenant, I think. I just wish Pérez would get him out of that treasury post." He rubs his thumb against his forefinger. "He has a little too much say in the amount of import duties we merchants owe."

"They're all the same," Gregorio says bitterly.

"Government officials have always been like that," Alma's mother says. "And there's always someone who doesn't like what they're doing. I doubt it's any different in Mexico City or California. I'm not going to allow a little political dissension to stop me."

The Englishman flashes her a sardonic smile. "It's your choice, but you can't say I didn't warn you."

She turns to Alma and Andrew. "It's past time for sleep."

# CHAPTER 13

The next morning they're back in the wagon and moving steadily through the mountains. It's piney and a little dusty and warm. It almost feels like home, although the hillsides are closer together here and it's hotter than it would be in the valley.

And there are more houses. Unlike the log cabin at home, most of these are traditional adobe like in Don Fernando de Taos. There aren't many. They're strung along the narrow river valley, each surrounded by its own outbuildings. At the village of Truchas, they're closer together. The house walls line the road on either side and come together in a tight cluster of walls and latticed windows at the top of the dusty hill. The scenery changes as they leave the village.

"Now that there's quite a sight," Old Pete says. He's taken over the wagon while Gregorio rides ahead on Pete's mule and monitors Andrew and the mastiff. The mountain man points his driving whip at the vista to the west.

The land slopes steadily down from here. The pine-covered slopes that hugged the right side of the road to this point have pulled back now and the Santa Cruz river valley on their left has widened. Further west, the hills on either side drop away entirely. Between the wagon and the hazy blue distance, sharp-sided flat-topped mesas jut up from the plain at irregular intervals. There are mountain peaks beyond them, but they're so far away they look like a mere suggestion.

The expansiveness queases Alma's stomach. She takes a deep, ragged breath and tries to straighten her spine.

Old Pete looks at her sideways. "Ain't like home."

"No," she whispers.

"Thank God," her mother says.

Alma's hands tighten on themselves.

"Some of us like more closed-in spaces," Old Pete observes mildly.

"I can't imagine why." Alma's mother leans forward a little, studying the road. "How did Ramón say you could find this woman who weaves?"

"She's about a mile past the El Cerro de Chimayó plaza. There's a good-size footpath that cuts around the bottom of the hill. He thought we might be able to drive it, but I'm not so sure that's a good idea. If we're spotted, folks in the plaza'll be wonderin' what we're up to." He glances at her. "I reckon we oughta go right through instead."

Alma frowns a little, confused, but as they drive into the village, she sees what Old Pete means. It's called El Cerro de Chimayó because it's built on a hill. The plaza is a hollow square of buildings like the one in Don Fernando de Taos, but here there are openings in the middle of the east and west sides, instead of at each corner.

The road goes straight through the plaza. Unlike Don Fernando, the center is filled with neatly laid out gardens. Tiny ditches alongside them carry water to the plants. Instead of people with goods to sell, children play in front of the houses. Three red-brown horses graze in a small fenced-off field.

Old Pete doesn't stop. Gregorio, Andrew, and Chaser Two drop back to pace beside the wagon. Alma turns her head to study the gardens. She can see corn, garlic, and chile. Then the wagon moves through the western gap and down the sloping road toward the fields and orchards in the valley below.

She can't see the mountains to the west at all now. But she's surrounded by greenery. To her left, cornfields stretch between the road and a distant row of gray-trunked, twisted trees with leaves that twinkle in the breeze. She looks at her mother. "What kind of tree is that?"

"Those are river cottonwoods. They're a kind of populus, or poplar."

"So they're related to aspens and our mountain cottonwoods?"

"Yes, but they have a broader leaf, almost a heart shape. There are some in Don Fernando, but not many. They like plenty of water."

"That there's the Santa Cruz River they're runnin' along," Old Pete says. "The same one we've been followin' from Truchas." He studies the road ahead. "Ramón said this widow lady lives right about here. Got a wall around her house topped with rocks."

He frowns a little as the road crooks around a large cotton-wood. Then he grins. "And there she is." He reins the mules in beside a tall wall that has pieces of rock embedded along its upper edge, sharp ends up. The big double wooden gate is closed up tight. Old Pete studies it for a long moment, then stands up on the buckboard and cranes his neck to peer over the wall. "Hello the house!" he calls.

After several long minutes, the right-hand gate creaks open just enough to let the old woman behind it peer out. Andrew, the dog, and Gregorio are standing beside the wagon now, Gregorio holding Old Pete's mule, and she gives them a hard look before turning to the wagon.

"Señora Juana Altagracia Ortega?" Old Pete asks.

She's thin, her brown face sharp as a hatchet, and her black-clad body straight as a young ponderosa. Her eyes snap as she runs her gaze up and down the mountain man and examines his battered brown hat and dusty clothes. Her gaze swings to Alma's mother, then back to Old Pete. "What is it you want?" Her voice has a grating, reluctant sound, like she's not used to talking and prefers it that way.

Old Pete is still standing. He takes off his hat. "I'm lookin' for weavin' to buy."

She sniffs. "I don't know you."

Alma's mother's hands lift from her lap, almost beseechingly. "I believe you are related to Juan Ramón Chavez of Don Fernando de Taos?"

"That one who worked for the New Englander?" Señora Ortega nods but her face doesn't soften. "The one María Encarnación Griego was to marry before she was murdered?"

Alma's mother leans forward slightly. "My father is the man from New England. Señor Chavez is a close friend of my family."

The woman's lips compress. Her gaze moves to Old Pete. "And who is he to you?"

"Ramón?" the mountain man asks.

Her lips tighten even more. She looks at Alma's mother and jerks her head toward Old Pete. "Who is he to you?"

The younger woman's lips twitch. She smoothes her skirt and takes a deep, quick breath. "He is a friend. I am Suzanna Peabody Locke." She nods toward Alma, then Andrew. "These are my children." Then she gestures toward Gregorio. "And I believe you know Jesús Gregorio Garcia."

Gregorio flashes the señora a winning smile, but she merely glances at him and bends her head in Old Pete's direction. "And this one?"

Old Pete takes off his hat. "Peter Andrew Micawber at your service, ma'am."

She sniffs and turns her sharp eyes back to Alma's mother, whose back stiffens slightly. "We have two purposes," she says formally. "Mr. Micawber is looking for woven goods to purchase. He has been so kind as to escort me here to you for my own mission."

Señora Ortega nods almost imperceptibly.

The younger woman's hands flatten on her skirt. "I am told you are a weaver of much skill. I wish to learn to weave in order to support myself and my children. I have come to ask you to accept me as your apprentice."

"At Ramón's suggestion?"

She hesitates, then nods. Alma glances at her in surprise. But the woman is watching her. And maybe Ramón did suggest that her mother talk to this old woman. Alma looks down at her own skirt and smoothes the cotton over her knees.

"It takes years to learn to weave fine cloth or blankets. You would start by learning to make jerga."

"Yes," her mother says. "He told me that would undoubtedly be the case."

"He's the only man I've ever known who had any sense." The señora glares at Old Pete. "I don't have anything to sell." Then she looks at Alma's mother. "However, for you I may have something to offer." She turns toward the gate. "Come."

Gregorio hands the mule's reins to Andrew and hurries to help Alma and her mother down from the wagon. Both the children move toward their mother, but Señora Ortega flaps a hand at them. "Tu madre and I will speak, then we will see." She glances at Old One Eye Pete, who's dropped back onto the buckboard's seat. "You will stay here until I've decided."

They all look at Alma's mother. She nods, gives them a quick, anxious smile, then follows the woman across the yard and into the house.

Alma turns toward Gregorio. He smiles at her encouragingly and goes back to Old Pete's mule. Andrew kneels beside Chaser and rubs the dog's ears. Alma drifts to the mules, scratches each one on the chin, then accepts Old Pete's hand to climb back up onto the wagon.

She wants to stand and peer over the wall into the yard, but this seems rude. If the señora comes out and finds her staring, she might not like it. Alma suspects there isn't much Señora Ortega likes. Certainly not men. And possibly not children, either. She sighs, put her hands in her lap, and forces herself to sit quietly. Her bottom is sore and her shoulders are tired.

"Travelin's hard work, ain't it, little missy?" Old Pete asks.

She looks up at him and grins. "You don't seem to think so."

"Well now," he says. "I been doin' it since I wasn't much older'n you. Got it in my blood. My pappy was a great traveler, too. Never could settle for long, that one. Nor his pappy before him. He come over the ocean from Scotland 'cuz he couldn't stomach bein' born on a land surrounded by water and nary a way t' get out."

Alma looks at him in surprise. She's heard a lot of stories from Old Pete but this is the most she's ever heard about his family.

"Guess it's just in my blood." He gives her a sideways, almost apologetic look. "That's why once you folks are settled here, I'll be makin' tracks."

She gulps a little. She's known from the beginning that he's going on, but still her lip trembles.

"A man's gotta make a living, same as everyone else." He turns and gazes at the road, where it extends on down the river valley. "I figurin' on bein' hereabouts a few days more, locatin' someone who'll sell me a passel o' woven goods, then light out for Santa Fe and throw in with a caravan south t' Chihuahua."

Alma nods. She studies her hands, forcing them not to curve protectively into each other.

"But I'll be back sooner or later," he says. "I ain't aimin' t' disappear and stay gone." When she doesn't answer, he says abruptly, "You know why the Injuns call me One Eye Pete, don't you?"

She looks up in surprise. "Because of what the bear did."

He runs a finger over the right side of his face. "Nah, that's just a scratch." When he grins, the scar twists his smile into a grimace, but his left eye still twinkles, partly with relief that she's not going to cry, partly with mischief. "There's more than one way of seein'. They also call me One Mind Pete."

"We all have only one mind."

"Most of us have half a dozen minds, and can't decide which one to listen to at any one minute. Run around like chickens after the hatchet's already hit their necks."

She giggles in spite of herself. Something loosens inside her chest. "That's true."

"I'm somewhat single-minded." He looks away, studying the señora's wall, the sharp stones along the top. "Makes me kinda stubborn."

She drops her eyes. "Like my mother."

"Well, now, I don't know about that." He chuckles. "Ain't nobody quite as stubborn as your ma." He pats her knee awkwardly. "But I do know this ain't the last time we'll be seein' each other."

# CHAPTER 14

The men and the mastiff stay with the mules and wagon as Señora Ortega takes the children and their mother inside. They enter a long narrow sala with a fireplace in the left-hand corner and a loom at the other end under a latticed window. Sunlight steams in, warming the cream and red partially woven blanket on the loom.

Beyond it is a small door to a storage area as deep as the living room is wide. It contains bales of wool and large earthenware pots almost as tall as the children. They're filled with beans, corn, and wheat and topped with well-secured wooden lids, but Alma can smell their contents. She and Andrew scoot up against a big black one to give their mother and the señora more space. It has the good smell of dried corn.

Señora Ortega points at a door in the far wall. "Mi cuarto de dormir," she says. She gives the children a sharp look. "No one enters there but me."

Alma's chest squeezes guiltily, even though she hasn't even thought about opening the door to the señora's sleeping room. She bites her lip and wonders how long it will take her mother to learn to weave. The old woman is staring at her expectantly. Alma nods to indicate she's heard the edict.

"And no getting into the supplies!"

Alma is suddenly aware that her skirt is pushing against the big black pot and that Andrew is snatching his hand away from its lid and moving toward their mother.

The señora turns to Alma's mother. "You and los chamacos will sleep here." Her eyes spark as she looks at Alma, then Andrew. "And there will be no meddling with my stores." She points at what looks like a stack of lumber in the far corner. "Or my old loom." She frowns at Andrew. "No climbing!"

Alma's mother rests her hand on Andrew's shoulder. "They are good children. They won't touch anything which doesn't belong to them."

The señora sniffs and jerks her head at the wall by the door to the sala. Part of the adobe has been hollowed out to form a narrow shelf. Beside it, four wooden pegs have been embedded in the wall. "You can hang clothes there."

"This will do nicely," Alma's mother says. "I am grateful to you."

Señora Ortega sniffs again and stalks back into the main room. Andrew and Alma turn to their mother. She puts her fingers to her lips. "We'll talk later." She pats Andrew's shoulder. "Let's get our things from the wagon."

"Where will you put your chair?" he asks.

She looks around the room and chews on her lower lip. "It's going to have to stay on the wagon for the time being. If we make sure it's covered well, it should be all right outside."

"And Chaser will be outside too?" But it isn't really a question. It's clear from Señora Ortega's attitude that the dog isn't going to be allowed in the house. There's no point in even asking.

His mother nods sympathetically, confirming his statement, and his shoulders slump.

He still looks sad when the children wake the next morning to a thumping sound coming from the sala. As Alma sits up on her pallet, Andrew opens his eyes. "What in tarnation is that?"

She shakes her head and they slip out of their blankets, tiptoe to the door, and peer out. The señora and their mother are at the near end of the loom, their mother studying it intently as Señora Ortega stands with each foot on a narrow board that extends under the heavy cottonwood frame. Ropes attached to the far end of the boards loop up into the workings. When the señora pushes down on her end, the boards move down on the other and thump onto the floor. The old woman looks almost like she's walking in place, though in slow motion.

She talks as she works, explaining the loom to Alma's mother. Finely spun yarn has been strung down the length of the flat wooden frame. The part closest to the women is filled with wool worked across it to form the pattern Alma's mother admired the night before.

"It's simple," the señora says. She points at the boards beneath her feet. "Cárcolas."

Alma's mother looks puzzled. "Treadles?"

The old woman acts like she hasn't heard. She shifts her weight to the left and the other end of the left-hand board drops. "Press down, the sections of the warp lift apart." She points to the thread that runs the length of the loom. When the board shifted, it pulled a lever that raised a crosswise wooden piece at the other end of the loom and the threads of wool attached to it.

Alma stretches onto her toes, trying to see. It looks like the stretched lengths alternate with each other. Half are still flat, while the other half have lifted with the crosspiece and formed a kind of V of empty space.

"That gap is the shed," the old lady says. She keeps her foot on the treadle as she leans to one side and grabs a hollowed-out piece of carved wood that's been lying on the loom's side beam. The hollow part contains a looped skein of yarn. One end trails from it to the already-woven section on the loom.

The señora looks at Alma's mother and hefts the wooden contraption. "La lanzadera. Americanos call it the shuttle." She leans forward and moves her hands across the empty space, leans further to the right, does something more with the yarn, and straightens up. She shifts her weight onto the right treadle and the bar at the other end drops, lowering the warp threads until they're all flat again.

Alma waits for her to start the next row, but instead the old lady reaches for another strip of wood that hangs from the top of the loom's frame. It's long and thin, with teeth like the comb Alma's mother uses in Alma's hair, only thinner.

"El peine," the señora says. She maneuvers the comb between the long threads of the flattened warp and pulls toward herself, snugging the newly inserted yarn tight against the cloth she's already woven. "That's the weft. Firm but not too tight." She shifts her weight to the other board under her feet. "Then press la cárcola and do it again."

She looks at Alma's mother, who nods. "Firm, but not too tight," she says.

The señora nods and wordlessly demonstrates a few more rounds, then steps away from the loom. "Try it."

As their mother moves to take up her position, she sees the children at the door. "Good morning," she says.

The señora turns and scowls at them. "No interrupting!"

Their mother grins at them conspiratorially, then turns to the loom and carefully positions herself on the treadles. She pauses, takes a deep breath, and shifts her weight onto the left-hand board. It moves slightly, then stops.

"Harder," the señora says. "All your weight." She peers under the loom. "Step forward."

Alma's mother readjusts her foot and leans to her left. The board drops sharply and hits the floor with a thud.

Andrew giggles and the señora scowls at him. His mother reaches for the shuttle and moves it carefully through the shed from right to left. When she reaches the end, she tugs on the yarn to pull it into place.

The señora jerks forward. "Not too tight! You'll ruin my work!"

She gingerly repositions the yarn and straightens to look at the weaving that's already been completed. "It's quite beautiful," she says. "I love the dark red stripes against the cream."

The señora gestures impatiently at the waiting shed and Alma's mother shifts her weight, closing the gap. She reaches for the comb and pulls it gingerly through the threads and up against the new line of yarn.

"Firmer," Señora Ortega commands. "Do it again." She turns her head, sees the children still watching, and flaps a hand at them. "Go away."

Alma and Andrew withdraw into the storage room. They turn away from each other to pull on their clothes, then work together to roll their pallets and stack them in the corner on top of their mother's. As they're folding the blankets, Andrew says, "Weaving looks like it's hard work. And complicated."

Alma nods wordlessly. There's a knot in the middle of her chest. It's going to be a long time before they return to Don Fernando de Taos. Even longer before they return to the valley. Her lower lip trembles.

"We can't stay in here forever," Andrew complains. "I need to make water." His face screws up. "If we go out there, she's going to yell at us again."

Alma's own bladder suddenly presses urgently against her pelvis, but she's almost grateful to it. It's a distraction from the thought of the valley and home.

She looks at Andrew and chews her upper lip. "We're going to have to be as quiet as possible."

He nods, his face anxious. "I don't want her to see me."

But when they slip through the door, neither woman glances up. The children find Gregorio outside and he takes them each by the hand to show them where to go to take care of their morning business.

On the way back to the casa, he points west, down the valley. "The village of Santa Cruz de la Cañada is there," he says. "It's larger than Chimayó and I have cousins there, Antonio Abad Montoya and his brother Desiderio. Primos my age but rico. I went to their house last evening and they invited me to stay and work with them."

His eyes shine when he looks at Alma. "If all goes well, I will have a horse of my own before winter." She smiles back at him, happy for his happiness, but her heart twinges at the thought of him not being close by.

"How far is it?" Andrew asks. "Can we come visit you?"

"It's about five miles." His eyes twinkle at Alma. "About the same distance as from the cabin to your favorite fishing spot."

She grins back at him. "Don't tell Mama it's that far, or I'll have to wear my sunbonnet when we come to see you."

# CHAPTER 15

Each morning, Señora Ortega rises before dawn, prepares the morning meal, sets the children's mother a weaving task, then disappears for an hour in the direction of the Chimayó plaza.

She comes back more thin-lipped than ever, corrects their mother's mistakes, and sets her another task. Then she gives the children their orders for the day: to gather eggs, chop wood, pull weeds, check on the mules in the pasture across the road, and anything else she can think of. There's no time to go visit Gregorio, even if their mother was willing to give them permission to do so.

When it's time to prepare the noon and evening meals, the señora sets Alma to making thin cornmeal atole, tortías, and beans, though the resulting mush is often lumpy, the tortías misshapen, and the beans crunchy. The old lady sniffs in disgust at the girl's ineptness but continues to call her to help.

After the evening meal, the women comb wool, spin it, or wind what is already spun into skeins. Or Alma and her mother do this while Andrew practices his penmanship and the señora does her colcha work, using the thinnest and most brightly colored strands of leftover yarn to embroider brilliant flowers and other designs on the cream-colored bedcovers she's woven.

On the Saturday evening after they arrive, she looks up abruptly from the rose-pink flowers she's working on and announces that Mass will begin at eight o'clock the next morning. They will need to leave early to get there in time. The church is in Santa Cruz and it's over an hour's walk, if they don't dawdle.

Alma looks up. Santa Cruz? Where Gregorio is? Her mother, who's beside her on the banco inspecting the wool Alma's just combed, looks up, too. "We aren't Catholic."

The señora's mouth purses. "This is méxico. If you're a citizen, you are católico. If you practice any other religion, you risk prison."

Alma's mother smiles slightly. "I know that's the law. No one worries too much about the religious regulations in Don Fernando. Except for Padre Martínez, of course. But even he realizes trying to enforce them is useless."

"Humph. Well, here in Chimayó, you'll find that we are a religious community. I go to morning prayers at la plaza capilla and we go to Santa Cruz for mass as often as the weather and our bodily condition allow." The señora snaps off the pink wool with her scissors, a sharp little click in the suddenly silent room.

Alma's mother's lips quirk with something between amusement and irritation. "I wouldn't want to embarrass you with our lack of knowledge of how to behave," she says mildly.

The older woman jabs her needle into the cloth in her hands. "You will embarrass me if you don't attend." She looks up. "And the priest and my neighbors will suspect you have something to hide." Her gaze hardens. "I will not protect you from the consequences."

So, early the next morning Alma and Andrew follow Señora Ortega and their mother down the dew-dampened road and then up a hill to the Santa Cruz plaza and the big church on its western edge.

It's a beautiful building. Its massive adobe walls and big wooden doors are somehow welcoming, even though the square tower that stands in the plaza in front of it gives the village a military air. People stream toward the church as the church bells ring across the village and over the river valley below. Alma pauses to watch the green fields and gnarled cottonwoods come to life in the morning sun.

But the señora is at the church door, turning back to make sure the children and their mother are still behind her. Alma hurries to catch up.

The church sanctuary is long and the ceiling high. The atmosphere is hushed and solemn. Alma slips to her mother's side. They stand at the edge of a cluster of people who seem to be Señora Ortega's friends, although there are no smiles or nods of acknowledgement. Everyone shifts to make room for the newcomers while remaining focused on the service at the front of the church.

Alma cranes her neck to study the wall behind the altar. It contains a ornamented wooden frame that contains pictures of various saints in long robes. A hand tugs her skirt. Alma startles into awareness. Everyone around her is kneeling. Andrew is pulling at her skirt and Señora Ortega, already on her knees, is glaring at her.

As Alma drops to the floor she sees that she's not the only person still standing. On the other side of the church, a thin, long-haired man is also just now sinking to the floor. His eyes twinkle as he winks at her. Alma flushes and looks away.

Her mother is paying no attention. Her eyes are fixed on the altar and the priest, her face tense and tired.

Alma suddenly feels sorry for her. What must it be like to learn to weave from a woman as exacting as the señora? Alma slips her hand inside her mother's, who gives her a startled look, then gently squeezes Alma's fingers. Señora Ortega glances toward them disapprovingly and Alma's mother half smiles, squeezes her hand again, then releases it.

When the señora has refocused on the altar, Alma turns her head to study the big room's whitewashed adobe walls. There are no windows. The only light comes from candles on simple wooden stands next to the altar.

There's another alter on her right. It also has candles. The big wooden frame on the wall behind it is marked off in sections and also contains a carved portrait in each rectangle.

But these paintings are simpler. More gentle, somehow. Maybe it's the colors, the soft reds, golds, and blues. Or maybe it's because they're closer, and the candles are right below them so she can see the pictures more clearly. Even Jesus on the cross seems gentle. It makes her feel quiet.

But the señora is looking at her again. Alma turns her eyes toward the front altar and its more elaborate decorations, but she's still feeling the power of the side altar when the service ends. She takes her mother's hand as they move slowly out of the church, following the hushed crowd.

Andrew is on her mother's other side. His shoulders slump with boredom as they reach the plaza and Señora Ortega begins introducing their mother and the children to first one, then another, of her friends, neighbors, and relatives. After the sixth or seventh person, and when she realizes Gregorio Garcia is nowhere to be seen, Alma doesn't even try to remember all the names.

Then the man who winked at her appears at the señora's elbow. "Aren't you going to introduce me to your new amigos?" he asks. Without waiting for an answer, he turns to Alma's mother, takes off his hat, and flips two shiny black braids over his shoulder. "Blas Lugardo Beitia at your service, señorita."

"Señora," the old lady corrects him, her voice sharper than usual. She gestures toward Alma and Andrew. "These are Señora Locke's children. They are guests in my home."

There's a warning note in her voice, but he doesn't appear to hear it. Instead, he bows gallantly to Andrew, then Alma. "I am extremely pleased to meet all of you." He turns back to their mother. "Locke? That name is familiar. Is Señor Gerald Locke, Jr. the man so fortunate as to be tu esposo?"

Alma's mother's hand tightens on hers as she nods noncommittally, but the man seems unaware of her reaction. He shakes his head. "A lucky man indeed. And two handsome children as well." He beams at Andrew and the boy smiles shyly back at him.

Señor Beitia turns to Alma's mother. "And how long can we expect to have the pleasure of your company in our midst?"

She looks at Señora Ortega, who frowns. "Señora Locke is here to learn to weave, not to keep company with the likes of you."

Even for the señora this seems unusually rude, but Señor Beitia only laughs. "It has been a long while since we have had a visit together, mi prima," he says. "I must come soon and purchase a blanket from you and also discuss the five fleeces that remain in my storage shed. Next week I will be clearing space for feed so the flock my herders bring down from the mountains will be well supplied this winter. Right now the wool is where the hay will reside." He winks at her. "I will make you a bargain."

She glares at him suspiciously but he only flourishes his hat at them all in an elegant bow, and walks off.

The señora sniffs, turns toward yet another group of friends, and begins more introductions. Alma stifles a yawn.

Then they are free and returning to the house and midday meal. There is no rest for their mother that afternoon. The señora may believe in going to mass on los domingos, but she apparently doesn't consider Sundays to be complete days of rest. She shoos the children outside so they won't interrupt the next weaving lesson.

"Señor Beitia seems nice," Andrew says as he perches beside Alma on the chopping block in the courtyard.

"Gregorio is nicer."

"Gregorio is busy with his new friends." He gets up to pluck a piece of kindling from the woodpile. "I wish I had a knife. This would make a great whistle." He tosses it back onto the pile. "Not that there's anyone here to teach me to carve one."

"Don't you still have the whistle Old Pete made you?"

He shrugs without looking at her. "I can't play it."

"It doesn't work?"

He shrugs again and scuffs his feet in the sandy dirt. "It makes my throat hurt." He turns abruptly and heads toward the animal sheds behind the house. "I'm gonna check on the wagon. I ain't seen Chaser Two all day."

"Haven't," Alma says automatically, but he doesn't even turn around to stick his tongue out at her. She sighs and pushes herself off the chopping block. If she was home, she would be fishing. But she's not. And the fields around the señora's house belong to the farmers who till them. She can't go exploring. Alma's shoulders slump as she drops back onto the big block of wood and stares at the rock-encrusted adobe walls.

# CHAPTER 16

Señor Beitia shows up three days later. Although Señora Ortega doesn't appear pleased to see him, Alma's mother greets him with a reserved smile, and Andrew is happy to discover that the man knows how to carve.

"I need a new whistle," he says, eyeing him.

Señor Beitia flips his right braid over his shoulder and reaches into a pocket. He pulls out a small but wickedly sharp knife. "I have just the blade for creating whistles." He gestures toward the door to the courtyard. "Let's see if you know your wood well enough to find me a good piece."

As Andrew goes outside, his mother looks up from her work. She looks very domestic there on the banco, her drop spindle moving steadily as she creates more thread. "That's very kind of you," she says.

Señora Ortega is sitting at the table supervising Alma as she combs wool. She sniffs loudly, but the other two adults ignore her.

Andrew comes back inside and hands Señor Beitia a short thick piece of smooth cottonwood.

"Ah, that will work well," the man says. He glances toward Andrew's mother. "He has a good eye, this one."

"My papa taught me," Andrew says.

Señor Beitia gives him a sharp glance and begins to poke his blade at the wood. Andrew watches him silently. After a bit, he says, "May I ask you a question?"

117

Señor Beitia winks at him. "You can ask and I will decide whether to answer."

"I—" Andrew gives him an uncertain smile. "I want to know why you wear your hair in braids."

"Andrew!" his mother protests, but the señor only raises his head and winks at her, too.

"A man needs to learn to ask questions, if only of himself," he says. "It's how he gets at the truth of things." He flips his head, which bounces his left braid off his back and onto his chest, and looks at Andrew. "It's a custom of those of us who live along el río de Santa Cruz." He jerks his head toward Señora Ortega. "Her husband the buffalo hunter wore them, too. Before he died at the hands of the Navajo."

She scowls at him and pokes a finger at Alma's work. "You've left a snarl," she says. "This fleece may be from a churro sheep and easy to comb, but you still need to pay attention to what you're doing."

Alma bends back to her task as Señor Beitia continues, although he's looking more at her mother than Andrew. "There are some who say we wear braids because there are genízaros among us and Indians are more comfortable in braids," he says. "But I am a well-read man and know that los españoles who settled here three hundred years ago also wore their hair long."

Andrew looks at his mother. "They did?"

Her brow wrinkles, then she nods. "I think they wore a single braid down their back. That would be a question to ask your Grandfather Peabody."

"It is a symbol of my heritage," the señor says. "A reminder that I am of el español blood. A symbol of my manhood and prowess."

Señora Ortega and Alma's mother exchange an amused look.

"I want to grow my hair long, too!" Andrew says.

His mother chuckles. "Your hair is too bushy and curly to grow long. I doubt it would ever make braids like el señor's."

Señor Beitia nods. "Your hair would grow straight out from your head, not flat and silky like mine."

The señora rises abruptly from the table. "This household retires early." She gives the man a sharp look. "It's time for you to be gone."

There's a small, shocked silence, then he throws his head back and laughs. Alma can see his strong white teeth. "Ah, señora!" he says. "You are so straightforward. It is a pleasure to deal with you!"

She stands immobile, watching him with a cold face. He smiles at her amiably, thrusts his knife back into his pocket, and hands Andrew the piece of wood. "If you will keep that safe for me, muchichito, I'll be back in a few days and we'll finish it."

And he does return, shortly before the evening meal a few days later, and finishes the whistle. In another few days, he's back again, this time with a basket of wild plums.

"I hoped to bring you more," he says, though he seems more filled with pride than apologetic. "These were all that were ready to eat."

Alma's mother reaches for the nearest one and sniffs at it appreciatively. "They're quite ripe for this early in the season."

He grins and winks at Señora Ortega. "They're from my secret grove, which always ripens earlier than anywhere else."

The old lady humphs impatiently but takes the plums while Alma's mother smiles, seats herself on the banco, retrieves her spindle from the basket of combed wool at her feet, and asks for news. The señora carries the fruit to the corner, then moves to the fireplace, adjusts the pot and stirs the stew. Alma and Andrew go

119

back to the table, which is littered with their slates and school-books.

"Ah, news." Señor Beitia flips his braids over his shoulders and drops into the chair nearest the fire. He grins. "La Cañada is receiving attention from His Excellency the governor and everyone's talking."

"What is Governor Pérez concerned about?" Alma's mother asks.

His face loses his mischievous look. "He's decided we're too savage to govern ourselves. The alcalde we chose to judge our disputes must be overseen by a man of the governor's appointment."

The señora turns, a big wooden spoon in her hand. "You speak of Prefect Abreú. He was appointed a month ago. Has it taken you this long to realize he was given the office and by whom?"

"It has taken this long for him to show how much he means to insert himself into our affairs," Señor Beitia says. Then his lips quirk sardonically. "Or perhaps for the governor to finally realize Antonio Abad Montoya is no longer in prison for those trumped-up charges for which he was jailed in December."

Alma and Andrew look up when they hear the name, but the adults pay them no attention.

"The charges the governor told him he'd have to appeal to the national Supreme Court?" Señora Ortega asks.

"Sí." His face is dark with anger. "Don Antonio may be a rico but he doesn't have the money to travel that far and to hire lawyers to defend him."

"Especially since he believes he did nothing wrong in the first place."

Señor Beitia scowls. "He believes correctly."

"Of course, since you know so much about the law." She turns back to the stew.

He looks at Alma's mother and rubs his thumb and fingers together. "Montoya spoke his mind about the so-called contributions the governor was demanding for the militia and Pérez slapped him in el calabozo." He shrugs and chuckles. "But Don Antonio Abad and Juan José Esquibel are cousins. It is common for cousins both to give each other gifts and to provide assistance when it is needed."

Then his face sours. "He understands nothing of honor. Don Antonio won't disappear. But the governor has decided Antonio Abad gave the alcalde a bribe. His Excellency is not from Nuevo México and doesn't care to learn our customs." His mouth twists. "He is from Vera Cruz and a colonel, as well. He has fancy clothes and an expensive Saint Louis carriage with matching horses to draw it. He is superior to all the vecinos of Santa Cruz de la Cañada together."

"Yes, yes," Señora Ortega says impatiently. "We know you dislike the man. But he was bound to hear that Antonio Abad is no longer in jail. Did you think a governor would ignore such flouting of his authority?" She turns to Alma. "Get the bowls, child. And the spoons."

Alma puts her slate aside and crosses the room to the wooden cupboard in the corner.

As she opens the door, Señor Beitia says, "It's not just the Montoya matter into which the new prefect is inserting himself. He's also countermanding every decision Alcalde Esquibel has made. Some hombre from Don Fernando de Taos claimed two Santa Cruz men owed him money. When Esquibel didn't rule in his favor, the stupid Taoseño appealed to the governor. He complained that the alcalde's judgment must be confused because the debtors were his relatives."

The señora snorts derisively. "Everyone in Santa Cruz is related to Juan José Esquibel or his wife. That's why he's the alcalde."

Señor Beitia laughs. "It is true. You are a smart woman, señora." Alma carries a bowl of stew to him and he accepts it, lifts the spoon delicately to his lips, then sucks greedily, making slurping sounds. "And an excellent cook as well."

She sniffs disdainfully and hands Alma a bowl for her mother, who places her spindle on top of the wool she's spun and gives the girl a conspiratorial grin as she takes the food. Alma suppresses a giggle and turns back to the fire. The man's flattery is hilarious, but the old woman's response to it is almost as funny.

Señor Beitia lifts his head from his bowl. "So now the governor has directed the prefect to overturn the alcalde's ruling and make the men pay the Taoseño. And he's ordered Esquibel to return Don Antonio Abad to el calabozo and also pay a fine for releasing him."

Señora Ortega shakes her head. "I have known Juan José Esquibel since he was a child. He is not one to take orders."

"Again, you see things clearly, señora. The good alcalde has refused most firmly to send Don Antonio back to jail or to pay such a fine. As he should." He slurps another spoonful of soup. "Excellent," he says. Then he shakes his head at Alma's mother. "This federalism, this centralizing of the government into the hands of a few, is a disease. They are taking away our liberties and bringing in foreigners who know nothing of our customs. Appointing men to oversee us as if we are children. Always before, those over us have been chosen from among the citizens they will judge."

His voice rises and his hands grip the bowl and spoon, but he's no longer eating. "We have governed ourselves for hundreds of years, fending off the Apache and the Navajo. Protecting the nation's interior from the savages. And in return for our service, they arrive in their carriages and their satins and silks and order us around like we're a lot of slaves!"

He pushes himself up from his seat. What's left of his soup slops dangerously at the edges of the bowl. "Slavery has been abolished in this great country of Mexico, as well it ought to be, and we will not be told what to do as if we are children. We will resist the tyrants to our dying breath!"

They all stare at him, their eyes wide. Then the señora breaks the silence. "Big words," she sniffs. She dips her spoon into her stew.

He blinks and glances apologetically at the children, then their mother. "Perdóneme. I fear my enthusiasm for justice causes me to speak impulsively." He transfers his bowl to his left hand and places his right over his heart. He gives her a meaningful look. "What I feel, I feel very deeply."

"And I feel tired," the señora says impatiently. She stops eating, rises, and takes the bowl and spoon from his hands. Then she waves them at him with a shooing motion. "Go now. It is late and time for us all to be sleeping."

He smiles at her genially, as if still trying to apologize for his outburst, and goes to the door. He lifts his hat from the wooden peg in the adobe wall, then turns to Alma's mother with a beseeching smile. "On a more pleasant note, before I leave I would like to invite you to accompany me in ten days time to la plaza del cerro for el Día del Santiago. I hope you and your children will do me the honor of attending the fiesta as my guests."

She glances at Señora Ortega. "I am in training, señor. My time is not my own."

The señora is still clutching his bowl and spoon in her bony hands. She scowls at Señor Beitia. "They will attend the feast as my guests." She turns to Alma's mother. "Santiago is the patron saint of el cerro de Chimayó. There is no working on his feast day." She permits herself a small smile. "Though there is much work to prepare for it." She nods toward Alma. "This one can help me bake."

Señor Beitia steps forward. "But I will escort you all if you will do me the honor." He turns to the señora. "If you would so honor me."

She gives him a disapproving frown, but then nods. "Another pair of hands to carry the food will be useful."

He beams at them all. "It is settled then." He flips a braid over his shoulder. "I am expecting to be occupied with business and political affairs in the interim, so I will not be able to give myself the pleasure of your company during that time." He bows again, flourishing his hat at Alma's mother. "But when el Día del Santiago arrives, I will be here as soon as the sun's rays have kissed the top of the eastern peaks, so that we may enjoy the day together, you and I."

Then he is gone before anyone can raise an eyebrow at his eloquence. Alma stifles a giggle as the door shuts behind him.

"Men," the señora sniffs. "You'd think they invented the world."

"But you were married yourself."

"And would still be, if he'd listened to what I had to say." Her lips tighten. "He wanted to go buffalo hunting on the plains. Easy, he said. Meat enough for the winter, he said. He'd never gone before, but he was sure it was a simple matter, that those great beasts were stupid and not dangerous." She looks at the loom. "A man strong and smart enough to build a loom could manage a bison easily enough."

"How long ago was that?"

"Thirty years, more or less. We were mere children. I was pregnant for the first time." She pauses. "The only time. They buried him out there." She turns abruptly away.

"And your child?"

"A son. Dead at three years." The woman's voice is dry as dust, as if she is reporting facts from a century ago. "Of a fever."

"I'm so sorry."

The black-clad shoulders shrug again. "God gives and God takes." But she says nothing more for the rest of the evening.

# CHAPTER 17

The next week is a busy one. As her mother continues her weaving lessons, Alma learns to make bread. Señora Ortega uses a large cottonwood bowl to mix the flour, water, and starter. Then she sends Alma into the storage room for an even larger black-and-tan pottery one that's so wide Alma can barely carry it.

She carefully sets the bowl on the table and runs her finger over the geometric designs that dance along its rim. "It's very pretty."

"It comes from the pueblo of Pojoaque south of here," the señora tells her. "Hold it steady." She lifts the kneaded dough from the floury table and drops it into the bowl.

"There's so many pueblos," Andrew says. He dumps the load of firewood he's just brought in beside the hearth. "It's confusing."

"There are so many," his mother corrects him from the loom. She leans forward to comb the weft into place.

Señora Ortega glances at her, then the boy. "Stack that."

"Yes, ma'am." He kneels to arrange the wood. "There are a lot of pueblos." He glances at his mother, but she's studying her work. "I wish I could see them all."

"You're still young," the señora says. "When you're grown, no doubt you'll wander. Alma, hand me that cloth."

"I won't wander," Alma says as she gives the old lady the thin cotton cloth and watches her drape it over the bowl to keep the bread warm while it rises. Alma lifts her chin. "I'll go back to the valley and stay there the rest of my life."

"Men are born to wander," the señora says, somewhat bitterly.

"And to protect," Andrew says.

The two women look at him in surprise. The señora's eyes soften a little and there's a pause before Alma's mother pushes a treadle down again. The long board thuds like a dull drum against the packed-dirt floor.

"Like Santiago." Señora Ortega begins scraping the table top clean. "You know of Santiago?"

"I know it means Saint James," he says.

"He is the patron saint of la plaza del cerro." She gestures to Alma to put the flour barrel away. "He was a disciple of Jesus. After Santiago died, a miracle took his body on a ship from Jerusalem to Spain and that's where he was buried. He has wrought many wonders there."

The two children share a skeptical glance. They know Grandfather Peabody would have a different story to tell about St. James. They look at their mother, but she's absorbed in her work.

"Santiago helped to push the Moors out of España," the señora continues. "He rides a great white horse and carries a sword. He even helped defeat the infidels at the pueblo of Acoma."

Andrew raises a skeptical eyebrow. "He was here in Nuevo México?"

"He appeared in order to help our troops. It was a miracle."

Andrew frowns and opens his mouth to ask another question, but Alma intervenes. "Why is he the patron saint of Chimayó?"

Señora Ortega shrugs. "He always has been. He watches over our crops and protects us from los indios bárbaros, those marauding tribes, those dark-hearted heathens."

"What are Moors?" Andrew asks.

"They're Muslims," Alma says. "Mr. Irving talks about them in his Alhambra book."

The señora purses her lips. "They were people from Africa who took over España. Muslims and infidels, all of them. Santiago appeared in the battles and helped Queen Isabella push them back to where they came from."

His eyebrow is up again. "How did—"

Alma picks up the barrel of flour. "What else do we need to do to prepare for the feast?"

The morning of the feast day dawns bright and clear. As Alma follows her mother and the others up the hill to the plaza, her head lifts. From here she can see over the cornfields and treetops and across the valley to the dry hills on the other side.

Instead of a sunbonnet, she's wearing a rebozo the señora has lent her. The long piece of cloth drapes demurely over her head and shoulders, but doesn't block her face. It's nice to be able to see.

Her mother didn't object to the big scarf, even though it won't protect Alma's skin from the sun. She touches the heart-shaped freckle on her cheek. She's been inside so much lately, it's probably faded. That's a good thing, although she can't help but wonder what kind of fish swim in the river beyond the big cottonwoods.

She takes a deep breath, tasting the fresh air. It feels good to see something besides adobe walls, even though the mountains to the east aren't home, the hills to the south are brown, not green, and the view west is much too open. A mist rises from the river and fingers through the cottonwoods and across the tops of the rows of corn. It's pretty, but it's not home. She almost wishes she'd worn her sunbonnet.

She turns to trudge up the hill after the others and focuses her senses on the pastries in the basket she's carrying. Their sweet yeasty scent is delicious, even more so because she helped bake them.

Up ahead, her mother glances around at her and smiles. Señor Beitia turns, too. He breaks into a wide grin. "Come, come!" he calls. "You'll get left behind if you don't hurry!"

Alma's smile falters, then she looks at her mother, who smiles more widely and gestures for her to catch up. The señora and Andrew are well ahead of them all, each carrying more food.

"I'd never leave you behind," her mother says as Alma reaches her. "Is that basket getting too heavy for you?"

Alma shakes her head. "It smells good."

"The work of our hands always smells best, doesn't it? I'm glad the señora has taken the time to teach you to cook."

"And you?" Señor Beitia asks. "You don't cook, Doña Suzanna?"

She chuckles. "I am no fine lady, señor. My father chose to keep me away from the kitchen and my mother, who he felt was a bad influence in other matters. Instead, he taught me to read and write."

"Reading and writing are valuable skills," he says. "Not many women are given that luxury."

"And I treasure them and make sure my children also have those skills. But unfortunately I never learned to cook much of anything." She smiles at Alma. "This one will be better prepared for the world."

"Ah, but you have spirit and what the americanos call gumption."

She smiles ruefully. "Others have been known to call it stubbornness."

He laughs and is about to speak again, when Señora Ortega reaches the entrance to the plaza. She turns to frown at them.

"You are talking instead of walking. We must hurry to put the food in its place or we will miss the procession."

"And the race!" Andrew says.

His mother lifts an eyebrow at him.

"They have a race to catch a rooster! The señora told me about it!"

"So you were talking and walking yourself," Señor Beitia teases the old lady.

She gives him a withering look. "My cousin will be waiting for the food." She turns and they follow her into the big square.

The plaza is busy. Children pop in and out of the house doors, most of them carrying platters or bowls of food to and fro. A woman pulls fat rounds of bread out of a beehive oven like the señora's . A group of men cluster near the road in the center of the plaza, then turn to greet others as they ride in from the east. A shout goes up and is followed by laughter and loud voices. On the slope Alma and her family just climbed, there's the sound of singing as more people approach.

Alma's breath catches. She's never seen so many people in one place. Andrew turns and grins at her, his eyes shining. Then they follow their mother and the señora into a cool adobe room and wait for the black-clad women inside to lift the baskets and bundles of food from their arms.

A tiny old lady with salt-white hair smiles at the children and hands them each a bizcochito. "You have worked hard, carrying such heavy loads so far. You deserve a treat." She pats Alma's shoulder and disappears into the crowd of women preparing the feast.

"Come," Señora Ortega says to their mother. "You can stir the stew."

Alma's mother moves toward the fireplace in the far corner and the children exchange looks, shrug, and head for the door. "Stay inside the plaza!" their mother calls after them.

There's no need to go beyond the house door, much less the plaza. There's plenty to see. Alma stands with her back against the building's warm adobe wall, and watches the people of Chimayó and their guests move between the neat garden plots and back and forth across the road.

Andrew finishes his cookie, pulls out his whistle, and adds to the noise. Alma eats hers slowly, savoring its buttery licorice scent and taste.

The number of men in the center of the plaza has increased. Señor Beitia and others have joined them. They chat amiably, the younger ones affectionately slapping each others' shoulders. Then another group of riders enters the village, this time from the west. The men in the plaza fall silent, their faces carefully blank.

The tiny white-haired woman who gave the children the cookies comes out of the house and shades her eyes with her hand. "Welcome, Prefect Abreú!" she calls. Her voice is loud in the stillness. She walks toward the newcomers like a little black bird.

As she gets closer, she tilts her head back to look up at the only rider with a plumed hat. He is slim and elegant in his dark red cloak. "You honor us, prefect" she says.

The man's horse reaches to sniff at her. She bats its muzzle away and smiles at the man. "Although you should teach your horse better manners." Then she makes a welcoming gesture with both hands. "But come! Come! You can't feast on the back of a horse! Besides, he should rest up for the rooster race!"

The prefect is tall on his horse but short when he dismounts. He flings his cloak over one shoulder, exposing a white linen shirt and embroidered satin waistcoat. The men with him swing off their animals. Andrew nudges Alma's side with his elbow. "Look at that tall one."

She squints toward the road. "That's the man we met in Don Fernando."

"The soldier," Andrew says, standing a little straighter. "Señor Donaciano Vigil."

"I wonder if he's been in Don Fernando recently. If he's seen Grandfather Peabody."

But the newcomers aren't moving toward the house and the food. They're mingling with the men in the plaza, greeting and being greeted. Alma watches them with a little frown. The people in Señor Beitia's group are polite enough, but they're certainly not as relaxed as they were before the prefect and his little troop arrived.

The old lady skirts around a garden plot and heads back to the house door. As she reaches the threshold, she gives Alma a smile and a wink. "We women have more power than men think," she says conspiratorially before she disappears inside.

Alma's forehead wrinkles. Then she spies another group of people entering the plaza from the west, several men and two women, one of them holding the hand of a girl about Alma's age.

Andrew sees them, too. "Gregorio!" he shouts.

Gregorio Garcia is at the edge of the group of newcomers but he doesn't see the children or hear Andrew's shout. His head is bent toward the younger of the two women, who is wearing a black lace mantilla that cascades from a tall silver comb perched high on her head.

"Gregorio!" Andrew calls again. Then he darts across the plaza, winding his way between the gardens. He's halfway to the road before Gregorio looks up.

The woman and child have already moved away toward an open door, but the one with the black lace remains. She's perhaps fifteen, still really a girl. Alma is well behind Andrew and sees her face crinkle disapprovingly as Gregorio grabs the boy in a hug, then swings him into the air before setting him back on the ground and beaming at him.

Even with her nose wrinkled, the girl is pretty. She has a heart-shaped face, large brown eyes, and smooth black hair woven into a kind of braided crown on top of her head, where the silver comb is perched. She stands very straight, with her chest out. She has curves like a woman, not a girl.

Alma's throat suddenly feels as if it's still full of bizcochito crumbs, but they're dry now, and choking her.

Somehow she manages to smile at Gregorio as he greets her, both hands extended. "Nita!" he exclaims. "I had hoped to see you here!" He turns to the others. "These are the friends I accompanied here from Don Fernando de Taos." He smiles at Alma, then the girl in the mantilla. "The reason I'm here."

He turns back to the children. "Andrew, Alma, these are my cousins on my mother's side, the Montoya brothers, Don Antonio Abad and Don Desiderio." He reddens a little as he looks at the young woman. "And their cousin on their father's side, Señorita Gertrudis Leonarda Fajardo." It's an ugly name, but the way he says it, Alma knows he finds it beautiful. She gives the girl a begrudging nod.

Then Andrew distracts them all by turning to the taller of the two Montoyas and saying, "I heard you were in jail!"

The curly-haired man throws his head back and laughs. Then he glances around the square, pretending to look carefully from side to side. "Don't tell anyone, but I'm out again." He nods toward another cluster of people who are just now entering the plaza. "He's the one who's supposed to be in jail!"

A stocky middle-aged man comes toward them, his hand extended. "Desiderio," he says genially. "And Antonio Abad. You're looking well, primo. I see you have our young Taoseño friend with you." He smiles at Gregorio and pumps his hand.

"Señor Alcalde Esquibel," Gregorio says. "It is an honor."

The man's chest puffs out with pride, but he waves his hand as if brushing the titles away. "Formalities, formalities." He peers into Gregorio's face. "I hope you plan to stay with us permanently, amigo. We need more men of enterprise and good looks in the valley of the río Santa Cruz." He smiles meaningfully at Gertrudis Fajardo. "Don't we, señorita?"

She dimples at him but doesn't speak. Alma's hands clench against the sides of her skirt.

But the older Montoya brother is speaking to her. Don Antonio Abad's eyes twinkle as he beams down at Alma and her brother. "I have a daughter just about your age." He waves a hand at the plaza. "She and her mother are around here somewhere."

"Only a girl?" Andrew asks.

Alma glares at him, but the tall man just laughs and turns to grin at his companions. "I'm working on getting a boy."

Gertrudis' cheeks color. She reaches for the arm of her other male cousin. "If you are going to be vulgar, I and Desiderio will follow your wife."

Antonio Abad laughs again and winks at Alma. "I'd better go along to protect myself." He gives the children and Gregorio a jaunty wave and takes Gertrudis' other arm.

As the little group moves toward the opposite side of the square, Gregorio says, "She's very pretty," with a longing in his voice that squeezes Alma's stomach. She bites the insides of her cheeks.

The Montoyas disappear through a door on the far side of the plaza. Gregorio pats Alma's shoulder goodby and follows them. Alma turns away, suddenly tired.

But Andrew has twisted around and is staring at the building nearest them, where a carved wooden door stands slightly ajar. Inside, a man is singing in a high, sweet tone. Other voices join in. As the sound swells, the plaza quiets and all the faces turn toward it, listening.

Then the music is interrupted by another rider, this one from the plaza's east entrance. Silver buttons run down the side of his trousers and his waist-length coat gleams with embroidered silk flowers. His white horse shines with good health and a newly-brushed coat. Its mane is carefully braided with blue and red ribbons and its saddle and bridle sparkle with bits of polished silver. Everyone watches as the horse moves regally down the road and past the children to the carved wooden door.

The door opens all the way. Two men come out, carrying a small brightly-painted wooden statue between them. They carefully lift it to the rider, who grasps it firmly in one arm while he holds the reins with the other hand. When he clicks his tongue, the big horse turns obediently back to the road.

While this has been going on, Alma's mother has joined the children. As she reaches for their hands, more riders enter the plaza from the east. The man with the statue waits until they're almost to him, then proceeds ahead, out the west entrance. More men stream out of the chapel and fall into line behind.

Señora Ortega is now standing behind the children and their mother. "It is the bulto of Santiago," she explains in a hushed voice. "They take it to the fields now, to bless the crops for the harvest."

"Why do they carry it on a horse?" Andrew asks.

"Santiago is the patron of horses as well as soldiers and la plaza del cerro."

The rest of the people in the plaza are moving past them now, following the men who followed the horses. The children, their mother, and the señora join the procession.

Below the hill of Chimayó, the fields stretch rich with corn. The leaves on the cottonwoods beyond are thick and green. They sparkle in the sunlight. Alma has a sudden yearning for her own valley, its green aspens, black pines, and craggy mountain peaks. She bites her lip and tries to make herself appreciate the warmth of the day, the sunlight on the leaves, the press of people as they walk slowly behind the saint and his attendants.

# CHAPTER 18

Finally, the fields are all blessed and the procession has returned to the plaza. The little carved saint is placed back in its chapel, the horses are released into the corrals outside the plaza, and everyone's voice is louder and more cheerful.

The children and their mother follow Señora Ortega into her cousin's house, where they're given a seat at the table. The stew is thick with meat and fresh corn, and hot with green chile. When the señora passes the platter of bread, she says, "And here is some the americano child helped to bake," and everyone laughs kindly.

As Alma dips a piece into her bowl, Prefect Abreú enters the house. Donaciano Vigil stoops through the door after him.

"Ah, Don Ramón!" the host says. "You are most welcome! And Señor Vigil as well!"

The prefect gives the sergeant a quizzical look. "Señor Vigil? You've come up in the world, Donaciano. Or else he's angry at you. I thought you were his cousin."

The host flushes. "I was just being polite. In honor of his companion."

The big soldier puts a hand on the man's arm. "It's only me, primo. There's no need to stand on ceremony." He looks at Ramón Abreú. "I believe you know everyone here, Excellency?"

The prefect looks around the room, smiling and nodding to those at the table as well as the women who are serving. Then his eyes reach the children and their mother. "I don't believe I've had the honor of meeting this young woman and her siblings," he says gallantly.

Donaciano Vigil and Alma's mother exchange a wry grin. "Suzanna Peabody Locke, may I introduce our prefect, Don Ramón Abreú," he says formally.

"I'm pleased to meet you." She touches the children's shoulders. "These are my children, Alma and Andrew."

The prefect's face tightens slightly. "You are of the family which squats in the mountains east of Don Fernando de Taos."

Her hand is still on Alma's shoulder. Her fingers tighten into Alma's cotton dress, but her voice remains calm. "We reside on the border there, guarding the Passes," she says evenly. "And maintaining friendship with the Utes."

The prefect breaks into a smile. "Ah, well put! Keeping an eye on things for us, are you?" He spreads his hands. "But you are here, not there watching!"

"My husband and father-in-law are there."

"They are business partners with Juan Ramón Chavez," Donaciano Vigil interjects. "Juan Ramón is my cousin on my mother's uncle's side."

Prefect Abreú laughs and slaps his thigh. "You people! I have lived here all my life and still I cannot grasp the way you are all so connected!"

"Live here long enough and you will find it is the same for yourself," his host says. "But please, be seated and take a bite and talk with us. Perhaps you will find that you're related to someone here after all."

"I'm sure the Sergeant will be!" Ramón Abreú says. "But I'm afraid my duties demand that we continue on our way. However, I thank you for the kind invitation."

As the host walks the two visitors to the door, Señor Vigil turns and grins at Alma's mother, then gives Alma a wink. She smiles back at him shyly. He's almost as nice as Gregorio.

"I wonder where Alcalde Esquibel is eating," someone at the other end of the table says in a low voice.

"Down by the river, I hope," a man answers. "Where he can escape."

Alma's mother sends them a sharp look, then leans toward the woman sitting opposite her. "Can you explain this corrida del gallo to me?"

Andrew stops eating to listen.

The woman glances at him, then says reluctantly, "It is a horse race, but they do not race to see who finishes first. Instead, they chase each other to capture the prize."

"And the prize is a rooster?"

The other woman nods. She glances at Andrew again before she answers. "The rooster is pegged out on the ground and the initial contest is to see who can get to him first and grab him up while the rider is still on his horse. Then the second part is to try to grab the bird from the rider who has him."

"How do they decide who wins?" Andrew asks.

The woman moves her spoon through her stew. "I've never known for sure."

Andrew frowns. "There must be rules."

The woman looks away. "I think it's when the rooster gives up."

"Gives up the ghost?" his mother asks quietly.

"Something like that."

Andrew is looking at his mother, waiting for an explanation.

She grimaces. "When the rooster dies."

"Oh." He puts his spoon in his bowl. His hands drop to his lap. Then he pushes back from the table. "May I be excused?"

She nods and he maneuvers around the other diners and out the door.

"Lo siento," the woman says apologetically.

Alma's mother shakes her head. "You only spoke the truth, and that as gently as possible. He has an adventurous heart but a tender soul."

"Pobrecito," the other woman murmurs.

Andrew has disappeared by the time Alma and her mother return to the plaza. Men on horseback mill in groups up and down the road, Señor Beitia among them. Alma spies Alcalde Esquibel in the middle of a cluster at the eastern end, leaning forward from his saddle to shake someone's hand.

Then she's distracted by Gregorio, who appears at her mother's elbow with Señorita Fajardo on his arm. The girl dimples at Alma, then her mother. Gregorio is opening his mouth to make introductions when silence falls over the plaza.

Prefect Abreú is back on his white horse, once again riding in from the western entrance at the head of his blue-jacketed soldiers. Donaciano Vigil brings up the rear. There's something about the set of the men's shoulders that says they're not here for a rooster race. Gregorio's breath hisses between his teeth as they pass.

The only sound is the clomp of horses' hooves on the dirt road, then the prefect pulls up in front of the group that contains Juan José Esquibel. Words are exchanged, too low for Alma to hear. The alcalde's chin lifts angrily and the prefect turns his head and barks a command at the blue-coated men behind him. The soldiers' horses move nervously, but not forward.

The prefect scowls. "I said, take him into custody!"

Sergeant Vigil's horse edges around the soldiers and draws alongside Alcalde Esquibel's. "Perdóneme, primo," he says courteously. His voice echoes across the plaza. "We have come to place you in safekeeping until the events of recent months can be investigated and addressed."

The alcalde's eyes narrow. He shakes his head. Alma stiffens. Will there be a fight?

But then he smiles. "Ah, amigo," he says. "You have a rare gift for words. It's too bad you insist on working for men who know so little of honor."

The prefect's head jerks. He scowls at Esquibel, then the sergeant. "I said, arrest him!"

Donaciano Vigil looks at the alcalde and shrugs eloquently. He turns his head, studying the men in the plaza, the women at the house doors, the children. When he turns back to Señor Esquibel, his face is grave. "I believe it would be best if you come with us quietly, amigo."

The other man glances around the plaza, then nods. He reins his horse past Ramón Abreú without looking at him and heads toward the western exit. As he passes Alma's little group, he spies Gregorio. He leans from his saddle. "Get word to the Montoyas."

"Silence from the prisoner!" the prefect shouts. He spurs his horse into a trot and moves past the soldiers and the alcalde. The big white breaks into a canter as it passes the houses and heads down the hill.

In the plaza behind him, voices erupt. "What about the rooster?" someone calls.

"Oh, just let him go," a man answers. "We have more important races to run now."

Señor Beitia's horse trots toward Alma's mother. The man's eyes flash with something between anger and excitement, but he speaks calmly enough. "I'm afraid there will be no more festivities today," he tells her. "The prefect has used the feast for his own ends and spoiled it." He turns to Gregorio. "But we know what to do in response, do we not?"

Gregorio's eyes are hooded and his jaw tight. He looks at Alma's mother, then Gertrudis Fajardo. "It may be best for you to return home. I fear events may take an ugly turn."

"Or at least the discussion will be ugly." Señor Beitia's voice is grim and excited at the same time. "Decisions must be made."

Gregorio frowns. "I must seek out the Montoyas. I believe they are in the eastern orchards arranging for the race and this evening's dance." He looks at the señorita. "Let me return you to your cousins and give them the message." He turns to Alma's mother. "Will you go back to Señora Ortega's house?"

"I will escort las senoras y los chamacos," Señor Beitia says officiously. He swings off his horse and bows to Alma's mother.

She gives him a brief smile and nods to Gregorio. "We will be fine. Go safely." She turns to Gertrudis Fajardo. "I hope we will meet another day." Then she holds out her hands to Alma and Andrew. "Come along, children." She glances at the senora. "That is, if you are ready to leave?"

Senora Ortega's face is grim and irritable at the same time. She nods and turns away abruptly to lead them down the hill.

# CHAPTER 19

It's another three days before they see Señor Beitia again or hear any news.

"We are gathering," he tells them. His very braids bristle with excitement. "The new taxes were bad, and the appointment of Ramón Abreú as prefect was worse, but this jailing of the alcalde, a man we elected, this is the final indignity."

"And what will you important men do in response?" the señora sneers. "You will talk and then talk some more, and finally wear yourselves out with talking while the harvest rots in the fields."

He ignores her and focuses on Alma's mother. "The alcalde is still in el calabozo, but the Montoyas are discussing what steps to take and when to enact them." He shakes his head admiringly. "They are natural leaders, those cousins of your young friend."

She frowns. "I hope they don't lead Gregorio into trouble when he's just beginning to develop an interest in an eligible girl."

Señor Beitia waves a hand, brushing her concerns aside. "Oh, the girl's not a problem. Her father is one of us."

"So her father's a fool as well," the señora sniffs as she turns toward the fireplace and the stew pot. She waves a hand at Alma. "Get the bread, child."

Alma helps to organize the meal as the man continues to talk. "Don Antonio Abad has asked me to reconnoiter the jail and determine the most effective way to accomplish the alcalde's release."

"Release?" the señora hisses at the fire. "What idiots!"

But he's looking only at Alma's mother. "I have relatives who guard the prisoners in the jail, so my knowledge is superior to that of other men."

As Alma places the bowls around the table, she glances at her mother, whose forehead is wrinkled with concern. "That seems dangerous," her mother says. "If the authorities discover you've been spying for the Montoyas, they could throw you in with the alcalde."

"And we would be good company for each other!" he laughs, slapping his thigh. "But there's little danger. Prefect Abreú has skulked back to Santa Fe. Only those who can be trusted are aware of what's about to transpire."

"Transpire!" Señora Ortega snorts as she ladles stew into a pottery serving bowl. She looks over her shoulder at the señor. "And of course you can't tell us what you're up to, can you?"

"Oh, it's not that I don't trust you, señora." He smoothes a braid and gives Alma's mother a meaningful look. "I would trust you with my life, you know that." Then his back straightens. "But I have given my word to speak only to the other conspirators about the plans that are unfolding."

"Humph." The señora moves toward the table, the serving bowl in her hands. "Well, in the meantime, food is necessary to prepare even foolish bodies for action. Let us eat!"

Although Señor Beitia can't tell them what the Montoyas plan to do, he has apparently not been barred from predicting the end result. He finishes his meal, then leans back in his seat and says, "Changes are coming and they will be important ones." He looks at Alma's mother. "You see before you a man who will be central to future events."

She raises a questioning eyebrow at him, but he merely smiles mysteriously and asks, "How would you like to live in the capitol?"

"Mexico City?"

"La villa real de la santa fe de Francisco de Asís!" The words roll off his tongue as if they're sweet as candy. He beams at her. "I can not only transport you to the capitol but also provide you with the best of everything there."

She pushes away from the table and stands, one hand on the rough planks. "I am married, señor. It is inappropriate for you to suggest such a thing."

"It's not a suggestion, it's a proposal."

The señora makes a hissing sound. The others ignore her. Alma's hands clench, her nails biting into her palm. She doesn't dare look at Andrew, but she can feel him, sitting very still on the other side of the table. Her mother turns abruptly and begins pacing the floor between the fireplace and loom.

Señor Beitia watches her, smoothing his braids. He leans back in his seat. "You must ponder the future, señora," he says quietly. "Your children will not be with you forever. And what then?"

She makes an impatient gesture and stops, one hand on the loom frame and stares at the rough jerga she's been working on.

"The girl will be married and off your hands in five or six years at the most. She's not very pretty, it's true. But she's a hard worker and mi prima has taught her the rudiments of cooking. And the boy can be apprenticed when he's twelve or thirteen."

Her head moves slightly. Señor Beitia's voice changes, reassuring her before she can object. "We'll find him a good patrón, someone who will teach him a trade. I have plenty of contacts who'll be glad of an extra pair of hands. They won't care about the color of his skin, as long as he stays away from their daughters." He chuckles. "Though that might be hard for him. African blood can be lusty."

Her head jerks. She turns to face him, one hand clenching the loom. Her eyes are wide, as if she's seeing him for the first time. "What in tarnation did you just say?"

He spreads his hands. "I'm willing to take you even with your mulatto children. I'll provide for them well, even after we have some of our own. I know you're not pureblood yourself, but I'm prepared to overlook that." He smiles disarmingly. "Your beauty and education overcome the savagery of your mother's ancestors."

Her mouth opens, then shuts again. She turns abruptly back to the loom, her head down. Her foot taps the floor.

In the silence, Señora Ortega leaves the table and crosses to the banco. She drops onto it without taking her eyes off Alma's mother and the señor and puts her hands in her lap as if she's watching a play.

"I know you would like to be independent, to rely on no one but yourself," Señor Beitia continues. "But you cannot truly make a living with your loom. Not any time soon. It takes years of practice to become an accomplished weaver. In the meantime, you and the children will starve and your beauty will fade. And then no man will want you."

She turns, her eyes furious black slits. "How dare you!"

He stares at her uncomprehendingly.

"You insult me and my children, señor. We may have impure blood, but we would never speak to another person as you have spoken just now." Her hand lifts from the loom and points at the door to the courtyard. "Get out!"

Señor Beitia glances at the señora. She nods, her eyes hooded. He rises from his seat, bows stiffly to Alma's mother and then, more gallantly, to the old woman and crosses to the door. He claps his hat on his head, turns back into the room, and opens his mouth. Alma's mother glares at him, her eyes snapping. He shrugs, yanks the door open, and disappears into the night.

"Well!" Señora Ortega says. "You certainly expressed your opinion about that clearly enough."

The younger woman looks at her contritely. "I apologize, señora. It is your house, not mine. It was not my place to tell him to leave."

The old woman shrugs. "It was your conversation, not mine. There was no other way to end it. Except, of course, to accept his offer." She nods toward the children. "Beitia's right, you know. You can't raise these two by weaving alone. Even if you were skilled, it would be a difficult life. He's not a bad man, though he's a vain one. You could do worse."

"You forget that I'm married."

"And where is this man you are married to?"

Her lips tighten. "He is taking care—"

"You have left him. You can take another if you prefer."

Alma's mother shakes her head and turns back to the loom. She rubs her hand over her face, then strokes the loom's thick side beam.

"Señor Beitia is not the most well-spoken of men, but he does speak the truth," Señora Ortega continues. "Except about himself." She snorts. "Pure blood. What foolishness. He and I share a forebear, an Apache girl captured by the Utes and sold in Don Fernando de Taos to a man who named her María Juana. She was my great-grandmother. And Beitia's, too." She nods at Alma's mother. "We're descended from genízaro, people of the indios bárbaros captured by the Spanish and civilized. Same as you."

"I'm not—"

"Your mother was half Navajo, wasn't she? Her mother was captured and sold, same as my mother's grandmother. Padre Martínez has the baptism records tucked away in a cupboard in the Don Fernando church. I'm sure of it."

Alma's mother bites her lip, nods, shrugs, and turns back to the loom.

"Genízaro, same as me. We may have more Spanish in us by now than from the marauding tribes, but we'll never be Spanish. We have wild blood, genízaro." The old lady gestures at Alma and Andrew. "We're mixed blood, same as them. Except some of their blood is negro."

Their mother's head snaps around. "My children aren't negro!"

The señora gazes at her implacably. "You can say what you like, the fact remains."

"I won't have them looked down on!"

"I didn't say they were good or bad, ugly or beautiful. I simply stated the obvious."

"I don't know that it's so obvious."

The old woman snorts and waves a hand at Andrew. "You can call those blond curls Irish if you want too, but that nose is negro. And the girl. Those so-called freckles. I've seen those before, but not on a Spanish girl. On a negro slave woman at Bent's Fort."

Alma looks uneasily at her mother, whose eyes flash with anger, but the old woman's gaze is calm and steady. "Your husband. He is not full-blood?"

Alma's mother looks away. "His mother was Irish. His father is the son of a runaway slave and a Cherokee man."

"He's a quadroon."

"I suppose so." She shrugs. "It's not obvious. I didn't see it."

Señora Ortega sniffs. "Because you didn't want to see."

"He lied to me!"

"Did he actually tell you he was something else?"

She doesn't answer.

The señora purses her lips. "Not quite a lie." There's a long pause, then she adds, "I hope you realize that Beitia is vain enough to return with his proposal. If you aren't willing to go back to your husband, what he has suggested may be the most sensible thing you can do. Especially if you plan to stay in the valley of the Santa Cruz." She nods toward the children. "Their negro blood is not important to me, but to others here it will be a matter of comment. And perhaps more. You will need protection."

Alma's mother stares at the old woman. Her chest heaves once, then twice. Then she jerks away from the loom and stalks into the sleeping space beyond. Alma and Andrew rise from the table and silently follow her. As they go through the door, a log drops into the fire behind them with a thud.

Their mother doesn't turn her head when they enter. They undress without looking at her or each other and crawl into bed. Alma crosses her arms across her churning belly and forces her eyes to close.

She doesn't sleep well. She dozes, wakes, and dozes again. When her eyes open again, it's still dark outside. Someone is crying, but the sound is suppressed, as if they're trying not to be heard.

Alma lifts her head. On the neighboring pallet, Andrew breathes steadily. There's a ragged sigh from the other side of the room. "Mama?" she whispers.

Her mother sniffs. "Go back to sleep." Her voice is muffled and scratchy at the same time.

Alma shivers, then slips out of her blankets and across the room. She kneels beside her mother's pallet and tugs gently at the wool blanket.

Her mother sniffles again and lifts the cover. Alma crawls into the warmth of her arms. They lie there a long moment, Alma's face tucked into her mother's chest, her mother stroking her hair.

"Why are you crying?" Alma whispers.

"Because I love you." There's a helplessness in her voice and a kind of regret.

"Don't you want to love me?"

Her mother's breath catches. "Of course I want to love you, niña. I'm crying because I want you to have a happy life."

Alma goes still. Now is the moment. "I was happy in the valley."

"I know." Her mother's hand smoothes Alma's hair. "But you and Andrew can't stay there forever. You'll grow up. I want you to be happy no matter where you go."

"I don't know about Andrew, but I'd be glad to stay in the valley forever."

Her mother chuckles wryly. "You are your father's child." Then she sighs. "But I can't go back." There's something between sadness and anger in her voice now.

Alma's breath catches. "Never?"

Now it's her mother's turn to go still. "Not yet, anyway." She moves her hands to Alma's shoulders. "Don't ever let a man lie to you, niña. Don't let there be any secrets between you." She sighs again, a ragged breath from deep in her bones. "Even my father lied to me."

Alma bites back sudden tears, feeling her mother's pain. But she also feels strangely secure, wrapped as she is in her mother's arms. Gradually, she relaxes into sleep.

When she wakes, her mother is already up and dressed. The window shutter has been pulled back, even though the sun isn't truly up yet. The sky is a white haze trying to turn blue. Her mother moves quietly around the room, taking clothes from the pegs on the wall and folding them carefully into a basket.

"What are you doing?" Andrew asks from his pallet.

His mother looks up. Her face is strained and tired, but there's a determined set to her jaw. "I'm packing. We're going to Santa Fe."

Santa Fe? Alma's stomach clenches. She pushes into a sitting position as Andrew throws off his blankets and demands, "When do we leave?"

"The day after tomorrow. I've already sent word to Gregorio Garcia, asking him to accompany us."

"He might not be able to," Alma says hopefully. "The Montoya brothers may need him to work."

"Then we'll go alone. With luck, we'll be in Santa Fe by the first of August. The beginning of a new month and a new chapter."

Alma's stomach twists, but Andrew's eyes are bright with excitement. "We'll have Chaser to protect us," he says.

His mother chuckles, but her face is still sad. "That's true."

"Have you told the señora?" Alma asks.

She nods without looking up. "We've spoken." Then she lifts her head. "Now get up and get dressed. We have much to do before we leave. We'll need to do some washing, I need to finish the weaving I've been working on, and the señora has agreed to bake some bread for us to take along." She raises her head. "And Alma, you'll need to locate your sunbonnet."

# PART III

## AUGUST–DECEMBER 1837

## SANTA FE

# CHAPTER 20

Gregorio sends word that he can't come for them until early Tuesday. Alma's mother accepts this grudgingly and goes back to the loom to finish the piece she's been working on. She and the señora speak to each other only when necessary.

And then it's Tuesday morning and Gregorio is standing in the doorway with his hat in his hand and smiling down at Alma, who's been waiting since sunrise for his knock.

Her mother comes forward. "Thank you for coming."

He smiles at her. "For you and your family, I would come from farther away than Santa Cruz and go further than Santa Fe."

At the table, where she's wrapping tortías for the journey, the señora sniffs derisively. "Such eloquence."

Gregorio turns toward her. "Señor Locke saved my life. I would protect his family with mine, if it were necessary."

Her hands stop moving as her sharp eyes search his face. Then she nods abruptly and returns to her work.

He turns back to Alma's mother. "I can also accompany you back to Don Fernando."

Her chin lifts. "I will not return to a place where I am treated like a child who must be protected from the truth."

His mouth opens, then shuts. He gives Alma an apologetic glance.

The señora sniffs again.

Alma's mother glares at her. "And I will not remain in a place where my children are considered inferior to others because of who their great-grandmother was." She turns to Gregorio. "The buckboard is behind the house and the mules are in the pasture across the road. If you'll get them into their harness, the children and I will gather our things."

Gregorio nods reluctantly. He makes a small formal bow to Señora Ortega and goes out the door, closing it carefully behind him.

The señora gives the younger woman a sharp look. "You have much to learn."

She glances at the loom. "I've learned the basics. I can manage from here."

The old lady sniffs and moves to the fireplace. "That isn't what I meant and I believe you know it."

Alma's mother doesn't reply. Instead, she waves her hands at the children, shooing them toward the sleeping room. "Go make sure we haven't left anything behind."

The señora turns from the fire, the poker in her hand. She points it at Andrew. "That old loom in the corner of the store-room. You tell the Garcia boy to rearrange what's still in the wagon and pack the loom in the bottom so it will be well protected. And make sure he lays all the pieces flat."

The children stare at her, then their mother, whose face is flushed with embarrassment. "Señora, I can't accept—"

The old lady waves the poker at her. "It isn't a gift. It's what I owe you in exchange for the rest of the money you paid me."

Her mouth opens, then shuts again. She chews on her lower lip. "Gracias," she whispers.

"And you, girl." The señora directs her poker at Alma. "Take that old wooden bowl you've been using for the bread. You're going to need it and I have another just like it."

Alma nods obediently. She crosses the room to retrieve the big cottonwood bowl from its shelf, then retreats to the storeroom with her brother. Her mother goes to the loom and begins carefully folding the piece she finished the night before.

Finally, everything is collected and in the wagon. Gregorio ties his little brown mare behind it and helps Alma's mother onto the seat in front. When he lifts Alma, his hands on her waist are comforting, though his eyes are cloudy with concern.

"All settled?" he asks. He turns away without waiting for an answer. "Andrew, are you riding or walking?"

"Riding," Andrew says. "I can see more from the wagon than I can on the ground."

When Gregorio lifts the boy into the back, Chaser Two rears up beside it. His front paws scrabble against the wood and he looks at Andrew imploringly. "You have to walk!" the boy laughs.

"He'll be joining you soon enough," Gregorio tells the mastiff. "He won't be able to sit still back there for very long."

Señora Ortega comes out of the gate. She's carrying the black rebozo Alma borrowed for the Chimayó feast. She hands it to the girl. "That's too short for me," she says gruffly. "You might as well get some use from it." Then she steps back abruptly, puts her hands on her hips, and glares up at Alma's mother. "Go with God."

The younger woman stiffens, then bites her lip and looks down at the señora. Her face softens. "I do appreciate all you've taught me, señora."

The old lady nods stiffly. Chaser trots over to her and sniffs at her skirt. She nudges him away with her knee.

Gregorio swings onto the buckboard, tips his hat to the señora, and snaps the reins. The mules move forward. The wagon creaks a little as the wheels begin to turn.

As they approach the first bend in the road west, Alma pushes the wings of her sunbonnet away from her face and turns to look back at the house beside the road. Señora Ortega is still standing outside the high rock-topped walls, watching the wagon. Alma lifts her hand in farewell, but the señora doesn't respond. Instead, she moves stiffly toward the gate without looking back.

The mules move quietly through the midmorning light. Dust puffs up from their plodding hooves. They seem to have caught their riders' pensiveness. Alma slips her hand inside her mother's and her mother pats it with a distracted air, as if she hardly knows it's there.

Finally, Gregorio breaks the silence. "I am sorry I couldn't come yesterday, señora. There have been developments in Santa Cruz and my presence was required."

Alma's mother looks at him blankly, then blinks. "Developments?"

"Sí." He returns his gaze to the space between the mules' ears. "Alcalde Esquibel is no longer in jail."

"The prefect thought better of his actions and released him?"

"The prefect does only as Governor Pérez instructs." Alma glances at him in surprise. His voice sounds different from the way it usually does. Bitter and amused at the same time.

"The governor has apparently decided our alcaldes have no authority to retain or release the prisoners in their jurisdiction," he continues. His face twists. "The concept of democracy no longer exists in Nuevo México."

Her mother's eyebrows rise. "But the alcalde is no longer in el calabozo?"

"That's right. He was released late last night by those most familiar with the case." Gregorio's face relaxes as his eyes twinkle. "It was quite an event."

"You were there?"

He smiles at her mysteriously.

"Isn't that risky? Participating in a jail break makes you an accomplice. You'll end up behind bars yourself!"

He shakes his head. "There's little danger. Even if the prefect could discover who participated, the jail would not hold us all."

She frowns. "If anything happens to you, your mother will be very unhappy with me."

"I am an adult. I make my own choices."

"You are here because you escorted me and the children to Chimayó. She will blame me."

He scowls and flicks the reins across the backs of the mules. Silence descends on the wagon. Alma studies the way the road curves along the edge of the river valley, between it and the small thinly grassed hills on their right.

They're almost to the road that leads off to the Santa Cruz plaza and church when a man steps into the road ahead of them and stands waiting. It's Señor Beitia. Alma looks sideways at her mother, whose spine straightens.

Gregorio reins in the mules and the señor approaches her mother's side of the wagon. She sits perfectly still and looks down at him inscrutably.

He takes off his hat, clutches it to his chest, and looks up at her with beseeching eyes. "I wish to speak to you, señora."

"You've already spoken."

"Sí, sí. It is that of which I wish to speak." He twists the hat. One hand goes toward his braids, then stops abruptly. He takes a deep breath. "I have wronged you." He half turns and gestures toward the village on the hill above. "I have spent much time in the church these last three days, praying the rosary and contemplating my sins." He looks up at her. "I have come to offer my sincere apologies for what I said to you about your heritage and about your children. It was wrong of me. We are all God's children and should be treated as such."

She studies him for a long moment. Then her face softens. "I agree with you, señor. We are indeed all God's children. Who our grandparents or great-grandparents were is not as important as how we treat those around us."

His face brightens, then sobers. "And I have another apology to make. It was wrong of me to tempt you to leave the father of your children."

She bites her lip and looks away. "I accept your apology."

"Good!" he says. "It is good." He gives her a brilliant smile. "I am much relieved by your forgiveness." He sweeps his hat to one side in a courtly bow and steps backward, to the side of the road. "Safe journeys, señora. May God go with you and keep you safe in these troubled times."

She smiles at him and Gregorio speaks to the mules. The wagon moves down the road.

"What did he mean about troubled times?" Alma asks.

Gregorio glances at her. "The alcalde has called for a rebellion. Men are meeting today at Santa Cruz to decide how best to proceed."

Her mother stiffens. "Rebellion?"

"That may not be the best word. The alcalde's arrest is only one of many insults and aggravations and los paisanos have had enough. They are demanding change." He shrugs. "Although, if the governor doesn't listen to them, there may well be a revolt."

"Surely they won't succeed."

160

He shakes his head. "It is well known that the governor has disbanded the presidio troops for lack of funds. The militia across Nuevo México is made up of men like us here in Santa Cruz, people who were already barely scraping by and are now threatened with more taxes and no more protection." His voice rises. "And now we aren't even allowed to govern ourselves. Everything must be decided in Santa Fe!"

Alma and her mother stare at him in surprise.

Other people apparently feel as Gregorio does. Beyond Santa Cruz, the valley fields are scattered with small camps. The men in them aren't harvesting. Instead, they're clustered in small groups, talking, waving their arms, and looking angry.

The travelers meet more men and even a few women, as they move onto the road that will take them south to Santa Fe. Everyone nods politely, but they look grim. The men carry spears, machetes, and an occasional gun. Some of them are Puebloan, with blankets over their shoulders and eyes that glance politely away.

Andrew stays in the back of the buckboard more than he did between Don Fernando and Chimayó. Chaser Two also hovers nearby. Though he doesn't bark at any of the strangers, he's alert to their presence and keeps a close watch.

There's another road south, one that swings toward the río Grande and follows its course, but Gregorio takes the more direct route across a series of rocky hills scattered with juniper. As the wagon crests yet another slope, Alma looks longingly at the mountains to her left. They're craggy and green-black and remind her of home.

Gregorio chooses this moment to point to the long strip of green in the valley on her right. "That's the río Grande del Norte," he tells her. "See how beautiful the cottonwoods are at this time of year?"

Alma nods. They look just like the trees along the Santa Cruz river: gray trunks, green leaves that are starting to brighten as they begin to turn toward Fall. A flat-topped mesa juts up from the flat valley, blocking the view of a good section of woodland. The outcropping is black and ominous in the sunlight.

"What's that?" Andrew asks.

"That's La Mesilla," Gregorio says. "What Old Pete would call Black Mesa. It's sacred to some of the pueblos here. There are two close to it, San Ildefonso and Santa Clara. And some rico haciendas, too." A kind of wistfulness creeps into his voice. "Some of them are quite beautiful. " Then he slides Alma a smile. "Almost as beautiful as your valley."

"Nothing is as beautiful as the valley," she says stoutly.

"Woof!" Chaser Two says from beside the wagon, and even her mother chuckles.

The road dips across the green and fertile pueblo of Pojoaque and up into dryness again. Chaser Two wanders off the road to sniff at a small wooden cross that's been stuck into the dirt and braced with a cluster of rocks. He lifts his leg and Gregorio calls sharply, "Chaser! No!" The mastiff drops his foot, gives the wagon a puzzled look, then snuffles away.

"What's a cross doing beside the road?" Andrew asks. "There's no church around here, is there?"

The wagon is level with the marker now. "Was someone buried there?" Alma asks.

"I think it's a descanso," her mother says. "I haven't seen one of those since I was a child."

Alma shivers.

"They aren't buried there," her mother tells her. "It's a kind of memorial."

"In the past, the word 'descanso' meant a place where the men carrying a casket stopped to rest on the way to the cemetery," Gregorio explains. "But now we also use it to speak of a cross that's put up by a person's relatives as a kind of remembrance of where they died. I think that's what this is."

Alma looks back at the little weathered cross. It tilts slightly to one side. "It looks so sad."

"Someone comes and tends it," Gregorio tells her. "That's why it's there. To comfort the family of the person who died and to remind us that life is short."

She shivers again in the bright air.

# CHAPTER 21

Early the afternoon of the next day, the wagon trundles into Santa Fe plaza. The space is big and virtually empty, very different from Don Fernando or Chimayó. A cluster of mountain cottonwoods in the northeast corner and a flag on a pole in the center are the only things that brighten it.

All the low brown buildings are more or less connected, but the one closest to the wagon is clearly not a house or a store. It takes up the entire north side of the square and has only one door under the portal that runs along its front. The door is actually two pieces that together are almost as wide as a courtyard gate. They're massive carved things and look important.

As Alma studies them, the door on the right swings open. She jumps in surprise. "Oh!" she exclaims.

Her mother's head swings, following her gaze. "Well, of all people!" she lifts an arm. "Pete! Old One Eye Pete!"

The mountain man crosses to the edge of the porch, stares at the wagon, then pulls off his battered brown hat and lopes toward them with a broad smile. "Well, I'll be! I never thought t' see you here, of all places!" He reaches up to shake Alma's mother's hand, then leans toward the back and ruffles Andrew's hair. "The sight of you all is as welcome as a fair sunrise!" He beams at Alma and her spine loosens. The plaza seems much less strange now.

"And Gregorio Garcia!" Old Pete adds. "And here I thought you'd of gone over to the rebels 'n all!"

Gregorio frowns slightly, but doesn't reply. Old Pete turns back to Alma's mother. "What are you all doin' here? I thought you'd be headin' on back t' the valley about now!"

She frowns. "Why would we do that?"

"Well, everybody's sayin' there's gonna be trouble in Santa Cruz and the Chimayosos are at the bottom of it." His smile fades. "I've been a worryin' 'bout you all and wishin' I'd been able t' get up there and see how you was doin' before I headed south."

"You're still going to Chihuahua?"

He nods. "Got me some tradin' goods and a place in a caravan that's leavin' tomorrow." His face darkens. "Caravan's gonna need all the men they can find t' get through, what with all this commotion goin' on. News is, the Apaches and Navajos are already reckonin' on how they can take advantage of the troubles here." He turns his head and spits into the dirt. "Cantóns and proclamations. What balderdash."

Her brow wrinkles. "Cantóns?"

"You ain't heard? Well now—" He turns and surveys the plaza. He points at the cottonwoods at the other end of the long building. "Whyn't you all ride on over there and take a break from sittin' and give those mules a rest? I'll go back int' the governor's palacio here and see if I can't find someone to hunt us up somethin' to eat and drink. Then we can talk."

Gregorio flicks the reins and the wagon moves along the portal to the tall trees. Old Pete disappears through the massive doors. A few minutes later he comes back out with a small boy. He hands the boy some coins and the child dashes off. Pete heads toward the travelers. He swings Andrew out of the back of the buckboard as Gregorio helps Alma and her mother down from the seat.

"Feels good to stretch your legs a little, now don't it?" Old Pete beams at Alma's mother. "It sure is right good t' see you." Then he sobers. "Though I wish you'd of gone home."

Her face darkens. He raises his hands, warding her off. "I know, I know. I reckon you're still mad at him and I ain't sayin' either one of you's right. But the valley'd be a heap safer than here in Santa Fe, even if the Injuns up there get contrary, too. Your man's got a way with the savages, and they trust him. That's all I'm sayin'."

The small boy appears at his elbow, a jug of water in one hand and a large white cloth parcel in the other.

"Ah, here we go," the mountain man says as he takes the goods. "Thankee, boy."

The child nods, gives Alma and Andrew a friendly grin, and runs off.

They gather in a small circle under the trees. Old Pete passes the water jug around and places the bundle on the wagon's seat. There are two fat loaves of bread inside. He pulls a long knife from his waistband, and begins cutting and distributing.

The bread is still warm and slightly sweet. As it hits her tongue, Alma realizes just how hungry she is. Old Pete chuckles and hands her another piece. "Sure do like to watch you enjoy your food, little missy."

Alma smiles at him, but her mother interrupts. "What were you talking about when you said 'cantóns and proclamations'?"

"I'm surprised you ain't heard. I guess the news flew right on past you."

She gives him an exasperated look. "So what is this news? I suppose it's from Santa Cruz."

"Yep." He looks at Gregorio. "Those friends of yours must of put together their little proclamation right about the time you left town."

"Proclamation about what?" Alma's mother demands.

Old Pete cuts into the bread again and hands Andrew another slice before he says, "Let's see now. They got twelve men together, like they're Jesus' disciples or somethin', and they wrote up a 'noucement sayin' they believe in God and the country, but they ain't puttin' up with people tryin' to rile 'em and get 'em all mad at each other. Somethin' like that, anyway. Also, they ain't payin' no taxes, neither."

Gregorio grunts and lifts the water jug to his lips. She looks at him. "You knew about this?"

He lowers the jug. "I knew there was talk of it. I wasn't sure they would do it."

"And they've sprung that Juan José Esquibel from the calaboose," Old Pete says.

She nods.

Old Pete looks at Gregorio. "You in on that?"

"Never mind that now," Alma's mother says. "It sounds as if we left just in time, although we didn't know about this proclamation or the cantón." Then she frowns. "Why are they calling themselves that?"

Old Pete shrugs. "Settin' themselves up as a separate state like in Switzerland, I reckon. Means 'region' don't it?" He squints at her. "You may be right about gettin' out in time, but I wish you'd of swung north instead of south. Gerald must be worryin' like hell about you and the young uns right about now. You send word to him about where you were goin'? "

She lifts her chin.

He starts to shake his head, then seems to think better of it. Instead, he says, "So what're you gonna do now?"

"Just what I was already planning to do." She turns her head and looks around at the plaza and its adobe buildings. A chapel stands on the side opposite el palacio, between two adobe buildings with big double gates. "We'll need to find a place to live. Something small but large enough for a loom."

"So you got taught to work one, huh? Good enough to keep you and the kids?"

"Do you know of a place I can rent?"

He pushes his battered hat away from his face and scratches his forehead. "Might be. Let me talk to a couple people and see what we can rustle up. Shouldn't take more'n a day or so."

"But your wagon caravan. Don't you need to leave tomorrow?"

"Another day or two won't make no never mind. I can catch up to 'em." He looks around the plaza. Three men come out of a door and stop to stare at the wagon. Old Pete turns to Alma's mother. "For tonight anyway, you'd best stay west of town by the river. There's a spot along side of mine." He looks at Gregorio. "I'm guessin' you're in a hurry to get back up north and it'd prob'ly be a good thing if you did. Rebels ain't too welcome in this town right about now."

Gregorio's face twists in irritation, but then he nods and moves toward the mules. Alma looks up at the buckboard seat and wrinkles her nose. Gregorio sees her expression and grins. He turns back to Old Pete. "Is it far, this campsite? I think we are all tired of sitting."

Old Pete chuckles. "It ain't far." He offers Alma's mother his arm. "And I ain't escorted a pretty lady anywhere in a good while."

She laughs and shakes her head at him. "You never change."

"Never have yet," he answers. "Why should I start now?"

The campsite he leads them to is green and cool and within a stone's throw of the Santa Fe river. Alma eyes the stream and wonders where her fishing tackle is. A blue jay scolds from a broad-leaved cottonwood and Andrew laughs and declares they should just live here, instead of finding a house. His mother ignores him. When Old Pete arrives the next morning with news of a rental, she leaves the children with Gregorio and heads off to make the arrangements.

When she comes back, her whole body seems brighter than it has in days. She gives Andrew a mock frown. "I'm afraid we won't be living in Santa Fe," she says.

Alma looks up from the trout she's cleaning. "We're going home?"

Her mother's eyes stay on Andrew. "We'll be on the road to Santa Fe. Close enough to walk into town when we want to. Our new casita is on the road to Chihuahua."

Disappointment stings Alma's throat but Andrew's eyes widen. "The one that goes all the way to Mexico City?"

She nods.

"Well, I'll be!" he says.

His mother laughs. "You sound like Old Pete!"

Andrew grins at her. "Can we go now? Right away?"

"First, I'll need to put the mules back into their harness," Gregorio tells him. "Do you want to walk or ride?"

"I want to walk! Come on, Chaser Two!"

Alma looks down at her fish.

"Those will make a good evening meal for us," her mother says above her. Alma doesn't look up.

The house Old Pete has found is one of a string of homes scattered along the road between Santa Fe and the village of Agua Fría. It's a two room casita, one for sleeping, the other just large enough for eating and the loom, which Gregorio sets up before he leaves late that afternoon for Santa Cruz.

The walled courtyard is small and made smaller by the heap of firewood tossed in the far left-hand corner. It has two entrances: an unpainted double gate that opens onto the road and, next to the beehive-shaped oven, a single one which leads to the sheds and animal enclosures.

A battered wooden bench sits by the wall beside the gate. After Gregorio says goodby, Alma climbs onto it and watches him and the mare until they're over the first small hill heading north and out of sight. Then she steps down into the yard and looks blankly at the small and untidy space with its well in the far corner, opposite the pile of wood.

Andrew appears at the gate to the back. "Come and see the corral!"

She follows him, feet dragging, though she perks up a little when she reaches the back. There's another adobe wall around the animal enclosure. A narrow row of prickly pear cactus has been planted along its top edge. No one's likely to bother the mules, who are in a fenced-off area at one end.

While she's on tiptoe looking at the cactus, Andrew disappears into an adobe shed at the back of the casita. "We should get chickens!" he says as he emerges from its shadows. "There's perches already set up!"

"There are perches," she corrects him automatically. Then she frowns. "We won't be staying long enough to need chickens."
He looks at her impatiently. Then his head tilts. "I wonder if Old Pete's caravan has chickens. Won't they need eggs?"

# CHAPTER 22

Alma's mother has negotiated a low rent payment with Don Salvador Martín in exchange for teaching his grandchildren to read and write. Even though there's a school in Santa Fe, he wants his flock educated at home. She will go to his compound each afternoon to give them their lessons. Alma and Andrew will go with her and learn alongside the others.

They start the next afternoon. With Alma and Andrew, there are eight scholars altogether, ten when sixteen-year-old María Paula Ortiz and her fourteen-year-old sister María Salome can be spared from their household tasks. Eleven-year-old Rafaela Montoya is their cousin. There's only one girl, Rosario Martín, who's Alma's age. The other two are younger by at least a year.

The boys are all older than Andrew. Esquipula Montoya and Jesús Silva are both nine and their cousin Felix Urioste is ten. There's another boy, José Martín, who's fourteen, but he also has duties that make him unlikely to be in the classroom every day. He's learning to manage his grandfather's laborers and works alongside them in the fields that circle the house and stretch along the road between the Martín compound and the village of Agua Fría.

The children nod shyly to each other as they file into the room that's been set aside for them and exchange covert glances while their new teacher calls first one, then the other, to her chair and runs them through a short list of questions to find out how much they know. Finally, she waves them outdoors into the sunshine while she decides how to organize their work.

In the courtyard, Alma and Rosario smile at each other. "I like your hair," Rosario says shyly. "I wish mine was curly."

Alma wrinkles her nose. "I wish mine was less curly. It's hard to comb."

Rafaela turns toward them. "I hate combing my hair," she says. "It takes so much time."

Andrew, Jesús, and Esquipula have scuffled into acquaintanceship and are now bent over a sling Andrew has rigged with a piece of leather given him by Old Pete and some scraps of yarn from his mother's weaving.

"You can use it when the fighting starts!" Jesús says.

Alma's head jerks. She and Andrew stare at the other boy. "What fighting?" Andrew asks.

"The governor is sending out runners to tell everyone to hurry to Santa Fe to fight the rebels." Jesús flings an imaginary rock toward the wall as Esquipula thrusts an imaginary sword into the air. "They'll send those insurrectos running back to the hills they come from!"

Gregorio is a rebel. The courtyard is warm inside its enclosed adobe walls, but a shiver runs down Alma's spine. Just then her mother appears in the classroom doorway. "Estudiantes!" she calls. "Let us begin!"

Alma follows the others into the room, but she hears little of the lessons that afternoon. All she can think of is Gregorio heading back to Santa Cruz and the men gathering in Santa Fe to fight him.

The next day is Saturday. While Alma's mother prepares lesson plans, she sends Andrew and Alma into the tiny front courtyard to stack the firewood. They leave the gate open to allow the air to circulate inside the walls.

Alma is positioning a piece of wood on top of the stack when she hears a chicken cluck. She turns to see Old Pete in the gateway, a chicken under each arm, one brown and one red. He grins at the children. "I brought you a present."

The red hen turns its head and pecks at his hand. "Ornery little things," Old Pete says. "Come and get 'em so I can go talk to your ma. She in the house?"

The children move forward and divest the mountain man of his burden, then he brushes himself off and heads inside. Alma and Andrew settle the birds into a pile of straw in the shed next to the corral, close the door behind them, and follow him into the house.

"So you're leaving today?" their mother says as they enter. She's moved to her rocking chair and picked up her knitting.

Old One Eye Pete sits on the tiny banco between the fireplace and the blanket-curtained door that leads to the sleeping room, his hat on his knee. "Don't got much of a choice. Caravan's likely t' be almost t' Alburquerque by now. Much past that and I'll have a time catchin' 'em before they get south o' Belen."

"We appreciate the chickens."

Even as he nods, his shoulders hunch forward. "I sure do hate leavin' you here like this, without a man t' keep an eye on things. 'Specially with everything that's happenin'." He nods in the direction of the front gate. "I'm guessin' there'll be strangers on the road out here in the next couple days, comin' in from Alburquerque an' all."

He looks around the little room, then squints his good eye apologetically at Alma's mother. "I wouldn't be leavin' you like this if I didn't have my goods already stowed away in Guadalupe Miranda's caravan, and him halfway to the pueblo of Santo Domingo by now."

She looks up from her work. "Well, at least he's not in Alburquerque yet. You'll be able to catch up with him easily enough."

He toys with his hat and looks at her sideways. "I don't s'pose you'd be willin' to pack up and come with me? I know it ain't the best solution in the world but I sure do hate leavin' you here alone like this."

Something like fire flashes across her face. Then she composes herself, though her rocker isn't rocking now and her knitting needles aren't moving. "I'm perfectly capable of taking care of us. The loom is set up and I have employment teaching the Martín grandchildren. Besides, we're on a main highway. There's nothing to fear."

"And now we have chickens!" Andrew says.

His mother smiles. "And now we have chickens." Her eyes twinkle at Old Pete. "What more could we want?"

He gives her a appraising look, then looks at Alma. She forces herself to smile, though it's a small one. He squints at her, then looks at her mother and stands up. "Well, then, I guess I oughta mosey on out o' here and go and catch myself up t' my goods."

He claps his hat on, then turns back to her mother. "Elisha Stanley says he's stayin', regardless. He's got a shop there by the plaza, and goods he's gotta protect. He's a sharp trader but he's a good man t' have beside you in a pinch. You go lookin' for him if things get bad now, you hear?"

Irritation flashes across her face again, but she nods.

Old Pete heads for the door. He pats Alma's shoulder as he passes and she follows him outside and across the courtyard. At the gate, he turns to look down at her. "I ain't leavin' you 'cuz I want to, little missy."

She nods and looks at the ground. Her eyes are wet and she doesn't want him to see. "I know," she whispers.

"What's that?" He reaches for her chin. His rough-hewn face is crinkled with concern.

"I know you don't want to leave," she says, more sturdily this time.

"An' I'll be back just as soon's I can."

She nods and slews her eyes away, trying to be brave.

He looks away. "The woman don't want my help and a man's gotta eat," he grumbles. Then he pats Alma on the shoulder and moves away. He's left his mule in the little verge between the road and the gate. It lifts its head and huffs at him impatiently.

"All right, we're goin'," Old Pete grumbles. He heaves himself into the saddle, then looks down at Alma. "You take care now, you hear?" He turns the mule's head south, down the dusty road toward the little village and beyond. Alma squishes her lips together to keep them from shivering into tears and leans against the gatepost until he disappears from sight.

The road is silent in the hot August sun and filled with a gigantic emptiness. A wave of longing sweeps over her for a small creek beside a narrow dirt track and a string of dripping, fresh-caught trout. She pushes her clenched fist against her lips and goes into the house.

# CHAPTER 23

Although their mother isn't a church-going person, she still believes Sundays should be a day of rest, at least for the children. They read quietly, do a minimum of chores, and are encouraged to stay close to the casa. She herself devotes the time to her weaving.

Andrew slips out to visit the chickens and Alma takes her book into the yard. The sunniest spot is by the woodpile, so she makes herself comfortable on the half stump that serves as a chopping block. But even Washington Irving's Alhambra stories can't keep her attention. The book drops into her lap and she tries not to think about what she'd be doing if she was home in the valley: climbing the hill behind the cabin to sit on the slab of sandstone and study the light on the western peaks; watching a coyote cross the hay meadow as Brindle and the other cows graze in the pasture and a raven wheels above the yard to croak at Chaser and try to get him to bark. Here there is only silence.

Silence and muffled footsteps on the road beyond the wall. Alma leaves her book on the chopping block, goes to the gate, and eases it open far enough to peer out.

A group of men has just passed the casa. Their backs are bare except for the leather arrow quivers slung over their shoulders. They carry bows and thick-handled spears.

One of them has a massive shaggy head. Buffalo horns stick out of on either side. She slips out the gate to get a better look. It's a buffalo headdress. Alma stares after them until the warriors disappear over the small hill north of the house. As she turns to go back inside, another group of men emerges from the village. Their bare chests and faces are also decorated with paint.

The Martín gate is open. Jesús and Esquipula peer out. Felix is right behind them.

The warrior closest to the boys is a tall, thick-chested man. He carries a small drum by a rawhide handle that curves out from one side. The drum dangles next to his leg. As the man passes the Martín gate, Esquipula darts out and jabs at the drum. The man scowls and lifts the instrument above the boy's head, then moves diagonally across the road, away from him.

Then he spots Alma. His eyes twinkle as she stares at his face. On his right cheek, black stripes have been carefully drawn around a set of puckered white scars that look like Old Pete's, although this man has both his eyes. "You won't try to touch my drum, will you?" he asks.

She shakes her head and he grins at her. Then he and the others continue on up the road. Jesús and Esquipula have followed them, with Felix, Rafaela and Rosario close behind. They all pause outside Alma's gate and watch the men disappear over the little hill.

"Who are they?" Alma asks.

"Warriors from the pueblo of Santo Domingo." Esquipula puffs out his chest. "And I touched their sacred drum."

"You did not," Rafaela says. "I saw you. You tried to touch it but you didn't. If you had laid your hand on it, your fingers would be burned off by now."

Alma giggles, then stops when she sees Esquipula's eyes. They're wide with fear.

"It's true," Rosario says. "María Paula told us. Pueblo drums are sacred. If you touch something sacred without respect, your hands will burn up. You'll wake up the next morning with no fingers at all."

Esquipula looks down at his fingers.

Felix's lips twitch. "But you didn't really touch it. So nothing will happen to you." Then he grins. "But you should be more careful next time."

"Those warriors are big!" Jesús says. "They'll protect us from the rebels!"

"They'll help my father protect us," Felix says. He looks at Alma. "My father is Manuel Miguel Urioste. He's a presidio soldier."

"And our Uncle Tomás is, too," Jesús tells Alma. "His full name is Josef María Tomás Martín and he's a presidio corporal!"

Esquipula bends to pick up a stick. He leaps around, thrusting it like a lance. "Take that!" he yells. "And that, you dirty-minded rebel, you chimayoso!"

Alma's stomach squinches. One of those rebels is Gregorio. Where is he now? She turns without saying goodby and hurries through the gate to the casita and her mother and brother.

The children are restless during their lessons on Monday. The governor and his men marched north that morning and the Martín grandchildren's Uncle Tomás is with them. Felix's father has been left behind with the force assigned to protect the capitol.

Jesús and Esquipula are twitchy with ideas of what a real battle is like, wondering what's happening. Their legs move restlessly as they try to focus on their work. When Alma's mother releases the children for a quick break, the two boys plunge into the courtyard and immediately begin a mock sword fight. "Vamos, Andrés!" Jesús shouts at Andrew. "You be a rebel!"

Andrew laughs, picks up a stick, and darts into the game. "Two against one, but I'm quicker! I can conquer you!"

María Paula appears in the doorway opposite, the one that leads into the kitchen. She has a jar on her slender hip and is clearly headed to the well for water. She stands watching the boys, her nose in the air. When they see her, they stop their play.

"Welcome, prima!" Jesús sweeps his free arm sideways and bends toward her as if flourishing his hat in an elegant bow. "Princesa Señorita María Paula, we your knights have swept your path free of all enemies."

She sniffs. "What enemies?" Then her gaze turns on Andrew. "Although I noticed last week that this one looks very foreign." Her lip curls. "What are you, part negro? Your hair is strange."

Andrew's chin jerks. "And you are very rude." He looks at Jesús and tosses his stick on the ground. "I don't want to play anymore."

"She was only teasing," Esquipula says, though he looks sideways at the girl.

Andrew moves toward the schoolroom door. María Paula sniffs. "It must be true, then," she says. Her gaze hits Alma and her shoulders twitch disdainfully. "I cannot imagine why my grandfather allowed you people to live so near to us."

Alma can think of nothing to say. She looks at Rosario and Rafaela for help, but the other girls stare at the ground. María Paula smirks and turns to the well. Alma puts her hand to her cheek as she follows her brother into the classroom. The other children slip wordlessly after them.

School the next day is a quiet affair. Salome has joined them but she seems to know about María Paula's observations the day before. None of the children look each other in the eye. During the break, Alma and Andrew stand together in the corner of the courtyard, not speaking. Alma is relieved when her mother calls them back inside.

But she doesn't immediately set them to their schoolwork. Instead she paces back and forth in front of the room. Alma frowns. Has her mother learned about María Paula's accusations? Is she going to address them? But when she turns to face the children, she isn't angry. Her face is tired and anxious. She leans toward them, bracing herself on her teaching table. "While you were playing, news came from the city."

The children stare at her. "I'm sorry to tell you that there was a battle this morning," she continues. "The rebels met the governor and his men just north of the pueblo of San Ildefonso at Black Mesa."

Alma's breath stops. Her mother goes on, talking about warriors who transferred their allegiance to the rebels, the government cannon that was captured, and the governor's hurried return to Santa Fe after the rebels won. Gregorio's side won. The fist in Alma's chest loosens a little.

Then Andrew raises his hand. "Was anyone hurt?"

"I don't know," his mother says. "I understand that Sergeant Donaciano Vigil was captured." She glances at Felix, the oldest Martín grandson in the room. "And possibly others."

Alma blinks at her. That look. She knows something about Tomás Martín. But the others don't catch her meaning. Alma closes her eyes. And Señor Vigil. It doesn't seem possible that a man bursting with such energy could be held captive by anything.

Then her mother says, "It's too soon to know much, except that some of the rebels are likely to reach Santa Fe this evening or tomorrow."

"Damn rebels!" Felix says. "My father will deal with them!"

Salome gives him a withering look. "There are thousands of rebels. Your father and the others aren't enough to defeat them."

"That's their job!" Esquipula turns to Alma's mother. "Isn't it, señora? Won't Tío Manuel and the other soldiers defend us against—" He squints, trying to find the right term. "Against pillaging?"

Her eyes twinkle a little at the big word from the child, but then her face becomes anxious again. "I don't know, Esquipula. All we can do is wait and see." She looks down at the table and the slates stacked there, waiting to be redistributed to the children with the corrections she's made. "In the meantime, let's try to get some work done."

It isn't a profitable afternoon. The children's thoughts are on the road from the north, the one the governor and his men marched out on just yesterday morning. The one the rebels will use to enter the city. Will there be what Esquipula calls pillaging? Alma shivers and tries to focus on the equation on her slate. The numbers jumble and she has to rub out her answer and start over again. She's glad when the school day is over.

Late that night, she rouses from a restless sleep. The day was warm. Her mother has left the window shutters open to allow the house heat to escape. Somewhere, an owl calls.

Hooves thud on the road beyond the casita walls, become louder, then fade into the darkness. A whole group of hooves. More than one man is riding south in the night. Alma shudders and pulls the blanket over her head.

But the wool smothers her with fear. She pushes it away, gasping for air, trying not to cry. Trying not to wonder where Gregorio is. Battles mean death and danger and wounds that kill, no matter which side a man is on, no matter who may have won.

Her breath catches again and she strains to hear any further movement on the road. But now there is only silence and the churning in her belly that threatens to burn into her throat.

# CHAPTER 24

Alma's in a daze the next morning, from lack of sleep and trying not to think about what happened the day before. She mixes the breakfast atole haphazardly and the thin cornmeal mush is both scorched and lumpy, but her brother and her mother don't comment. They seem distracted themselves.

After the meal, her mother goes down the road to the Martín compound. When she returns, she announces there'll be no school today. Things are too unsettled. Word has come that Tomás Martín was one of the men captured during the battle. Don Salvador is keeping everyone inside the walls and has advised the Lockes to do likewise.

"The governor and his men fled south last night," she explains. "The rebels will probably arrive today. No one knows what they'll do or what's happened to the captured men." She takes a deep breath. "There's nothing we can do but wait." She glances at the loom. "I can weave, though."

"And I'll cut kindling," Andrew says. "We can always use more."

His mother nods as if she hasn't actually heard him, her mind already on her work.

Alma chews her lower lip. This might be a good time to try to remember what Señora Ortega taught her about bread making. She holds her breath as she checks the starter she's been feeding each morning. It's nicely filled with tiny bubbles.

She carefully measures flour into the big wooden bowl and adds water and the starter. But when she dumps the mixture onto the table to knead it, the dough squishes under her hands and sinks into the miniscule cracks in the table boards. She's forgotten to put flour on the kneading surface first. Her hands freeze in the sticky mess. Tears bite her eyelids. She looks toward the loom, but her mother's head is bent over the threads, checking to see that everything's snug.

Alma's chin lifts. Her mother's doing her work to the best of her ability and Alma is going to do hers. She won't think about why they're here and why she's doing this now. Why she needs to stay busy. She won't wish for her father. Or Ramón. Her chin trembles. She bites the insides of her cheeks and gulps once, then twice, then pulls on the dough with both hands, trying to move it toward her and away from the table surface.

The mass of gooiness seeps away from her, oozing back onto the wood planks. The barrel of flour is on the stool on the other side of the table. Alma studies it. She desperately needs more flour, but it's too far away. If she releases the dough, it's going to make an even bigger mess to clean up.

The door opens and Andrew and Chaser come in. Andrew spots her and laughs. "That's a lot of bread!"

Alma scowls at him. "Stop laughing and help me."

He shakes his head. "I ain't gettin' my hands in that stuff. It's gonna be up to your elbows in a minute!"

She looks down. It's true. Her hands are sinking into the lumpy dough.

She jerks her chin toward the flour barrel. "Move that over here beside me and then put a big double handful on the table where the bread's sticking."

He grins at her. "You just need a man around to lift the heavy stuff, huh?"

She glares at him and he chortles and carries the barrel around to her side of the table.

"Wash your hands before you put them in the flour."

"You don't have time."

She hauls on the mass of bread dough, pulling it as close as she can, but it oozes away from her out from under her hands. It's surprisingly heavy. "Hurry up!" she snaps.

Andrew shrugs, trots outside to the water bucket, and comes back a minute later with dripping hands.

"Dry those first," she says. He grins at her, grabs a piece of her apron, and wipes his hands with it. Now her apron is wet, but at least he's helping. He dips into the barrel, comes out with a double handful, reaches across the dough, and drops the flour onto the table. It wooshes into the air in a soft cloud that drifts across Alma's face.

"You're all white now!" he laughs.

She raises a shoulder and swipes it at her face, but doesn't reach more than the side of her cheek. "Add another handful," she says grimly. "Slowly this time. That barrel's getting low. We don't need to waste it."

There's something about her voice that tells him she's not going to take anymore teasing. He dips into the flour again and carefully pours it onto the table. "Is that enough?"

She pushes the mass of dough and almost immediately feels it change and become more solid and pliable. "That's good." She pulls her sticky fingers out and grins at him. "See, I have my hands back."

"Sort of."

Her fingers and palms are lined with sticky goop. She dusts them with flour and goes back to work, kneading the dough.

"You want me to get the fire going in the horno?"

Her hands stop moving as she stares at him. "Tarnation! It should already be started. I forgot that part." Her shoulders sag. "The oven takes three hours to heat properly."

He looks at the mound of dough. "How long will it be before that's ready?"

"After I knead it, it'll have to rise." She glances toward the sleeping room. "I'll put it in there, in the coolest spot I can find. Maybe it will take a long time."

"So we have time."

She nods. "Thank you," she says softly.

He grins at her. "De nada."

He and Chaser trot out the door again and Alma goes back to work, pushing the bread away from her, adding more flour, working it into the dough. The motion feels good. Strong and steady and physical. As the dough becomes more solid and pushes more firmly against her hands, the anxiety loosens from her shoulders and neck.

The shadows are lengthening across the courtyard by the time the horno is ready for the bread, which Alma has punched down twice to keep it from getting too spongy. Her mother stops her work to help scrape the fire coals and ash out of the oven and swab it clean. Alma carefully slips the loaves inside and her mother scoots them a little farther in, then places a small wet blanket over the opening. She's closing this off with a special-ly-shaped wooden cover when a sharp knock sounds at the gate.

Alma and her mother freeze in place. They look at each other anxiously. Alma's throat is so dry she can't breathe.

"Señora?" a man's voice calls. "Señora Locke?"

"It's Gregorio!" Alma darts forward.

Her mother is right behind her, grabbing her arm. "Slow down!" she hisses. "You don't know—"

"But it's Gregorio!"

"You don't know for certain it's him, or who he's with." She releases Alma's arm and gives her a little nudge toward the casa. "You stay back."

Alma nods reluctantly but she doesn't move away. There's another knock, then the same low voice. "Señora?" It's Gregorio. She's sure of it.

Her mother straightens her skirt, lifts her chin, and moves to the gate. There's a crack between the boards just at her eye level. She peers out, then moves to lift the wooden bar and ease the gate open a few inches.

"I am alone, señora," Gregorio says. "It is safe enough."

She swings the gate wider and he slips through. His trousers are covered with dust, a shirt sleeve is torn almost completely off, and a ragged blue cloth is wrapped around his head. He makes no effort to help to close and bolt the gate. Instead, he leans on his crooked walking stick and blinks as if he can hardly see.

Alma runs toward him. "You're hurt!"

"It's all right, nita. The stick is because it's a long way from San Ildefonso to here."

"But your head!"

"It's only a scratch. The bandage is larger than was truly necessary but there was no médico to deal with it properly."

Her mother turns from the gate. "Come inside and I'll see to it."

He smiles for the first time. "That's one of the reasons I came to you." He looks around the tiny courtyard. "That and to assure myself that you are safe."

"From the rebels?" Alma asks.

He glances at her, then her mother. His eyes are shadowed by more than exhaustion. "The governor tried to escape south last night but was turned back this morning. He and those with him scattered in every direction. Some of his men have already been caught. As for Pérez, the warriors of Santo Domingo are tracking him. They say he's returning to Santa Fe. This is the only road from that direction. "

Her mother looks at the gate as if to reassure herself that it's truly closed. Then she turns back to Gregorio. "Come inside."

His wound is more than a scratch, but Alma's mother says it looks worse than it really is. She washes it carefully with water that's been boiled and cooled, and puts one of her special salves on it.

When she wraps a clean white cloth around his head, Andrew laughs. "You look like a Turk!"

Gregorio's lips smile but his face is pale and tired. "How do you know what a Turk looks like?" he asks, his eyes half closed.

"Felix Urioste says they wear turbans."

Gregorio's eyes snap open. He looks at Alma's mother. "This Felix is the grandson of Salvador Martín?"

"Yes. I'm teaching his grandchildren in exchange for rent."

He nods, then winces as if nodding makes his head hurt. He closes his eyes but keeps talking. "Sí, I remember. There is talk in the camp about Old Martín. He has many fields and horses and is known as a man who turns no one away. Also he has a son and a son-in-law in the presidio troop."

She nods. "The son was captured yesterday."

His lips tighten as if he's forcing himself to speak against his weariness. "Pérez is on foot now. They captured his horse, which he gave to someone else to care for. Because the Martín house is outside Agua Fría, it's easily accessible to anyone who doesn't want to be seen. There's speculation the governor will take refuge there before going on to Santa Fe."

Her brows contract. "If he does and the rebels find him there, won't they take revenge on the Martín family?"

"And anyone associated with them." He opens his eyes. "That's the other reason I came here."

She stares at him, then glances at the children and rises from her seat. "We should eat something. You must be starving." She looks up at the latticed window. "The light is fading. It must be almost sundown."

"And Alma has made bread!" Andrew says.

Gregorio looks at Alma. A faint smile lights his face. "Just knowing there's bread makes me feel better."

In spite of everything, her heart sings a little as she smiles back at him.

Gregorio rests a little while they wait for the bread and feels well enough to accompany them into the yard to uncover the horno. Alma's mother has just lifted the wooden cover when the shouting and neighing begins. The adults exchange anxious looks and move across the courtyard. Gregorio raises the bar and opens the gate just enough to peer out. Alma's mother stands on tiptoe and cranes to see over his shoulder.

Alma heads toward them, but her mother turns and shakes her head. "No!" she hisses. "Stay back!"

Alma bites her lip and drops onto the chopping block. In the road, a man shouts. Is it a cry of warning? Defiance? All she knows is that hearing it makes her stomach clench. She hunches her shoulders and wraps her arms around her belly.

A gun fires. Then there's another shot. Someone shrieks in pain. Alma's throat is sharp with sourness. She looks toward the gate. Her mother has stepped back, her knuckles to her mouth.

Gregorio is still watching. His hands are tight on the gate, ready to slam it shut if he needs to. "He has a sword," he says over his shoulder. "He may be a bastard, but he can fight." His voice is low, but there's an excitement in it that Alma's never heard before. Her stomach squinches even further.

Then a horse screams and there's more shouting. "The horse is down," Gregorio says, more slowly now. "Pobrecito."

Something thuds on the other side of the wall. It's a dull, deep sound. Alma shudders. It's not wood against wood. Wood against flesh?

Gregorio turns his head toward the courtyard, as if he can't bear to see any more. As Alma rises to go to him, there's a crashing sound, but this time it's behind her. She whirls, her heart pounding. Andrew is on the ground at one end of the wood pile, which is now strewn around him. His face is white and he looks like he's about to be sick.

His mother dashes toward him. "Are you all right?"

He nods and shoves firewood away from his arms and feet. He pushes himself up and brushes at his trousers, which are littered with remnants of bark and wood.

She kneels in front of him. "Are you hurt?"

He shakes his head, but doesn't look at her.

"Andrew?"

He looks at Alma instead. His face is pale. His mouth wobbles. "I saw them. Two men shot. The horse, too. And they were beating it with sticks." He sways a little and his eyes close. "And swords. They have swords."

There are more shouts from the road, but their mother doesn't turn. Instead, she stands, puts a hand on Andrew's shoulder and moves him toward the casita. "Come inside." She looks back at Alma. "Both of you. I should have sent you in when it began."

Alma looks at Gregorio, who nods grimly. "I'll be here, nita. I won't let them in."

She shudders. There are men dead out there. But his hand is firmly on the gate and his shoulders fill the gap. She moves reluctantly toward the house door.

It's at least an hour before he follows. The children are on the tiny banco with their mother between them, her arms around their shoulders. The last bit of sunlight trickles through the still-open shutters. The fire has died to a bed of hot coals.

Gregorio drops into the rocking chair and closes his eyes.

"Children, go get ready for bed," Alma's mother says. They shrink against her. She drops her hands behind their backs and pushes gently. "Go," she says softly. "It's all right."

Gregorio looks around the room as if he's seeing it for the first time. He pushes himself from the rocker. "I'll close the shutters and bring in more wood." Then he grins slightly. "And the bread."

She nods and shepherds Alma and Andrew into the next room, kisses them each good night and goes out, adjusting the blanket door behind her. Andrew crawls between his blankets on the other side of the sleeping space and is instantly asleep, but Alma's eyes refuse to close. The head of her pallet is near the fireplace and the words of the adults drift from the joined chimney whether she wants to hear them or not. She curls herself into a ball under her blanket and tucks her head toward her chest.

"He fought like a mountain cat," Gregorio says. "But they got him in the end. The head—"

"The governor?" her mother asks.

There's a pause, then Gregorio's voice again, thick with emotion but trying to be matter-of-fact. "They cut it off. Used his own sword against him and carried it bleeding toward the plaza."

In the other room, Alma's throat fills with bile. She forces it back and pulls her blankets higher over her shoulders.

"Tarnation!" her mother says.

"Though, the last I saw, they weren't actually carrying it." He sounds as if he can't believe what he's saying. "They were tossing it between them, like a ball. Then one of them dropped it and started—"

The rocker squeaks a little, then there's the thud of wood dropping onto the fire. Gregorio speaks again. His voice is louder now. He must be leaning against the fireplace. He sounds like he's going to be sick. "He started kicking it. The head rolled away, up the road. Then someone else kicked it, moving it forward. Like it was a game."

"Savages!"

Gregorio doesn't reply. After a long while, Alma's mother says, "Will you stay here tonight? I can bring you blankets and you can sleep in front of the fire."

Alma can hear them moving around the next room. After a while, her mother comes in and begins preparing for bed. Alma rolls over and pushes her face into her pillow. It smells vaguely of the chicken feathers it's stuffed with. Of home.

She shudders. The valley. Where her father didn't want her to stay because it wouldn't be safe for her there. She bites the insides of her cheeks to keep the tears from coming and shudders again.

# CHAPTER 25

Gregorio is gone when Alma wakes the next morning. The house feels empty without him. The gate is firmly closed and the crossbar is dropped into place..

"You are both to stay in the courtyard," their mother tells the children. She gives Andrew a sharp look. "And no climbing onto the woodpile or the bench to see over the wall."

He nods without meeting her gaze. His face is pale and there are shadows under his eyes. He slips outside to gather the eggs and make sure the mules have what they need. She watches him go, then sighs and turns to study the fire. "Is there enough wood in here to cook a meal?" she asks Alma.

Alma gives a little start. There's wood, but she has no energy for cooking. "There's still bread. Will that be all right?"

Her mother sighs again. She wipes a hand across her face. "I'm sorry," she says. "I'm sorry I brought you here and this has happened." She turns to Alma. "I wish—"

But then there's the sound of pounding from the front gate. Her mother jerks toward it. "I wish I had a gun," she mutters. She takes a deep breath and moves across the room. As she swings the house door open, a man's nasal voice bellows "Open up dammit!" from the road.

Alma laughs in sheer delight. "That sounds like Old Bill Williams!"

Her mother's shoulders relax. "It certainly does." She grins at Alma and nods toward the fireplace. "He's going to want more than bread for his breakfast."

Alma's breath comes more easily as she hurries to reheat the beans left over from the night before.

When the rangy mountain man stoops through the door, he gives her an approving nod. "Hard at work, youngling?" He shoves his shaggy red braids away from his chest. "You're a righteous sight for sore eyes, and no mistake."

Over breakfast, he explains that he's passing through on his way to Don Fernando de Taos. "There's someone I need t' re-acquaint myself with up there." Then he frowns at Alma's mother. "When I heard you were here, I was righteously sur-prised. I thought you were tucked up safe and sound in that valley of yours, out of this confounded rebellion and away from the so-called cantón and its damnable proclamations."

"It's not my valley," Alma's mother says. In the fireplace, the teakettle begins to spit hot water. She pushes back from the table and goes to lift it from the flames. "Alma, bring me a pad to set this on."

Alma leaves her place to rummage in the cupboard and comes back with an early piece of her mother's weaving. Old Bill nods at the piece of wool. "That your work?" he asks her mother.

She nods. "Tea?"

"If that's all you have available." He grins at her. "I don't suppose you have anything more powerful in this here domicile of yours."

Her eyes twinkle back at him. "Not even coffee." She nods at Alma, who lifts the little wooden tea chest from the shelf, sets it beside the kettle, and goes back to retrieve the teapot.

Old Bill reaches across the table and rubs a finger across the weaving. "That's well-constructed work."

"It's not quite as even as it should be. That's an early piece." She spoons tea leaves into the pot and adds water from the kettle.

Old Bill pulls the cloth toward him. "It's a likely piece of jerga. Not bad at all."

"It's good enough to serve as a table protector, anyway."

He grins and pushes it back into place. As she places the kettle back onto it, he turns his head and studies the loom. "You settin' up to make enough t' sell?"

"That's the idea. I'm teaching to cover the rent, but we'll need to restock our food supplies before winter sets in. I have some pieces that I think are good enough to sell as floor coverings, but I haven't had a chance yet to find a buyer." She gestures toward the door and the courtyard beyond. "We've been somewhat preoccupied with recent events."

He grimaces in acknowledgement. She hands him a cup of tea and he folds his long fingers around it. "I still think you'd better off at home in the valley."

She glares at him.

"All right, all right," he grumbles. "I know it ain't righteously my business. But I do dislike the idea of you and the younglings here by yourselves."

Her lips tighten but he scowls right back at her. "I wouldn't like you bein' here even if Santa Fe was a nest of twittering friendly robins. But it ain't. It's quiet enough at the moment, but I righteously doubt it'll stay that way. Right now the place is more like a nest of snakes waitin' for the sun to come out."

She reaches for the teapot and pours herself a cup. Silence stretches across the room.

Old Bill grunts in disgust and shakes his head. "Well, if you're so set on stayin', you might as well have enough to keep body and soul together. I reckon I might be acquainted with someone who can assist you in that endeavor."

She raises an eyebrow at him.

"There's a Missouri merchant in town by the name of Elisha Stanley. He's been in and out of Santa Fe since 1823 and has a shop off the plaza. I've done business with him and he's a man to be righteously trusted. I reckon he'd give you a fair price for your productions."

She's sitting up straight now, eyes shining.

But when they enter Señor Stanley's mercantile that afternoon, she seems uncertain, almost as if she's bracing herself to be turned down. She's carrying samples of her work and is two steps behind Old Bill, an unusual place for Alma's mother.

Though Alma also finds the store rather intimidating. It's more like a wide hall than a room and it's crammed to the rafters with goods. On each side long wooden counters run from the front to the back of the store. They're layered with small rugs and other woven goods. Behind them are shelves crowded with bolts of brightly colored cotton, stacks of canned and boxed food, and other items. Surely this merchant has enough of everything for sale.

But then Old Bill coughs and a man in an American suit like her Grandfather Peabody's materializes from the back of the store. He's about Old Bill's height, but thicker. Older, too. His hair is certainly shorter and neater. But his eyes and mouth are what catch Alma's attention. There's a kindness there that reminds her a little of Ramón. Though there's caution, too. Not like Ramón when he looks at her. She bites her lower lip.

Old Bill explains what they're after and Mr. Stanley turns to her mother and takes her samples. He moves to the door, examines them in the light, and comes back with a pleased smile.

"I'll be happy to take whatever you can bring me, Mrs. Locke," he says. "It will be my pleasure to do business with you." He nods toward the woven goods on the counter. "As you can see,

I have plenty of fine items, but there is a need here and in Missouri for jerga for floor coverings. If you could provide me with that type of item, I believe we can be of mutual assistance to each other."

He names a price and her mother's face tightens a little. "I can provide you with wool," he adds. His eyes twinkle. "It's something people often bring in to trade, but it's bulky to ship and there's not much of a market for New Mexico wool in Missouri." He tilts his head. "Same price, but I provide the wool." He gestures toward his stocked shelves. "And I can give you credit for what you may need in the way of foodstuffs and other goods, as an advance on your work."

She smiles and nods. "I am grateful, señor. I will do my best to give you a sellable product. In the meantime, I have some already completed that I can bring you tomorrow."

"Excellent!" he says. "Excellent! Come into my office and we'll write this all down, so I won't forget what we've agreed to. And Old Bill Williams here can act as signatory." He grins at the mountain man mischievously. "I hear you have quite an elaborate signature."

"I know my letters," the mountain man says stiffly, but he follows the other adults into the back.

The children stray into the sunshine out front. They lean against the adobe wall below the mercantile's wood-grilled window and watch the street.

It's crowded with people, though they all seem to be men. Men carrying guns and spears and wearing all sorts of headgear, from old metal helmets to what look like pieces of knit stocking. The men ignore the children, though many of them gaze at the shops and buildings as if they've never been in Santa Fe before. They're all headed in the same direction, toward the east side of town.

Andrew wrinkles his forehead. "Where're they goin'?" He steps into the street and leans forward to peer up the road. He's not paying attention to the men coming toward him, and an old man with his hat pulled low walks right into him.

Andrew leaps back. "Perdóneme!"

The man shoves his hat off his forehead and grins at him. Two of his teeth are missing. "De nada," he says. "What are you looking at, muchichito?"

Andrew drops his gaze. "I was curious."

"Curiosity can be a dangerous thing."

Andrew shivers. "I know it."

"But you are wondering where we are all going and why?"

Andrew nods without looking up.

The old man waves a hand toward the plaza. "We go to the parish church to celebrate our victory."

Andrew flashes him a glance, then looks down again. "You are rebels?"

The old man chuckles. "We are of the cantón. It is a question as to who is the rebel now. Some of those who oppressed us are dead, this I know."

Andrew gulps and nods. He turns and moves back to his sister.

The old man watches him go, then shrugs and joins the parade up the street.

There's a long silence. More men walk past. Alma looks at her brother. "What all did you see yesterday?"

He studies his feet and shakes his head. When Alma touches his shoulder, he jerks away. She opens her mouth to ask again, but just then her mother comes out of the mercantile.

Elisha Stanley is behind her and Old Bill is behind him. All three carry baskets of spun wool. The merchant has two small ones, which he hands to the children. The adults say their goodbyes and then Alma and Andrew trail after their mother and Old Bill, moving against the wave of men still going to worship.

As they reach the edge of town, the rebels thin out. Alma and Andrew draw level with their mother. She's deep in conversation with Old Bill and has a lightness to her that Alma hasn't seen since they left Chimayó. It's almost as if she's forgotten the events of the last few days. She asks Old Bill about his recent travels and comments on the way an individual branch of a big cottonwood beside the road has already started to turn gold even though the rest of the tree is still green.

Old Bill is his usual loquacious self. In response to the comment about the tree, he launches into what he says is an old Osage legend about why the leaves change color each year.

Alma grins up at him. "Is there anything you don't have a story about?"

He chuckles as he scans the road ahead. They're almost to the top of the small hill north of the casita, but still far enough below it that Alma can't see the houses. "I've picked up a fair amount of information in my travels," he says. Then he stops abruptly. "Damn!"

Alma's mother frowns at him in disapproval, but he gives her a dark look and jerks his head southward. "Look there." He steps back, taking the children with him.

She moves up the rise and stands for a long moment, then turns back to him, her face stricken. "What should we do?"

"Go through the fields, maybe. Come in behind the casita and get in through the back, by the corral."

She looks at the baskets of wool they're all carrying. "The crops are still standing. It would be hard going."

"Men can be righteously bestial," he says grimly. "And some of them have the conscience of a rattler." He looks sideways at the children, who stare at him in confusion. Then he grimaces. "The younglings might as well learn it now as later."

"What is it, Mama?" Andrew asks.

Her face twists. "When we came out through the casa gate, Old Bill was careful about where he stood, so you wouldn't see—"

"Is it still there?"

She stares are him. "Is what still where?"

"The governor's body." He looks at his feet. "I saw when they stabbed him. After he fell." He glances at her, then looks away. He gazes at the cottonwoods beside the road. "That's when the firewood slipped." His face twists. "They were pulling off his clothes."

"Damn!" Old Bill says again.

She crouches in front of Andrew. "You saw it?"

He nods, his eyes on his feet. A tear rolls down his cheek. He wipes at it with his sleeve.

She rocks back on her heels and takes a deep breath. "I—"

Andrew lifts his head. "It's all right, Mama. I know things get killed. Like the mountain cats with the calves if we don't bring 'em in at night. Or the eagles with the prairie dogs."

"They could of at least buried him or carried him off the road," Old Bill growls.

She shakes her head as she gets to her feet. "The rebels won't be in any hurry to do that. The governor's body is a symbol, an example to his officials and anyone associated with them. The rebels will want to leave him for a while. And no one will risk burying him without permission. Doing so could put them and their families at risk."

The mountain man huffs in disgust, then says, "Well, at least we don't have to look at him close up. He's nearer the Martín place than the casita."

Loretta Miles Tollefson

Alma takes a deep breath and steadies herself. "That's just his body," she says firmly. "It's not him." She's not sure she feels this, but she knows it must be true.

Her mother smiles at her but Old Bill mutters, "What's left of his body, at any rate." He turns back toward the hilltop and hefts the basket he's carrying. "Come on then, let's get this righteously over with."

They follow him silently, trying to watch the road at their feet and not look ahead. But in spite of her best intentions, Alma's eyes lift as she nears the casita gate. Her stomach twists. Blood splotches the center of the road. On the far side, a man's body sprawls on its back in the dirt. It's still wearing trousers, but what's left of the chest is bare and there's a gaping black hole in the center, just below the ribs. Where the man's belly is visible under the dried blood, it's pale and bulging in the sunlight. Bloated.

Alma jerks her eyes away, toward the governor's face, but a black-winged vulture sits where the man's head should be. The big bird's scaly red forehead and wrinkled neck are spotted with black. The scavenger stares at Alma disdainfully, then its hooked beak darts forward and tears into the empty space at the top of the governor's torso.

Beside her, Andrew makes a gagging sound.

"Damn it all anyway!" Old Bill moves forward to block the children's view as their mother darts to the gate, drops her basket, and fumbles at the latch.

"You don't have to keep staring at it," Old Bill grumbles. "Look away, younglings. There ain't no righteousness in studying on somethin' that ain't worth your while."

200

Finally, the gate swings open. The adults hustle the children into the quiet courtyard where the two chickens peck peacefully at the dirt by the woodpile.

As Old Bill drops the crossbar into place, their mother moves to the casita door. "It seems to me that we're all due for a bit of a rest and something cool to drink," she says. "Alma, will you draw the water?"

Alma nods unwillingly. The courtyard is still too close to the road and the governor's body.

"I'll do it," Old Bill says. She smiles at him gratefully and follows her mother into the house.

The casita feels empty when Old Bill leaves after the evening meal. Her mother is busy gathering the finished goods she'll take to the mercantile the next day. After the dishes are cleaned and put away, there's nothing much for Alma to do. When she tries to read, she can't concentrate. When she tries to spin, her fingers fumble and break the yarn.

But when she goes to bed, she can't sleep. Her mother is still moving around in the other room. Andrew is curled into his blankets, but Alma's eyes are wide in the darkness. She forces them shut, breathing slowly in and out, trying to relax. But as she drifts off, the image of the governor's gaping chest, the black eyes of the vulture, its wrinkled red head and angry beak flood into her mind and she jerks wider awake than before.

She shudders and claws her blankets around her shoulders, trying to find something good to think about. There's Old Bill. There's her father. But he's not here. She turns her thoughts resolutely toward something more pleasant. Gregorio, his beautiful eyes, kind smile, and steady hands. His hands on her waist as he lifts her down from the wagon.

But he's a rebel. Rebels killed the governor. And left him there to be pecked at. Eaten. Bile rises in her throat. Alma swallows hard, forcing it away.

On the other side of the room, Andrew whimpers in his sleep. Alma sits up, swings her blankets over her shoulders like a cape, and slips across the room.

He peers up at her and scowls. "I wasn't crying."

"I know," she says. "But I'm cold. Can we share?"

He nods and she settles down beside him. A hand creeps out of his blanket and into the middle of her back. Gradually, her body relaxes and she drifts into a dreamless sleep.

# CHAPTER 26

When she wakes in the morning, the pallet beneath her is damp and smells of urine. Andrew kneels beside it, looking down in dismay.

Alma sits up. "It's just sweat because we were both on it. It's just the heat from our bodies." He sniffs and she scrambles to her feet. "The pallets all need to be aired anyway. We'll put everything out in the courtyard. Mama's, too."

Their mother doesn't question what the children are up to. She's busy measuring the work she's completed and folding it into baskets. When she's ready, she orders Chaser to stay in the courtyard and she and the children slip out the gate. They carefully avoid looking in the direction of the Martín compound and move quickly up the road to Santa Fe.

Alma breathes a small sigh of relief when they're over the rise north of the casita. She can't turn back now to see if the governor's body is still there. Beside her, Andrew points out a hawk perched high in a dead tree. The day is sunny and the sky overhead a clear blue. The occasional adobe houses shine golden-brown in the light.

Then they round a bend and see a group of men moving toward them. They're carrying spears and bows and arrows. One of them is wearing a shaggy buffalo headdress. Alma's stomach tightens. Andrew darts behind her to their mother's other side.

She shifts the basket she's carrying and touches his shoulder. "It's all right," she says. But he sticks close even after the warriors have moved past them. He's still hovering next to her when they reach Elisha Stanley's mercantile.

The merchant greets them affably, enters the value of what they've brought into his account book, subtracts the price of a dozen apples and a bag of salt, and hands Alma's mother a few silver coins. He shakes his head as he closes the book. "I'm happy to take anything you can bring me, but I wonder if it would be kinder of me not to purchase your work."

She raises an eyebrow.

"Santa Fe doesn't seem like a very safe place for a woman alone these days," he explains. "What with the rebels and all." His eyes wrinkle with concern. "It seems to me that a woman of your education and background would be better off back East, in a more civilized environment."

She smiles a little at the compliment, but shakes her head. "I have no family back East."

"From what I understand, you have plenty of connections there. Ceran St. Vrain's family. And the Bents' relatives, as well." He hesitates, then adds, "There's a merchant train leaving to-morrow for Missouri. Some of the men from it came in late yes-terday for last minute supplies and I mentioned that you were here. They said they'd be glad to take you along and help you get settled back in St. Louis or thereabouts." He spreads his hands on the counter, palms down, and leans toward her, his face puckered with concern. "It would be safer for you there."

She shakes her head again.

He glances out the mercantile window. The street is empty. The sun slants brightly on the adobe wall across the way. "I admit the rebels have been well behaved so far. But who can predict what the future will bring? I doubt the fighting is over. The ricos in Alburquerque and the rest of the lower river are bound to try to retake control."

She looks at the children, her eyes lingering on Andrew's head. She chews on her lower lip and looks at the merchant. "I do worry."

"You can find the train on the west side of town, camped by the river. They aim to head out at first light, but if you sent word, I'm sure they'd wait. One day is much like the other. They never start early that first day. It's generally as late as noon before the teamsters are over their final-night drunks and on the trail." Her eyes twinkle and he hastily adds, "It's only one or two that are like that. On the whole they're good men."

"Though they are men." She reaches for the apples and salt and glances down at Andrew. Her face sobers and she nods to the merchant. "But I'll think on it."

Andrew and Alma follow her out of the store. In the street, Andrew says, "Are we really going on a wagon train?"

Alma looks anxiously at her mother, whose forehead is crinkled with anxiety. Then her mother turns away. "It might be for the best," she says abstractly. She moves down the street.

The children follow at a distance. Alma's throat is dry. Missouri is so far away. She stares at her mother's back, willing her to speak, to turn, to say the merchant's suggestion is a preposterous one. But there's only silence. They leave the town and follow the dirt road toward Agua Fría. As they approach the little rise north of the house, Alma's chest tightens.

Suddenly, Andrew moves closer to their mother. "My belly hurts."

They all stop and look at the little hill. The governor's body waits on the other side. And the vultures. Alma suppresses a shiver.

"Tarnation!" her mother says. Then her chin goes up. "When there's no way around a thing, the only thing to do is face it." She looks down at Alma, then Andrew, half in question, half in command.

Alma takes a shaky breath and nods. Andrew does the same thing. "Let's go," he says.

They move forward steadily, three abreast. Because their mother is taller, she can see over the little hill before the children can. They're two-thirds up the slope when she stops abruptly and takes a deep breath. "What a relief!"

Then she frowns and gestures to the children to stay back. She moves forward another couple steps, then stops to stare at the landscape below, studying the road and the nearby fields. Finally, she turns to the children. "It's gone," she says wonderingly. "It hasn't simply been dragged off the road. It's actually gone."

They edge toward her until they also can see the track ahead. It sweeps past the casita and straight on to the Martín compound and Agua Fría beyond. There's nothing on it except a pile of horse dung. Even the blood spots have disappeared, faded into the ground or covered with dirt by whoever took the body away.

But Alma still doesn't want to look too closely. Until they reach the casita, she keeps her eyes fixed on the trees and fields beside the road or on her feet in the rocky dust. And she's first through the wooden gate.

Her mother shuts it behind them, her face tired. As they enter the house, she looks around the room speculatively. "I wonder if there'd be wagon space for a loom," she mutters.

Alma bites the insides of her cheeks and turns away. Her stomach is sour with fear. She pushes past her brother and into the courtyard. Chaser snuffs at her skirt and she impatiently shoves him away. She moves to the bench by the gate, drops onto it, and wraps her arms around her chest. Her stomach churns.

"Please, no," she whispers. "Please, no." Tears well into her eyes. Yes, she's frightened to stay here in this place where men are killed and beheaded and left for the vultures to eat. Where girls like María Paula think who a person's grandparents were is all anyone needs to know about them. Where kind men like Gregorio can become a rebel and join in a fight where men are killed. Can be hurt himself.

But she doesn't want to go anywhere but home, to her father and her valley. Certainly not St. Louis, Missouri. It's too far. It's simply too far. Her shoulders shake with silent sobs.

Then there's a knock at the gate. Alma wipes her tears on the back of her sleeve and goes to answer it.

It's Old Bill Williams again, grinning at her through a crack in the boards. The very sight of his weathered face and sharp but kindly eyes makes her feel better. She smiles back at him and lifts the bar.

"Well, youngling," he says. "Thought I'd drop in before I take off for Don Fernando. How are you?"

She shrugs and looks at the ground. He reaches for her chin and she lets him take it, but she doesn't meet his eyes. "Hmm," he mutters. "What's that Mama of yours up to now?"

But he doesn't confront her mother directly. Instead he says his hellos, settles himself on the banco, and puts his hands on his knees. Alma's mother is in her rocker, knitting madly, as if trying to finish the socks she's making in a single session. Alma drops onto the bench at the table, next to Andrew, who has his slate out and is filling it with carefully drawn arrows.

"So are you settled in tight now?" Old Bill asks their mother. "You comfortably assured you'll make out all right?"

The knitting needles glint in the firelight. "We'll be fine. With the proceeds from the weaving, I can keep food on the table. Thank you for the introduction to Elisha Stanley." She adjusts the end of the stocking in her lap.

Old Bill nods and looks around the room. "Not much light in here to weave by or for los chamacos to do their schoolin'." He gives her a sharp look. "You're still teachin' them, aren't you? You ain't lettin' their education slide in favor of Marteen's grandkids?"

Her lips tighten. Her needles drop into her lap. "Yes, I am making sure they do their lessons. They participate fully in the Martín classroom and I also set them additional work here at home. I am fulfilling my obligations as their mother."

"Humph," the mountain man says. "That's as may be." He stretches out his legs and studies his mocassined feet.

"I'm doing the best I can." The needles begin clicking again. "And if I decide to, there's still enough money to get us to Missouri and start fresh."

Old Bill's head jerks up. "Missouri? And why in the name of all tarnation would you want to go there?"

She keeps her eyes on her work. "Mr. Stanley has pointed out that Santa Fe is not the safest place I could choose for myself and the children. There's a wagon train leaving soon for Missouri. He believes we could find a place on it. It's possible we could settle there or even go on to New England, eventually. Some place more civilized than here."

"Civilized!" He's sitting straight up now. "Are you crazy, woman?"

She glances up at him, her lips thin.

He doesn't even seem to see her annoyance. He leans forward. "Suzanna Peabody Locke, I've known you since you were a pup and that is the most righteously idiotic idea I've ever heard come out of your stubborn mouth! I thought you were smarter'n that! Bein' here in Santa Fe is bad enough, but Missouri! Are you loco?"

She drops her knitting. Her eyes are black and cold. "You presume too much on our friendship, Mr. Williams."

He glares right back at her. "Now you can just get right down off your high horse, young woman! Gerald's shown a strong toleration of your ways, and I don't righteously know why, but I ain't about to! Gallivanting off to Missouri is just about the most damnably stupid thing I've ever heard word of!"

"Rosa Villalpando went there," Alma interjects. She doesn't want to go to Missouri, but she's never heard Old Bill speak so harshly to anyone, let alone her mother.

Old Bill swings his red head toward her. "That was a righteously long time ago," he says, his tone slightly softer. "And she was Spanish, not part Navajo. Also, when she went there she was married to a rich white man. Missouri's not a place for a woman to be goin' alone."

"I said perhaps New England," her mother says.

His head swings back to her. "Well, that might be a slight improvement. At least there you'll only be second class citizens and not as likely to get slapped into chains."

She blinks at him. "What are you talking about?"

"Well, probably not you, seein' as you're part Navajo, not African." He waves a hand toward the children. "But these two are, and there's not much likelihood they'd pass as White. Especially in Missouri. They could get snatched up any time, regardless of what kind of papers you might invent for them."

"Snatched up?"

"Missouri's a slave state, girl! Even if you were headin' straight to New England, you'd have to pass through it! Or have you forgotten those miniscule pieces of useful information in your unfortunate attempt to escape who you and they are? You'd end up workin' as a maid for some rico. Or worse." He pauses and looks away. "Just to keep food in your mouth." His chin lifts and his blue eyes spark as he glares at her. "At least here you've got some kind of dignity, even if you don't have enough sense to go home to where you righteously belong!"

She's still as a portal post now, and just as stiff. But her eyes are alive with something between confusion and fury. She opens her mouth, closes it, then opens it again. When she finally speaks, her words are clipped and precise. "I thank you for the information regarding the current state of affairs in Missouri or the geographic position of New England, Mr. Williams. And I'll also thank you to keep your opinions about my mental faculties to yourself. No matter what opinion you may think of my abilities, I do have the right to make my own decisions."

His lips twitch. "You do at that. But you might want to remember that the reason you have that right is because you're livin' here in Mexico, not the United States. If you were back East, you wouldn't be allowed to traipse around the country wherever you want without your husband's permission. Especially with his offspring in tow."

She stares at him, then looks down at her work. Her knitting needles begin moving again, though more slowly now.

There's a long silence. Alma suddenly realizes that Andrew's hand is clutching hers. A log falls in the fireplace.

Old Bill stirs and rises to his feet. "Well now," he says, his voice calmer now. "It seems to me that we've said just about all we're about to righteously say on this matter."

Her lips quirk. Then she shakes her head and gives him a tired smile. "I know you mean well, but this is something I need to decide on my own."

"You can always just go back home."

Her smile drops. "No. No, I can't."

"Why not?"

"That's not your concern."

His eyes narrow. "He don't know exactly where you're at, does he?"

"He would if he bothered to inquire."

Old Bill shakes his head. "You are the most righteously stubborn woman I've ever known." He turns and looks at the children, who gaze back at him. "If those two weren't so obviously well and cared for, I'd kidnap you all and take you back to Gerald myself."

Her eyes narrow. "I'd like to see you try."

He lifts a hand. "It was a joke."

"It didn't sound like one."

"You have certainly dispensed with your sense of humor," he says sourly. He nods to the children, then their mother, and turns to the door. "Good night."

A cold draft of wind swings through the entrance as he goes out. A shiver runs down Alma's spine. Her mother's eyes are closed. Moisture sparkles at the end of her lashes. The children look at each other and creep quietly out of the room and to bed.

# CHAPTER 27

The next morning, Alma wakes to the sound of the loom thudding in the other room. As she sits up, Andrew slips in, looking petulant. "What's the matter?" she asks.

"We ain't going with the wagon train." He waves his hand at his bedroll, which is carefully rolled and tied and leaning against the wall by the door. There's a small bag of clothes beside it. "I packed and everything."

The surge of relief is so strong that Alma has to bite the insides of her cheeks to keep from laughing.

Three days later, she's still smiling. Gregorio has come by to check on them. His head wound is healing nicely. While school is less pleasant than it was, no one has made any more comments about her and Andrew's grandparents. Truly, the only thing she could wish for now is to go home.

But at least she's still in Santa Fe and Gregorio's nearby. Alma hums a wordless tune as she scatters feed for the chickens. Then there's a knock at the gate. She drops the remaining grain onto the ground and runs to peer through the cracks between the boards.

It's Old Bill. She lifts the crossbar and he pushes through the gate and bends to hug her close. She breathes in the good wood-smoke-and-tobacco smell of him. "I thought you were in Don Fernando."

He chuckles. "What with one thing and another, I haven't made it up that far yet. And since there's no predicting when I'll be back down this direction, I wanted to lay eyes on you one more time before I head out."

"Mama's in the house."

He squints at the door. "I don't know that she righteously wants to lay eyes on me just now." He squeezes Alma's shoulder. "We'll just sit out here in the sunshine for a while, shall we?"

She nods, not sure why he's come, but glad all the same.

He leads her to the bench by the wall. "I saw your face when I said all that about Missouri the other evening. It got me to worrying that you'd be righteously chewing on it and fussin' in your mind about what I said." He looks at her sideways, crosses to the woodpile, and picks up two pieces of kindling. He returns to the bench, pulls out a pocketknife, and begins whittling. "I knew what your daddy was the first time I set eyes on him."

She stares at him.

He points the knife at her. "That's a good man, your pa. Straight as an arrow and made of heartwood all the way through. He don't have a speck of badness in him." He chuckles and shakes his head. "Though he is a stubborn one. Once he gets an idea in his head, he don't let it go."

He holds up the stick he's working on and runs a finger over a rough edge, then begins chipping tiny flakes off it. "I cogitated right off that your pa was part African. There's a certain look you can see, if you've been around 'em some and paid attention. Same as the different Indian tribes." He glances at her. "Andrew's got some of it, though you don't really. Except for the color of your skin."

Her hand goes to the heart-shaped freckle on her cheek but he doesn't appear to notice. The kindling is a mere splinter now. He drops it and reaches for the other piece.

"I've been around a good many men in my day," he says. "White ones and red ones. Brown ones and black ones. And I figured out long ago that what a man does and what he is inside is a righteously more essential matter than who his granddaddy or his great-grandma was. I also know for certain sure that no one of us ought to be owned by anyone else. It's a righteously outrageous thing, this buyin' and sellin' of human beings."

He turns what's left of the stick over and squints at it, then looks at her. "If your pa knew your ma was figurin' to haul you younglings East, he'd be down here to put a stop to her tomfoolery faster'n you can say 'tarnation'."

She smiles a little at this use of her mother's favorite expletive. "She's decided not to."

"Well, I'm glad t' hear it. I just wish Gerald had reined in her conniptions before she decided to bring you down here to Santa Fe." He shakes his head and tosses what's left of the piece of wood onto the ground. "Your pa." He glances at her, then his gaze moves to the well, on the other side of the yard. "I know he's your pa and he's righteously shiny in your eyes, but he's not one to kick up a fight if he can help it. He may be stubborn, but he also likes things peaceful-like."

Her jaw juts out. "He killed that Enoch Jones when Jones was goin' after Gregorio."

The mountain man smiles at her. "I didn't say he wasn't brave. He did what needed doin'. Tried his righteous best, anyway. We all thought Jones was sure enough dead. And your pa's your hero, which he righteously ought to be." Then he shakes his head. "But he don't like conflict and that's a fact. He put up with my jawin' all one winter while we were trappin' and never said a word of complaint, even when I was bein' as full of ornery opinionations as I could righteously think to be."

Alma giggles in spite of herself. It's true that Old Bill is opinionated and ornery sometimes. Even when he's feeling sweet-tempered.

214

He slides her a sideways grin. "You can't argue with me about that, now can you? You and your pa are two sides of the same peso. Too obliging for your own good."

She bites her lip and looks away.

Old Bill's voice changes. "And she never sent word to him about comin' to Santa Fe."

It's not a question. Alma follows his gaze toward the well.

Old Bill clicks his tongue disapprovingly. "Well now, that's just righteously loco. Your ma's not makin' good sense."

Alma bites her lip. "It just happened. He knew we were going to Don Fernando, and then she decided to go to Chimayó, and then—"

"Then the folks in Santa Cruz and Chimayó started their rampage and she didn't head home. You all came here instead," he finishes. "And that Gregorio Garcia went back to Santa Cruz to join up with the rebels instead of staying on and keeping an eye on you all. He ought to've known better. But I reckon he got a mite sidetracked by all the fightin' words bein' bandied around up river. He's just a kid still."

Then his jaw tightens. "But Old Pete knows better'n to behave like that to an old pal. When he found you here, he should've got you settled safe enough and then headed right back up into those mountains to give your pa the news he deserved. Instead, Pete joined up with Miranda and headed south and righteously left you to fate."

"He didn't have time before the caravan left," Alma points out. "It was already almost to Alburquerque before he left to catch up to it. Besides, Mama would've been mad at him if he'd told Papa where we were."

"Because she didn't want your pa comin' after her." Old Bill shakes his red head. "Let me tell you something, youngling. Secrets are trouble. And there ain't any secret too small not to cause tribulation." He scowls at the woodpile. "Besides, wantin' to take you out of the country without telling him is a righteously bigger secret than your pa's was. Gerald's gonna be in a fine pucker when he hears about this."

Now it's Alma's turn to scowl. "Well, she decided not to, didn't she? And besides, he hasn't come looking for us. And he must know about the rebels by now."

Old Bill gives her an impatient look. "Your ma told him she was goin' to Don Fernando, now didn't she? Not Chimayó, of all the righteously cussed places."

Her chin wavers, then lifts. "It was her decision to make. He let us go." Her stomach squinches even as she says it, because somewhere deep inside, she knows both her parents have handled this badly. She sucks in her cheeks, against the tears.

Old Bill glances down at her, then swiftly away. "Both of them are acting like a couple of sanctimonious greenhorns," he grumbles. "Secrets!" He spits to one side and pushes himself off the bench. "We'll just see about that!" Then he stalks out of the little courtyard without saying goodby.

With his going, Alma's lightness of heart evaporates completely. As she mulls over their conversation, she realizes just how unlikely it is that her parents will ever get over their quarrel. He's right. They're both stubborn. And now so far apart.

She droops around the casita, only half a mind on her chores. The only sound is the thud of her mother's loom, turning out yet another piece of jerga, and Chaser barking at Andrew as they roughhouse in the yard.

Her only comfort is Gregorio, but that isn't much. He brings them a load of firewood, then disappears north to Santa Cruz. He promises he'll be back later in the month, when the Montoya

216

brothers come to Santa Fe to participate in a special meeting the new rebel Governor has called. But Alma doesn't know whether to believe him or not. None of the adults in her life seem very dependable these days.

# CHAPTER 28

She breathes a sigh of relief when Gregorio comes back and seems inclined to stay around. Santa Fe is filling up with ricos from as far south as Belen, coming in for Governor Gonzales' meeting. Gregorio needs a place to sleep. He offers to bring Alma's mother more firewood in exchange for a bed in the storage space behind the casita.

Alma's mother frowns. "That shed is not an adequate sleeping location."

He chuckles. "It's better than the fields outside the Rosario church, where most of my fellow rebels camp in Santa Fe."

She chuckles. "In that case, the shed is all yours. And any meals you'd like to take with us." Her eyes twinkle. "Alma's doing the cooking, not me."

He looks at the children. "I'll need help bringing firewood in from the mountains. Is anyone interested in joining me tomorrow at first light?"

Andrew and Alma beam at him. "Certainly!" Alma says. Then her face drops. She looks at her mother. "It's a school day." She tries to keep her voice neutral. Her mother doesn't need to know how much school has changed since María Paula decided Andrew and Alma aren't pureblood. It's not as if she can do anything about it, anyway.

"I can manage without you for a day," her mother says and a little burst of pleasure pings in Alma's chest.

They set out right after breakfast the next day. As their mother follows the children and dog into the courtyard, Andrew offers to make Chaser Two stay at the casita, but she smiles at him sadly and says, "I'll be perfectly safe here, son. Take him with you."

Andrew studies her, his blond brows knotted. "If you're sure."

"I'm sure." Then she gives him a sharp look. "Now you pay attention to Gregorio and do what he tells you, do you hear? No wandering off out of earshot to look at bugs or other wildlife."

Andrew grins back at her. "Yes, ma'am."

She gives Gregorio an amused look. "Have fun."

He chuckles and clucks at the mule they're taking to carry the wood. The animal is carrying only an empty aspen pole frame and a handsaw, but he still sniffs disdainfully and shakes his head at Gregorio's signal. Gregorio grins. "If I have trouble, it will be with this one, not los chamacos."

They head through the gate and across Santa Fe to a road that straggles east from the plaza into the foothills. As they climb into the woods, Alma sniffs the air appreciatively. It smells of pine and, in the damp places, green growing things. Like home.

She bites her lower lip and forces her mind away from her sorrow. She has this day. And Gregorio, striding ahead with the mule, turning his head now and then to make sure she and Andrew are still following. The next time he looks back she smiles at him and is rewarded with a sympathetic grin. Warmth quivers in her belly and something loosens in her chest.

Gregorio finds the mountainside spot he's looking for and gets to work, cutting already-downed timber into pieces the right length for stacking onto the frame on the mule's back. The sun dapples the ground under the trees and glints off the saw blade.

While he cuts, the children collect the thin branches that litter the ground where the wind has tossed them or others have harvested. When they've gathered a good-sized pile, Gregorio pulls out a roughly woven bag and Andrew and Alma begin filling it with pine cones. Chaser snuffles the ground nearby, following interesting smells here and there.

They stop for a cold midday meal of tortías and beans, then Gregorio cuts the children's branches into packable pieces and they stack everything onto the mule, with the bag of cones on top. The animal huffs a little, then settles when he realizes he has no choice. The load isn't all that heavy, it's just cumbersome.

When Gregorio moves the mule and its burden onto the trail back to town, Alma heaves a deep sigh.

Gregorio glances at her. "Are you all right, nita?"

"It's nice up here," she says.

"It is congenial, isn't it? Sometimes I wish I could spend all my life in the woods."

"I wish that all the time. The mountains, anyway."

He ignores her reference to the valley and holds out his free hand. "But your mother will wonder where we are."

She takes his hand and walks beside him down the mountain. Andrew and the dog trail behind, investigating whatever takes their fancy. Alma hardly notices them.

Gregorio drops her hand before they reach the plaza, but she still feels a deep well of contentment. Until she sees the Montoya brothers and their Fajardo girl cousin moving across the plaza in her direction.

Padre Martínez and Donaciano Vigil step out from the palacio portal right then, but Gregorio doesn't see them. He has eyes only for the Montoyas. He raises a hand in greeting and pulls the mule to a halt.

"You've been busy!" Antonio Abad greets them jovially. He runs a hand through his curly black hair and claps Gregorio on the shoulder. "Good man!" He grins at Gertrudis. "See, Trudes? I told you he had something better to do than squire you around!"

She tosses her pretty head at him. Tiny silver hoops dance from her earlobes. "I only mentioned that I hadn't seen him since we arrived," she says with a pout. She looks through her eyelashes at Gregorio. "We wondered if you would be coming to el baile tonight."

His face brightens. Then she looks away and adds, "I was trying to determine how many of our friends would be attending. It will be uncomfortable if too many people are there. The Rosario camp is filling up again because of the governor's meeting, and they all seem to be invited, along with most of Santa Fe."

Gregorio's narrow face drops. Alma feels a sudden urge to kick the young woman in the shins.

Then Desiderio Montoya says, "At any rate, all the women in Santa Fe will be attending, so there will be plenty of partners."

Gertrudis turns pointedly to look at the buildings that line the plaza. "But I won't be able to go if I can't find the ribbon I need to trim my new dress." She slides a look at Gregorio. The worshipful look on his face makes Alma want to kick him, as well.

"Well, then, we'd better hurry along," Antonio Abad says, grinning. "Knowing you, it will take most of the afternoon to identify just the right ribbon."

Gertrudis flashes her dimples at him. "I'm sure there will be more choices here than there would be in Santa Cruz. And I intend to examine them all!"

He laughs and the little group moves off, angling across the square toward the street that contains Elisha Stanley's mercantile.

This is the route to the Locke casa too, but Gregorio doesn't cluck the mule into motion. He stands watching the Montoyas and the girl. Then he looks at Alma. "She's very beautiful, isn't she?"

Alma nods without meeting his eyes, but he doesn't seem to notice where she's looking. The Montoyas disappear around the corner before he clucks at the mule again and moves forward.

The few remnants of Alma's earlier good feelings evaporate completely as her own little group passes the mercantile and moves south toward Agua Fria. But she cheers up that evening when she realizes Gregorio isn't going to attend the Santa Fe dance after all.

He's very quiet, but at least he's here in the casita, sitting at the table fiddling with a piece of harness that's developed a weak spot. She's perched on the banco spinning more of the endless wool into yet another swirl of yarn for her mother's loom.

But early the next afternoon, when she and her mother and brother head out the gate to the Martíns' and school, Alma stops short. Gregorio stands in the middle of the road south of the compound, his head bent attentively toward Gertrudis Leonarda's heart-shaped face. It's turned away from him, studying the road to the north, but Alma can see the girl's dimples even from here.

"I see Gregorio has a friend," her mother says.

"Yes," Alma mutters.

Her mother lifts an eyebrow, then looks at Andrew.

"She's the cousin of the rebel leaders, those Montoya brothers," he says. "The ones Gregorio works for."

"The ones we met at the Chimayó feast," she says. "I remember." She studies the couple in the road ahead. "I hadn't realized. I wonder if his mother knows her." She glances at the Martín gate. "We have a few minutes. I think I should get reacquainted with this girl." She advances purposefully down the road. Andrew stays beside her but Alma hangs back.

Gregorio is so busy paying attention to Gertrudis that he doesn't notice Alma's mother until she's almost at his elbow. She coughs discretely. He glances up in surprise. His face breaks into a confused mix of pleasure and embarrassment.

"I wondered where you had disappeared to so early this morning," she says in amusement. "I thought you might be retrieving more firewood."

"No, I—" He glances at the girl. "Perdóneme, señorita. I don't believe you have met Señora Locke, who is renting the casita of Don Salvador Martín and schooling his grandchildren."

He turns to Alma's mother. "Please allow me to introduce Señorita Gertrudis Leonarda Fajardo. She is a cousin of Antonio Abad Montoya and his brother." He glances toward the village behind them. "She is staying here in Aqua Fria for the duration of the governor's conference."

The woman nods to the girl. "I believe we met at the feast at Chimayó in July," she says politely. "For just a moment, before events overtook us." She smiles. "It sounds as if we are both strangers here."

"Oh! I am not a stranger," Gertrudis says. "I am staying with my mother's widowed cousin."

"Ah, I am glad you are comfortable." Alma's mother smiles at her, then at Gregorio. She glances toward the Martín gate, where Felix and Rosario are now looking out. "My scholars await me." She nods to the girl. "It was a pleasure seeing you again." Then she turns to Alma and Andrew. "Come children. We're going to be late."

She moves off, but Alma lingers a moment, long enough to hear Gertrudis say in a low, disapproving voice, "That is not a Spanish name."

They see little of Gregorio during the next week and a half. He's either running errands for the Montoyas while they confer with the governor and Nuevo México's other leading men or he's accompanying the Fajardo girl to various dances, puppet shows, or other entertainments.

However, by early September the meetings are over and she and her cousins have returned to Santa Cruz. Gregorio reappears at the casita, arranging for more hay for the mules, delivering jerga to Elisha Stanley and returning with corn and other groceries, and bringing in more wood from the forest. But it's not the same as before. He's physically present, but his mind is clearly elsewhere.

Alma's mother is acting the same way. She's distracted even in the classroom. María Paula Ortiz and José Martín join the other scholars the second full week of the month and the sixteen-year-old girl watches Alma's mother with narrowed eyes. While the children are taking their mid-session break on Wednesday, she sidles up to Alma and asks, "Just what is your mother's connection to Señor Gregorio Garcia?"

Alma looks at her in surprise. It's the first time since they've met that the other girl has spoken to her directly. "He's my father's friend."

The older girl tosses her sleek black hair over her shoulders and narrows her eyes. "You know Garcia is a rebel, don't you? And the rebellion has ended without a shot. After all the fuss about that meeting late last month, the important people in Tomé where my aunt lives met and decided enough was enough. All they had to do was say the word and the rebels' so-called governor left town."

Alma frowns in confusion. Is any of this true? The other girl smiles with satisfaction. "My grandfather knows all the important people, even Manuel Armijo, who was Governor before and is bringing soldiers from Alburquerque to reinforce the presidio troops." Her mouth twists. "The stupid rebels have all fled back to

Santa Cruz. Except for your father's friend. Is he a spy for them? Is that why he stayed, so he can help try to retake Santa Fe after Armijo's troops arrive?" She flicks her hair again. "He'd better hurry and join them while he can, because they're sure to fail this time and then he'll be captured and given the punishment traitors deserve."

Alma stares at the other girl blankly, her mind whirring. Is this why Gregorio has been so preoccupied? Are soldiers really coming? Will the rebels come back and fight for the capitol? Her stomach tightens. Is Gregorio truly in danger?

María Paula is still talking, looking at Alma through her long lashes and saying something Alma doesn't understand. Something about where Gregorio sleeps at night. "But then, your mother isn't very particular, is she?" the girl adds. She sniffs and gives Alma a sideways look. "After all, she married a mulatto, of all things."

Alma blinks. "What?"

Just then her mother appears at the schoolroom door, calling the children inside. María Paula moves away, her skirt swishing. Alma follows, her lips numb with shock.

The rumor María Paula had repeated about the troops from Alburquerque is true. The next day, they march past the casita, raising a haze of dust on their way to take control of the capitol. Alma's fear for Gregorio's safety pushes the girl's other comments to the back of her mind.

He's still staying at the casita, bringing wood from the mountain, helping local farmers with their harvests, and generally finding reasons to remain in the area. "You're very quiet," he tells Alma one night as he snags another tortía from the platter in the middle of the table. He waves it at her. "These taste well tonight. You're becoming quite a good cook."

The food is dry in her throat. She stares at him, at the way the firelight highlights the planes of his narrow brown face.

He gives her a puzzled look. "Are you well?"

Her mother looks up. "Are you ill?"

Alma shakes her head and looks down at her food. Her eyelids tingle. She swipes at them with the back of her hand.

"What is it, nita?" he asks.

She clenches her hands together in her lap. "Are you safe?" She raises her eyes to his. "Now that the Alburquerque militia has have come?"

He and her mother exchange a glance. "I am not an important person," he says gently. "The soldiers do not care about someone like me. As long as I don't try to attack anyone, I am safe enough." He looks a little sad as he says it. "And I'm not likely to do that. I support the rebel cause, but I'm not bloodthirsty." He glances at her mother. "From what I've heard, General Armijo hopes to address the cantón's complaints peacefully. He and the men from Alburquerque and further south are here to look important but not to actually fight." He refocuses on Alma. "There's no need to worry."

"But I will be worried if you don't eat," her mother tells her.

Alma nods and reaches blindly for another tortía, but when Andrew asks to be excused, she follows him into the yard. They sit side by side on the bench and silently watch the sky grow dark. When the stars begin to brighten, they wordlessly carry more firewood inside and get ready for bed.

Alma runs her fingers through her curls to smooth the worst of the tangles, then bundles it into two loose braids. Her hair really needs to be combed properly in the back, but she can't do it herself. In the other room, the loom treadles thump the floor. She ties the ends of her clumsy braids with bits of string and crawls into bed. Andrew is already snoring on the other side of the room.

She drifts into sleep and dreams of Governor Pérez's bloated and blood-splashed body sprawled in the dirt and a sharp-eyed vulture hunched where the man's head should be. In the morning, Andrew again needs help drying out his pallet and airing his blankets. She's almost grateful to him. The task keeps her mind off her roiling stomach.

Two full weeks go by and nothing happens. Alma's stomach starts to settle. Former governor Manuel Armijo has arranged a truce with the rebels, one that includes jailing Alcalde Esquibel and both the Montoya brothers. Groups of refugees begin to trickle in from the south. With their militia in Santa Fe, people around Alburquerque are now worried about Navajo raids.

Alma doesn't understand why the men don't leave the capitol and go back to guarding their home towns against what Senora Ortega called los indios bárbaros. The rebels won't do anything more now that their leaders are locked in the Santa Fe jail.

Alma's breath tightens when she thinks of them. She liked Antonio Abad Montoya when she met him. And his brother seemed nice enough. It seems cruel to lock them up. Also, they're Gregorio's employers. And his cousins. Isn't he at risk, too?

But he doesn't seem concerned about the danger to himself. He visits the Montoyas almost every day. In fact, they ask him to act as courier between them and their families in the north. The correspondence is reviewed by General Armijo or the presidio commander first, but it's still allowed to go out.

"I'll leave early again tomorrow," Gregorio says one night at the evening meal. "Don Antonio is anxious to get news to his family."

"Does his family include cousins such as Señorita Fajardo?" Alma's mother asks mischievously. "I'm sure she and her parents are quite concerned about their primos here in the capitol."

Gregorio keeps his eyes on his food. "Don Antonio and Don Desiderio are well known throughout the upper river region and have many friends and family there. All of them are concerned about the brothers' well-being."

Her smiles drops. "This must be difficult for Antonio Abad's wife."

Gregorio nods. "Yes, it is hard for her, though she has her daughter and her parents are nearby, so she isn't lonely. It's his sister María Catarina who is most anxious. She and José Ramón Vigil have just had a little boy, and her worries beset her. But Trudes—" He catches himself. "Señorita Fajardo was in Santa Clara with her the last I heard, assisting her with the infant and their four-year-old, and that must help a great deal."

Her eyes twinkle again, but Gregorio keeps his gaze firmly on his food and she says nothing more. Alma bites the insides of her cheeks. She doesn't want to think about Gregorio travelling to Santa Cruz. And she wants even less to think about the dimpled Gertrudis at Santa Clara or wherever she may be.

# CHAPTER 29

Gregorio is away on another trip for the Montoyas a few mornings later when there's a knock at the gate.

Andrew and Alma are in the courtyard, Alma coming from the back with a small basket of eggs and Andrew drawing water from the well. Alma stops in the little doorway as Andrew sets the bucket on the side of the well and crosses to the gate.

"Buenos días," a man's voice says. Andrew swings the gate open and Don Salvador Martín appears. He's a short, kindly looking old man with thick white hair and an anxious expression in his eyes. He smiles at the children. "I see you are industrious niños," he says, a little too heartily. "And your mother? Where will I find her?"

There's something about his tone that says he has bad news. Alma gestures wordlessly toward the casita door.

Andrew has felt it too. He gives her an anxious look, then collects the bucket from the well. They're right behind the old man when he knocks and enters to their mother's summons.

She's standing by the fireplace, the poker in her hand. "Don Salvador!" she says in surprise. She leans the poker against the wall and moves toward him. "How nice to see you so early in the morning!" Then she stops and studies his face. "Is something wrong?"

He turns and looks at the children. Andrew sets the bucket on the table and Alma places the basket of eggs beside it. Don Salvador turns back to their mother. "I would prefer that we have this conversation alone, señora," he says gravely.

She raises an eyebrow, then nods to the children, then the door. "It's cold outside," Andrew objects.

Don Salvador glances at the blanket-covered door to the sleeping area and shrugs slightly.

Their mother makes a shooing motion at the children. "Go on."

They do as they're told, but she begins speaking before the blanket drops between the two rooms. "What is it?" she asks.

"It has come to my attention—" the old man says.

Andrew edges the blanket away from the doorway and peers out. Alma pokes him in the ribs and shakes her head. He scrunches his face at her and drops the blanket, but doesn't move away. Alma bites her lip. But then, if her mother really didn't want them to hear the conversation, she would have sent them outside in spite of the cold.

Alma leans toward the blanket. Andrew grins at her. Then the old man's voice rises. "You did not seek my permission and I would not have granted it if you had! Such a thing is disgraceful!"

"Such a thing?" their mother's voice is icy. "To provide food and lodging to a friend?"

"My wife—"

"Yes?"

His voice is pleading now. "It has the appearance of a great impropriety, señora. She seeks to provide our grandchildren with only the purest of examples."

"Your wife has never entered this casita or spoken more than a few words to me." Her voice is dangerously calm. "She has never entered my classroom. How could she know what kind of example I may be setting?"

"The children—"

"The children? Which children? If I am to be accused, I would know the names of my accusers, at least."

"The oldest of the girls under your tutelage. María Paula Ortiz."

"The child who has been present in the classroom perhaps a total of ten days since I began teaching there."

"Sí, this is so." He sounds grumpier now. He's clearly not used to being spoken to like this by a woman. "She is a conscientious girl who my wife has trained carefully to pay attention to events and personages. And she has seen this Gregorio Garcia leaving your gate in the early morning hours, slipping out as if he does not wish to be observed."

Alma sniffs. Just what was María Paula doing abroad at that hour? But her mother doesn't ask this question. Instead she says, "And so we are to leave the casita." Her voice hardens. "I suppose you or your wife have already found someone who can pay in coin instead of in kind. There must be any number of refugee families in the city searching for space to lay their respectable heads."

"No, señora, I am not so mercenary," he says stiffly. "I would not turn you out. But I cannot allow you to return to the schoolroom. I will resume responsibility for the education of los chamacos. As for this casita, we must make another arrangement."

"Another arrangement." Her voice is still flat, but there's a note of caution in it, too. Perhaps hope.

"I thought it might be possible for you to pay a small rent in place of the schooling. I see you have set up a loom and my wife tells me you have made arrangements with Señor Stanley—"

"Your wife certainly seems to know a great deal about me."

Now his voice sounds as if he's doing his best to be patient. "We are a small community here, Señora Locke. It behooves us in these days to pay close attention to those with whom we associate."

"And your wife has heard that Gregorio Garcia has visited the Montoya brothers in jail." She chuckles. "Is the señora Gertrudis Fajardo's has been visiting friendly with your wife, by any chance? Even though the Fajardos are related to rebels?"

Don Salvador doesn't respond. A log falls noisily into the fire.

When she speaks again, her tone has changed. "Perdóneme, Don Salvador. I spoke hastily because I am anxious. I must look after my children and I have few resources."

"Sí, señora." He sounds a little sulky. Then his voice changes. "But I am a magnanimous man and I will turn no one into the street, no matter what accusations are made against them. Not until the charges are proven. You may stay here, but we must discuss another arrangement regarding the rent."

"How much?"

He snorts with laughter. "I had forgotten how straightforward you can be, señora. You have so few feminine wiles and dissimulations."

Behind the curtain door, Alma rolls her eyes. Is that a compliment or an insult?

But her mother ignores his remark. "If we are to come to an agreement, we should waste no time. I must return to my loom so I can earn the necessary funds."

"I will consider the matter and let you know tomorrow," he says. "In the meantime, there will be no more schooling. Adios, Señora Locke."

There's a pause, then the door thuds shut. The children draw away from the curtain, drop onto their pallets, and stare at each other. "No more school!" Andrew chirps.

The curtain lifts. Their mother says, "I suppose you heard all that. Now we can concentrate properly on your lessons. Schooling the others has been a distraction."

Andrew's face falls and Alma laughs at him in spite of her anxiety. She looks up at her mother. "But the money?"

"We'll manage. We'll have to."

Three days later, she's setting up her loom for yet another piece of jerga and the children are studying at the table when Gregorio returns from Santa Cruz. It's midafternoon. He's saying, "Slow down, now," and looking down at Chaser as he opens the door, and is halfway into the room before he sees Alma and Andrew watching him.

He stops and stares at them, then swings toward the loom. "I thought you'd be at the Martín's at this time of day!"

"So did we," their mother says. Then she smiles, trying to soften her tone. "There's been a slight change in our arrangement."

Gregorio absentmindedly pats Chaser's head and crosses to the fireplace to warm his hands. He looks at Alma's mother, who has returned to her work. She carefully winds the warp yarn around the pins set into the front of the loom and feeds them down to the other end. As she moves back and forth, Gregorio raises his eyebrows at the children. They both shrug, glance at their mother, and return to their work.

"What has happened?" he asks.

She keeps her head down. "Don Salvador has decided he would rather have cash rent than education for his grandchildren."

Gregorio frowns. "How strange. I thought he was a person of means and ambition."

She shrugs and moves to the other end of the loom.

"Will you—" He stops, looking embarrassed, then tries again. "Is the rent an amount you can pay?"

She looks up, then down at the wool in her hands. "As long as I'm able to weave and Elisha Stanley is willing to pay me for what I produce, we'll have enough."

He nods and looks at the children. They're not even pretending to study. He raises his eyebrows and tilts his head at Alma questioningly, but she glances at her mother and drops her gaze to her book.

He turns back toward the loom. "Is there anything I can do to help?"

Her hands stop moving. "Oh, Gregorio. You have been such a help already. I can't ask you to do more."

"In return you have provided me with shelter and food. It is a fair exchange. And I have an obligation to your husband which I can never repay."

"That was a long time ago."

"He saved my life. I am indebted to him and all those who belong to him." Alma glances up and finds his eyes on her. He smiles at her and a squiggle of warmth touches her chest. He looks at her mother. "For that and for past kindnesses, I will not desert you."

She's at the front of the loom now, positioned to begin weaving. "You are most kind, but I'm sure we can manage." She leans into the first treadle. "You must be hungry." She nods at Alma. "Heat up something for him." As she bends to her work, Gregorio and the children look at each other with somber eyes.

Early the next day, Gregorio announces that he's going to the forest for more wood and asks if the children can accompany him. Their mother looks as if she'll be relieved to get them all out of the house, and they set off.

They take both mules this time, Gregorio leading one and Andrew the other. The air is cold and a little damp. The sky is a dull gray. As they enter the forest, Alma finds herself shivering even though she's well wrapped in the rebozo Señora Ortega gave her. The shawl covers her head and reaches below her waist, but she's still cold. Gregorio is lost in his thoughts and doesn't notice her discomfort even when the ground becomes soggy with the remnants of a recent snow.

There's been no snow at the casita, so Alma is a little startled when the path slips under her feet. She looks at the mud in sad amusement. It's mid-October now. In the valley, the ground around the cabin would already be icily solid.

They pass the spot where they collected wood in August. Half a mile later, Gregorio turns up a rocky gully. They climb for another quarter mile to a stand of charred pine.

"Was there a fire?" Andrew asks.

Gregorio nods. "But the trees are still alive." He tilts his head back. "See the green tops?"

The children follow his gaze. The dark green needles are somber under the overcast sky, but they're still there. Only the tree branches and outer bark are marked by the fire. "It's incredible how plants and animals can survive events that seem to offer certain destruction," Gregorio says. He turns to remove the saw from the side of his mule. "We'll take the lower branches." He glances around. "While I cut, you can pick up the limbs that have already fallen."

They nod and wander away through the trees, searching for windfall. The nearby pieces are black with soot and Alma's hands and skirt are soon streaked with the greasy residue. She finds a bit of damp grass and wipes her palms as clean as she can, then ties her rebozo in a knot on her chest so it won't slip off her shoulders.

There isn't much she can do about her skirt except try to be more careful.

She makes a tired face at it and goes back to work. Her fingers are stiff with cold and it's hard to pick up the wood. The sky overhead is now a cloudy, dim white that hurts her eyes when she looks at it. This isn't as much fun as it was in August.

The mules don't like the cold either. They snuffle at her when she drops an armload of wood beside them. She puts her hands up to their nostrils and they nose her palms, but even this makes her sad. They're looking for treats she doesn't have. She's glad when Gregorio decides they've collected enough wood and can go home.

It starts to snow as they reach the plaza. There are only a few flakes, which float lazily through the air as if they're not sure they're really snow. "Look at that!" Andrew says in delight, but Alma just shivers. She's dirty and tired and cold.

The plaza is full of people, as it has been ever since the refugees began arriving. People and wagons and cows and pigs. Gregorio and his mule move ahead. Alma sticks close beside him as Andrew and the other mule follow. They maneuver through the crowd, angling toward the street that will take them past the Stanley mercantile and on to Agua Fría.

Then Gertrudis Fajardo appears, slipping between the wagons and people. She's headed in Gregorio's direction, a finely woven bright red rebozo draped over her head and shoulders. She stands out in the crowd and looks quite pleased with herself, although she seems unaware of Gregorio and his load of firewood.

Alma shrinks against the mule as the girl gets closer, but Gregorio pulls to a stop. He's between two carretas, one filled with chickens in woven willow cages and the other with bundles of wool. Gertrudis will have to squeeze between him and the carts if she doesn't see him in time to skirt around them.

She's watching where she walks, not where she's headed. Then her eyes flicker over the chickens and land on Gregorio. Her chin lifts. She turns her head to avoid his gaze and steps sideways to edge around him.

Alma's breath catches. She resents the insult to Gregorio, but she also doesn't want the girl to speak to him.

He moves to block Gertrudis' path, forcing her to look up.

"Hola, señorita," he says quietly. "I see you have returned." There's an almost menacing tone in his voice that Alma's never heard before.

Gertrudis' chin lifts. "Buenos días, señor. Let me pass, por favor."

"I would speak to you a moment."

"And I would not listen."

He seems larger, somehow, his eyes darker, his shoulders more solid. "The ladies of Agua Fría are spreading tales that are both unkind and untrue."

"I know nothing of such tales."

"But you know me. And you know I would not harm another soul, much less a woman."

"I thought I knew you." She looks past him, toward the governor's palace. "Certainly, you will harm no one. Not even those who have imprisoned my cousins, to whom you owe service."

"And who I continue to serve as best I can. But your cousins are rich men." He glances at Alma and Andrew. "Others have fewer resources."

Gertrudis looks at Alma and her filthy skirt. Her lips twist with contempt. Then her gaze lifts to Gregorio's. For a moment, there's something else in her expression. Pain? Sorrow? Her mouth tightens. Now there's only anger. "Their mother seems to have resources enough."

He jerks back as if she's slapped him. "How can—"

But she takes advantage of his movement to slip past him and the mule. Then she stops and turns. Her hands clutch the red rebozo to her chest. "Not that her choices affect me at all." Her chin lifts. "I'm going home tomorrow, to where I belong!"

"Going home? Who will be your escort?" There's real anxiety in his voice. "The roads aren't safe for a woman alone."

She draws herself up. "How I travel is no concern of yours!" Then she turns in a swirl of skirts and disappears around a brace of oxen driven by an American teamster. The man whistles as she passes but she only lifts her head higher.

Gregorio stands for a long moment, staring after her, oblivious to the crowd. Then he turns, clucks at the mule, and moves on, the children following.

A week later, he goes into the mountains alone to collect wood. When he returns, he has news from the plaza. Rebellion has broken out again, this time in Las Truchas. There is also unrest in Don Fernando de Taos. General Armijo, who's now calling himself Governor, has threatened to execute the Montoya brothers and the other rebel leaders if the cantón marches on Santa Fe again.

This is the most Gregorio's spoken since he and Gertrudis met in the plaza. In spite of the bad news, Alma's pleased that he seems more energized. Her pleasure dims when he announces that he's going to Don Fernando. "I must check on my mother," he says. "She'll be worrying about events here and how I am faring. If the rebellion has truly spread that far north, it may not be safe for her there."

Alma's mother looks up from the loom. "Surely the cantón members there will know you're one of them and won't harm her."

He shakes his head. "Nothing is certain. It depends on who's leading the rebel faction there."

Her eyes twinkle in her tired face. "And the Fajardo hacienda is on the way."

He looks at her stonily.

She turns back to her work. "Will you take a letter to my father for me?"

"And one to the valley as well?"

She doesn't look up. "If there is a message waiting at my father's, you may send word that we are well." A treadle board thumps to the floor.

Gregorio glances at Alma, who's moving the soup pot from the fire to the table. "Let me help you with that, nita."

She smiles at him as he takes the pot and sets it on the table. "If you see Papa, tell him I miss him," she murmurs. He glances at her mother and shrugs.

It's snowing hard the morning he leaves. Alma stands outside the gate, watching. At the top of the little rise north of the casita, he turns and waves. As she turns to reenter the courtyard. there's a shout from the road by the Martín compound. Esquipula and Jesús are throwing snowballs at each other.

They look so warm and contented and secure. Alma clutches her rebozo and shivers as she returns to the house. She's using ground corn to make tortías now, trying to make the little wheat flour that's left last as long as she can. Her mother leaves the single window in the main room open each day until the very last bit of light is gone from the sky, weaving until she can't see anymore, until she has only the firelight at the other end of the room. Alma and Andrew have to huddle near the flames to stay warm. The grill over the window does nothing to block the cold.

The days grow shorter and colder. Gregorio doesn't return. Her mother goes to the Martín casa to pay the rent and returns looking grim. She's up early each morning to set the children's schooling tasks for the day, then places herself in front of the loom and stays there.

Alma is actually grateful for the amount of time her mother spends working. When she does stop weaving at midday to eat and review the children's lessons, she snaps at Andrew for his sloppy penmanship and scrawls a big X across Alma's sums. "Pay attention!" she tells them. "You know how to do this!" Then she pushes away from the table and heads back to her work. "Do it again!" she says over her shoulder.

Andrew's chin wobbles and Alma stomach's tightens. She bites back her tears and bends over her slate.

Later, when Alma goes outside with the empty water bucket, she finds her brother sitting on the bench by the wall. He's hunched into himself, arms crossed over his chest. When he sees her, he straightens and he swipes at his face with his sleeve.

She drops down beside him. "It will be all right," she says, trying to sound more convinced than she feels.

"No it won't."

She stares blankly around the courtyard. It's full of late afternoon shadows.

"I wish Papa was here," Andrew says.

Alma looks at him in surprise. "You're not mad at him anymore?"

He looks away. "I wish he would come."

"Maybe Gregorio will go to the valley and tell him."

"Tell him what?"

"Where we are. That we need him."

"Mama told him not to."

"Maybe he'll go anyway." But she knows he won't. He won't go against her mother's expressed wishes. He's like Old Pete that way. Alma doesn't dare speak. She rises from the bench and numbly carries her bucket to the well.

# CHAPTER 30

And still Gregorio doesn't return. At first, Alma thinks hopefully that he's defied her mother's wishes after all, gone to talk to her father, and been delayed. The valley snows are unpredictable this time of year.

Then she begins to suspect he's never coming back, that he's decided to stay in Don Fernando with his mother. She shivers. She's heard Elisha Stanley and her mother talking in the mercantile. Although General Armijo didn't execute the Montoya brothers as he'd threatened to, the rebels in Las Truchas are still restless. Also, Navajos have struck settlements in the upper río Grande and even into the mountains. Will they venture through the mountains as far east as the valley? Are Papa and Grandpa Locke and Ramón even alive?

The thought closes her throat. Her stomach churns. She forces herself to breathe. Someone would have brought news if disaster had hit the valley. Grandfather Peabody would have come to find them.

If he can get here. He can't ride well anymore. He'd have to take the wagon and use the mountain route from Don Fernando. The snow must be deep there in winter. Impassable.

She bites the insides of her cheeks and blinks hard to bring the Latin on her slate back into focus. She needs to do the translation her mother set for her and keep watch on the beans in the pot so they won't boil dry.

The days drag on, filled with meaningless chores. Alma's stirring more water into the beans one afternoon when Chaser Two begins barking outside.

Andrew, who's at the table practicing his 'F's' and 'L's', looks up. "Someone's at the gate."

Their mother leans forward to run the shuttle across the loom. "Go answer it," she says absently.

Alma starts toward the door, her long wooden spoon in her hand, but Andrew has already scrambled off the bench. He runs outside and returns a few minutes later, the house door shutting behind him. "It's Gregorio!" Then he turns to his mother, hesitation in his face. "With a lady."

"Well, let them in." She leans forward again and moves the shuttle the other direction without looking up.

By this time, Gregorio has guided the woman with him into the casita and they're taking off their wraps. "Why, Antonia Garcia!" Alma's mother says.

The woman lifts her black rebozo from her gray-streaked hair. She's plump in a friendly way and her hands are work-worn. The smile in her dark brown face is warm and kind. "Buenos días, Suzanna," she says. "It has been a long while since we have seen one another."

"It certainly has." Alma's mother leaves the loom, crosses to the older woman, and gives her a hug. "It has been too long." She turns to the children. "This is Gregorio's mother, my good friend Señora María Antonia Garcia." She smiles into the woman's eyes. "I have known her a very long time."

"Since before you and Gerald met." There's a smile on Señora Garcia's face, but also a kindly sternness as she says it. Alma feels a sudden surge of hope. This is a woman who knows both her parents and isn't afraid of her mother.

"What brings you to Santa Fe?" her mother asks. Then she holds up a hand. "But you must be tired from your journey. And hungry." She turns to the children. "Andrew, take their wraps. Alma, is the food ready? Are there tortías left from this morning?" Her voice has a lilt in it Alma hasn't heard in weeks. She hurries to check on the food.

Over the meal, Gregorio explains that things in Don Fernando are not only tense, but the threat of Navajo raids is real. Even with the difficult roads between Santa Fe and there, he was uncomfortable leaving his mother in her out-of-the-way casa. Señora Garcia lifts her work-worn hands and shows them to Alma's mother. "And there's so little laundering to be done that my hands have become positively soft!"

The younger woman laughs. "They aren't as red as I've seen them in the past. But it's about time you had a little rest."

Antonia Garcia glances at her son, then at the loom. "You certainly don't seem to be resting."

"Gregorio told you about the teaching and the rent?"

"Sí. This Señor Martín seems to have a difficult household."

Alma's mother throws her head back and laughs for the first time in months. "That's one way to put it!" She wipes at her eyes with the tips of her fingers and smiles at the other woman. "It is so good to see you."

Señora Garcia smiles and pats her hand. "I do have a small problem, though." She glances at Gregorio. "Santa Fe is filled with refugees like me. I have nowhere to lay my head."

Alma holds her breath. Surely they have room for one more. "And if you are here, the gossips will be silenced," her mother says.

The señora smiles. "Perhaps not silenced, but at least subdued."

Alma's mother looks at Gregorio, then at his mother. "You are truly a good friend."

Señora Garcia waves a hand at her son. "It would be a help to him as much as to you." She grins. "He speaks often of this Fajardo girl. I need to learn more about her, even though he seems angry with her a good deal of the time."

"Madre!" Gregorio protests indignantly. "The girl is nothing to me!" The women's eyes twinkle and he scowls at them both.

Alma giggles in spite of herself. She doesn't want to hear about Gertrudis. Surely Gregorio can't really care for her, after that scene on the plaza. But she's so glad he's returned that she almost doesn't care what the adults talk about. Even the Fajardo girl can't make her unhappy.

And she soon discovers that Antonia Garcia is an interesting combination of tact and blunt speaking. The woman takes over much of the marketing and cooking, which is a relief to both Alma and her mother. She lays her sleeping pallet near the fire in the main room each night and rolls it up and tucks it into a corner each morning as if she's a servant with no space of her own. But she's not afraid to confront Alma's mother about her actions and attitudes.

One of her laundering customers has paid her with a fleece and the señora has brought it with her to Santa Fe. She has it flat on the table and she and Alma are picking it clean the morning she tackles the younger woman.

"Perdóneme, Suzanna," she says, not sounding at all apologetic. "But it still isn't clear to me just why you are here in Santa Fe and not in the valley con tu esposo."

Alma's mother is in her rocking chair in front of the fire, taking a short break from the loom while she knits a stocking for Andrew. She glances up in surprise. Then her lips tighten and her chin juts out. Her eyes hold a kind of stubborn wariness. She looks just like Andrew when he doesn't want to admit he's done something wrong. "He lied to me."

"Hmm." The señora glances down and points at a small prickly seed in the fleece. "Be careful with that," she tells Alma. "It may be sharp." Then she looks up at Alma's mother, who's staring at the fire. "You've never lied to him?"

"Not about something like that."

"But he didn't actually lie, did he? He simply didn't tell you the truth."

Alma's mother glances at her, then down at her needles.

"And have you never kept things to yourself? Simply because it made life easier?"

"No, I haven't."

"You're the first woman I've ever met who can say such a thing," Señora Garcia says drily. "I certainly can't." She pauses. "I wish I could."

The knitting needles stop clicking.

Antonia Garcia looks down at her work. She moves her fingers carefully through the long strands of the fleece. "Gregorio's father wasn't my first man." She looks up at Alma's mother. "I never told him." A pleading note enters her voice. "It was important to him that I be pure. And in my heart, I was. I loved only him. But I was afraid that if I told him I was not virgin, he wouldn't want me."

"Did he find out?"

Her hands are still now. She nods. "The other man was from Abiquiu. I met him when he came through Don Fernando with the militia to help patrol for Comanches. He returned to the area two years after I met Matias."

"And Matias found out?"

"He—" She shifts on the bench. "I don't know for certain. He was very quiet, and then he went with the militia himself and was killed in a fight with the Navajo." When the señora looks up, there are tears in her eyes. "He did not tell me he loved me when he left. I still wonder if he died thinking the worst of me." She shakes her head. "I have confessed my sin and completed mi penitencia, but still I wonder."

Alma's mother stares into the fire. "It isn't quite the same. I am in Matias' place, not yours."

Señora Garcia runs her hand over the fleece on the table. "I tell you this to explain that someone may withhold information out of love and desire," she says gently. "Not to cause pain."

The younger woman doesn't turn her head. "But it was still withheld. And it did cause pain. Secrets cause pain. It's that simple. No secret is too small that it can be ignored."

"What about the secrets we hide from ourselves?"

Her head swings toward the table. "What?"

"The things in our hearts we don't want to admit." The señora's hands are flat on the table now. She leans slightly forward, as if she wants to push her words into the other woman's heart. "I remember the stories of your courtship, how you said who his people were and where he came from didn't matter. But apparently it did. It seems to me that you weren't truthful with him or with yourself."

Alma's mother doesn't respond. She looks down at her work but doesn't pick it up.

Señora Garcia straightens and begins to run her fingers through the fleece again, searching out any bits of dirt or grass seed. "None of us know our own heart completely," she says. "Gerald's family history must have worried you on some level, or you wouldn't have been so adamant about not wanting to know more about it."

She looks up at Alma's mother, who's still staring into the fire. Her voice softens. "I suspect you didn't inquire further because, like me, you were afraid. In my case, I didn't tell the truth. In yours, you didn't want to hear it, so you pretended you didn't care. You lied to yourself and everyone else in the process." She sighs and looks down at her work. "It's the secrets we don't tell ourselves that are the most dangerous."

The younger woman's head turns. Her eyes are large and black. Her lips twitch. "I—" She covers her face with her hands.

Antonia Garcia leans forward, her hands on either side of the shaggy fleece. They press so hard on the table boards that her knuckles are white. "It pains me to say this, because I believe you love Gerald deeply. And you are part Navajo. I'm sure you know what it is to experience the condemnation of foolish people due to no fault of your own. Just as I have felt the barbs of comments about the darkness of my complexion or the wrinkles on my face." She looks down at her fingers. "Or the roughness of my hands." She refocuses on the rocking chair. "But I must ask it. Are you quite sure you aren't secretly angry because Gerald's father carries African blood? That the thought of that blood in your children' veins is repulsive to you?"

"I love my children with my entire soul!"

"I know. I suspect that is why fully acknowledging their forebears is so difficult for you."

Alma's mother springs from the rocker, which tilts dangerously to one side. She yanks it back into place. "You know nothing about my feelings and motives!" She stalks to the loom, where she stamps onto the boards, slams her right foot down, and yanks the shuttle through the shed.

At the table, the señora sighs and looks down at the fleece. She nods toward the edge nearest Alma. "I think there's another burr buried inside that knot," she says. "Be careful. Those things hurt if they catch under a fingernail."

# CHAPTER 31

Her mother settles down more quickly than Alma expects, although she does ban Chaser to the courtyard and the animal pens behind it. There's simply no room for the mastiff in the casita.

Antonia Garcia doesn't object. As nice as she is, she isn't a dog person. Chaser doesn't—or perhaps doesn't want to—understand. He hovers around the casita door and tries to slip in whenever someone enters.

He does it again the morning Gregorio comes inside with an armload of split cedar. "Perdóneme," the man says, closing the door in the dog's face. As he adds the wood to the stack by the fireplace, he looks at his mother, who's standing next to the table, combing Alma's hair. "I should go to Don Fernando to check on the house," he says. "Some of the Santa Cruz rebels are moving north. They'll be looking for shelter as winter sets in. An empty casa will be an attractive place to camp, especially one as out of the way as ours is."

She frowns. "Perhaps I should have stayed there."

He shakes his head. "It's not safe. Even though you're the mother of a rebel, there are different opinions among us about what should be done next. Those who disagree with my views would be quick to abuse you for the sake of their own."

"Sheer foolishness," she mutters. She begins braiding Alma's hair into one thick plait.

Gregorio straightens. "What was that?"

"War and rebellion." She finishes the braid, puts her hands on her hips, and scowls at him. "It's all foolishness."

He shakes his head but his voice is patient. They've clearly had this discussion before. "Sometimes there is cause for rebellion. Especially when the governing have forgotten they do not live only for themselves."

"Did Governor Pérez forget?"

He snorts. "I don't think he ever knew. With his clothes and his finery and his demands for obedience, he was not a man to listen to reasonable concerns." He turns back to the little pile of wood. "And now Manuel Armijo, even though he was born in Alburquerque and comes from a long line of nuevomexicanos, is turning out to be the same way. He hasn't changed the rules about voting, returned our right to choose our own judges, or done anything about the taxes, as far as I know. He's simply waiting for the soldiers from Chihuahua to arrive. Then he'll suppress what little remains of the people's voice."

Alma's head jerks toward him. Soldiers? Chihuahua? At the other end of the room, the loom stops thudding.

But Gregorio is focused on stacking the firewood and doesn't notice. "However, Padre Martínez isn't waiting to express his opinion," he continues. "He doesn't seem to think he needs soldiers to keep us in our place. Which is probably why there are so many rebels headed to Don Fernando."

"What soldiers from Chihuahua?" Alma's mother demands. Her voice rises. "The governor has sent for more soldiers?"

He stands and turns toward her. "Oh yes. And they're coming. It's only a matter of time."

But Señora Garcia is focused now on the last part of what he said. "Padre Martínez? They're going after the Padre now?"

"He won't stop talking." Gregorio sounds more frustrated than angry. "He preaches against us at every opportunity. Every mass, every baptism. Even at weddings."

"What does he say?"

"That we should all submit and be respectful citizens and obey those God has set over us."

"Which would be him." Alma's mother's voice is dry and amused at the same time.

"Which would be him." Gregorio chuckles. "Perhaps not Manuel Armijo, but definitely the Padre. Those of us who live in his parish should do as he says, at any rate."

"He's only trying to protect you." Señora Garcia doesn't sound as if she fully believes this, but she's a church-going woman and wants to think the best of her priest.

He shrugs. "That may be true, but there are rebels who see him as the governor's puppet and therefore someone to be silenced."

"He's a priest. Surely they wouldn't—"

"Men do foolish things when they're afraid," Alma's mother says grimly.

The two women share a long look, then the señora turns to her son. "Please be careful."

Alma closes her eyes, willing the prickling tears not to fall.

He sets out the next day. The casita seems colder without him. A kind of waiting gloom descends on the women and children. They celebrate Alma's ninth birthday on December 14th with nothing more than a few tiny pieces of brown loaf sugar and a kiss on her cheek from each of the women. Andrew gives her an awkward hug instead. He's too old for kisses. When Alma goes outside, Chaser Two makes up for this lack by thoroughly washing her face with his tongue.

But the next morning, the gloom descends again. The days are even shorter now and her mother's nerves are frayed. When Andrew pushes his slate aside, folds his arms on the table, and lowers his head to them, the thump of the loom stops abruptly.

"What in tarnation are you doing?" his mother demands.

He raises his head. "I'm wishing for Papa. I wish he would come for us."

"Even if he did come, we couldn't go back with him. You heard what Gregorio said. The mountain route is impassable, and the track by the river is too stony and narrow for wagons or any other kind of conveyance."

"He could still come."

Then Antonia Garcia enters, fresh from her morning visit to the Agua Fría mission chapel, and stops short. She looks from the children to their mother and her face loses its sparkle.

The other woman doesn't appear to notice her. She's staring at Andrew, her lips twitching. Alma braces herself, but her mother only sighs and says, "And if wishes were horses, beggars would ride."

"But then, sometimes we do need to ask for what we want," the señora says. She lifts her rebozo from her head and shoulders and hangs it on a peg beside the door.

"And sometimes we shouldn't have to," Alma's mother says. The loom treadles begin thumping against the floor again, more sharply now.

The other woman stands watching her. Then she moves to the end of the loom, puts a hand on one corner, and studies the younger woman's face.

"He has sent no word." Alma's mother bends forward, slips the shuttle through the shed, switches feet, then yanks the comb toward her, shoving the new strand of yarn against the old. "He has made absolutely no effort to contact me or arrange for us to go home."

Andrew and Alma exchange a glance. This is the first time she's sounded as if she wants to go back to the valley. Hope twinges in Alma's chest.

But then the señora speaks. "You have sent no word. Gregorio wanted to take a message, but you told him—"

"I'm not going to beg." The opposite treadle thumps against the floor. Alma's mother bends forward to pull the comb through the growing cloth.

Señora Garcia lets out an exasperated breath. "Or are you afraid of how he might respond?" She pauses. "Or not respond?"

She flashes her an irritated look. "I have no idea what you're talking about."

"Don't you wonder if he even wants you to return? A man can be pushed too far, Suzanna."

Alma sucks in her breath. Andrew's slate jerks against the table, scraping the boards, but their mother doesn't look up. The treadle boards pound the floor.

That night, Alma's nightmares return. She wakes with her blankets twisted around her pounding chest, her fingers stiff from clutching the rough wool.

She can just see her mother's sleeping form on the other side of the room. Andrew huddles beside her. The night is cold. Alma's breath hangs in the air, but she's drenched with sweat. Images churn in her head. A man's half-naked body on the blood-spattered dirt road. The vulture's wrinkled red neck stretched toward an empty neck.

And the silence. The frozen shock of a landscape afraid to breathe. Silence broken only by the chuffing wings of ravens wheeling overhead, waiting their turn. Papa so far away. And

Gregorio. Suddenly, last night's tortías and beans burn her throat. She clamps her jaw against them and stumbles out of her blankets to the door.

Señora Garcia is already awake and moving quietly around the outer room. She looks up. "Hola. How did you—" Then she sees the child's face, reaches for a nearby rebozo, and throws it over Alma's shoulders. "Go quickly. As far as you can from the door."

Alma nods, clutches at the long shawl, and hurries outside. When she returns, she accepts a cup of water and drinks it greedily, feeling the clean wash of it down her throat and into her sore belly.

The señora watches, her eyes dark with concern. "You are unwell?"

Alma shakes her head. "Not now." She tilts the cup again. A shudder runs through her body. Water spills down her chin.

"But you are chilled." She turns to the fireplace, crouches to add more fuel, then eases the thin pottery comal griddle onto three rocks carefully positioned to support it over the heat. "Come and sit."

Alma moves to the banco and settles herself, pulling her knees to her chest and tucking the edges of the rebozo around her feet. She should be helping, but it feels good to relax into the warmth and watch the señora's deft hands prepare the morning tortías. As the first pale yellow round touches the hot comal, she breathes out in a deep sigh.

Señora Garcia smiles at her sympathetically. The knot in Alma's chest relaxes a little further. This woman won't be cranky with her for voicing her fears, the way her mother would be. Yet it seems disloyal to say all the things she wants to say, to ask the questions that haunt her. Besides, only her mother can answer most of her questions.

There's only one she wants to put to Señora Garcia. Alma wets her lips with her tongue. "Is Gregorio safe?"

The woman's hands stop moving. She stares at Alma with wide eyes. The tortía on the comal hisses and a scorched smell fills the air. She looks down, lifts, and flips. She watches it for a long moment, then eases the golden disk off the hot surface and onto the waiting platter. But she doesn't continue her cooking. Instead, she drops her hands into her lap and looks at the girl.

"I am certain he is well," she says firmly. "I am his mother. I would know it in my heart if something happened to him." Her eyes close and her lips move silently. Then she crosses herself, takes a deep breath, and returns to her work. "I pray we are through with battles and rebellions," she says, more to the masa than the girl. "But of course that is for El Dios to decide."

"If there is a God."

The señora looks at her with raised eyebrows.

"He seems very far away."

The woman nods sympathetically. "Much has happened to you these past months. Coming here without your father. Your mother forced to weave for your sustenance. The rebellion. And Governor Pérez killed on the road outside this very casita. It is more than a girl your age ought to be required to bear."

Alma nods and looks away. Suddenly, her eyes are burning and her lashes are wet. She puts her forehead against her knees and pulls her legs closer to her chest.

There's movement at the blanket-covered door, then her mother appears. "Alma? Come and get dressed, child."

Alma blinks away her tears and swings her legs off the adobe bench. She can feel the señora's gaze on her back. Her shoulders hunch against the cold.

But over the next few days, there is no more talk of sorrow and fear. Señora Garcia seems determined to put a cheerful face on things, especially with Christmas approaching. Alma's mother is busy at her loom, seemingly oblivious to the season. Elisha Stanley has asked her for more brown-and-red jerga and she's working hard to provide it by the new year.

"We need the money," she says when Andrew pleads with her to take the time to walk with him and Alma to the Santa Fe plaza. "I don't have two extra hours to meander to town and back. Not unless I have something to sell. You can go by yourselves."

His eyes drop from her face. "There might be rebels. Or robbers." His toe scuffs at the floor. "Or Navajos."

"It's perfectly safe. Alma will be with you and you can take Chaser."

Alma, who's at the table combing a fleece Elisha Stanley has sent, grimaces. She doesn't want to go either. Not without an adult.

Their mother's lips tighten. "Then don't go. You don't really have the time to fritter away, either."

Andrew looks up. His chin is out and his eyes are mutinous. "I've gathered the eggs, broken the ice on the mules' trough, and brought in more firewood."

"Have you split the kindling?"

"Alma did that after she folded the blankets and swept the room and helped with the cooking."

Señora Garcia is sitting on the banco spinning the fluffy combed wool piled in the basket at her feet. She looks up. Her hands move steadily, guiding the wool onto the long thin spindle and deftly twisting it into yarn. "They have been very helpful children this morning," she tells their mother. "As they are every morning. You have trained them well."

Alma's mother looks more annoyed than pleased. She doesn't like being placated, even by as good a friend as Antonia Garcia. She turns back to Andrew. "I don't have the time to go with you. If I don't weave, you don't eat. If you want to go, you'll have to do so by yourselves."

His eyes drop again and his shoulders droop as he drifts away, toward the sleeping room. As he passes the banco, Señora Garcia's hands falter. Alma glances at her in surprise. But then Andrew disappears into the other room and the señora's hands move again. The loom thumps steadily onward.

The tip of the spindle scratches the bottom of the little brown pottery bowl Señora Garcia uses to keep the stick and its burden of wool from dropping onto the floor. It and the thump of the loom treadles have a strangely calming effect, a rhythm that allows Alma's mind to wander. Images float in her head. The sleeping room, where her brother is crouched. Chickens pecking in the courtyard outside. A man's headless body.

Her breath hitches and her wooden comb jerks in the wool, jamming the long fibers. Alma's hands fall to her lap and squeeze the edges of her skirt. Her heart thuds against her ribs so hard it hurts.

Antonia Garcia looks up with a question in her face. Alma flushes and shakes her head. She's too old for daymares. Her mother will only scowl if she sees. Alma flattens her hands on the tabletop, closes her eyes, and forces herself to breathe deeply in and out. When she opens her eyes again, the señora is focused on her spindle. Alma steadies herself, swallows her memories, and reaches for the task at hand.

# CHAPTER 32

Three days later, it's the day before Christmas. Señora Garcia announces that there'll be no combing or spinning this day. "It is la Noche Buena," she tells the children's mother flatly. "A day to prepare for la Navidad and feasting and the giving of gifts."

"We don't have money for a feast." Alma's mother glances toward the children, her face suddenly tired and worn. "Much less the giving of gifts."

"We have the gift of each other and a roof over our heads. There's still enough wheat flour for a small batch of bread. And I have been putting aside an egg each day. If the hens are kind to us this morning, there will be enough for natías." She looks at the children. "Though I will need help stirring the custard to keep it from burning."

"We can do that!" Andrew says.

His mother shrugs and moves to her loom. She places her feet into position on the treadles, moves her head from side to side to ease her neck, then sets to work. The steady thump of the loom fills the room.

By the time the outdoor oven has yielded two loaves of yeasty bread and the egg custard is cooked and cooling, it's late in the day. Andrew hovers over the natías, sniffing appreciatively.

"That's for tomorrow," the señora tells him. "Tonight we will eat a little of the new bread with our beans, but tomorrow is the true feast day."

"It's going to be a long night," he moans. "I'm not going to be able to sleep."

She chuckles. "Perhaps that is why the priests hold la Misa del Gallo on la Noche Buena. So boys have something to do while they wait for the morrow's feast."

Andrew's forehead wrinkles. "La Misa del Gallo? The mass of the rooster?"

"Sí. The service begins at the first hour of the day and doesn't end until the rooster crows."

"The first hour? You mean midnight?" His forehead wrinkles. "You stay up all night?"

"That's a long service," Alma says.

The señora chuckles. "It is only a saying. I will be home before the rooster truly crows." She purses her lips and studies the children. "I am going to la capilla castrense, the military chapel on the Santa Fe plaza, with a friend from Agua Fría. Would you like to go with us?"

Andrew turns toward the loom. "Can we, Mama? Can we stay up all night?"

His mother's right foot pushes down, moving the warp threads apart. She reaches for the shuttle. The yarn inside it is a deep red. She runs the yarn through the V of the warp and snugs it into place, then looks up. Her eyes are smudged, as if she hasn't slept in a week. Alma's heart snags in her chest. Maybe she should stay here and keep her company.

"Who is going with you?" her mother asks.

"The widow who lives on the plaza near the chapel along with three of her grown sons and their wives and children. Two of the men are Presidio soldiers. We will be safe enough."

Alma's mother looks at Andrew, who's watching her anxiously. Her face softens. "Yes, you can go to the service."

"Will you come with us, Mama?"

She shakes her head. "I have work to do." She shrugs and looks away. "Besides, I would only spoil your fun."

"But you'll be alone. It won't be safe."

"I'll have Chaser to protect me." She makes a shooing gesture at him. "Go. I'll be all right."

He nods doubtfully, but he can't help but be intrigued with the idea of staying up all night. He grins at Señora Garcia and Alma expectantly.

The evening threatens to be a long one, since they won't leave for the chapel until well after dark, but the señora insists that Andrew and Alma nap a little beforehand. Then suddenly there are men at the gate and the children are wrapped well in extra shawls and bundled out into the cold.

There is no moon. The men on the edge of the little crowd are armed with knives, iron-tipped pikes, and torches, but the blackness beyond the flickering light still makes Alma shiver. Andrew feels it too. He stays close and slips his hand into hers.

They move through the night, up the dirt road and over the rise north of the house. Then the darkness ahead is broken by the glow of a bonfire. A guitar thrums and the men and women around the fire burst into song. The voices die out as Alma's group approaches.

"Feliz Noche Buena!" one of the widow's sons says gruffly.

"Greetings!" a man by the fire answers. He raises a wooden cup to them. "Come and drink with us!" He waves a hand toward a table half-hidden in the shadows. "Come and eat!"

"We thank you, but we are on our way to la castrense."

"Ah, it is a dark night for such a journey and the chapel will be crowded! Stay with us instead!"

"I thank you, but we must not delay."

"Safer with friends than in the dark!" the man persists. "You never know when a rebel might be lying in wait!" They all laugh uproariously as Alma's group continues on its way.

Her eyes swim, trying to adjust again to the darkness. The governor's decapitated body seems to rise out of the shadows, just beyond the men's torches. A shudder runs down her spine. Antonia Garcia pats her shoulder, but Alma hardly feels the woman's hand. She has a sudden urge to turn and run back down the road. All she wants is the warmth of the casita and the steady thump of her mother's loom. Or, even better, her father's arms. Gregorio's smile.

She bites her tongue against the sudden tears and trudges on, surrounded by Señora Garcia's friends and utterly alone. Even Andrew's warm hand between her palm and fingers doesn't dissolve the knot in her chest, the twitch of tears under her lids.

They pass more bonfires and the widow's sons turn down more invitations to stop, eat, and drink. "As if they don't remember what the purpose of the season is," the old woman sniffs.

Finally, the little group reaches Santa Fe's narrow streets. They pass Elisha Stanley's closed-up shop and enter the plaza. Here, the darkness is pushed back by the flare of more torches as other groups of worshippers move from every direction toward the chapel on the square's south side. Many are singing hymns accompanied by men and women strumming guitars. The voices aren't loud and some aren't very melodious, but there's a reverence in their tone and a solemnity in the singers' faces that makes the children look at each other in wonder. The plaza itself looks different tonight. Calmer. Less cluttered and dusty.

Alma's group is close to the chapel entrance, but they can't enter. Men in blue and red uniforms block the big wooden doors. Their gold-fringed shoulder boards glitter in the torchlight, making the soldiers wearing them seem bigger than they actually are.

Except for one, who is taller than the rest. Andrew sucks in an admiring breath. "That's Donaciano Vigil," he whispers in Alma's ear. "See him?"

But she doesn't have a chance to respond. Movement ripples on the opposite side of the square. A stout man in a swirling cloak and hat with a tall white feather moves toward the church, a soldier on each side and two behind. The crowds part to let them pass.

"Tarnation!" Andrew says. "Who is that? Is he a prisoner?"

"It is General Armijo," Señora Garcia tells him. "The men with him are his escort."

"To protect him from the likes of us," the widow adds drily.

The governor and his guard sweep past and into the chapel. Donaciano Vigil and the other waiting soldiers enter behind him. Now the way is clear for the populace. The singing stops and men douse their torches. In the sudden darkness, Señora Garcia puts a hand on each child's shoulder. "Stay close," she says in Alma's ear. "I don't want to lose you."

Alma nods numbly. The plaza's beauty has vanished. Now it's simply a dark and crowded space that contains too many people, all of them edging toward the chapel entrance. Everyone's very quiet and polite, but she still feels as if she can hardly breathe.

Then she's through the door and the señora has maneuvered herself and the children into a position halfway up the long narrow room but off to the right, next to the white adobe wall. If Alma lifts her fingers from her skirt, she can touch its smooth surface.

A woman behind them taps the señora on the shoulder. She turns and gasps in delight. "Mi amiga!" she exclaims softly. "It's been so long since I've seen you!" She twists farther toward the woman, to look at the youngsters beside her. "And are these your grandchildren?"

She's has released Alma and Andrew as she turned. Alma moves closer to the wall. All over the church, people are smiling and nodding and whispering to each other. Andrew is watching them with bright, curious eyes, but Alma feels only a dull loneliness. She wishes her father was here. Or Ramón. Or Gregorio. All three of them.

Finally, a priest in holiday vestments enters the chapel and stands before the altar. He raises his hands and the crowd flutters into silence.

Alma watches the ceremony and listens to the music and words in a kind of haze. She's tired from the walk and, although the warmth of the crowd seeps into her, it isn't a cozy feeling. If anything, it only makes her more anxious, more hemmed in. A tiny bird beats in her chest, searching for relief.

But there is no relief. She's old enough to know that help isn't coming, that grownups don't always resolve their differences. That her mother's worry and weariness and irritation aren't likely to lessen any time soon. And that her father may never come for them. Tears prickle her eyelids. She bites the insides of her cheeks and tries to focus on what's happening at the far end of the room, beyond the gold shoulders of the men in uniform.

The congregation is kneeling now. She drops with them and peers at the candle-lit altar. The priest's back is to the congregation. He raises a shining cup. Her gaze moves beyond it.

The wall behind the altar isn't smooth white adobe like the one next to her. It's rock. A tall expanse of stone as wide and almost as tall as the room that towers over the priest and the table below.

Alma sucks in her breath. Every inch of its surface is carved with designs and figures that seem to dance in the candlelight.

The decorations aren't random. The flat surface is divided into two rows of three shallow rectangular niches set on end. The center bottom space is deeper and there's a statue in it. Alma can't see what it looks like because the priest blocks her view.

But she can see most of the spaces. Each contains a carved and painted stone picture. In one, a man holds up a cross. There's a shell of some kind in his other hand. Worshippers kneel at his feet. In the niche above him, a man holds a cross in one hand and a plant of some kind in the other.

Alma smiles. He must love plants as much as her mother does. Her smile fades. There's been no planting or gathering since they reached Santa Fe. Will there ever be again? But she can't think about that now or the tears will start again. She concentrates on the carvings.

Her forehead wrinkles. Each picture by itself seems very simple and she doesn't understand what they mean. But together they do something calming to her heart. She looks around the room. The kneeling worshippers are focused reverently on the priest and the altar. They all seem so peaceful, so intent, so sure of what they believe. She feels a little envious, but also strangely peaceful herself. The bones in her chest loosen, making more space for her lungs.

The priest turns toward the congregation and raises his hands. They all rise. Alma doesn't understand the words he speaks, but she can sense the quiet joy in them, the confidence that he and the people he speaks to will have strength to face tomorrow. And that it will be a better day. She's not sure she really agrees with him, but somehow she does feel better. As if she can cope a little longer with her life and all its fears and confusions.

The crowd says something in unison, answering the priest, and sings a final hymn. Then the service is over. The people begin to stream out into the night. Señora Garcia nods goodby to her friend and touches Alma lightly on the arm. "Stay close now."

Alma smiles up at her and looks at her brother, who solemnly slips his hand into hers. She turns back to the señora. "We won't get lost."

# PART IV

## JANUARY—MARCH 1838

## SANTA FE

# CHAPTER 33

But within a week Alma's calm is shattered. The rebel leaders may be in jail, but their former followers have found another leader and he's issued a new pronouncement. This one accuses Manuel Armijo of taking his position by force and calls on the citizenry to march on Santa Fe.

"The goal seems to be to release the Montoyas and the others," Antonia Garcia says, repeating what she heard in the market.

Men marching means bloodshed. And Gregorio will be with them. He still hasn't returned from Don Fernando. Alma's knees feel weak. She sinks onto the banco by the fire and squeezes her eyes shut, trying not to see the headless corpse, the vulture's yellow eyes and wrinkled neck.

"I thought there were soldiers coming from the south," her mother says.

"Surely it won't come to that," Señora Garcia replies. "Surely General Armijo will be able to talk sense to these men."

"I wonder. He put the rebel leaders in jail and they simply found new ones. They don't go back to their homes and fields, they continue to agitate. I'm beginning to believe that nothing but a battle and bloodshed will end this."

Pain stabs Alma's stomach. She doesn't realize she's made a retching sound until her mother says, "Alma! Please! Not inside!" and Señora Garcia hurries toward her with a rebozo.

Alma pulls the big shawl around her shoulders and stumbles to the door. When the cold air hits her face she stops and gulps it in, forcing the nausea under control.

But then the tears threaten. She moves numbly to the courtyard bench, drops onto it, and closes her eyes. Bloodshed. Battle. Gregorio. The governor's bloated body. Her belly churns. She leans forward and covers her face with her hands.

The red hen clucks at her feet, then Chaser's nose sniffs her shoulder. Alma straightens and dully strokes the dog's ears. He snuffs at her again, then wanders off. She lifts the rebozo over her head and wraps it more tightly around her chest. She doesn't want to feel this way. She wants to feel quiet and sure, the way she felt after the mass at la castrense. Can she feel that again?

She takes a deep breath of cold cleansing air, then breathes out. The steam of it dampens her cheeks, but at least it's not tears. She pulls the cold in again, filling her belly with it.

Her stomach settles a little more. She closes her eyes, concentrating. The iron band around her chest relaxes a bit. She tries again. Gradually, her mind empties of everything but the feel of her breath rising and falling.

Another image—pine trees, needles underfoot, soft dirt. The peace of the woods. Gregorio's smile. Will she ever see him again? She shivers and opens her eyes. The casita door opens and Andrew appears with the water bucket.

He pauses before her, eyes wide with concern. "The señora doesn't think there will be fighting," he says reassuringly.

She looks at the chicken, which is still pecking the ground. "I'm all right."

His shoulders drop. He turns away. Alma shivers again, gets up, and goes into the house.

The cold she felt in the courtyard is followed by six inches of snow and a temperature drop that keeps Santa Fe and Agua Fría frozen in place. It's as if nature itself is waiting for something to happen. The women and children stay inside as much as possible and try to simply endure. Gregorio sends word that he's in Santa Cruz at the Montoya hacienda.

Señora Garcia's face pales a little when she gets the message and she slips to the chapel more often, but nothing else changes. Alma's mother weaves, the señora cooks and spins, and the children do their chores and study. Or try to. Alma has to work hard to keep her mind from wandering north.

Then one morning there's the sound of bridles and tramping men on the road beyond the casita wall. Andrew and Alma are in the courtyard, he chopping kindling, she collecting and stacking it.

As they turn toward the gate, Señora Garcia comes out of the house with an empty water bucket. She stops when she hears the noise in the road, then walks past the well to the gate. The children follow her.

She lifts the bar and opens the gate just enough to peer out, then swings it farther and moves slightly aside so the children can see, too.

"Soldiers!" Andrew breathes.

"Dragoons, I think," she says without turning her head.

Dragoons on horseback. And in uniform—green coats with red facings, gray and blue trousers with red stripes down the sides. Shiny boots with big round spurs attached. The men are very tall in their saddles. Their mustaches gleam under their big black hats.

One of the men is even taller than the others. He also has larger mustaches and a bigger, shinier horse. He watches Antonia Garcia and the children as his mount prances past the gate.

"We should return to our work," Señora Garcia says. She shoos the children away, but before she can close the gate, the tall dragoon has wheeled his horse and trotted back to the casa. He reins in and smiles down at her.

"Por favor," he says in a deep voice. His face is pockmarked and his nose is too big for his chin, but his eyes are eloquent. He nods at the señora's bucket and fixes her with a pleading look. "If you could spare a little water, you would be doing me a kindness." His mount bobs its head and the man chuckles. "And for El Burro, as well."

"El Burro?" Andrew asks.

"Because he is so small and so shaggy." The man may be answering the boy, but his eyes are on the woman. The two of them share a smile, although hers is a reluctant one.

"However, I have forgotten my manners." He looks into Señora Garcia's eyes. "My name is Sargento Eduardo Silva and I am a dragoon of the Vera Cruz regiment." He bends forward, bowing in the saddle. "I am at your service, señora."

Her hand goes to her hair, smoothing a stray lock from her face. Then she frowns. "And I am Señora María Antonia Garcia."

"And these are your children?"

"Oh!" She looks at Alma and Andrew as if she's never seen them before. Then she smiles at them apologetically and turns back to the man. "No, I do not have that good fortune." She pauses, as if confused, then says, "That is, I have a son, but these are not my children."

Andrew steps forward. He puts his hands on his hips and stares up at the dragoon. "My name is Andrew Ramón Locke." He waves his hand toward the house. "This is my mother's casita. Señora Garcia is her friend. If you would like water, we have plenty."

The man throws back his head and laughs. "Yes, that is the way to greet someone who is so impertinent as I!" He glances up the road. "But I'm afraid I must join my men." Then he refocuses on the señora. "I wish I could stay." He gazes at her, his voice low and intimate now. "Perhaps I may return for that drink of water?"

She lowers her eyes and nods. Her cheeks are tinged with pink but her lips are tight, as if she's angry with herself.

When he does return, he wants more than water. The refugees who crowded into the city last Fall are still there and the housing shortage has worsened with the arrival of the new troops. The January weather is too cold for the dragoons and artillery men to camp outside for more than a few nights.

"There are almost two hundred of us now, and more coming," the sergeant tells Alma's mother. "There is simply nowhere to house us all." He's so tall, he has to stoop slightly to keep from bumping into the casita's ceiling. He holds out a small piece of parchment. "We are authorized to offer payment,. It is not much, but all I ask is a place to lay my head."

"And your horse?"

He hesitates. "I can stable him elsewhere, if it would be more convenient for you. Somewhere in Agua Fría."

She shakes her head. "There is room. I only wondered about feed."

"I can provide that."

She looks down at the slip of paper. "There is no room in the house." She waves a hand around the room. "We have only this and the storage room where the children and I sleep." She glances at Señora Garcia. "It would not be appropriate for you to sleep here in the main room."

"Ah," he says. He glances at the señora, then quickly away.

Señora Garcia looks at Alma's mother and says reluctantly, "You need the money. There is the shed where Gregorio was sleeping." She glances at the dragoon. "My son. He is—"

Alma's breath catches. Surely she won't tell the tall dragoon what Gregorio is and where.

"Away tending to the señora's affairs," Alma's mother says.

The dragoon glances at her, then the señora, and nods.

"The shed isn't much," Alma's mother says.

He smiles at her. "I have been sleeping on the ground in the cold Nuevo México desert. A roof and walls are all I desire." His gaze finds Señora Garcia again, then he blinks and refocuses on Alma's mother. "That is, a roof and walls are sufficient to meet my needs." He stops again and looks away.

She glances at the señora and smiles faintly. Then sadness sweeps across her face. She turns away. "Let me just get my rebozo—"

But Andrew is already holding it out to her. "You'll have another animal to care for," she warns him.

"That's all right." He tilts his head back to look up at Señor Silva's. His shoulders straighten. "I can do that."

After the sergeant's new quarters are inspected and approved, El Burro is introduced to the mules, and Alma's mother's name is written on the piece of paper for the military accounts, Señor Silva heads into Santa Fe and the military headquarters at the presidio. Although it isn't part of the arrangement, Alma's mother invites him back to join them for the evening meal.

"Well, this should cause some gossip in the village," Señora Garcia says as the door shuts behind him.

"Ah, but this is different," Alma's mother says drily. "He's a dragoon, not a rebel. Therefore he can be trusted to behave as a gentlemen should."

"I'm sure he's trustworthy enough. Even if he is a government dragoon."

NO SECRET TOO SMALL

Alma's mother studies her for a long minute, her face a mixture of sympathy and amusement. Then she turns and goes to her loom.

The bit of extra money coming in puts her in a better frame of mind and Alma and Andrew both breathe sighs of relief. But then the cold weather continues and the firewood runs short. She has to pay someone to bring more. Prices are higher than usual because there's more demand now, from all the soldiers as well as the refugees. The man who brings the wood is apologetic but firm. He leaves with almost all of what's left of the Locke family savings.

When Alma's mother closes the door behind him, she doesn't go back to her loom. Instead, she drops into the rocking chair and stares gloomily at the fire. "We'll freeze to death if we don't keep it going," she says.

"We won't eat, either," Señora Garcia says. "We need to cook." She's at the table, dicing withered carrots for the stewpot. The children are opposite her, doing their lessons. "And if we let it go out completely, we'll have trouble getting it started again."

There's a long pause, with only the sound of her knife cutting into the food and the scrape of Andrew's chalk on his slate. Alma turns a page of her botany book.

"I'm just so tired," her mother says. "Everything feels so difficult."

The señora looks up at her. "Would you have married him if he'd told you the truth?"

She flashes her a surprised look., then returns her gaze to the fire. "I don't know. I hope so."

Alma and Andrew exchange a quick glance, then look down at their work. Alma's heart loses a little of its heaviness. Her mother doesn't say anything more. The only sound is the click of the

# CHAPTER 34

Even though her mother is oppressed with worry and the house is cold, when Señor Silva comes in each evening, life returns to the casita for a little while. Each day, he brings with him a new tidbit of information, all of it colored by his enthusiasm.

First, it's the cannon already in Santa Fe. Excellent equipment! he says. And in such good condition! Then he describes the enthusiasm of the populace. Admirable! And so well spoken! After that, he reports that the newly confirmed Governor Manuel Armijo has done a superior job of training Nuevo México's militia. And he looks every inch the general!

Also, the tall dragoon likes the weather of the place, the crispness of the air, and the chiles in the food. Also, the women here are prettier than anywhere else he's ever been posted. When he says this, he looks meaningfully at Antonia Garcia and she looks stubbornly away.

But then he brings sobering news. News Alma doesn't want to hear. The rebels are gathering again in Santa Cruz, and this time Governor Armijo has lost his patience. He seems to have thought the rebels would disperse once the troops from Vera Cruz and Chihuahua showed up. Instead, they're more defiant than ever. Alma looks at Señora Garcia, who turns her suddenly pale face resolutely away.

Señor Silva is even more sober when he comes in from the morning review of the troops two days later. "The rebels are moving toward Santa Fe," he tells Señora Garcia as he hands El

Burro's reins to Andrew. "The governor is marching to meet them tomorrow with every man at his disposal."

She closes her eyes. "I had hoped it wouldn't come to this."

"And I." He pauses. "Your son?"

Her face twists. Alma's breath catches. Will she admit that Gregorio is a rebel? Then her heart sinks as the woman says, "I can only pray he has returned to our home in Don Fernando de Taos."

The sergeant doesn't frown or act surprised. He almost seems sympathetic. "You've heard about the rebel threats there against Padre Martínez ?"

She shudders and turns away.

"There's no need to worry about the Padre," he continues, as if her shudder is for the priest, not her son. "He arrived in Santa Fe about a week ago. However, the news he brought and now the reports from the north have made Governor Armijo very angry. He's—"

Alma's mother comes out the house door. They all turn to look at her. She stops on the threshold. "What is it?"

Andrew moves toward her. "The rebels are coming."

She looks at Señor Silva, then Señora Garcia, who gestures wordlessly toward the dragoon.

"We're marching to meet them—" He glances at the children.

"We'll hear anyway," Alma says. She's afraid to know, but she feels as if she'll burst if she doesn't.

Her mother smiles ruefully. "There are no real secrets in this household."

The sergeant takes a breath, as if steadying himself. "That's not the only news." He glances at Señora Garcia. "The rebel prisoners have been executed. The Montoya brothers and Alcalde

Esquibel and the other man." He grimaces. "Instead of a review this morning, I and my men stood guard."

Alma's tongue is suddenly thick in her throat. She feels herself weaving, then curving forward. The señora springs toward her and eases her onto the courtyard bench.

"You could have said that more gently," she says over her shoulder.

"I'm sorry. I didn't want to say it at all. Is she all right?"

They're all looking at her. Alma nods and gulps back her tears. "The Montoya brothers? Both of them? Antonio Abad? The one with the daughter my age?"

"Daughter your age?" He gives her a confused look. "Do you know these people?"

"We met Antonio Abad and Desiderio Montoya when we went to the feast of Santiago at Chimayó in July," Andrew tells him.

Alma wipes at her face. "And we saw Señor Esquibel there. When he was arrested." Her voice quavers. "And now he's dead."

Señora Garcia turns to the dragoon. "How did they do it?"

He puts his hand to his throat.

"Beheaded?" Andrew's voice has a choked sound.

Señor Silva nods and looks away.

The señora takes a deep breath. Alma's mother closes her eyes. "Dear God in heaven." She looks at the sergeant. "Will there be a battle?"

He nods somberly. "I think so, yes. It is believed that nothing else will stop the rebellion from erupting again. It is time for it to end."

"Oh, santo Dios," the señora whispers.

Suddenly, Alma can't breathe. She leans back against the wall, her palms flat on the bench, fingertips digging into its rough surface. There's a roaring sound in her head like a million bees buzzing.

"Alma?" someone asks from a great distance, then the hard edge of the bench scrapes her back as she slides to the ground.

When she comes to, she's in the casita, half-lying on the banco. A rebozo envelops her like a blanket. Her mother bends over her, but her face is hazy. Alma blinks and the room comes into focus. "Gregorio," she whispers.

"Yes." Her mother glances toward the door, where Señora Garcia is standing close to Señor Silva, his head bent toward her. "Poor Antonia. A man on each side."

A shudder convulses Alma's body. Her mother drops onto her knees beside her. "I wish I could tell you everything will be all right."

"So do I," Alma whispers.

Then Andrew is there, leaning against her mother. She wraps them both in her arms as Chaser, who's slipped into the house in the confusion, snuffs at Alma's feet. She gulps back her tears. Even in her fear, the closeness feels good. But Gregorio— She shudders again and her mother hugs her closer.

Finally, Sergeant Silva leaves and Señora Garcia turns from the door. Her cheeks are wet. "Come," she says to Andrew. "I need water from the well." She looks at Alma. "Are you well enough to help with the tortías?" Alma nods and her mother heaves a tired sigh, releases the children, and goes to her loom.

Alma's dream returns that night. This time there's a head lying beside the bloated body. A man's head. One with curly black hair and eyes that no longer twinkle. But it still smiles. The lips twist up at the ends in a grotesque parody of amusement.

In the pale cold light that comes just before dawn, she wakes with tears on her face and a lump in her belly. She pulls the blankets more tightly over her chest. Antonio Abad Montoya, so full of life and good cheer. Gregorio's cousin.

Her stomach twists. Gregorio. What will happen in the coming battle? She can't bear to think about it. But when she forces her thoughts away from her friend, her mind turns to her father. His arms around her, his hand stroking her hair. She bites the back of her hand but the tears come anyway.

"Alma?" Andrew asks from the other side of the room.

She lifts her head. His eyes widen, then he scrambles off his pallet, slips across the room, and crawls into the blankets with her.

"Why can't adults get along?" she whimpers into his hair. They huddle together in the pale morning light. His arms are oddly comforting. Gradually, she drifts into sleep, Andrew's head heavy on her shoulder. When she opens her eyes, her mother is crouching beside them, her face anxious.

"Mama?" she asks.

"Did he have a bad dream?"

Alma shakes her head. "I did."

"Well, at least we won't have to air his bedding."

Alma grins in spite of the tightness in her chest. "You knew?"

Her mother chuckles. "There was no other reason for the two of you to be hauling blankets into the courtyard."

"I didn't want him to get into trouble."

"And I was busy." Her mother's face is sad now. "I'm sorry I'm so preoccupied these days." She strokes Alma's hair. "I miss combing this."

Alma feels a glimmer of pity. Then anger sweeps in instead. What is she supposed to say? It's all right? It isn't. But nothing she says will change anything. She moves her head slightly, away from her mother's hand. "It's all right."

Her mother smiles wearily. "You're a kind person, Alma." She touches Andrew's shoulder. "But you two need to get up now. We should try to follow our usual routine."

However, there's nothing usual about this day. The dragoons have marched north with Governor Armijo and the women and children can only wait. Her mother moves slowly and uncertainly at the loom, as if her feet and hands don't know what to do with themselves. Señora Garcia prepares the food mechanically and burns half the tortías.

The children hunch over their schoolwork. Andrew covers his slate with chalk circles and lines, boxes inside boxes. Beside him, Alma stares blankly at her book and wishes she could retrieve the peacefulness of that night in the Santa Fe chapel. Waiting is the hardest work in the world, she decides. That's why she feels so heavy, so tired. She and the others drift silently through the day, each of them lost in their thoughts, afraid to speak their fear.

But by the next morning, Antonia Garcia's distraction has turned to anger. "Women's breasts have more influence than oxcarts," she mutters as she sweeps the room. "If that little bitch hadn't interfered, he would be here."

Alma's mother is setting up her loom for another piece of jerga. She glances up in surprise. "Señor Silva?"

"Gregorio!" The broom jabs at a bit of dust caught in the corner by the storeroom door. "That Gertrudis Leonarda Fajardo. That señorita of the río Arriba. That princesa of her family and darling of her Montoya cousins." The broom straw stabs the hard-packed floor in front of the fireplace. "Damn her, anyway!"

Alma's mother stares at her. "I've never heard you speak in such a way of any human being."

The broom clatters to the floor. The señora drops into the rocking chair and covers her face with her hands. "Oh, my boy!"

When she looks up, her cheeks are streaked with tears. "What will I do if something happens to him?"

Alma's mother drops her work, moves down the room, and kneels next to the chair. She reaches for the other woman's hands. "I wish—"

"There's nothing to be said. I know it." Señora Garcia removes her hands and wipes at her face. "I know it. But waiting is so difficult." She sighs. "And the Fajardo girl isn't entirely to blame." She smiles a little and shrugs. "But I think he stays with the rebels at least in part because of her loyalties. Why else would he keep returning to Santa Cruz? And she doesn't seem to understand or appreciate my boy. Which makes me dislike her."

The younger woman's eyes twinkle. "She's clearly not a very intelligent young lady."

"Claramente," Gregorio's mother agrees. "Because, in my opinion, my boy is just about perfect."

At the table, Alma sniffs. The two women turn. She glances at them, then at her slate.

Her mother chuckles. "In your opinion, he *is* perfect."

Alma smiles bleakly and returns to her sums. Or tries to, anyway. Nothing makes much sense to her today.

# CHAPTER 35

They don't make much sense the next morning, either. Not after Elisha Stanley arrives to tell them the rebels have been defeated. Men on both sides have been killed and wounded.

"Though not as many as might have been expected." His voice is a little triumphant. Alma suddenly hates him. "Armijo didn't turn out to be much of a general," he adds. "But the captain of the Vera Cruz dragoons was. And they're saying the Chihuahua infantry fought valiantly."

Antonia Garcia is standing next to the table, her hand gripping its edge. "And the rebels?"

He turns to her. "They've been put in their place once and for all, and the head of their gang, that Jose Angel Gonzales, has been executed. Armijo made sure to take care of that, though they say he did give Padre Martínez time to hear the so-called governor's confession before he was shot."

"Padre Martínez was there?" Alma's mother asks.

"Oh yes. He offered to act as chaplain for the troops and Armijo took him up on it." The merchant's lips curl in disgust. "The good Father wanted to be on the winning side, I suppose."

"And the others?" the señora asks.

"The others?"

"Those who were wounded." She swallows. "Or killed. What of them?"

He shrugs. "I haven't heard anything about the casualties on either side. I expect we'll know more in the next several days."

Alma's stomach suddenly feels hollow. Several days? They've already waited forever. The days are an empty blank of waiting. Her lashes prickle with tears. She doesn't bother to wipe them away. It's just too much work.

She closes her eyes and sees Gregorio's narrow face, his broad shoulders, his hands on the axe, spangled with light. Then the glow of him fades into Señor Silva's kindly face, his mustache quirking as he smiles. Alma chokes back a sob. How is it possible to care so much for two people who are on either side of a fight?

But it's not just Gregorio and the dragoon. It's also her mother and father. She feels like a piece of paper with a single word written on it and the page ripped down the middle, the word itself torn in two.

She's only slightly less distracted two days later, when Andrew suddenly asks their mother, "What day is it?"

She looks at him blankly, then recognition dawns. "Today is January 30th. Oh Andrew, I'm so sorry. It's your birthday." She makes a hopeless gesture. "With everything else going on, I forgot all about it."

He nods. His face is somber, but his eyes don't leave her face.

"And now you're seven." She shakes her head. "It's hard to believe."

"And such a grown-up seven-year-old," Señora Garcia says. "You are such a responsible joven that I forget you're so young."

His chin lifts. "I'm not young. I'm seven."

Her eyes twinkle. "You certainly are. And a very mature seven-year-old."

"I'm afraid I don't have a gift for you," his mother says.

"That's all right." He puts his hands on his hips. "I have everything I need." Then his face falls. He turns away. "Almost everything."

"Everything I have the power to give you." Her voice is soft and sad.

He glances toward the door. "Can I bring Chaser Two inside? Can that be my birthday gift?"

She exchanges a look with Señora Garcia, who shrugs as if to say a dog in the house is the least of her worries. Then she nods at Andrew. "All right. But just for today."

The boy runs outside to call the dog, but when he returns, he's also accompanied by Señor Silva. The dragoon raises an eyebrow at the mastiff and Andrew grins at him. "It's my birthday, so he's allowed inside today."

The big dragoon's mustache quirks in amusement, but then Antonia Garcia comes in from the storage room. He crosses the room and takes her in his arms.

Alma, who's at the table studying, looks away. She's never seen two adults so close to each other or kissing like they are. Then the señora says, "Oh!" in a wounded voice.

Alma looks up. Antonia Garcia has pushed herself out of Señor Silva's arms. "But where is my son?" she demands. "The battle was Saturday. It's been three days, and I've had no word."

He reaches for her shoulders and pulls her to his chest. She doesn't resist, but she doesn't kiss him either. "I'm so worried." She looks up at him. "I've been so worried."

"I'm here now, my love."

"But Gregorio."

He pats her shoulder and looks around the room. When his gaze meets Alma's, he winces as if she's struck him. She wets her dry lips with her tongue. His eyes drop. Fear stabs her belly and her fingers tighten on her book.

"I don't know." He looks down at Señora Garcia, who has pulled back and is staring at him with frightened eyes. "I don't know, but I'll find out."

There's something about the way he says it that makes Alma shiver. He believes the worst. She's sure of it. Señora Garcia seems comforted by his words, but Alma's terrified.

The terror creeps into her dreams. That night, the headless man is not Governor Pérez or Antonio Abad Montoya. It's Gregorio, though she wakes before her dreaming gaze reaches his face. Even in her sleep, her eyes skitter away from the place where his head should be.

It's his hands she focuses on. His strong brown hands, cold and still, gripping dirt they can no longer feel. Vultures hop around them, scaly heads jerking back and forth on wrinkled red necks. Raven wings chuff overhead. The horror pitches her awake, sitting straight up, her breath catching, her stomach roiling.

"Alma?" Andrew asks. Then he's crossing the room and wrapping his arms around her and she's clinging to him, her tears falling into his curly blond hair.

She does her best to hide her distress during the daylight hours, especially around the adults. It isn't difficult. The women are preoccupied. There's still no word of Gregorio, and Sergeant Silva has been ordered north to ensure the rebels have truly dispersed to their homes. He has promised the señora that he will look on his own for her son.

When he returns a week later, his face is somber. Alma's mother stops working when he enters. Señora Garcia hurries toward him. Her face falls when he wearily shakes his head. "I can find no trace," he says.

Andrew and Alma are at the table, looking into the room, Andrew working on his penmanship, Alma combing wool. She can see only the man's back, but even his uniform looks defeated. It's wrinkled from long riding and streaked with dirt.

Antonia Garcia retreats to the banco, and sinks onto it as if she needs the wall's support against her back. She wraps her arms around her chest and shivers in spite of the fire's warmth.

"I'm sorry," the tall dragoon says helplessly.

She nods without looking at him. He turns and goes into the courtyard. The loom begins again, slowly, as if its operator is having trouble concentrating.

Señora Garcia bends forward and buries her face in her hands. Then she suddenly sucks in a deep gulp of air and looks up. "I hate war!" she says. "I hate it!"

Alma's mother puts her hands on the loom's wooden frame and gazes sympathetically at her friend. "Yes. And yet you love men on both sides. Men who believe different things."

The señora looks down at her hands. She turns them over as if she's never seen them before. "It's not their beliefs that I love about them," she says slowly. "It's their sense of duty and honor. Their passion to protect. To fight for a cause bigger than themselves." Her face softens. "I honor their sense of honor."

Then her mouth twists. "But I hate that our leaders and their officials refuse to find a way to make peace, must put the lives of my men in such danger! And Gregorio—" She covers her face with her hands. "To not know—"

Alma's throat tightens, burning with unshed tears.

Suddenly, Señora Garcia pushes herself to her feet and marches to the door. She lifts her rebozo from a peg and turns toward the loom. "I'm going to the village chapel."

Alma's mother nods. Then she steps away from the loom, fumbles in her pocket, and brings out a small coin. "Buy as many candles as you can with this."

The other woman's eyes glimmer with something between amusement and tears as she takes the bit of silver. "I thought you didn't believe."

"In a situation like this, even I find myself praying."

Now Gregorio's mother is even closer to tears. Alma gulps back her own. The señora looks at her. "And you? Will you pray?"

Alma nods numbly, though she's not sure how to go about doing so. But what she feels—the swallowed tears, the longing, the unspoken terror—must be a kind of prayer. Because it's all a fist-clenched breath-holding wish for Gregorio's safety and return.

But she can't sustain the tension of her anxiety. At some point, her body betrays her. In spite of her fear, she sleeps without dreaming that night as well as those that follow and wakes each morning to a gray dullness that feels as if it's always hovered over her and always will.

She wishes she could be like Señora Garcia and go each morning to the Agua Fría chapel and return slightly calmer. But Alma doesn't ask to go with her. She doesn't have the energy. And she doesn't really believe she could find peace in the little adobe building. She's not sure she can find peace anywhere.

But the excursions do seem to help the señora and they also provide her a way to gather news. One morning she says, "I saw Gertrudis Fajardo's mother's cousin at the chapel. She lost a son in the battle, as did Gertrudis' father's brother."

"I'm sorry to hear that." Alma's mother shakes her head. "So much loss."

The other woman sighs. "I suppose I shouldn't be so hard on the girl. I've never laid eyes on her, yet I've formed such strong opinions. At first, Gregorio seemed to believe she loved him, and then he only scowled when I mentioned her." She looks at Alma's mother. "You've met her. What do you think?"

The younger woman leans forward to straighten her warp thread. "I think she's sixteen and doesn't know her own mind."

Then she stops moving. Alma looks up from the wool she's combing. Her mother is staring at her work as if she's never seen it before. After a long moment, one foot slowly presses a treadle board and her hands move again across the cloth. There's a thoughtful look in her eyes, as if her mind is a million miles away.

Alma has a sudden urge to cry. She drops the wool and comb, and heads to the door.

"Rebozo!" the señora calls after her, but Alma pretends not to hear.

The usual February thaw has begun. The courtyard walls radiate early spring warmth tinged around the edges with coolness. The grass has hope, at any rate. Tiny spikes of green push through the soil at the foot of the old wooden bench.

Alma closes her eyes. None of it matters. She doesn't care about spring or plants or Gertrudis or whether the girl should be hated or liked. She just wants Gregorio to be here.

She crosses the yard and drops onto the still slightly damp bench. And her father. She also wants her father. Her father and Ramón and the valley. She shivers and wraps her arms around her chest. Chaser ambles across the yard and pokes his nose into her lap.

As she reaches for him, her tears start falling again. "I hate being a child," she tells the dog. "I want to make my own decisions about where I live!"

Not that being in the valley right now would tell her where Gregorio is. Even when she's grown she won't be able to control other people's decisions. Or their attitudes.

Her hand goes to her cheek. María Paula's words seem so small now, so unimportant. Yet Something in Alma's heart knows they'll begin to sting again when everything returns to normal. A shudder runs up her spine. If normal ever returns.

She bends toward the dog. "Where *is* he?" she asks. But all he can do is move his big head closer to be scratched.

# CHAPTER 36

Alma's in the courtyard again several days later, this time crossing it dully with a small basket of eggs, when the ungreased cottonwood wheels of a carreta squeal to a stop outside the gate. A hand raps tentatively on the wood.

Then she hears a man's thin voice. Gregorio? Her basket thuds to the ground as she runs across the yard. She wrestles with the gate and yanks it open, her heart pounding.

But it's only a young woman, so wrapped up in a big black rebozo that only her eyes are visible. She clutches the halter of a tiny brown burro who looks too small to pull the crude two-wheeled cart behind it.

The woman doesn't speak. Her shoulders slump with exhaustion. She simply plods forward, leading the burro and cart into the courtyard. There's an intensity in her weariness that compels Alma backward, allowing her in.

It's only after the cart is inside the walls that Alma sees Señor Silva, but even then she's barely aware of him. She's glimpsed the carreta's contents now, and nothing else matters. Gregorio. Relief floods her chest. Then her breath catches. He's so pale, yet flushed at the same time.

He opens his eyes. "Nita," he murmurs. He lifts his left hand and touches the right side of his chest like a child telling his mother where it hurts, then his eyes close. Alma's knees wobble. She turns toward the woman in the rebozo.

But there's no one there. She and Señor Silva are already at the casita door, the sergeant knocking briskly, the woman pulling her rebozo tighter around her shoulders, as if for protection.

Alma crawls into the back of the cart. "Gregorio?" she whispers.

His lips flicker. His eyes crease at the corner, smiling even though they're closed. "Yes, it's me," he murmurs.

She giggles in spite of her fear. "I would hope so!"

Then Antonia Garcia appears and Alma scrambles out of the way. Gregorio's mother leans in to kiss his forehead, then moves into position to help Señor Silva ease him out of the cart and into the house.

Inside, Alma's mother has sprung into action. There's a rough pallet of folded jerga beside the far wall and blankets nearby. When the tall dragoon carries Gregorio inside, she's kneeling beside them, folding a small piece of her softest weaving around a bit of wool to serve as a pillow.

Once he's settled, Gregorio's mother goes into action. She sends the children out for more water and begins heating the soup left over from yesterday's evening meal.

The woman who led the burro into the courtyard moves to the loom. She's still there when Alma and Andrew return with the water. She's lifted the rebozo away from her face now and has one hand on the big cottonwood frame, leaning against it as if she can barely stand. Alma's heart squeezes. Gertrudis Fajardo looks much paler than the last time she saw her and not nearly as haughty and pleased with herself.

Alma's mother moves toward the girl, her hands out. "Thank you for bringing him to us, Señorita Fajardo."

At the fire, Antonia Garcia's hands go still. Then she straightens and turns. "I am his mother," she says. It's more of an accusation than a self-introduction.

Gertrudis flinches, then bobs a slight curtsy. "I am happy to meet you. I am Gertrudis—"

"I know who you are." The señora's eyes go to her son, who seems to be sleeping. Her face tightens. "What I don't know is why you are here."

Gertrudis' eyes flash. "I brought him."

Señora Garcia's eyes move to Señor Silva. He nods. "I found them on the road from Santa Clara." He glances toward Gregorio. "He was very weak from his wound."

"We did everything we could, María Catarina Montoya and I," Gertrudis says. "But he wasn't healing and—"

"I wanted my mother," Gregorio says from the pallet.

"You could have sent word," she says. "I would have come." She winces, as if seeing him lying there is more than she can bear. "You were too weak to travel."

"There were soldiers searching the houses, looking for rebels," the girl says. "I was afraid of what they might do if they found him." She shivers. "Sargento Vigil was kind enough not to question us closely—"

"Donaciano Vigil?" Alma's mother asks.

"Sí." The girl's face is strained and anxious as she remembers. "He and others came searching. I believe he knew Gregorio was there. He sent his men outside and spoke to Catarina and me in a loud voice." A smile flickers on her lips. She glances at Gregorio. "Loud enough to be heard in the storeroom beyond, behind the bales of wool at the far end."

Then she closes her eyes. "He said we should be careful. That others might come searching and we might not have time to sequester our valuables." She chuckles and opens her eyes. "He's a good man, that Donaciano Vigil. He has a gift for saying much with a few words." She looks at Sergeant Silva. "And so Catarina and I smuggled Gregorio out of the house and I came south with him."

"They had only his horse," the dragoon says. "The riding re-opened the wound."

Her lips tremble. "When he began to bleed again, I was so frightened. And then Señor Silva appeared."

"I exchanged the horse for a carreta and burro," he explains. Then he grins. "I'm not sure the Pojoaque family I bartered with are especially pleased with their end of the deal. They need a cart more than a riding horse."

"We'll need to return it," Señora Garcia says absently. She swivels toward her son. "But first we need to take a look at that wound. And when was the last time you ate?"

A smile flickers across Gregorio's pale face. His gaze finds Gertrudis. "I told you she would be happy to see me." His eyes close, then he opens them and finds Alma's mother. "Señor Beitia—" he says.

Alma's breath catches. "In the battle?" her mother asks.

"Yes." His eyes close again. He's very pale.

A spasm of pain passes over Gertrudis' face as she gazes at him, then she turns to Alma's mother and begins winding her rebozo around her head and shoulders. "I must go to the casa of my mother's cousin and ask for shelter, and also send word to my parents and to María Catarina. I have much to explain."

Alma's mother blinks. "You left without telling them?"

"Catarina will want to know I am safe. There was no time to send messages elsewhere and we feared they might fall into the wrong hands."

Señor Silva glances at the window. "It is growing dark. If you will permit me, señorita, I will accompany you into the village."

"I would like that, señor." She turns to Alma's mother. "If you will permit me, señora, I will return tomorrow to see how he is and to assist in any way I can."

Antonia Garcia's hands stop moving among the goods in the cupboard. Alma's mother glances at her, then nods to Gertrudis. "We would be happy to see you."

She's back the next day and the day after that. Early each morning, Señora Garcia slips to the village chapel to light a candle of thanksgiving for her son's safe return and of petition for his continued healing. When she returns, Gertrudis is usually hovering by Gregorio's side, urging him to eat the thin cornmeal atole Alma has dished up for him.

Alma would like to serve him herself, but Gertrudis takes the bowl from her with such a winning smile that Alma almost forgives her for her intervention. The young woman clearly cares about Gregorio. Alma wishes she could be happy about that.

But Alma's more polite than Gregorio's mother is. Antonia sniffs disapprovingly when Gertrudis brings her the empty bowl and takes it without looking at the girl. "He's perfectly capable of feeding himself," she says.

"It hurts him to sit up," Gertrudis answers mildly. "I'll wash the bowl, if you like."

"I can do it."

Gertrudis returns to the pallet, where Gregorio is sitting sideways, his back against the wall. She kneels beside him and takes his hand.

"I do feel stronger," he says. "You and Mama are excellent nurses."

His mother's head snaps around, her eyes narrowed. He's looking at Gertrudis, reaching up to stroke a strand of hair from her forehead. "I wish I could draw," he says. "You are—"

She glances at the señora, then reaches out to touch his lips with a finger and smiles at him tenderly.

Señora Garcia's face darkens. She turns back to her work.

Because Gregorio's mother is preoccupied with his recovery, Alma's mother takes over much of the marketing. Money is tight again. The governor is sending Sergeant Silva and his men on extended patrols to take retaliatory actions against the Navajos and reassure people that the outlying areas are safe once again. There's no payment for his lodging if he's not in residence.

Also, she's reduced the amount of time she's weaving in order to allow Gregorio to sleep undisturbed. There's isn't as much cloth to deliver to Elisha Stanley as there would normally be, although she does have some knitted stockings to sell him.

She takes the children with her to the mercantile. "We'll need to bring back cornmeal, salt, and possibly some flour," she tells them. She looks at Andrew's pale face. "And we could all use the exercise."

He shrugs listlessly and follows his mother and sister across the courtyard. When Chaser Two trots toward them, Andrew pushes him out of the way. "You stay here. You don't really want to go anyway."

His mother looks at him in surprise, but doesn't say anything. Alma studies him. He's been acting strange the last several days. He didn't seem glad to see Gregorio and he's spending all his free time in the sleeping room. When she comes in to retrieve anything from the supplies, he doesn't look at her.

"He'll just wander off," Andrew grumbles.

His mother shifts the basket of jerga to her other hip. "Come along, then."

They trudge through a landscape that's cold and wet and seems to match Andrew's mood. Elisha Stanley's store is extra cozy and warm in contrast.

"I haven't brought you as much as I'd wanted to," her mother says apologetically. "We have a wounded man in the house—"

"Ah yes, so I've heard," the merchant says. "How is the Garcia boy doing?"

She raises an eyebrow. Mr. Stanley grins. "You know how it is. People talk. And the old lady his young woman's staying with was here yesterday to purchase a few items." He chuckles. "She seemed rather put out."

Her eyes spark. "Because Gertrudis visits my home?"

"It seems to have more to do with the señorita's journey to reach your casita. I gather the young people weren't chaperoned most of the way and then, when they were accompanied, it was by another man."

"Yes, I can understand why the circumstances of that journey would raise concerns," she says drily.

"The señora is very angry and apparently has expressed herself quite forcefully to the girl. And the girl's parents have ordered her to return home. But Señorita Gertrudis persists in remaining and returns each day to his bedside."

"Ah."

"The old woman can't understand how any young lady of the upstanding and patrician Fajardo family can be so deliberately disobedient and wanton." His eyes crinkle at the corners. "I'm not sure which angers her more, the journey or the visits to his bedside. She has strong opinions, that one."

298

"Yes, I believe she does." Alma's mother looks past him to the shelves behind the long wooden counter. "Besides the cornmeal, I need a small bag of salt. Our invalid seems to relish it just now."

He gathers their items, enters the tally into his book, and shows her the balance. "I can't go much lower than this," he says sorrowfully.

She sighs and nods. "I hope to bring you more goods in another two weeks." She turns to the children. "We'd best get home so I can get started on the next batch."

When they return to the casita, Gertrudis is there. Antonia sits on the banco, spinning wool and watching her son. He's sitting sideways on his pallet again, but this time his back barely touches the wall. Gertrudis is beside him with a book, bending toward him and reading in a low voice.

They all look up when the children and their mother enter the house. Gregorio smiles at them, then leans his head back and closes his eyes. Alma's heart squinches. She drops her bundle onto the table and crosses the room to kneel on his other side. "How do you feel?"

He smiles again and reaches to pat her shoulder. "I am better, nita. Truly. Soon I will be strong enough to go into the forest to collect wood."

Warmth spreads into her belly. As she squeezes his hand, she sees that Gertrudis is watching them with a fond smile. As if Alma is a child. She rises abruptly from the pallet. "I need to help put the things away."

"What a fine father you will make," Gertrudis murmurs as Alma moves off. Alma's hands clench her skirts. She has a sudden urge to turn and kick the girl right in the shins. No wonder Señora Garcia dislikes her.

But later that night, after Gertrudis returns to the village, Alma's mother repeats Elisha Stanley's gossip. The señora is sitting on the banco, spinning more wool. When the younger woman finishes speaking, there's a long silence. The only sounds are the tip of the spindle scraping the inside of the pottery bowl, the soft crackle of the fire, the whisper of the rocking chair, and the click of knitting needles.

Gregorio is asleep. The children are at the table, their schoolwork in front of them. Andrew stares blankly at the opposite wall. Alma watches Señora Garcia's face. A series of emotions play across her eyes and mouth. Irritation. Tiredness. Something almost like guilt.

Then her hands stop working the wool and she crosses herself. "I have committed a sin," she murmurs. She glances toward Gregorio. "The girl not only brought him to me, but she has continued to brave her family's displeasure to see him each day. She must love him very much."

"Enough to overcome her assumptions about what she thought he did when he was here last Fall."

The señora sighs and returns to her work. "The trouble is, I still can't find it in my heart to actually like her."

Alma's mother chuckles. "Now that may be a problem."

# CHAPTER 37

As Gregorio heals, Gertrudis Fajardo spends less time at the casita. Perhaps this is because she has no more excuses to give her relatives. Or she's worn down by Señora Garcia's still barely suppressed dislike. Whatever the reason, she reverts to her traditional señorita self and wheedles him into visiting her properly at the Agua Fría casa.

He hobbles out almost every day to see her, leaning on a thick stick. His mother's lips tighten as she watches him go, but her eyes brighten when he returns and she hurries to bring him a hot drink while he rests on the banco beside the fire.

He's there, his eyes closed and his head tilted back against the wall, the day Señor Silva returns. He's been gone three weeks. Señora Garcia's eyes brighten even more when Andrew opens the door to the tall dragoon's knock.

There's a kind of spark in the room when she and the señor look at each other. Alma, at the table combing wool, glances at them, then Gregorio. He's staring at his mother as if he's never seen her before. Then he focuses on the Sergeant. "You have returned." There's a note of caution in his voice.

"I have!" The dragoon crosses the room and bends to shake the younger man's hand. "And you! You look much healthier than when I last saw you!"

Gregorio smiles wanly. "In some ways, I also have returned." He waves a hand at the rocking chair. "Please, seat yourself."

At the loom, Alma's mother lifts her head. Her brows contract a little, then her lips quirk in amusement and she returns to her work.

Señora Garcia bustles around, taking Señor Silva's coat and hat, heating water for tea. "We have yerba buena and cota," she tells him. "Which do you prefer?"

He gives her a smile. "You know what I prefer."

Her face turns bright red. She glances at Gregorio and turns away. "The mint then."

The dragoon leans from the chair and half-turns to speak to Alma's mother. "I find the city is as crowded as ever. None of the refugees seem to want to leave. Is there still room for me here or would you prefer—"

She combs another row of thread into place without looking up. "The same terms?"

"Sí."

She glances at Gregorio, then his mother. "Then I believe we can accommodate you. Although that shed is still going to be cold."

He smiles and glances at the señora, who's suddenly busy moving things around in the corner cupboard. "I'm sure I'll be warm enough."

Alma looks at Gregorio, who's staring at the tall dragoon with an expression somewhere between surprise and irritation. Alma squirms uncomfortably, but then the moment is over. Gregorio's eyes close again and Señor Silva accepts a cup of hot tea from the señora.

In the coming days, the sergeant isn't actually around much. He's busy drilling his men and they're often sent out on short patrols to make sure the rebels don't regroup yet again. This seems less and less likely as the days go by. The January battles appear to have convinced them there's no further hope.

Andrew perks up for a few days after Señor Silva and El Burro return, but as time goes by, even caring for the glossy horse seems to lose its appeal. He goes back to spending most of his time in the sleeping room, or droops around the courtyard, even though the weather has turned cold again, as it tends to do in March. During his lessons, he draws endless boxes along the margins of his slate instead of the elaborate penmanship circles his mother has assigned him or the sums she's given him to complete.

One morning, she pulls herself away from the loom to check on the children's schoolwork and discovers he hasn't even begun the tasks she's set him. His slate is edged with a narrow row of careful boxes inside boxes. The sums remain in the center with no answers beside them. Her lips tighten. "What's this?"

He shrugs.

"Those sums won't complete themselves, Andrew."

"I'm tired."

She reaches for his chin and tilts his face toward hers. Her irritated look turns to one of concern. "You do look tired." She frowns. "You may be going into a growth spurt. Alma did that when she was about your age. She was tired a great deal and then suddenly shot up three inches. You should try to eat more."

He moves his head away from her fingers. "I'm not hungry."

She frowns. "You're always hungry."

"Not lately." Alma looks up. "He hasn't been eating much."

Her mother frowns at Andrew. "Have you been giving your food to the dog?"

He scowls at the table. "No."

"You haven't been playing with him, either," she says thoughtfully. "I have noticed that." She leans toward him, eyes dark with concern, and places the back of her hand on his forehead. "You don't seem to have a fever. Are you tired all of the time?"

He starts to shake his head, then nods reluctantly. "And my stomach hurts."

"Even when you eat?"

"'Specially then."

She chews on her lower lip, then pushes herself to her feet. "I'll make you some chamomile tea. That ought to help."

His shoulders slump and he sniffs audibly. She gives him a sharp look, but he's lifting his slate from the table and looking wearily at the numbers on it.

He and Alma are at their lessons again the afternoon Señor Silva returns from yet another patrol. He and Señora Garcia slip outside a few minutes later. When the señora returns, she's alone. Her face is flushed and her eyes are dancing, but she doesn't explain herself. If anything, she seems intent on keeping her eyes on her work and nowhere else.

But her smile disappears when Gregorio comes in a little later with Gertrudis. They're holding hands and looking shy and pleased at the same time. He nods to the children and their mother, who's at her loom. Then he turns to the señora, who's sitting on the banco spinning. "Mama, I have something to tell you."

She looks pointedly at the young people's linked hands. "I think you've already told me."

Gertrudis turns bright red and snatches her hand away.

Gregorio smiles at her, then his mother. "Sí. It is so." Then he looks anxious. "If her parents will accept my suit."

"And why wouldn't they?" She drops her spindle and stands, hands on her hips. "You are equal to anyone in the country!"

"It is a mere formality," the girl says reassuringly.

"I should hope so!" She moves across the room and begins rummaging in the food cupboard in the corner.

"We will leave tomorrow," Gregorio says.

She turns. "Leave?"

"I must go to Santa Cruz to speak to her parents. And it is time for Trudes to return to her family."

"And who will chaperone you?"

"Her mother's cousin goes with us."

"Humph." She turns back to the cupboard. "And what are your plans, once you are married?"

"The family of Antonio Abad Montoya has sent word that they are in need of assistance."

She stops moving. The whole room seems to freeze. Then she turns and faces him. "Santa Cruz? Not Don Fernando? Not—" She makes a gesture as if taking in the whole of Santa Fe and Agua Fria. "Not here?"

He drops his eyes. "No, Mama. I believe it would be better if we are close to the Fajardo hacienda." He looks at the young woman beside him. "For Gertrudis' sake."

His mother's face is stony. "I see." She turns back to the cupboard. "This is in complete disorder," she mutters. "It's going to take the rest of the day to straighten it."

"With your blessing, Mama?"

She takes the tin of salt from the cupboard. "And we need more salt."

"Mama?"

She doesn't turn. "Go, then," she says. "You'll do as you wish anyway."

Gregorio's lips twitch. It's not clear if he's irritated or amused. Gertrudis looks like she's going to cry. He looks down at her.

"It's all right," he says gently. "She's upset at me, not you. I was too sudden with my news."

Señora Garcia pulls the wooden tea box from the cupboard and wipes at it with a cloth. "Everything's dusty, too." She replaces it on the shelf and picks up another container. Then she looks around at Gregorio. "Are you still here? Don't you have a journey to prepare for?"

"Sí, Mama. I will send word when the date has been decided." He touches Gertrudis on the shoulder. As they turn toward the door, he catches Alma's eyes and smiles conspiratorially. She tries to smile back at him but finds herself staring instead at her slate. Her eyelids prickle.

She's dimly aware that the loom has stopped and her mother is at the door, congratulating Gregorio and wishing Gertrudis joy. Alma watches her out of the corner of her eye. Her mother looks happy and sad at the same time.

Señora Garcia just looks angry. She doesn't speak to Gregorio when he returns to the house to gather his things and retrieve the burro and cart. When Señor Silva comes in that night, she snaps at him too, until he gently takes her elbow and leads her into the courtyard.

When they return, he looks pleased with himself, but she still seems irritated. She waves a hand toward the loom, where Alma's mother is working. "Go on, tell her," she tells the dragoon grumpily.

He moves down the room. His cheeks are red above his big mustache. "Señora, I'm afraid I must move my lodging," he says formally. But he doesn't look sorry. In fact, his eyes are sparkling with delight.

Alma's mother frowns. "Is there a problem?"

"No! That is—" He looks at Señora Garcia, who has followed him as if pulled by a string. "You see, word has come that we of the Vera Cruz squadron are to stay in Nuevo México at least through the Fall and possibly longer." He reaches for the señora's hand. "I have been fortunate enough to persuade this good lady to take me as her esposo—"

Alma's mother's eyes widen. She looks at Señora Garcia, who blushes and looks away.

"It would not be—" His face is even redder than before. He glances toward the children. "It would be best if we—"

"You certainly can't set up housekeeping in the shed." She glances at the floor near the fireplace, where the señora usually spreads her pallet. "And you wouldn't have any privacy in here."

Now Señora Garcia's face is red. "It would be most incómodo," she murmurs.

Andrew frowns in confusion. He looks at Alma, but she's busy watching the adults. At the other end of the room, their mother is chewing on her lower lip. "This is all so sudden."

"I'm afraid we are bringing a hardship upon you, señora," the dragoon says.

"Although we are reducing the mouths you will need to feed." Señora Garcia's voice changes, hardens a little. "Especially now that Gregorio has gone."

Alma's mother flashes her a sharp look, but her voice is mild when she says, "He was bound to marry at some point."

"But such a girl and in such a way. And to live with her family, not his mother."

"I'm sure if you asked—"

Señora Garcia's chin lifts. "I will not ask that girl for anything." She shakes her head, then looks up at Señor Silva, who smiles down at her and puts an arm around her shoulders. She lifts her chin. "I have given enough of my life to that boy. It is time I pursue my own choices."

"Well, then." Alma's mother looks at the dragoon. "But it will take you time to prepare for the wedding and find lodging."

His face reddens again. "I have found lodging. It's not much more than a closet, but it is private and will be only ours." He looks at the señora. "As for the priest, we—"

"The formalities can wait," she says. The back of her neck is red. She looks at the dragoon, then Alma's mother. "We thought perhaps tomorrow."

The younger woman begins to laugh, then clamps her hand over her mouth. "I apologize. This is just so sudden and so—" She opens her hands, palms up. "So precipitate."

"Nothing like your own wedding," the señora says drily.

Alma's mother's hands drops to her sides. She frowns, then her lips twitch in amusement, as if she can't help herself. "Nothing at all." She grins. "After all, we were engaged at least a month."

There's a flurry of activity the next day as Señora Garcia and Señor Silva collect their things and say goodby. The casita seems very empty.

"It's just like it was when we first arrived," Alma says to her mother, who's sitting motionless in the rocking chair. Alma's on the banco spinning. The señora has left her the little brown pottery bowl that supports the spindle's base. "But it feels so much more lonely," she adds softly.

"Yes." Her mother considers the room. "The cabin feels like this sometimes, when you're all out and about and I'm the only one there. Like a coat that's too big for me."

Alma is careful to keep her voice neutral, although she has to fight to breathe. "Do you miss it?" She forces her fingers to keep plucking and twisting the wool.

"Sometimes." She looks down at her hands. "I miss gardening. As I suspect you miss fishing."

Alma's face brightens, but before she can respond, her mother pushes herself out of the rocker. "I wonder if I can get that blue and tan piece done before the light fades completely."

Alma looks up at the open window. "The days are starting to get longer."

"Not long enough." Her mother moves toward the loom. "It's still March. The way those clouds are building up outside, I suspect we're going to get rain tomorrow. And possibly snow. And probably the day after that."

"Ramón would know for sure." Alma says it to herself, but she glances at her mother to see how she'll react.

She doesn't turn. "He probably would." She reaches the loom, positions her feet on the treadles, and goes back to work.

The rain does come the next day. And the day after that, and the day after that. But there is no snow. The moisture falls softly and steadily, soaking into the ground and raising fingers of grass along the base of the courtyard wall. The chickens peck at it hastily, as if they're afraid someone else will get to it first.

"It's a good thing that's not Mama's lettuce," Alma says to Andrew as she stands watching them. The rain has let up and it's merely cloudy now. She has a basket of eggs in her hand.

He looks up from the chopping block, where he's slicing kindling from a chunk of twisted cedar. "She didn't bring any seeds. We weren't supposed to be away this long."

"You wanted to come. It was going to be an adventure."

"Some adventure. Chopping wood, hauling water, doing sums."

"You could go out with Chaser if you wanted to."

He gives her a impatient look and swings the hatchet into the cedar. The blade sticks in the wood, wedged between two contrary grains. "Damn thing is too twisted!" The wood lifts with the buried hatchet when he raises it. He slams the edge of the cedar against the chopping block but the blade doesn't budge.

Alma glances toward the casita. She can hear the thump of the loom treadles through the open window. "You'd better not swear too loudly," she warns.

"I don't care." He drops the hatchet and wood onto the chopping block. The ground around it is covered with a litter of thin pale sticks. "She doesn't care. She's too busy weaving."

"She's trying to keep a roof over our head."

"We could just go home. People there don't care who our great-grandparents were."

Alma stares at him. There's a knot in her chest that won't let go. And a lump in her throat. She moves blindly to the bench by the wall and drops onto it. She looks into her basket. Four eggs, two speckled and two brown. Yet they're all eggs. It's not the outside that matters.

Her brother picks up the hatchet and its connected twist of wood and begins wiggling the handle, working the blade out of the cedar. "I reckon I can get used to people looking at me like I'm some kind of freak, but he hasn't sent for us. And he hasn't come. Maybe he doesn't want us anymore."

Her lips quiver so she can hardly speak. "Do you really think that?"

"I don't know. I don't know what I think." The wood releases the blade with a protesting squeal. He places the hatchet on the chopping block and drops the chunk of cedar beside it. As he squats to pick up the already-cut kindling, the rain starts up again. His shirt clings to his thin body as he carries an armload into the house.

Alma wipes the moisture from her face. If she thinks about Papa, the tears will start again. She forces herself to look into her basket. When she adds these eggs to the ones she's been setting aside each day, there'll be two dozen to take to the mercantile tomorrow with her mother's woven goods. Maybe they'll help eliminate a little of the debt in Elisha Stanley's big book.

And they do help, but not much. The merchant looks after them sorrowfully as her mother hurries the children out of the store. She's silent on the way back to the casita and hardly glances up when Alma points out that the currant bushes near the river are starting to leaf out. Their twisty branches shimmer with green.

"Mama?" Alma prompts.

Her mother has always been alert to the first signs of spring, especially when those signs are plant-related, but now she barely lifts her gaze. "I see it," she says absently. But she's not looking at Alma, much less the plants. "We need to get back. I want to set up the loom for the next batch of jerga before nightfall." She grimaces. "Not that it will do any good. I can't seem to make enough to pay the rent and also feed us."

"Is there something I can do to help?"

"You already do more now than you should." She looks at Alma, then Andrew, whose eyes are on his feet. "You both do." She sighs. "You aren't experiencing much of a childhood."

"It's all right," Alma says, but her mother only shakes her head.

Andrew looks up. "You could write him a letter."

She glances at him, then looks resolutely at the track ahead. "I did."

The children stop and stare at her. She keeps walking. "In December," she says over her shoulder. "I sent it with Gregorio to give to my father."

"Maybe the Pass is snowed in and he hasn't received it," Alma says.

Her mother looks at her sideways. It's the end of March and starting to warm up. "Perhaps." There's little chance that Palo Flechado Pass is impassable.

"Maybe it got lost," Andrew says.

Her lips twist. "Perhaps."

Alma's stomach growls. She presses her hand against her belly to silence it, but her mother doesn't seem to hear it, anyway. At the top of the rise north of the casita, her mother looks down at her. "We'll manage somehow," she says, but tears sparkle her lashes.

## CHAPTER 38

When Alma goes out to the well the next morning, she hears the squeal of carreta wheels going by on the road outside. Andrew, who's coming from the corral where he's been checking the mules, hears it too. The children move to the gate and edge it open enough to peer out.

Three men ride past, south toward Agua Fria. Then another cart rumbles down the little hill to the north. A boy is perched in the back, on top of a crate full of chickens. He waves gaily at them. As the cart gets closer, he shouts, "We're going home!"

The woman walking beside the cart frowns at him but he only laughs and waves at the children again. "Alburquerque!" he yells as the cart trundles past. He circles his mouth with his hands and lifts his face toward the sky. "Alburquerque!"

Alma chuckles. He says it the way she would shout "Moreno Valley!" if she was going home. Her eyelids tingle and she bites the insides of her cheeks. Then she feels her mother's hand on her shoulder and half turns.

Her mother looks out the gate, over the children's heads. "They must be refugees."

"They're going home," Andrew tells her.

She nods but doesn't answer. Alma looks up at her. The bright spring light is unkind to the new lines on her mother's face, the shadows below her eyes.

There's a break in the activity on the road, then a man and two boys come from Agua Fría, herding a bunch of goats. Three of the floppy-eared animals break toward the casita gate, then stop abruptly. Their noses go up, sniffing at the children and their mother.

She opens the gate further and reaches for the closest head. She's scratching it between the ears when one of the boys runs over. "Perdóneme señora," he says breathlessly. "I hope they will be better behaved by the time we reach Taos."

"You're going to Don Fernando?" Her head goes up, searching for the man in charge. "The roads are clear?"

"Sí, señora," he says as he approaches. "The snow is gone from the mountain route. I wouldn't want to herd this bunch over the hills above el río del Norte. They'd all be trying to get down to the river, goats and boys alike." He waves his walking stick at the loose animals and the child. "Get back on the road now." He chuckles as they trot toward the rest of the herd, then turns back to her. "The way is a little muddy still, but it's clear enough to travel."

She nods thoughtfully and bids him good day. Her face looks more tired than ever as she watches them go.

Andrew is looking down the road, toward Agua Fría and the Martín house. "There's Esquipula!" He frowns. "He's waving at me."

"He wants you to come and play."

Andrew draws back, into the yard. His mother looks at him, her face shadowed even more than before.

"I have chores to do," he says without looking at her. "They'll just want to play rebels and soldiers and make me the genízaro. The one who gets killed."

She nods and silently helps Alma swing the gate shut.

It rains again the next morning, but still the refugees move south. The sounds come over the wall—boys calling to straying animals, carts squealing, harnesses jingling. It all gives Alma a heavy, sad feeling. Of course, the rain doesn't help. The weather here isn't so different from the valley, really. There's less snow, but spring is the same everywhere. It may come earlier here, but it's still wet. And the wet is cold.

Or maybe she feels cold because she's tired. The endless round of chores here isn't as satisfying as it is at home. She knots her rebozo more firmly over her head and shoulders and pulls the bucket from the well once again.

Her mother's mood this morning is even darker than Alma's. She was at her loom when Alma woke and she's been there ever since, shoving the treadles with her feet as if she wants to dig a trench into the floor. She's been like that ever since she shut the gate yesterday.

Chaser Two nudges at Alma's arm, seeking attention, but she elbows him out of the way. She's tired and sad and wet. She doesn't want to play. She heaves the bucket from the well, sets it on the ground, and gazes around the dingy courtyard with its stacks of wet wood and mud-spattered walls. The rain drizzles onto her rebozo. How she wishes—

But nothing she can do will change anything. And standing here won't help, either. She gives herself a little shake, picks up the bucket, and heads into the house. When she opens the door, she realizes the loom has gone silent. She was so busy feeling sorry for herself, she hadn't even noticed.

Her mother is sitting at the table, a handful of coins spread before her. She's sorted them into two little groups and is moving them aimlessly back and forth. Andrew sits opposite her with his slate. He's watching his mother and drawing endless circles with his chalk.

Alma crosses the room, places the bucket on the floor near the fire, then goes to the table and drops onto the bench beside her brother.

Her mother slides the stacks of coins together and looks up at the children. "We have enough for the rent for another month, or enough to pay Elisha Stanley what I owe him." She glances at the coins. "At least, I hope there's enough to pay him. It depends on what he gives me for this batch of goods." She sighs and shakes her head, then refocuses on the children. "So I have a decision to make."

Alma sits a little straighter. There's a new tone in her mother's voice. Determination? Hope? Not tiredness and irritability, at any rate.

Andrew's chalk stops moving. "What decision?"

His mother picks up a coin. "I can pay the rent and we can try to survive another month or I can pay the account with Elisha Stanley and we can go north."

"Home?" Alma doesn't ask it as much as she breathes it. Like a prayer.

Her mother's lips twist. "Don Fernando, anyway." She glances away. "I don't know if your father—"

Alma's breath catches.

"He might," her mother says quickly. "It's just that I don't know. We haven't heard from him and he hasn't—"

Alma glances up. Her mother's mouth works as if she's afraid to say the words.

"He hasn't come," Alma whispers.

Her mother nods and looks away again. Then her chin lifts. "But we don't have to sit here and wait forever. We have choices. We can at least go to Don Fernando." Her voice changes. "Where the people who know us aren't quite as obsessed with the purity of their own blood, much less anyone else's."

"Grandfather didn't want us," Andrew mutters to his slate.

His mother tilts her head. "He wanted us to go back to the valley. He thought I would give up the thought of leaving if he wasn't too welcoming." There's a glint of amusement in her eye. "He should have known better."

Alma grins, then sobers. She tries to keep the excitement from her voice. "When can we leave?"

"We can't go by ourselves," Andrew says. "It's not safe. We had Old Pete and Gregorio with us before, and that was before the rebellion."

His mother takes a deep breath. "The rebellion is over. Even the refugees are going home. But yes, it will still be a risk."

"We could wait until Old Pete comes back from Chihuahua."

"We could. But we don't know when he'll return."

"It could be months and months," Alma says. As much as she loves Old One Eye Pete, she doesn't want to wait for him or anyone else. "It could be a year."

Her mother chuckles. "It could. There's no telling with him or Old Bill."

Old Bill. Alma's eyes close. He'd said he was going to talk to her father. But her father hasn't come. Wasn't Old Bill able to get through to the valley? Or maybe Papa really doesn't want them. She bites the insides of her cheeks, fighting the panic.

"Alma? Are you all right?"

She doesn't mean to ask it, but she blurts it out anyway. "What if he really doesn't want us anymore?"

Her mother doesn't ask who 'he' is. She just wraps her arms around herself and bows her head. "I'm sorry," she whispers. "This is my fault."

Alma starts to shake her head, then stops herself.

Andrew's slate scrapes the table as he shoves it to one side. "It was Papa's fault too."

Alma nods. Yes, both their parents are to blame. But it doesn't matter who's at fault. Not really. Not anymore. It just needs to end. She looks at her mother's sad head. So strong and yet so weak sometimes. So human. "But we still love you," she says in a small voice.

Her mother lifts her head and gives Alma a watery smile. Then she looks at Andrew and gives a sharp little nod. "So we'll go north."

But it's not quite that simple. When their mother goes to the Martín hacienda to tell Don Salvador they're leaving, he comes back to the casita with her. To inspect the premises, he says, but really to try to persuade her to stay.

"You have two more weeks on your rent, señora," he points out. "And I can extend that, if you wish it." He hesitates. "And I can speak to my wife about returning again to our previous arrangement. I truly don't have the time to attend properly to the children's lessons."

She smiles wryly. "Even though Gregorio Garcia is no longer here, I'm not sure your wife would appreciate my influence." She looks toward the fireplace, where Alma is tending the beans. Andrew is adding wood to the stack along the wall. They're both watching the adults out of the corners of their eyes. She turns back to the old man. "I appreciate your offer, but I believe it's time to return north."

"You will go back to your valley, then?"

Her chin goes up. "We will return to Don Fernando and my father, at any rate. People there need jerga, too."

Finally, he leaves. She stomps to her loom. "'Your valley,'" she mutters. "As if it was ever mine, and not Gerald's." She shoves the right-foot treadle down and jerks the shuttle through the narrow passage between the warp and woof. "As if he has any right to know where I'm going and what I'm planning to do!"

She maneuvers the comb into place to tighten the weaving, but the warp thread is too loose, and the comb can't push it smoothly into position. "But I can't finish this if it tangles," she grumbles. She glances up at the children, who are standing side by side now, watching her.

She takes a deep breath and shakes her head at them. There's a sparkle in her eyes in spite of her irritation. "That man is annoying, but we'll soon be away from here." She hefts the shuttle in her hand. "If I can finish this piece tonight, we'll take it to the mercantile tomorrow and settle up with Mr. Stanley. Then we'll pay Antonia Garcia a quick visit to say goodby, and come back and pack up."

She studies the loom's support timbers. "I think we can get this apart and into the wagon by ourselves." She looks at the children. "Though it will take all three of us and maybe Chaser, too."

They grin back at her. Alma's chest swells with hope.

The final piece of jerga is finished late the next morning. When the children and their mother set out for the Santa Fe plaza, the sun is shining on a rapidly drying world. Small birds twitter in the still-barren cottonwood trees. Alma isn't wearing her sunbonnet or the rebozo. There's a feeling of freedom and hope in the air.

That hope is squashed when the merchant finishes tallying the amount for her mother's work and the money she's brought against what she owes. He turns the account book so she can read it. "This still remains."

Her lips tighten as she studies the total. Her eyes flick over the columns and the neat entries for flour, cornmeal, beans, and salt. She looks up at the merchant. "I would like very much to close out my account with you, señor."

His eyes widen in alarm. "I am not displeased with our arrangement," she says hurriedly. "I—" She glances at the children. "We are returning to Don Fernando de Taos and I don't want to leave with a debt on your ledger." She nods toward the big book. "But as you can see, I owe you money I don't have. Even if we stayed, with the cost of provisions what they are, that isn't likely to change." Her brows contract. "I'm afraid all I have to offer you in exchange for this balance is a couple chickens and what remains of our firewood."

Andrew sucks in his breath when she says "chickens" but the adults ignore him. The merchant looks down at the account book. When he raises his eyes, he says cautiously. "When I visited your casita last Fall, I noticed you own a rocking chair."

She nods, her eyes wary, her voice neutral. "Yes. It's of mahogany and was imported here from St. Louis."

There's a little pause, then he clears his throat. "I don't suppose you would be willing to part with it."

She studies the amount in the book. "It's worth a good deal more than this balance."

He nods and gazes out the open door. A carreta passes in the street, its wheels complaining noisily. The sound fades toward the plaza. The merchant looks at Alma's mother. "I can return a quarter of the money you've given me in exchange for the chair, the chickens, and the firewood."

Her eyes narrow. "Half the money for the chair only. And you'll need to come get it."

320

His head tilts to one side. "A third for the chair and the firewood. I'll send someone for them this afternoon."

She nods. "All right."

After she and the children leave the mercantile, they make a quick stop to say goodby to Antonia Garcia, who is delighted to see them. When Alma's mother explains why they've come, the señora's eyes widen with even greater delight, but she's successful in her effort not to appear too smug and Alma's mother still seems glad about her decision as they head back to the casita.

In fact, she seems positively buoyant, moving quickly down the road and debating with Andrew about what to do with the chickens. She wants to give them to Señora Garcia.

"She doesn't have room for them!" he protests.

His mother chuckles. "You've turned them into pets, haven't you?"

He shrugs and looks at the ground.

"We can take them with us," she says more gently. "I'm just not quite sure how."

"We can put them in a basket," he says eagerly. "When we stop for the night, I'll let them out and watch to make sure they don't get away."

She chews on her lower lip. "We'll need to clip their wings so they won't be able to fly off."

He frowns. "I don't know how to do that."

"I'll show you."

And that's what they're doing when the cart shows up for the firewood and chair later that day. The two men the merchant has sent are quick and efficient. They leave enough wood for the evening and morning fires, fill the cart with the rest, wedge the rocking chair on top, and head out.

Alma follows her mother back into the house and watches her cross to the spot in front of the fire where the chair has stood all these months. She looks down sadly, turns, and goes to sit on the banco. She leans forward slightly, her hands gripping the curved edge of the seat, closes her eyes for a long moment, then opens them again, gazes around the room, and pushes herself to her feet. "Time to start dismantling that loom," she says briskly. She turns to Alma. "Run and fetch your brother. This is going to take all three of us."

# CHAPTER 39

They pull out late the next morning. Don Salvador is there to see them off. He hands Alma's mother a carefully tied cloth bundle. "Some bread and some sheep cheese," he says. "My wife sends them with her best wishes. María Paula made the bread and asked me to bring it to you." He pauses. "She really is a good girl."

Alma's fingers clench. If it was her, she'd throw that bread right in the old man's face. But her mother only says, "Gracias," and takes the food.

They harness the mules, place the chickens in their basket, and climb onto the wagon seat. Chaser Two leads them out the gate, which Don Salvador swings shut behind them.

They're only a few yards from the gate when Andrew demands, "We're not going to eat that bread, are we?"

"Hush," his mother says. "We're still within hearing distance."

"I don't care! That María Paula said mean things and made the other kids look down on us, and you lose your job, and now she's a good girl because she baked bread! She probably poisoned it!"

Alma leans forward to peer at him around her mother's hands. His face is twisted in something between anger, fear, and disgust. He glares at her. "She might have!"

"She's mean and stupid," Alma says. "But she isn't stupid in that way. Everyone knows who made the bread."

Their mother chuckles. "I'm sure the bread is fine." She looks at Andrew. "I'm sorry she said those things about you. She's only repeating what she's been taught and that plenty of other people believe. Remember Señor Beitia? He also believed in the importance of his Spanish blood." She shakes her head. "Poor Don Salvador. He has two difficult women on his hands."

"Stupid!" Andrew spits.

"That's not a kind word, but I have to admit it seems to apply."

"But Don Salvador lets them act like that," Alma says. "Shouldn't he at least try to make them be nice?"

Her mother smiles sadly and flicks the reins at the mules.

They camp in the sand hills south of Pojoaque that night, near a spot they used coming south. Alma didn't feel afraid then, but tonight she does. She moves a little closer to the fire.

Her mother gives her a sympathetic look. "Cold?"

"It seems very lonely here."

"It does. I suppose we've become accustomed to being surrounded by adobe walls."

"I wonder where Old Pete is."

"Someplace in Chihuahua. You should get some sleep, child."

"So should you."

"I can't. There are too many things on my mind."

"Like Don Fernando?"

"Yes. And Santa Fe. What I subjected you children to."

"And Papa?"

"That also."

"I'm sorry you had to leave your rocking chair behind."

Her mother stirs on the log she's sitting on and wraps her skirts more firmly around her legs. "I'll miss that chair, but it's not as important as keeping you and Andrew safe and fed."

"And going home?"

There's a little pause. "Perhaps."

Even the hope of hope quickens Alma's pulse. She never wanted to leave the valley in the first place, but now more than ever she wants the comfort of it. The things María Paula said will linger inside her a long time. Maybe forever. But the mountains and streams of home and the friendship of men like Ramón, Old Pete, and Old Bill, will go a long way toward healing the pain. She stands, stretches, circles the fire, and drops a kiss on her mother's head. "I love you."

"I love you, too." She squeezes Alma's hand. "Good night, niña." It's Alma's father's nickname for her, not her mother's. The word and the sad tone send a tremor through the child's heart. Her shoulders drop. Her mother has said only "perhaps" about returning to the valley, not "yes." And she sounds so sad. As if going home may be impossible.

Alma's throat closes. And it might be. After all, Papa hasn't come for them or sent word. Her stomach twists as she lays out her blankets and crawls between them. She's too old to cry. But the darkness still seems too large, somehow, and she can't help shivering in the empty night air.

She's tired the next morning. She doesn't want to think about what lies ahead or anything else. Andrew feels it, too. There's no energy in either of them. The excitement of the initial leaving is over and now the journey stretches ahead with no certain destination. The mules are recalcitrant and it takes all her mother's ingenuity and the children's assistance to get the animals connected to the buckboard again.

They move slowly up the dusty rock-ridden road. Alma and Andrew sit on opposite ends of the plank seat, their mother between them. Alma sinks into a dull half sleep. Her head lolls to one side and bumps against and then away from her mother's shoulder. The wagon climbs a hill, descends, then climbs another. There are faint whiffs of pine and the stink of juniper, but mostly there's only dust in the air. Alma sniffs, wakes, and closes her eyes again.

Then suddenly her mother is saying, "What in tarnation!" and pulling hard on the reins. "Whoa!" she says. "Whoa now!"

Alma frowns, straightens, and rubs the sleep from her eyes. The buckboard is at the top of a small thinly-grassed hill. The road tilts down from here and dips across a muddy arroyo. At first, Alma thinks her mother's concerned about the depth of the mud. Then she hears the cattle.

She squints past the arroyo bottom to the opposite slope. A small herd of perhaps twenty animals mills on the hillside. Then one breaks away from the others and trots purposefully down the hill, its brown-and-black head swinging from side to side.

Andrew leans forward. "That steer looks like Brindle."

"Yes," his mother says without turning her head.

Then a man on a chestnut horse with a star-shaped white blaze on its forehead tops the rise above the herd. Alma jerks to her feet and Andrew leaps from the wagon. He and Chaser race down the hill. "Papa!" he yells. "Papa!"

The man gallops toward them, cattle scattering out of his way.

Now Ramón's big black horse appears at the top of the slope. He swings a slow lariat at the cattle, hazing them back into some kind of order. Alma waves both arms over her head and he drops the rope to his side, lifts his hat, and waves it back.

Her father rides up to her mother's side of the wagon. Andrew is settled in the saddle in front of him, squashed against the pommel. He grins at Alma triumphantly, but she's watching her father's face.

"Suzanna," he says quietly.

"Gerald." Her voice is frighteningly noncommittal.

But he doesn't look afraid. If anything, he looks stronger than ever. There's a stillness about him that Alma's never felt before. It's not that he's braced for what's coming. It's more like he's rooted where he is and not planning to go anywhere except forward.

"We're headed to Santa Fe," he says. "Can you get that wagon turned around or do you need help?"

Her mother looks at the mules. One of them twitches an ear and the other shakes his head. "It would be easier if I had help." She's clearly talking about more than the buckboard and mules. A small flower of hope blooms in Alma's chest.

Her father eases out of the saddle, leaving Andrew with the reins. "Go give Ramón a hand," he says.

"Yes, Papa." Andrew flashes Alma a delighted smile and trots away, with Chaser right behind.

Her father moves toward the wagon.

"You're limping!" her mother says. "What happened?"

He grimaces. "It's always worse when I've been riding." He reaches the wagon and braces himself against the side. "Help me up?"

The minute he's on the wagon seat, Alma stumbles around her mother's legs and into his arms. He pulls her to his chest and bends his face into her hair. "Mi alma," he whispers. "Can you forgive me for taking so long to come to you?"

She clutches at him. "Don't let her go away again," she whispers. She pulls back and looks into his face. "Please, Papa."

There are tears in his own eyes now, though he's smiling through them. "I'll do my best," he murmurs.

"Are you two talking about me?" Her mother sounds like she wants to laugh and cry at the same time.

# CHAPTER 40

"I was a fool," her mother says to her father. "Can you forgive me?"

Alma and Andrew exchange a surprised look. They've never heard her say those words before. Alma shoots a sideways look at Ramón, who's on the log beside her, whittling a new whistle for Andrew. He smiles at her and looks down at his knife.

Her parents are side by side on a dead log with no space between them. Their arms are around each others' waists. A sturdy walking stick leans against his end of the log.

"I was a fool not to have told you about my father in the first place." Her father grimaces. "As Old Bill informed me at righteously considerable length when he came through last Fall." He pulls her mother closer. "He also told me you were in Santa Fe. I thought you were still in Don Fernando." He shakes his head. "We knew about the Santa Cruz rebellion, but I thought you were still with your father. He didn't send word that you'd gone south."

She bites her lower lip. "I asked him not to. That was wrong of me. You had a right to know."

"I would have come sooner, but I have to admit I was feeling fairly aggravated myself. Around the time my temper died down and I could think straight again, winter set in." He gestures at his leg. "Then this happened."

She raises her eyebrows questioningly and he looks a little sheepish. "Some shingles on the barn roof had worked loose and what with one thing and another, we didn't get to them before the first snow."

Ramón looks up. "Those shingles might have held if the wind hadn't been so strong." Alma creeps toward him and he sets aside his work and puts an arm around her shoulders. "It was stronger than usual for the time of year."

"I should have gotten to them earlier, but with one thing and another—" Her father straightens his leg and winces. "I went up to try to patch the roof and it was icier than I thought. I slid all the way down."

Alma's mother winces. "I'm surprised you didn't break both legs."

"I expect I would have if I'd hit the ground itself. It was frozen solid by then. But Papa broke my fall."

She sucks air between her teeth. "Tarnation!"

Ramón nods. "He was worried the ladder wasn't steady and would slip on the frozen ground, so he went out to brace it." He gestures toward Alma's father. "When he saw this one sliding, he rushed to catch him."

Alma winces as she pictures it. The horror of the slow slide, Grandpa Locke running across the yard's frozen ruts toward the barn.

Her mother is looking at her father. "He caught you?"

He chuckles. "Well, not exactly. He had his arms out wide enough, but I came down at an angle and he read it wrong. I ended up slamming into his chest and one arm." He grimaces. "I heard his arm snap just before my leg splintered."

Alma's stomach squinches. "Oh, Papa!"

Ramón pats her arm. "It's all right, nita. It was a clean break."

"It's much better now, niña," her father says. "Ramón had the worst of it, what with two men to nurse and the animals to care for, too." He chuckles and looks at the other man. "Though it was probably a relief to be in the barn instead of the cabin. We Lockes aren't the best of patients."

Ramón grins back at him but doesn't reply. He reaches for his knife and the whistle and goes back to work.

"Why do you have Brindle with you?" Andrew asks.

His father moves slightly and reaches for his pipe and tobacco. "Just about the time I was up and around again, we had a visit from a man sent by Padre Martínez." He glances at Alma's mother. "He brought that letter you sent with Gregorio Garcia."

She looks as if she's about to speak, but then Andrew's forehead crinkles. "What does that have to do with Brindle?"

"Brindle was always intended as a meat cow," his mother says gently. "That's why he was gelded."

Andrew looks at his father.

"Padre Martínez sent word that there was a food shortage in the Taos Valley, partly because of the Navajo raids and partly because of the rebellion."

As he tamps the tobacco into his pipe, Alma's mother picks a splinter of wood from the ground and leans to the fire to light it. She hands it to him and he smiles tenderly into her eyes as he takes it. Then he looks at Andrew. "There weren't enough people in the valley last fall to properly bring in the harvest. The Padre wanted to buy a few beeves to feed the poorest of his parishioners."

As he draws on the pipe, he and Ramón exchange a glance. "After we made those arrangements, we learned that the government was paying a good price for beef in Santa Fe, to feed the troops." He gestures at his leg. "This was finally healed up enough that I could get on and off a horse, so we decided to gather up what we could and head this direction." He glances at Alma's mother a little guiltily and wraps an arm around her again. "It was a good excuse to come find you."

Alma narrows her eyes at him. He didn't need an excuse. But he's too busy looking at her mother to notice. As she looks away, Ramón squeezes her arm companionably. "I've missed you, nita."

She leans toward him. "I've missed you, too."

"Getting those cows through the canyon was another story," her father says from the other side of the fire.

Ramón chuckles. "A long one."

Her mother looks from one man to the other. "What happened?"

"My leg wasn't quite as healed as I thought." He grimaces and stretches it carefully toward the fire. "So that slowed us down. Then the cattle didn't much like being pushed down the valley to Palo Flechado Pass. There was still plenty of mud and snow in that direction. They figured the barn was a more sensible place to pass the time. Then when we finally reached the top of the Pass, we were hit by a late snow squall."

"But surely things settled down once you got onto the Don Fernando river side," she says. "The canyon would keep the cattle funneled west to Don Fernando."

Ramón chuckles. "You would think so."

Alma's father grins around the stem of his pipe. "We weren't counting on that catamount and her youngsters."

"Ah," her mother says, understanding.

Alma frowns. "What did they do?"

"Those cats harassed that herd all the way down the canyon. The cattle panicked, of course. There's nothing like the scream of a mountain lion to make a cow nervous. Especially when there's three of them."

332

"Horses don't like it much either," Ramón says drily.

"Mine certainly didn't." Alma's father takes the pipe from his mouth and shakes his head. "I thought that chestnut was smarter than that. He carried on like every minute was his last."

"He sounds pretty smart to me," Andrew says.

"Me too." His mother snuggles closer to his father's shoulder. "But you made it all right."

He leans his head toward hers. "I'm sorry it took so long."

Alma's eyes are suddenly itchy with tears. She looks away. Ramón pats her shoulder.

"It was a long time," she says into his ear.

"It's over now, nita."

"I hope so."

"But now you're here," her mother says to her father.

"Now we're here." He pulls her closer. "And we're on our way to Santa Fe with enough cattle to feed the troops for a few weeks and also put some money in our pockets." He glances sideways at her. "Our half should be enough for glass windowpanes."

She goes very still, stares up at the stars, then gives a little sigh and nods. "That would be good." She tilts her head toward him, little frown on her forehead. "If it won't stretch us too far in other directions."

"We should be fine."

There's a pause, then she says hesitantly, "And how's your father?"

"His arm healed up pretty quickly. He stayed behind to take care of the place." He grins. "We talked about windows before we left and calculated what size pane to get and how many, but he's more ambitious than that. He believes it's time you and I had a bedroom of our own. The ground's still too frozen to set posts, but he figured he could get some logs cut, at any rate." He nods toward the wagon, where the side sections of the loom jut into the darkness. "He's also planning to just about double the floor space in the main room, so there should be plenty of room for your contraption, as well."

She nudges him playfully with her shoulder. "It's not a contraption. I'll have you know that I can now weave a competent piece of floor covering and I'm almost ready to try making a blanket." She makes a little face. "I doubt I'll ever have the skill to create a weave fine enough for clothing, but I can create usable jerga. We'll just need to find a good source for wool."

Ramón clears his throat. "With my portion of the cattle proceeds, I may purchase a few churro." He leans toward Andrew and hands him the new whistle. "There's room in the valley to graze sheep as long as we can keep the mountain cats away."

Andrew sits taller. "Chaser and I can help!"

"I had planned to use the milk for cheese and sell the new lambs for meat." Ramón's eyes twinkle as they look across the fire. "But now that we have a weaver in the valley, I'll have to teach myself again how to shear."

"And I can help comb it and spin it," Alma says.

"She also cooks a little now, too." Her mother smiles at her. "She's much more competent than I am."

"I'd say you're very competent," Alma's father says. "And brave."

She grimaces. "Not brave enough to admit when I'm wrong." She looks him in the eyes. "I'm sorry."

He removes his pipe from his mouth and bends toward her as if pulled by a magnet. Their foreheads touch. Andrew and Alma glance at each other, then away.

Then their mother straightens and looks into their father's eyes. "I need to apologize to your father. It wasn't his fault I didn't know. It was unfair to be so angry with him." She looks down at her hands. "I wasn't quite as unbiased as I thought I was. Deep down, there were assumptions based on nothing more than arrogance and stupidity."

"I wouldn't go that far."

"I would." The fire pops in the silence that follows. One of the horses huffs. A cow moos in the distance. Chaser barks once, then twice, then silence settles again.

"I learned something while we were gone." She stares into the fire. "Something I'm not proud of. I thought my father's New England forebears somehow made me better than other people." Her voice wobbles. "I didn't know I believed that, but I did." She looks at the children, then their father. "I was a fool. This experience has reminded me that we are all the same under the skin. And that it's a person's heart that matters most of all." Her lips tremble. "And that I love you all so much, I can hardly bear it."

There's a little pause. A log drops in the fire. Sparks shoot into the night. Then Alma's mother grins at Ramón. Her voice changes. "Did I tell you that Antonia Garcia is in Santa Fe and she's fallen in love with a Vera Cruz dragoon? He has an ugly face but quite a magnificent uniform!"

"And a heart that's pure gold," Alma says.

Her father smiles at her. "One heart recognizes another." Then he looks at Andrew. His voice drops. "So that's why we have Brindle with us."

Andrew's shoulders straighten. "I always knew he was a beef cattle." He lifts his new whistle. "See what Ramón's done made me? Do you wanta hear it?"

"Ramón's made for me," their mother corrects him absently. The children exchange a grin.

# CHAPTER 41

They return to the Agua Fria casita to use up the rest of their rent. Don Salvador meets them with open arms and helps the men negotiate a good price for the cattle. Then they visit Elisha Stanley's mercantile and arrange to buy back the rocking chair and also purchase glass for the new cabin windows.

When they leave the casita the second time, the children from the Martín compound are on hand to see them off, all except María Paula. Rosario and Rafaela smile apologetically at Alma and shyly press dried flowers of remembrance into her hands. She can barely whisper her thanks.

Esquipula, Jesús, and Felix scuffle with Andrew and Chaser in the dirt road. Alma gazes at the spot beyond them, the place where Governor Pérez died. It's just a patch of dirt now.

A raven caws overhead. Ramón looks up at it. "It's saying goodby to you," he says.

Alma shivers in spite of the warm spring air. He looks at her questioningly, but she turns away. He raises his voice toward the boys. "Come and help with the churros, chamacos. At least to the top of the hill."

Alma looks up. "Can I come too?"

He grins at her. "You might as well ask me if you can go fishing as soon as we reach the valley. Could I stop you?" Then he tilts his head. "Do you need to fetch your sunbonnet?"

Her face falls. But the sun is bright in the sky. She really ought to wear the floppy hat. Her skin will get blotchy. She turns toward the wagon, where her mother is reaching over the sideboards to stow the last of the items from the casita. "My bonnet," she says in a small voice.

Her mother turns and looks at her. Her eyes rove across Alma's face. "I don't know that you need it. Your skin is just fine the way it is." She pulls her arms out of the back of the wagon, drops a kiss on Alma's head, and then turns to jiggle a bundle closer to the rocking chair, wedging it in more firmly.

Something lifts in Alma's chest. She turns to Ramón, whose eyes twinkle as he waves her toward the sheep. "Go on, then," he says. "You and your friends."

The children and Chaser shoo the churros away from the verge where they've been milling and onto the road behind the wagon and its precious cargo of glass. Her parents climb into the wagon and they set off. When they reach the top of the hill, Alma runs to catch up to the buckboard and scramble onto the seat beside her mother. She turns to wave goodby to the Martín grandchildren, then faces forward. The mules bob their heads as if they too are eager to move out.

Perhaps that eagerness speeds their journey. The little cavalcade makes good time in spite of the sheep. By noon the next day, they're almost to Pojoaque.

Andrew has left the sheepherding duties to Chaser for a while and is on the wagon beside his father, learning to handle the reins. He's paying more attention to the mules' heads than the road, so when Alma points out the crosses, he looks up in surprise.

Then he sees them. His eyes widen. Wooden markers no taller than the mule's withers line both sides of the rocky track. Some are painted white. Others are stained with red earth. The ground is rocky here and many of them are stuck into small piles of stone instead of soil. Most of the crosses have flowers tucked around their base and feathers tied to their crossbars, floating like prayers on an indefinable breeze. The markers disappear up ahead where the road curves, but at the top of the next hill they appear again, silhouetted against the turquoise-blue sky.

"Memorial crosses," Alma's mother says. "Descansos."

"There are so many," Alma murmurs.

Her father nods. "We saw them as we were coming south. Someone told us they're for the people who died in the January battle."

Alma studies the one nearest her. As they pass, a hawk feather flutters in the wind. It's tethered by a thin leather strap. "They look so lonely."

The reins are slack in Andrew's hands now. His father gently removes them and takes over. The boy doesn't seem to notice. "They're all dead?"

"Yes." His mother's voice is sad and grim at the same time. "All of them. This is what war does."

"Because two groups of people couldn't bring themselves to talk to each other like rational adults," his father says.

Alma bites her lip and looks at her parents, but they're studying the crosses. Then she sees that her mother's hand has crept into her father's lap. He gives it a squeeze before he goes back to the reins.

"I wonder if there's one for Señor Beitia," she says.

Her father glances at her. "Who?"

"Someone we met in Chimayó," her mother says. "A relative of Señora Ortega."

The wagon jolts on a rock. Andrew grabs the edge of the seat to steady himself and glares at the symbols of death. "I hate war!"

"I'm glad to hear it," his mother says. "So you don't want to be a soldier any longer?"

His chin quivers. He shakes his head. "No." After a long moment, he leans out so he can see around his father, and grins at her. "But I would like to go trapping with Old Pete."

She chuckles. "Well, we'll have to see what we can do about that."

"Will we stop in Santa Cruz?" Alma asks.

Her father looks at her quizzically.

Alma's cheeks feel hot. She glances at her mother.

"Gregorio Garcia is working for the Martínez family in Santa Cruz," her mother explains. "The ones who helped lead the revolt and were executed in January. He's hoping to marry their cousin."

"Ah. Good for him! We should stop and wish him luck."

"He may need it, though his intended seems to care for him very deeply." She glances at Alma. "It would be good to see him again."

Alma's chest is suddenly tight. She bites the insides of her cheeks.

Her mother leans toward at her. "He'll always be your friend," she says gently. "Even after he's married."

Alma nods and looks away. Her mother reaches for her hand. Alma squeezes it. She can't tell Gregorio her secret, how she feels about him. But she's glad her mother knows. Somehow, it makes it easier to bear.

Her father glances at them. "While we were convalescing, Papa told me stories about his parents and grandparents," he says. "They experienced some interesting times."

Her mother tilts her head. "Really? What happened?"

## THE END

339

# NOTE TO READER

The 1837 rebellion in New Mexico was one of a number of flare-ups across Mexico in the second half of the 1830s. By 1835, independent Mexico was moving away from its democratic origins to a more conservative centralist structure. The result was rebellion in, most famously, Texas, but also in Zacatecas, California, and New Mexico.

Mexico's Congress plunged ahead with its changes anyway. The Federal attitude was perhaps most clearly expressed in the seven constitutional measures Congress adopted in late December 1836. These laws replaced the more democratic 1824 Constitution and were popularly known as the Seven Plagues. They included a number of changes designed to reduce local autonomy, including restrictions on who could vote or hold office, and the abolition of elected councils in towns with populations under 8,000, communities that had been largely self-governing since the early 1820s.

Since independence, the smaller communities in New Mexico had been administered by a locally elected alcalde who served as a sort of combined mayor and adjudicator. The new laws replaced this position with a justice of the peace appointed by the area's prefect, a position appointed by and answerable to the governor, who in turn was named by Mexico City. Now only Santa Fe had a council, one heavily influenced, if not downright controlled, by recently appointed Governor Albino Pérez.

In addition to restrictions to local autonomy, there was the threat of taxation. Because New Mexico had long acted as the

341

first line of defense against the First Nation tribes to the north, east, and west, it had been exempt from Federal sales tax for most of its existence as a Spanish and then Mexican political subdivision. The most recently enacted tax exemption was set to expire in the summer of 1837. At their February meeting that year, New Mexico's Departmental Council requested a ten-year extension, but Governor Pérez didn't see fit to send their request on to Mexico City until late May.

This may be because New Mexico's coffers were running low and Pérez saw the new taxes as another revenue stream. It's not clear if the budget situation was the result of poor management, manipulation of the funds derived from customs duties, limited attention from the central government, or simply New Mexico's traditional poverty. At any rate, by the spring of 1837 the situation was so dire that there was no money to pay the Presidial troops garrisoned in New Mexico.

Pérez reacted to this particular crisis by furloughing the soldiers. As he'd done in previous years, he also obtained credit from American merchants in Santa Fe for personal as well as governmental needs, and exacted enforced loans from New Mexico's ricos.

None of these actions made him popular, except possibly with the small group of men who held the appointments at his disposal. Across New Mexico, the average working class family faced new taxes and restricted rights, and richer families were subject to random demands for yet another "loan."

Attitudes toward Governor Pérez were also tarnished by the perception that he and his officials were "not from here." Certainly, his lifestyle seems to have been quite different from everyone else in New Mexico. He'd spent time in Mexico City, where the display of personal wealth, fine clothing, and imported buggies from St. Louis was acceptable and even admired behavior for men in power. In New Mexico, this type of splendor tended to breed resentment.

The impact of Pérez's choices was exacerbated by the New Mexican tendency to be suspicious of people without strong family ties to the region. There was a general feeling that people from elsewhere couldn't truly know New Mexico or have her best interests at heart. This attitude became more intense when the men in question began implementing changes that seemed to cut to the heart of New Mexico's self-sufficiency—increasing taxes and eliminating the people's ability to govern their communities themselves. There was even some suspicion that Pérez was making changes without the approval of Mexico City: being harsher than the Federal Government intended, or perhaps not reflecting Congressional edicts at all.

These suspicions grew throughout the early months of 1837, especially in the upper río Grande Valley, or río Arriba. In the area around Santa Cruz de la Cañada, this distrust was reinforced by the administration's response to the local alcalde's ruling in the Taos debt collection matter and his decision to release Antonio Abad Montoya from jail.

When Esquibel was incarcerated, things reached a boiling point. Given the prevailing sense of injustice and what was perceived as the administration's heavy-handedness, the Santa Cruz citizens' decision to free the alcalde from jail and the events of the following days seem almost inevitable.

The various historical sources don't agree about the exact sequence of events prior to the Tuesday, August 8, 1837 battle at Black Mesa. For example, there's disagreement about when Alcalde Esquibel made his debt collection decision as well as when and how he was arrested. Part of the challenge of researching this novel was integrating the various narratives into a cohesive sense of what happened and when. However, there's little disagreement about what occurred at Black Mesa and in the following days.

Governor Pérez lost that battle when New Mexico militia members and Pueblo warriors who'd marched out of Santa Fe with him switched sides. The next day, Wednesday, August 9, 1837, after an all-day flight from the men shadowing him, the governor died gruesomely on the road outside the Salvador Martín house north of Agua Fria, a small village south of the capitol.

On Thursday the rebel army completed its occupation of Santa Fe and went to mass to celebrate their victory. They didn't hold the city for long. In mid-September, former Governor Manuel Armijo marched into town with militia from the río Abajo, or lower river valley, and took the capitol without firing a shot. Later that month, when the rebels began moving toward the city again, he talked them into surrendering and also exchanging the now-jailed rebel governor José Angel Gonzales for Antonio Abad and Desiderio Montoya, as well as Alcalde Esquibel and a man named Juan Vigil.

It was a temporary and tenuous peace. Many of the rebels didn't go home. They went back to Santa Cruz and regrouped. They still controlled the Santa Cruz Valley, including Chimayó and Truchas. They also had a strong presence farther north in the Taos Valley, although Padre Antonio José Martínez did his utmost to challenge that control. As the local priest and the oldest son of a leading rico family, Martínez used his position to resist the rebels, incurring their wrath and bringing threats down on his own head, as well as that of his brother, the local sub-prefect.

During this time, the First Nation groups New Mexicans referred to as the "wild tribes"—the Apaches in the south and the

Navajo in the west—took advantage of the unsettled conditions. While the Apache seem to have contented themselves with raiding Chihuahua-bound merchant caravans, the Navajo raided the Spanish settlements, venturing as close to Albuquerque as Bernalillo and as far north and east as the Taos Valley. The regional unrest was a great opportunity to supplement their sheep herds and perhaps also pick up a few captives to replace those taken by New Mexicans in earlier raids.

Since the militia tasked to protect these communities was now in Santa Fe with Armijo, New Mexicans who could afford to do so followed them there. These are the refugees whose presence causes the housing shortage and rise in prices that create additional pressure on Suzanna and her children during the winter of 1837/38 and result in their sharing the casita with Gregorio, his mother, and eventually Sargento Silva.

While the tall dragoon is a fictional character, the men he arrives with in January 1838 are not. I have no evidence that Vera Cruz and Chihuahua troops were housed with local residents, but it seems likely. Certainly, the presidio barracks wouldn't have been large enough to house them all, and typical January weather in Santa Fe does not make camping outside a reasonable alternative for any extended period of time.

Santa Fe was crowded that winter. The flood of refugees must have made Elisha Stanley and the few other American merchants who'd remained in town glad they'd done so. They'd had some anxious moments in August when the rebels took over, but the merchants and their goods weren't molested. Given the influx of refugees and soldiers, trade must have been brisk. The men who headed south with Guadalupe Miranda's train on August 4th or back to Missouri eight days later—the train Suzanna considers travelling with—missed out on a great opportunity.

However, the Americans who went south with Miranda did run a risk. A number of officials in Mexico believed Americans had instigated the revolt in order to pry New Mexico away from Mexico, either by annexing it directly or helping it to set up as an independent country the way Texas had. There seems to be little factual support for this suspicion. In fact, Elisha Stanley is said to have turned down the rebel governor's plea for American assistance in late August 1837.

The very fact that Governor Gonzales made this overture indicates the rebels knew within days of capturing Santa Fe that their insurgency was unlikely to succeed long term. Ultimately, it did fail, although the rebellion wasn't completely crushed until late January 1838 at the battle of Pojoaque where Gregorio is wounded.

Ironically, although the rebel movement collapsed, their discontent was noted and responded to in Mexico City. By late Spring 1838, the administration had confirmed Manuel Armijo, scion of an old río Abajo family, as political and military governor and, more importantly, extended New Mexico's tax exemption for another seven years. In many ways, the insurgents had accomplished their goals.

But the new Republic of Texas had also taken note of the restlessness on their western border. New Mexico's rebels were quiet, but that didn't necessarily mean they were satisfied. They might still welcome a change in government. If so, Texas was ready and willing to assist them and perhaps even annex New Mexico itself. In 1841, three years after this novel ends, Texas President Mirabeau Bonaparte Lamar launched what came to be called the Texas-Santa Fe expedition—a group of 320 men sent to New Mexico ostensibly to explore the potential for trade, but also to test the possibility of closer connections.

That expedition didn't go quite as planned. In fact, it led to wholesale disaster for the Texans involved. Guadalupe Miranda, the trader who headed out of Santa Fe before the rebels arrived there, received the Mexican Cross of Honor for his actions in response to the Texan incursion. But, as Old Pete would say, that there's a subject for a whole 'nother book.

# HISTORICAL FIGURES IN
## *NO SECRET TOO SMALL*

**Abreú, Ramón (1806–1837)** Brother of New Mexico justice and former governor Santiago Abreú. Ramón Abreú was named prefect of northern New Mexico in Summer 1837 and was killed on August 9 at the rebel camp west of the Santa Fe plaza.

**Armijo, Manuel (1790–1853)** The only man to serve as Governor of New Mexico three times: from 1827 to 1829, from late 1837 to 1844, and from 1845 to the American invasion in 1846. Although Armijo's reputation is tarnished by the fact that he relinquished New Mexico to the invading Americans in 1846 without a fight, in 1837/38 he does seem to have kept the region from going up in flames.

**Beaubien, Charles 'Carlos' (1800–1864)** Quebec-born trapper of aristocratic French descent who arrived in New Mexico in early 1824, then turned to retail, becoming a merchant in Don Fernando de Taos.

**Bent, Charles (1799–1847)** Mountain man turned merchant who arrived in New Mexico in 1829. He and Ceran St. Vrain were business partners in a venture that included a store on the south side of the Don Fernando plaza as well as Bent's Fort, an important stop on the Santa Fe Trail.

**Duran y Chavez, Fernando (?–?)** Spanish man to whom the Crown granted land in the Taos Valley prior to the 1680 revolt, when he left and did not return. What is now known as the village of Taos was originally called Don Fernando de Taos in his honor.

**Esquibel, Juan José (1788–1838)** Alcalde of Santa Cruz de la Cañada in 1837 and a leader of the revolt that Fall. Some historians report that his first name was Diego, but the more definitive sources say his name was Juan José, which I have chosen to use in this story. His wife, María Rafaela Martín Sangil, was a member of a large family, most of whom lived in the Santa Cruz area, making her husband related to many of the local residents.

**Gonzales, José Angel (1799–1838)** A buffalo hunter, or cibolero, from the Taos area. A widower, in 1837 Gonzales had recently married a widow from Chimayó. After the rebels captured Santa Fe in August 1837, he was named governor. He served in that capacity until September 11, when word arrived that the ricos south of Albuquerque had identified Manuel Armijo as New Mexico's interim leader and head of the loyalist armed forces. Gonzales was jailed, then released in late September. He returned to Santa Cruz, where he helped organize the January 1838 insurgency. He was captured and executed following the battle at Pojoaque Pass.

**Martín, Jesús María y José (1823–after 1855)** The oldest son of Salvador Martín's first-born, José Ramón. He was 14 in the Fall of 1837.

**Martín, José María Tomás (1808–1845)** Corporal, or cabo, in the Santa Fe presidio troop in 1837 and the youngest of the Martín sons who lived to adulthood. José María Tomás Martín was captured by the rebels in August 1837 but returned to Santa Fe later that Fall.

**Martín, María del Rosario (c. 1830–after 1846)** One of Salvador Martín's granddaughters. María del Rosario was the daughter of Ramón Martín and María Josefa Tafoya. I have been unable to identify a precise birth date for María del Rosario, so have made her eight years old for the sake of this story. She married Juan Luis Rafael Romero in December 1846.

**Martín, Salvador (1763–after 1837)** The man outside whose home Governor Pérez was killed on August 10, 1837. Martín, known as "Tio Salvadorito," and his wife María Antonia Chavez y Armijo had thirty-one living grandchildren by 1837, most of them in the Santa Fe/Agua Fría area. The family's baptism, marriage, and census records identify their last name as both Martín and Martínez. For the purposes of this novel, I've chosen to use the shorter version.

**Martínez , Antonio José (1793–1867)** Member of a prominent Taos Valley family and the Catholic priest there from 1826 to 1857. By 1837, he was also a member of New Mexico's Legislative Council. A strong personality from a wealthy family, Martínez worked to suppress the 1837 revolt in the Taos area. He also volunteered to act as chaplain for the government forces in January 1838 and is said to have heard José Angel Gonzales' confession prior to his execution.

**Miranda, Guadalupe (1810–1888)** Merchant, trader, and schoolteacher who would receive the Mexican Cross of Honor for his actions during the 1841 Texan invasion of New Mexico. He and his wife María Francisca Rascon had nine children together. Their third, María Francisca Concepcion, was born in Chihuahua on October 27, 1837, which may explain why Miranda was in such a hurry to leave Santa Fe in early August that year.

**Montoya, Antonio Abad (1813–1838)** One of the leaders of New Mexico's August 1837 revolt. Montoya was the oldest of four siblings. He and his sister María Catarina were married to María Dolores and José Ramón Vigil respectively, siblings who were cousins of Donaciano Vigil. Montoya and his wife had one child, a daughter named María Ygnacia, who was about 7 years old in 1837. He was executed, along with his brother Desiderio, just prior to the final rebel battle in January 1838.

**Montoya, María Catarina (1819-after 1866)** The oldest of the two younger sisters of Antonio Abad and Desiderio Montoya. She married José Ramón Vigil, the brother of Antonio's wife, in 1830 and by 1837 had one child, a little boy named José Francisco, and another on the way. Nicolas Antonio was born that June.

**Vigil, José Ramón (1805-after 1866)** María Catarina Montoya's husband. The marriage record indicates that his parents were residents of Santa Clara, so I've placed the couple, who were still in the first decade of marriage in 1837, in the Santa Clara area during the events covered by this story. My sources indicate that José Ramón owned a ranch in the valley north of Santa Clara in what is now the town of Española.

**Montoya, Desiderio (1816–1838)** Younger brother of Antonio Abad Montoya who was jailed with him in Fall 1837 as a leader of the August 1837 revolt. They escaped execution in October that year only to die just prior to the final rebel battle in January 1838, shortly after Desiderio's 22nd birthday.

**Montoya, José Esquipula (1828–after 1862)** One of Salvador Martín's and María Antonia Chavez' many grandchildren. In 1837, the nine-year-old José Esquipula was the oldest living son of Salvador Martín's daughter María Barbara and her husband Juan Manuel Montoya.

**Montoya, María Jacinta Rafaela (1826–after 1846)** José Esquipula Montoya's older sister and María Barbara Martín's and Juan Manuel Montoya's oldest daughter. She was 11 years old in 1837 and married José Francisco Baca nine years later, in 1846.

**Ortiz, María Paula (1821–1880)** Daughter of Salvador Martín's oldest daughter, María de la Luz, and her husband Ignacio Ortiz. Sixteen years old in 1837, María Paula, also known as Pablita, would go on to marry Juan Ortiz in 1843. I have found no record of María Paula's attitude toward others based on their heritage. My description of her in this novel (other than her age) is completely imagined.

**Ortiz, María Salome (1823–after 1846)** Another of the Martín granddaughters. She was the younger sister of María Paula Ortiz and turned 14 in October 1837. She married José Duran in 1846.

**Pérez, Albino (?–1837)** Governor of New Mexico from Spring 1835 to August 1837, when he was killed during what is popularly called the Chimayó rebellion. He is said to have left behind a wife in Mexico City and a child in Santa Fe, the son of his housekeeper, Trinidad Trujillo.

**St. Vrain, Ceran (1802–1870)** Don Fernando de Taos-based trapper and trader who grew up in St. Louis and arrived in Santa Fe in March 1825. He remained in New Mexico the rest of his life, eventually settling in Mora.

**Sarracino, Francisco Antonio José Felix (1790–after 1850)** Governor of New Mexico, 1833 to 1835. He was replaced by Albino Pérez, who named Sarracino the New Mexico Subcomisario, or Treasurer in 1835. In April 1836 Sarracino was charged with malfeasance and temporarily removed from office. He was reinstated in late July 1837. Sarracino was wounded at the battle of La Mesilla and briefly captured. He escaped to his home in Pajarito and stayed there until he resurfaced in late September, when he put in a claim against Governor Pérez's property, specifically the large gilded mirrors Pérez had borrowed from him.

**Silva, Jesús María (1828–after 1846)** Another grandson of Salvador Martín. Silva was the son of María Dolores Ygnes Martín and José Dolores Silva and was nine years old in Fall 1837. He married Juliana Padilla in 1846.

**Smith, Thomas Long 'Peg Leg' (1801–1866)** Trapper who would become famous as the mountain man with the missing foot, hence the nickname "Peg Leg." In 1836, Smith travelled to California to procure horses by trade and other less legitimate means. He and his partners then drove the herd to Bent's Fort and sold them, no questions asked.

**Stanley, Elisha ( 1790–1874 )** Merchant in Santa Fe in the 1830s and 40s with a store near the Santa Fe Plaza. Stanley arrived in New Mexico in 1823 and seems to have returned East shortly after the events of 1837/38. He never married. He is said to have had a gentlemanly deportment and a generous nature.

**Urioste, José Felix (1827–after 1879)** Oldest child of Salvador Martín's daughter María Guadalupe and her husband Manuel Urioste, a presidio soldier. He turned 10 in late February 1837, so was almost 11 that Fall.

**Urioste, Manuel (?–after 1850)** Presidio soldier who was married to Salvador Martín's daughter María Guadalupe. José Felix was their oldest child.

**Valencia, Tomás (?–after 1837)** The man who gave Donaciano Vigil a job in his Santa Fe mercantile after the presidio troops were furloughed in early 1837. He and Vigil were cousins by marriage: Valencia's wife Josefa Vigil and Donaciano Vigil were both descendants of Don Francisco Montes Vigil.

**Vigil, Donaciano (1802–1877)** Presidio sergeant who was captured at the battle of La Mesilla and served as Secretary of State under rebel governor José Angel Gonzales and also Manuel Armijo. Tall, well-spoken, and well-educated, Vigil held a number of government positions under both the Mexican and United States administrations, most notably as civil governor following Charles Bent's death in 1847.

**Villalpando, María Rosa (1742–1830)** Young woman who lived in the Taos area in 1760 and was captured by Comanches that year. She was traded to the Pawnee, with whom she was living when she met French trader Jean Sale dit Lajoie. She and Sale dit Lajoie married in 1770 and moved to St. Louis, where she died at age 88.

**Williams, William Sherley 'Old Bill' (1787–1849)** Garrulous mountain man with a gift for languages who was active in New Mexico from the early 1820s to 1849. Williams is believed to be the father of a little boy born to Antonia Baca at Don Fernando de Taos in March 1833. In 1837, Williams had just returned from a two-year trapping expedition in the northern Rockies. By late summer, he was at Bent's Fort, where he took charge of a wagon train going to Santa Fe. Earlier that year, Antonia Baca had borne a little girl by an unknown father. Williams may very well have gone to Don Fernando that Fall to address his relationship with Antonia and determine how his son was faring.

**Workman, William (1800–1876)** Mountain man and merchant from northern England who settled in the Taos Valley in the 1820s and owned a distillery there.

# GLOSSARY OF SPANISH AND OTHER TERMS

abuelo – grandfather (Spanish)

Alburquerque – city south of Santa Fe which is now the largest in New Mexico. In 1706, it was named for the Viceroy of New Spain, who was also the Spanish Duke of Alburquerque. Some time during the 1800s, the city name lost its first 'r' and became 'Albuquerque.' I use the older form in this book.

alcalde – a magistrate who served as justice of the peace and head of a town's municipal council (Spanish).

americano – any non-Spanish speaking White person in New Mexico (Spanish)

amigo/amiga – friend (male/female) (Spanish)

atole –cooked cornmeal cereal or mush (Spanish)

baile – dance (Spanish)

banco – adobe bench built along a wall near a fireplace (Spanish)

bizcochitos – rolled and cut cookie flavored with anise and cinnamon (Spanish)

buenos días – good day, good morning (Spanish)

bulto – image of a holy person carved in the round (Spanish)

cabo – military corporal (Spanish)

calaboose – jail, prison, lockup (American mountain man slang derived from Spanish)

calabozo – jail, cell, dungeon (Spanish)

cantón – region, district, administrative district (Spanish)

capilla – chapel (Spanish)

cárcolas – treadles on a foot-operated weaving loom (Spanish) carreta – two-wheeled wooden cart (Spanish)

casa – house, dwelling, building (Spanish)

casita – small house, cabin (Spanish)

católico – of the Catholic faith (Spanish)

chamacos – kids, children (Spanish)

Chimayoso – someone from the village of Chimayó (Spanish)

cibolero – buffalo hunter (Spanish)

claramente – clearly (Spanish)

comal – flat hot surface used for cooking tortías over the fire (Spanish)

compagnons d'armes – companions in arms (French)

con – with (Spanish)

corrida del gallo – rooster race (Spanish)

cota – wild herb with small yellow flowers that's used for medicinal tea (Spanish)

cuarto de dormir – bedroom (Spanish)

mi – my (Spanish)

cussed – nineteenth century somewhat socially acceptable swear word meaning cursed, contemptible, mean, etc. (English)

damn – swear word that was less socially unacceptable in the nineteenth century than now (English)

daymare – distressing experience similar to a bad dream, occurring while one is awake. Anxiety attack (English)

de nada – you're welcome, don't mention it (Spanish)

descanso – a kind of shrine for the dead usually marked by a wooden cross and flowers and other mementos (Spanish)

domingo – Sunday (Spanish)

don – title of respect for a man with money and family connections that's used only with his first name (Spanish)

Don Fernando/Don Fernando de Taos – aka Taos. Through the centuries, what is today known as the town of Taos has been called Don Fernando de Taos, San Fernando de Taos, and also San Fernandez de Taos. In the 1800s, the First Peoples pueblo of Taos three miles northeast of the village was more likely than the town to be called simply Taos. In this novel, I generally use Don Fernando de Taos or simply Don Fernando to refer to the town.

doña – title of respect for a lady with money and family connections which is used only with her first name (Spanish)

el cerro de Chimayó – the village or plaza of Chimayó, literally "the hill of Chimayó" (Spanish)

el día del Santiago – feast of Santiago, or St. James, the patron saint of Chimayó (Spanish)

El Dios – God (Spanish)

España – Spain (Spanish)

español/españoles – Spanish/Spaniards (Spanish)

esposo – husband (Spanish)

estudiantes – students (Spanish)

excelentisimo – most excellent (Spanish)

fandango – a dance that generally involved hard liquor, gambling, fistfights, and the presence of americanos (Spanish)

feliz – happy, as in "Happy Christmas" (Spanish)

gallivant – to wander about seeking pleasure or diversion (English)

genízaro – nomadic First Nation person captured by Spanish settlers and Christianized, or someone descended from these captives (Spanish)

gouverneur – governor (French)

gracias – thanks, thank you (Spanish)

hacienda – farm, plantation (Spanish)

hola – hello (Spanish)

hombre – man (Spanish)

horno – large outdoor beehive-shaped oven made of brick-size adobe blocks (Spanish)

hoyden – boisterous, bold, and carefree girl; a tomboy (English)

incómodo – incommodious, inconvenient, uncomfortable (Spanish)

indios bárbaros – unacculterated First Nation groups. The term usually meant the Navajo, Apache, and Comanche but could also refer to other groups (Ute, Kiowa, etc.) who weren't Christianized. (Spanish)

insurrecto – rebel (Spanish)

jerga – a kind of sackcloth, a coarse woolen fabric used for floor coverings (Spanish)

joven – young man (Spanish)

lanzadera – shuttle that held the yarn or thread for weaving and was passed across the loom and pressed into the growing cloth to become the weft, or crosswise thread (Spanish)

likely – good looking (English)

lo siento – I am sorry (Spanish)

loco – crazy, insane (Spanish)

madre – mother (Spanish)

mantilla – woman's silk or lace head scarf worn over the head and shoulders (Spanish)

masa – a kind of corn paste used as the main ingredient in corn tortillas (Spanish)

médico – a medical practitioner (Spanish)

mi – my (Spanish)

muchichito – boy (Spanish)

natías – a kind of vanilla pudding or custard cooked on top of a stove or over an open flame (Spanish)

negro – black (Spanish)

niña – darling, apple of the eye, used to refer to a female (Spanish) niños – children (Spanish)

nita – little sister, dear sister (Spanish)

Noche Buena – Christmas Eve (Spanish)

Nuevo México – New Mexico (Spanish)

padre – father, priest (Spanish)

paisanos – country men (Spanish)

palacio – palace, royal residence. In New Mexico, this word referred specifically to the Santa Fe offices and residence of the governor. The building is now home to the New Mexico Museum of History. (Spanish)

paraje – camp, camp ground, resting stop (Spanish)

patrón – master (Spanish)

peine – long fine-toothed wooden comb used in weaving to position the weft threads against the growing cloth (Spanish)

penitencia – penance (Spanish)

peón – farm worker, unskilled laborer, any person of low social status (Spanish)

perdóneme – pardon me (Spanish)

plaza del cerro – the plaza of Chimayó, literally "the plaza on or of the hill" (Spanish)

pobrecito – poor little one, used to refer to a male (Spanish)

por favor – please (Spanish)

por qué – why (Spanish)

portal – covered porch (Spanish)

prefect – a type of regional justice of the peace or administrator appointed by and answerable to the governor (Spanish)

presidio – military garrison (Spanish)

primo/prima – cousin (male/female) (Spanish)

princesa – princess (Spanish)

pucker – a state of irritation or anger (English)

quadroon – a person with one-fourth Black ancestry (English) queso – cheese (Spanish)

rebozo – a kind of long woven shawl (Spanish)

rico – rich, opulent, wealthy (Spanish)

río – river (Spanish)

río Arriba – district in New Mexico upriver of Santa Fe (Spanish)

río del Norte –river that flows from north to south through New Mexico, also called río Grande del Norte, or río Grande (Spanish)

río de Santa Cruz – Santa Cruz River (Spanish)

sala – hall, drawing-room, parlor (Spanish)

santo Dios – gracious God (Spanish)

sargento – sergeant (Spanish)

señor – mister, also used in the sense of "the gentleman" or "the man" (Spanish)

señora – married woman, mistress, or Mrs., also used in the sense of "the lady" or "the woman" (Spanish)

señorita – unmarried woman, young woman, or miss, also used in the sense of "the young woman" or "the girl" (Spanish)

sí – yes (Spanish)

squire – escort (English)

Taos – small town in northern New Mexico also known as Don Fernando de Taos, San Fernando de Taos, and San Fernandez de Taos. . In the 1800s, the First Peoples pueblo of Taos three miles northeast of the village was more likely than the town to be called simply Taos. In this novel, I generally use Don Fernando de Taos or simply Don Fernando to refer to the town.

Taos Lightning – hard liquor made from wheat grown in the Taos Valley (English)

tarnation – euphemism for damnation widely used throughout the 1800s (English)

tío – uncle, brother of one's mother or father (Spanish)

tortía – tortillas (Spanish)

tu – your (Spanish)

vamos – let's go, come on (Spanish)

vecino – citizen, friend, neighbor (Spanish)

viga – ceiling beam (Spanish)

villa real de la Santa Fe de Francisco de Asís – royal city of the holy faith of Saint Francis of Asisi, or Santa Fe for short (Spanish)

weft – crosswise thread of a piece of weaving (English)

yerba buena – spearmint (Spanish)

Loretta Miles Tollefson

# LIST OF SOURCES

Brooks, James F. *Captives and Cousins: Slavery, Kinship, and Community in the Southwest Borderlands.* Chapel Hill: University of North Carolina Press, 2002.

Chávez, Fray Angélico. *But Time and Chance: The Story of Padre Martínez of Taos, 1793-1867.* Santa Fe: Sunstone Press, 1981.

Kraemer, Paul. *An Alternative View of New Mexico's 1837 Rebellion.* Los Alamos: Los Alamos Historical Society, 2009.

Lecompte, Janet. *Rebellion in Río Arriba 1837.* Albuquerque: University of New Mexico Press, 1985.

Lucero, Helen R. and Suzanne Baizerman. *Chimayó Weaving: The Transformation of a Tradition.* Albuquerque: University of Mexico Press, 1998.

Márquez, Rubén Sálaz. *New Mexico: A Brief Multi-History.* Albuquerque: Cosmic House, 1999.

Read, Benjamin M. *Illustrated History of New Mexico,* Santa Fe: New Mexican Printing Company, 1912.

Simmons, Marc. *New Mexico: An Interpretive History.* Albuquerque: University of New Mexico Press, 1988.

Stanley, F. *Giant in Lilliput: The Story of Donaciano Vigil.* Pampa, TX: Pampa Printing, 1963.

Twitchell, Ralph Emerson. *Old Santa Fe Magazine, Vol. 2.* Santa Fe: Old Santa Fe Press, 1914-1915.

Twitchell, Ralph Emerson. *The Leading Facts of New Mexican History, Vol. 2.* Cedar Rapids: The Torch Press, 1912.

Usner, Don J. *Sabino's Map: Life in Chimayó's Old Plaza.* Santa Fe: Museum of New Mexico Press, 1995.

Weber, David J. *The Mexican Frontier, 1821-1846*: *The American Southwest Under Mexico.* Albuquerque: University of New Mexico Press, 1982.

Weigle, Marta, Ed. *Telling New Mexico.* Santa Fe: Museum of New Mexico Press, 2009.

Made in the USA
Las Vegas, NV
19 November 2020

11128425R00205